Earthedge

Books by Ivan Blake

The Mortsafeman Trilogy
Dead Scared
Dead Silent
Dead Reckoning

Novels
Earthedge

Coming Soon!
The Man Who Made an Angel

For more information
visit: www.SpeakingVolumes.us

Earthedge

Ivan Blake

SPEAKING VOLUMES, LLC
NAPLES, FLORIDA
2025

Earthedge

Copyright © 2025 by Ivan Blake

All rights reserved. No part of this book may be reproduced or transmitted in any form or by any means without written permission.

This novel is entirely a work of fiction. All characters, and incidents in the story are the work of the author's imagination. The names of several well-known historical figures are used in the story. However, the characters to whom the names refer populate an alternate reality and in no way represent real persons, either living or dead, in our reality. The publisher does not have any control over and does not assume any responsibility for author contents.

ISBN 979-8-89022-234-3

For Heather

Introduction

Earthedge is a work of fantasy and alternate history full of mischief and nonsense. The central proposition in the story is absurd, but in the alternate reality I've concocted the proposition is true, and my hero must fight to reveal this truth because that's what heroes do. No matter the context, real heroes perform the same function: they fight for what is true and to undo the damage done by lies.

You're about to read a sprawling tale of war and exploration, intrigue and youthful romance. As such it has many, many characters. You need not fear, however, since most of them make only brief appearances and then disappear back into the storytelling ether. The few characters with whom you will become very familiar are the following:

- Stalwart Wordsmouth, an Earthedger and our hero
- Marigold Springpeeper, an Earthedger and Stalwart's girlfriend
- Lollipop Crossingguard, an algorythy (mathematician) employed by the Royal and Ancient Academy
- Lord Edmund of Muckyheath, Chancellor of the Royal and Ancient Academy
- Hobby Natterer, an Academy smartypants (security guard) and Lord Edmund's righthand man

All the other characters in the story are far less important and their only function is to populate the world in which our tale unfolds. If, however, you do like to keep track of all the characters mentioned in a story, then I've provided a complete list of both the consequential and inconsequential characters at the end of the book.

A word about the characters' names in this alternate reality. In our world, many names harken back to ancient trades (like Fisher, Smith and Farmer), familial relationships (like Fils du Roy or Fitzroy, Erik's son or Ericson), nature (like Rose or Willow) or virtues (like Grace, Joy or Hope). Why, I thought, might their world not follow a similar course when coming up with names, except that they might look to such things as condiments (Tartarsauce), conveniences (Fireplug) or engineering devices (Armature). Anyway, I had fun creating them and I hope you enjoy encountering them.

You're also going to come across a lot of peculiar terms for everyday items in this alternate reality, terms like medicator (doctor), bookylearn (school), diplomatize (graduate) and impracticum (college). It is their world after all, and they have every right to call things whatever they choose. Most, I'm sure, won't cause you any grief since you're likely to be able to intuit their meaning quite easily.

And finally, a note about scientific terminology in our story. Earthedge exists in an alternate reality in which much of the science and invention that has happened in our world has been stifled by the nefarious Royal and Ancient Academy of Knowledge in theirs. What little technology that does exist is largely the creation of the creative minds of Earthedge, and that tiny community certainly won't have come up with the same names for such things as microphones, internal combustion engines and transformers as we have. Hence, the curious names like 'exagifier' and 'watchycallit' and the 'cans and fans' engine. Here again, my hope is that you will be able to intuit what the device resembles in our world.

The End

Would that we grasped the middle
When we're standing on the side,
The ups, the downs, the ins, the outs,
When we're on some other tide.

The good, the bad, the feigned, the true,
The fact, the false, the dark, the light,
When each is mere perspective,
A trick of failing sight.

But pray the end remains concealed,
Unknown 'fore we depart—
That we're never told the outcome,
The end—before we start.

—Stalwart Wordsmouth

Chapter One

London, 1957

Twenty-first year in the reign of His Majesty King Edward VIII[1] and the tenth since the Scratchybottom Armistice ended the Realm's third war with America[2]

Lord Edmund of Muckyheath, Chancellor of the Royal and Ancient Academy of Knowledge and the United Kingdom's greatest scientist since Leonard Diggs[3], dipped the last of his marmite toast in the runny yolk and murmured, "He simply has to die." After a foul night of dithering and second-guessing, the necessity of Grimly Wordsmouth's death now seemed as obvious as the bowed legs on a beggar's brat. Just as Edmund had cracked open his soft-boiled egg for breakfast, so he'd have to crack open Wordsmouth's skull by teatime. And what a relief it will be to finally put an end to all that fopdoodle's pontificating.

"Truth," Edmund grumbled, "what does that cretin know of truth? Truth is what I say is truth."

Morgurt, the downstairs maid, popped her head around the morning room door. "Steam carriage is here, your Lordship."

The bone-jarring carriage ride across London was nauseating. Edmund regarded the city as one enormous heap of filth and a labyrinthine warren for

---

[1] Edward VIII ascended the throne on the twentieth of January 1936. His marriage to twice-divorced American socialite Wallis Simpson almost ended his reign, but the king stared down his constitutional critics and eventually prevailed. Wallis Simpson never enjoyed much public regard, however.

[2] The Scratchybottom Armistice was named for the tiny Dorset fishing harbor, Scratchybottom, where it had been signed.

[3] Leonard Diggs (c.1515–c.1559), a surveyor, was credited with the invention of the theodolite, a device to measure angles between points at a distance.

vermin, both two-legged and four. Every minute spent chugging along squalid lanes, over cracked cobblestones, past gaunt and grubby denizens, and through the stench of a thousand cesspits and the smoke from a thousand coal fires further poisoned Lord Edmund's already dyspeptic stomach and corrosive disposition.

That said, the trip afforded his Lordship a final few solitary moments in which to collect himself before the bedlam of the Royal Academy's annual conclave commenced. Edmund's determination—the single-minded, ruthless, cold-eyed determination he'd nurtured since childhood—was as steely as ever. But today was going to be the most severe test of his leadership in a lifetime of blood-soaked accomplishments.

Today, that worthless slug, Grimly Wordsmouth, was going to challenge the awesome authority Edmund had dedicated his life to preserving. Doubly galling was the fact that Wordsmouth was a nobody, a worm with neither an impracticum appointment nor Royal Warrant. And worst of all, the cursed slug, the mewling biddy, the ass end of a prized porker, actually had the means to do precisely what he'd threatened—to humiliate and even obliterate Edmund's beloved Academy.

***

After its Order of the Garter, the Royal and Ancient Academy of Knowledge was the British Empire's most powerful body. The Academy authorized all academic inquiry. It dictated the Realm's scientific agenda. Above all, it prescribed established truth. Simply by its presence, it had unquestionably saved the kingdom vast wealth. Without its oversight, how much treasure might have been squandered on fruitless, garden-shed variety tinkering, frivolous rainbow-chasing, and feeble investigations? In a thousand years, there had never been an instance of unapproved research, nothing of consequence anyway, not before this sniveling, bog-dwelling, damnable mathematography teacher, Grimly Wordsmouth, appeared on the scene.

And who could the chancellor blame for this first instance of bald-faced rebellion in a thousand years? No one but himself. One stupid lapse in his own judgment had spawned this upstart.

Earthedge

From the outset, Lord Edmund had been uncomfortable with the space cannon project, and he'd told everybody so. But then the small boy in him overwhelmed an old man's apprehension. As a child, he'd stared endlessly at the heavens from the roof of his parents' orangery. What child hasn't wondered what lies beyond the great crystal dome? And so, like an ignorant bumpkin, he'd approved the idiotic space cannon.

Against all odds, the enormous cannon's projectile achieved orbit and managed to circle the planet twice. Its courageous cannonaut also survived his ride among the stars long enough to make several sketches of Earth from the heavens. But then the damned fool, as his last coherent act, had secured his drawings in a leaden casket before the projectile's fiery tumble to Earth. The projectile's recovery team seized the casket from the crash site but not fast enough.

For *stercus*[4] sake, Grimly Wordsmouth was a nothing, a mere worldyforms and mathematography teacher. He'd labored in the employ of an industrialist with the misguided notion of providing free primary education to the offspring of his workforce. Then fate had struck.

While on a midwinter working holiday in the Carpathians, Wordsmouth witnessed the projectile's flaming descent to Earth. He'd trekked across snow-covered mountains in pursuit of what he'd assumed was a shooting star. After two days and nights of hard slog, he'd reached the village of *Svinjac*. The destruction visited from space upon their neighbors still rattled its inhabitants. The projectile had killed a widower, his spinster sister and her cat, and demolished a farmhouse, a chickencoop, and a clothesline of clean wash.

Wordsmouth arrived no more than an hour ahead of the projectile recovery team, but time enough for a glance at the cannonaut's drawings. That's when Wordsmouth first got wind of the Academy's darkest secret, and from that day forth, he was a driven man.

---

[4] *Stercus* is Latin for, well, for human excrement.

As soon as Lord Edmund was informed someone might have seen the cannonaut's drawings, he'd ordered his most trusted Academy smartypants[5]—Hobby Natterer—to hunt down the culprit.

Hobby Natterer had earned a barely respectable impracticum diploma. As a consequence of his indifferent academic performance, he'd forsaken any real opportunity of a scientific career. Even so, he still fancied he might one day get a second chance. Until then, however, he'd wear the tartan pantaloons of an Academy smartypants proudly and prosecute every assignment with bloodthirsty resolve. Or so he'd assured Lord Edmund. Natterer's willingness to employ violence earned him Lord Edmund's trust, and after receiving his new assignment, Natterer hadn't taken long to identify the chancellor's prey.

Grimly Wordsmouth's sudden resignation from the Millworth Bookylearn had raised the suspicions of his colleagues. The prospect of earning a pound or two from the Shared Secrets Program of the National Police had been too enticing for some to resist: *Print what you've Seen, pop it in the Box and pick up a Bob.* Three colleagues popped cards into the bookylearn's Shared Secrets box. One of Wordsmouth's drinking chums knew precisely where he'd gone.

Wordsmouth's wife had recently inherited some property in the Scottish Highlands. Natterer soon located Wordsmouth, his wife and their brat at the western end of the Great Glen near Fort William. There, they were living in a croft out on the Old Military Road. For nearly a year, Natterer observed the rebel scholar's activities from a sheepcote high up the slope above Wordsmouth's hidey-hole.

---

[5] The Corps of Smartypants was the Academy's enforcement arm. Dubbed smartypants for the Corps' founder, Brigadier Hironimus Smarty (retd), the Corps had been established in 1820 to quell an outbreak of unauthorized experimentation and grave robbery spawned by the literary fantasies of a libertine named Mary Shelley. Brigadier Smarty had prescribed the Corps' distinctive pantaloons in his clan tartan because, as a Scot and an avid golfer, he'd wanted to be able to gallop from parade square to golf course without changing attire.

Lord Edmund was livid to learn Wordsmouth had already begun his unsanctioned research. According to Natterer's encrypted reports, the bastard devoted nearly every waking hour to his studies. He reviewed all the atlases, topographical calculations, and travelers' accounts he could find. He waded through subjects as diverse as magnetism, optical illusions, and mass hallucinations. And he walked, walked day and night, for miles and miles, for months on end. He muttered to himself, stopped to scribble notes, and made innumerable observations of the sun and moon. Even when accompanied onto the hills by his young son, Wordsmouth continued his observations and calculations. And then, as abruptly as his research had begun, it ended.

One crisp morning in early December, Wordsmouth emerged from the croft with a battered suitcase. He embraced his wife, kissed his son, and set off on foot down the muddy track to Fort William. There he caught the weekly Gale and Northern Wind Wagon for Edinburgh.

With a bit of physical persuasion, Natterer extracted Wordsmouth's destination from the ticket agent, then watched from the station's weather tower as the great yellow sails of the lumbering wind wagon slowly disappeared around the side of Ben Nevis. At the Royal Semaphore Shoppe, he sent an urgent message to Lord Edmund, saying Wordsmouth was on the move. Academy eyes were upon Wordsmouth the moment he disembarked his Dregs Class coach in London.

From a dosshouse on St. Pancras Road, Wordsmouth wrote first to the king, then to the Talkyhall Primus Speaker, and finally to the Royal Academy's Board of Regents. He requested meetings to discuss, as he put it, "the shape of the Earth." Neither the king nor the Primus Speaker bothered to reply. Most Royal Academy Board members wished to reject Wordsmouth's request out of hand. How many other blithernits over the decades had asked for the Board's time to air their views on the state of the world? The request rattled Lord Edmund, however.

"Shape of the Earth," the upstart had written. It appeared the chancellor's worst fear might have been confirmed: the bastard knew. Lord Edmund promptly replied, 'We'll meet alone." Thank Combe he'd had the good sense to stipulate "alone."

Their meeting in Putney Old Burial Ground went catastrophically wrong. Accusations, insults, and curses echoed across the tumbled markers and collapsed graves. Even so, Lord Edmund's threats of endless lawsuits and physical violence had done the trick. He'd silenced the bastard, for the time being at any rate. Wordsmouth had agreed to delay his public pronouncement. More importantly, Lord Edmund had bought the time he needed to conjure a strategy and prepare for this day. Wordsmouth had vowed to make his devastating discovery public at the Royal Academy's annual conclave and Lord Edmund had sworn retribution if he did.

And so today, their battle would be joined.

***

Trundle Cobble Lane stretched from the stinking fog of the Thames Valley up Snapthrottle Hill to the vast estate of the Royal and Ancient Academy of Knowledge. Since before dawn, the procession of steam carriages had clogged the ancient thoroughfare. Puffing great clouds of sulfurous smoke, each carriage in its turn rumbled to a halt before the Academy's broad marble staircase. A dozen automata, gears whirling and drive belts twisting beneath scarlet uniforms, greeted every elderly scientist. The automata then lifted the greybeards from their carriages and carried them up the steps to the immense Palladian complex.[6] There, the frock-coated gentlemen awaited the opening of the Academy's annual conclave and exchanged opinions on prospects for yet another war with America.

"Frankly, I can't see how having an American-born queen has ever helped our relations with the Yanks," said one old gent.

---

[6] Venetian Renaissance architect, Andrea Palladio, reinterpreted the architecture of ancient Rome for his own time. His distinctive use of columns and covered porticos became known as Palladian style. The Royal and Ancient Academy was designed by one of Palladio's English adherents, Sir Burntumber Autumnleaves, who unfortunately had none of his master's sense of proportion and symmetry. Nicknamed the Milk Bottle Travesty, the Royal Academy Portico had too many marble columns by half and resembled a dairyman's delivery basket. Not infrequently, portly greybeards got stuck trying to squeeze between the portico's oversized columns.

"No indeed," said another. "In fact, lots as still believe Queen Wallis may have caused the last war. It's said she turned away the advances of their president's virile young son. The boy was so bewildered by the rejection that he ran sniveling to daddy. The story goes, daddy then found a pretext for war."

"Well, I place little stock in that tale," replied a third particularly distinguished gentleman. "Since when has our queen ever turned away the advances of any man, virile or otherwise?" he said to the snickers of some.

"Of course, Lord Bilbury," said a fourth greybeard, "you'd know that better than most," which occasioned raucous laughter from everyone within earshot and a self-satisfied grin from Lord Bilbury.

The greybeards' procession was largely ceremonial since most of the aged academikers already lived in residence. Those who did not, however, joined their colleagues in Academy rooms for the month-long conclave in order to give their undivided attention to the state of British science.

A large crowd of well-wishers had congregated outside the gates. Some of the less shabby were permitted to enter the estate and line the Grand Avenue. They applauded Academy members and chanted the names of the more famous. Some even waved posters imploring the kingdom's brightest minds to address one or another especially pressing social ill.

Beloved Scientists, Please Invent a Better Poultice for the Pox.

Distinguished Greybeards, When Shall We Have a Cure for Dropsy?

The arrival of Lord Edmund's steam carriage—a crimson Trevithick Steameater, a five-ton double lunger with six iron wheels and emblazoned with the Academy's coat of arms—drew the loudest approbation and most fervent appeals.

Beloved Chancellor, can you not rid the rats from our borough?

Lord Edmund, Why Can't We Clean the Thames?

As the Realm's most prestigious scientist, Lord Edmund certainly didn't have time for trivial matters like rats or the Thames. He was far too busy perfecting his wind-driven calculating engine, now miraculously smaller than a back-garden privy. In Britain's unusual autumn heat, Lord Edmund's ankles were already rubbed raw by the cogs in his clockwork walking pants. Even so, he declined the automaton's lift to acknowledge the posters and their bearers with a smile and a wave as he staggered up the steps in agony.

Nurturing the good auspices of the rabble was the duty of every chancellor. The ignorant masses' veneration of their intellectual superiors remained almost as unwavering in 1957 as when William the Conqueror first convened his Assembly of the Brilliant in 1072. The public's acquiescence had sustained the Academy in its near limitless authority for a millennium, and nothing was going to change that. Certainly not during Lord Edmund's tenure as chancellor, and most especially not today.

Damn it, not at my conclave!

"Scribben! Scribben!" Edmund shouted as he reached the top of the stairs.

His aide pushed his way through a gaggle of greybeards, "Over here, your Lordship, here."

Edmund grabbed Scribben by his faded green livery and growled, "After my opening remarks I'll need to rest, but while I'm napping, I want automata posted at every entrance and all smartypants to be on the lookout for that weasel, Wordsmouth. They can take whatever measures they fancy to restrain him until I'm ready to deal with him, but Wordsmouth must not get into the Academy. Understood?"

***

The frantic pounding on his office door roused Lord Edmund from a mouth-watering dream about kippers and cream. "Chancellor sir!" Scribben, his aide, shouted from the other side of the door. "He's here. He's at the conclave!"

"He? Who?" Lord Edmund grumbled as he rubbed his eyes and ran his fingers through the remaining wisps of hair on his wrinkled scalp. But then, of course, he knew: Wordsmouth!

Scribben bustled into the room as Lord Edmund was attempting to dry his feet. He'd dozed off soaking his inflamed ankles in a basin of hot potato water and seaweed.

"Quickly man, help me dress!" Lord Edmund bellowed.

Scribben rubbed ointment on Edmund's ankles and then shook the crumbs from the chancellor's robe of office.

"Wordsmouth's here? How is that possible?" Edmund grumbled as he pulled on his piss-prevention pants. Without them, he'd never make it to noon. "Did I not give strict instructions to post automata at every entrance? Did I not say that?"

"Yes, sir, and we did, sir," Scribben replied as he laced up the chancellor's whalebone girdle and knotted his garters. "But Wordsmouth was already inside. He'd slipped in during an early-morning scuffle in the foyer. A ménage of sex researchers and a collection of librarians clashed over the classification of certain … um … illustrated texts. The pictures being tossed about may have distracted our more excitable colleagues."

The chancellor sighed, gargled with oysters and rainwater, spit into his washbowl, and asked, "So where is he now?"

"In Mary Toft Hall, sir, he's on stage. Grabbed a panelist's megaphone, he did, and then said he's going to blow up the Academy!"

"Oh, *stercus*!" Lord Edmund muttered as he pulled the scarlet gown of office over his girdle. "*Irumbado*[7] *stercus*!" Then tugging the enormous top hat of royal appointment down over his ears, he stormed from the study. Despite his girth, Edmund jogged away toward the theater.

"Where's my gun?" he bellowed as he rumbled through the Hall of Heroes. "Get my damned gun! And arm the automata!" As he pounded across the Pantheon and entered the Wing of New Miracles, he cried, "And get Natterer here! I need Natterer now!"

At the sculpture of Mary Toft, Lord Edmund paused to catch his breath and mop his brow.[8] Then, in expectation of gunfire and explosions, he burst

---

[7] *Irumbado* is Latin for, uh, 'intimate relations', here used as an adjective.

[8] In 1726 Mary Toft claimed to have given birth to rabbits. A local surgeon investigated the matter and notified several prominent physicians, including Nathaniel St. André, surgeon to King George I. St. André concluded Toft's case was genuine and

through the theater door and immediately dropped to his knees. He crouched behind a very large colleague seated on the aisle and awaited the whistle of passing bullets.

Instead of gunshots, he was greeted by utter silence and a thousand terrified faces.

"Ah, here you are!" The amplified voice echoed through the great hall. "Why are you on your knees? Isn't that a rather undignified position for a man of your years?"

Edmund struggled to his feet. He looked first at the stage. There, five old men sat—frozen more like—in red velvet armchairs. They appeared utterly bewildered. But a gun-toting Wordsmouth wasn't among them. Edmund then glanced up at the plafond, the ceremonial dais suspended over the audience and the chancellor's place of honor.[9]

Even in the flickering glow of a hundred coal-oil lanterns and the watery green daylight from a dozen enormous windows, it was difficult to make out much of Grimly Wordsmouth, standing as he was in heavy shadow on the edge of the dais, save that he was short, thin and with closely cropped hair.

"Yes, Lord Edmund, I've taken your spot," said Wordsmouth through a megaphone. "Oh, and I've had that ridiculous golden staircase removed. Its presence might have posed too much of a temptation for some foolhardy soul."

---

in Toft's honor, George I gifted the Royal Academy its grand theater and her sculpture.

[9] Since Toft Hall's construction, every chancellor had presided over the assembled Academy from the plafond. An imposing onyx disk, a cubit thick and six cubits in diameter, the plafond dangled on silver chains, some 66.6 cubits long, from the ornately carved and colorfully painted ceiling of the cavernous hall. The dais swayed slightly, and each new chancellor required a month or so to develop their plafondilly legs. But that was, after all, the job of a chancellor, to "hold sway" over the brightest minds of the Realm.

Chancellors customarily ascended from the stage to the plafond up a suspended staircase. It was then swung away during debates to prevent any aggrieved presenter from attacking the chancellor. Early in Lord Edmund's tenure, he'd had the stairs gilded. An extravagance admittedly, but Edmund hadn't done it for himself; he'd done it to reinforce the dignity of the chancellor's office and to remove any doubt as to the absoluteness of a chancellor's authority.

Grimly Wordsmouth swept his hand across the thousand terrified faces below him. "Quiet, aren't they." He shook his head. "But you should have heard them ten minutes ago. Bellowing at one another over … what was it? Ah yes, whether that old man on the right," Wordsmouth pointed at one of the panelists as he spoke, "should be permitted to repeat a recent German experiment in making a new metal called steel in quantity. Or, as the nutter on the left would have it, the Academy should ban any talk of new metals as a betrayal of good old British iron. Ban a metal? Can you believe it? Our science has come to that!"

Scribben slipped into the theater and crept up behind Edmund. "Sir," Scribben whispered, "I have it."

"Is that a gun?" Wordsmouth shouted. "Is your lackey trying to slip you a gun? Well, I suppose that's only fair." Wordsmouth pulled a revolver from his belt. "Since I have one of my own."

Greybeards gasped and whimpered.

"Is that it? Is that what you want?" shouted Lord Edmund, "a gunfight right here between you and me? Because if so, you need to know I was grouse shooting champion of my school for six years, and you were what, needlepoint champion?"

"I don't want to shoot anyone," replied Wordsmouth. "You know that very well, Lord Edmund, even if you'd like nothing more than to shoot *me*."

Several voices immediately shouted, "But he *does* want to hurt us, he said so! He has a bomb! He said he's going to destroy the Academy!"

"I did. I did say I was going to destroy the Academy, but not with a bomb. I have another device in mind, and the chancellor knows what I mean, don't you, Chancellor?"

At the news the interloper had no actual bomb, many greybeards jumped to their feet, shouting and waving their arms. "If there's no bomb, then get the automata in here. Hurry now! Bring the stairs back. Take this madman away."

One of the panelists—a striking man with an elegant bearing and full head of salt and pepper hair—stood up and raised his arms for silence. No other member, save the chancellor himself, could have quieted the Academy so quickly. But this panelist wasn't just anyone. He was Lord Bilbury, the scientist who'd overcome the innate human dread of imbalance and invented the Bilbury Tricycle, the most widely used mode of transportation in the Realm and the scientific breakthrough for which he'd been awarded the King's Medal for Cleverness. And more galling still, Lord Bilbury had once been Lord Edmund's closest rival for the post of chancellor. Edmund knew only too well there were many members present who still resented his victory. When quiet was restored, Bilbury called out, "You know this man, do you, Edmund? So, what is he talking about? If he has no explosive, then what sort of weapon does he have?"

From the plafond, Wordsmouth echoed Bilbury's question with blatant mockery in his voice, "Yes, Chancellor, what sort of weapon *do* I have?"

Lord Edmund took a long breath, drew himself up, walked to the stairs, and climbed onto the stage. Standing in front of the panelists and looking out over the crowd, he started to speak. "This man has information—"

"Can't hear you!" members called from across Toft Hall. "Too quiet! Speak up, your Lordship!" A panelist passed his megaphone to Lord Edmund, who took a moment to gather his thoughts and then recommenced.

"As I was saying ... this man has learned a secret no one else has known for 500 years, no one except for the honorable gentlemen who have held the office of chancellor of our august Academy. Since 1571, every chancellor in his turn has had to make the difficult decision to either keep that secret or divulge it, and each has made the same choice: the decision to keep it. But now, this man wants to make that secret public. And, like every chancellor before me, I fear the revelation will destroy our Academy, and very possibly, the Realm."

Earthedge

"Oh please," Wordsmouth replied, "you're being far too dramatic. When have facts ever been costlier than falsehood? And so, what if this particular fact breaks the stranglehold your precious Academy has around the neck of rigorous research? You've had it for far too long. So what if unbridled inquiry is restored to the Realm, what harm could there be in that?"

Again, bedlam reigned. Hundreds of greybeards screamed, "Blasphemy! Heresy! Madness! The man is a lunatic!"

The chancellor hushed the crowd. Old men fell back into their seats, huffing and wheezing.

"Before we go any further, young man," said Lord Edmund, "may I ask that the gentlemen of the broadsheets be escorted from the room?"

Wordsmouth nodded, and several automata immediately jerked to life. There followed much shuffling at the back of Toft Hall as a dozen flustered scribblers with their chalkboards and writing boxes were summarily marched from the theater.

When order was restored, the young man on the plafond spoke.

"Chancellor, I've allowed you to expel the scribblers because I know with certainty there is nothing you can do to conceal the truth much longer. Before entering this chamber, I slipped new punch cards into two of your automata, instructing them to distribute a thousand copies that I had several pennyinkmen in Doodler Lane make at my own expense. They're replicas of a sketch made by that pathetically suicidal sop you sent up in your space projectile, copies of the one sketch your recovery team did not retrieve."

Lord Edmund's skin crawled.

That damned cannon again! Stercus!

Grimly Wordsmouth looked out across the crowd. "Did any of you even know that your cannonaut made sketches of the Earth during his orbits? It was the one achievement that might have given some meaning to his pathetic sacrifice—if, that is, the world had been told of it. During the poor fool's state funeral, your chancellor made no mention of the sap's gift to humanity, the first truly human glimpse of our planet from the beyond! How arrogant you all are! If you never actually wanted to see what he saw, why did you send a man? Why didn't you simply send a chimp?"

Doors opened on each side of the great hall, and in marched two automata carrying sheaves of paper.

"Ah, right on time. So, now let's light the fuse, shall we?" said Wordsmouth.

The automata moved haltingly down the aisles, passing a stack of sketches to each row in its turn. The first automaton to reach the stage handed several sheets up to the chancellor.

One glance at the sketch and Lord Edmund knew the end was at hand.

Oh stercus! Stercus, stercus, stercus! There is nothing to be done.

"Will we get a copy, Edmund?" Bilbury asked.

Lord Edmund spun about. "Oh, yes, of course," he said and passed the remaining copies to the panelists.

Bilbury is enjoying this!

There was much muttering across Toft Hall as greybeards cleaned their specs, squinted at the drawing, and whispered to one another. The buzz grew in intensity until, at last, someone called out, "What are we looking at? Is it a pie? What has a pie got to do with anything?"

Wordsmouth was now seated on the edge of the plafond with his legs dangling over the side. He called down to Lord Edmund, "Shall I tell them what they're looking at, your Lordship, or would you prefer to do the honors?"

"Edmund," Bilbury shouted, "surely this is a joke. It's a cartoon. It cannot be the Earth."

Hubbub everywhere until Lord Edmund cleared his throat, and the hall fell silent.

"No, Bilbury, it is not a cartoon. It is indeed the Earth ... as seen from space by our courageous cannonaut."

"But then why is it shaped like ... like a fruit flan?" Bilbury snorted at his own wit. "The heat in the capsule or the pressure or a lack of phlogiston must have driven the man mad before he tumbled from orbit."

Wordsmouth called out, "The cannonaut drew the Earth like a flan because that is what it looks like."

Earthedge

"Flat ... like a ... a dinnerplate?" exclaimed Bilbury. "And this ... this ridiculous cartoon is what you fear might threaten the Academy?"

First, there were sniggers, then chuckles, and finally, gales of laughter. Ancient academikers guffawed and then gasped for breath. They wheezed and then held their sides. They doubled over and grasped their nether parts for fear of having an embarrassing accident.

"Yes," the chancellor replied.

"You can't be serious," sneered Bilbury. "Your young friend is mad. He's wasting our time with this rubbish. Have him tossed out, and let's get back to business."

"Ah, but Lord Bilbury," Grimly Wordsmouth shouted from the plafond, "There is proof! Your poor cannonaut was not impaired or mad or anything else. He drew precisely what he saw as he spun around the rim of the Earth. The Earth is *flat*. When I saw this sketch I was at first confused, but then I began my own calculations and I have confirmed what your cannonaut observed. But when I brought my work to Lord Edmund's attention, he admitted that he already knew the Earth was flat and that he had proof of his own. Don't you, Lord Edmund."

"This is preposterous," exclaimed Bilbury. Academy members across Toft Hall bellowed their agreement. "There can't be such proof, young man, because it couldn't possibly exist."

"I regret," said the chancellor softly—the chamber immediately fell still— "I regret to say ... he is right, I do have proof."

"But that's absurd!"

Edmund spoke almost apologetically. "The proof is the work of Abd Allah Muhammad Ibn Al-Bedriddon. He was a Muslim Berber, a scholar and an adventurer who died in 1364. He'd explored the entire known world and reported his findings in a manuscript entitled, *A Gift to Those Who Contemplate the Marvels of Traveling and Believe the World to be Round*. It came into the Academy's possession in 1571, after its discovery in the ruins of a former Templar stronghold outside Auriac-du-Périgord."

"And you believe this ... this Musselman?"

Edmund hesitated. Until now he'd been able to ignore Ibn Al-Bedriddon and his inconvenient discoveries. Locked away in Edmund's vault, the Arab's proofs had seemed as dead as he was. Now, to have to admit publicly that he believed the Arab would be to take ownership of a fact Edmund had spent his entire life rejecting. But what choice did he have? The importance of the Academy's mission to maintain orderly inquiry and constrain impulsive curiosity transcended the significance of a lot of mathematical blather about a flat Earth. All that mattered was maintaining the Academy's mandate even if Edmund was going to have to admit to concealing this one awkward fact.

"Yes, I do believe it," he said, although he nearly gagged on the words.

"But our ships sail across the globe," blustered Lord Bilbury. "Our navigational instruments work flawlessly. We have time zones and telescopes. And none of our world travelers, not one of them," he repeated for emphasis, "has ever fallen over the edge of your flat Earth."

Wordsmouth chimed in again. "No one has ever fallen over the edge because no one has ever even approached the edge. That's because the Earth's magnetic fields function to confine us within a veil of confusion. Magnetic fields prevent us from seeing distortions in the size and scale of distances in the same way the moon looks so much larger when it is near the horizon, or heat rising from a cobbled lane makes our vision ripple and roll."

"And you think this information could destroy the Academy."

"It will," Wordsmouth shouted, "when the king and the broadsheet publishers and everyone else come asking for the evidence Lord Edmund has locked up in his safe, including, I might add, the other sketches your cannonaut made during his two orbits around the rim of our flat Earth."

"I don't understand," Bilbury said with obvious irritation. "If the proof is so compelling and every chancellor since 1571 has believed it, then why was it suppressed in the first place?"

"Because," Edmund avowed, "our beloved chancellor of the day, Earl Henry Percy, was concerned for the very survival of the Academy."

"That's not an answer!" replied Bilbury with a vigorous shake of his head. "Why was he so afraid of the Arab's work?"

"Because, Bilbury, releasing the Arab's work would have meant taking on the whole damned world. Need I remind you that everyone in 1571 believed the Earth was round? Everyone!" shouted Lord Edmund. "Greek astronomers had said so in the third century BC. The entire medieval world believed it. By the sixteenth century, every posh person in Europe owned a Dutch-made terrestrial globe, and in 1522 Captain Elcano claimed he'd circumnavigated the world. To top it off, the Roman Church believed it. Their priests insisted the world was spherical because the scriptures refer to Christ's "spheres of blessings."

"*That's* what Chancellor Percy confronted in 1571 and he knew full well how dangerous it would be to announce that the Earth was flat based on the work of some unknown Muslim explorer. The news would have pitted our Academy against the Church, the Realm and even the simple-minded masses just at a time when the world was already being ripped apart by that madman Copernicus and the rest of his heliocentric mob. It took the Inquisition a century to settle that mess."

Despite Edmund's rage, Bilbury still wouldn't shut up. He seemed determined to prolong Edmund's discomfort. "But even if this news might have ruffled feathers, if it's a fact the world is flat, then didn't the Academy have a duty to say so?"

At this point, Edmund's anger was on full display. "Earl Percy didn't give a steaming heap of donkey's dung whether a flat earth was a fact or not. But he did care about this institution and he agonized over its preservation. I know because I've read his diaries. He realized that announcing the world is flat wouldn't merely "ruffle feathers," as you put it. It would look like the Academy had cast its lot with the heliocentric mob and other such disrupters of established truth when rabble-rousers like Copernicus and his toady, Galileo, were already in full retreat. Percy concluded this one revelation—whether it be true or not—wasn't worth opening old wounds and bringing the wrath of the entire world down upon the Academy. And so, he concealed the manuscript." Edmund paused for moment, and then bellowed, "Because that's what chancellors do! We defend the Academy … no matter the cost!"

"And all Percy's successors went along with his decision?" Bilbury asked in a tone of incredulity.

Edmund let out an audible sigh and said, "Percy hoped the day would come when one of his successors would be able to release the manuscript without harm. But that day never came."

Bilbury still wouldn't let it go. "So for five hundred years, all our beloved chancellors have been sitting about, waiting for some other nation to reveal the news and claim the credit?"

"What other nation was going to discover the truth?" responded Edmund with a dismissive wave of his hand. "The Americans? They don't have a single impracticum worthy of the name and besides, there's nothing original about their science. They copy everything from us. The rubber-band rocking chair? Ours. Lime-burning theater lights? Ours. The clockwork page turner. Ours. So then what about the Russians, you might ask? Too primitive, mired as they are in their theocratic peat bog. And France? If it can't be seared or poached or glazed, they're simply not interested. And as for the rest of the world? Well, if we don't already own it, then no one does and it's not worth having. And besides, no one would believe anything that came out of those barbaric lands anyway."

Lord Edmund's lengthy reply seemed to provide Bilbury with the time he needed to cook up a proposal. "Well Edmund, perhaps the day Earl Percy had hoped for has now arrived," he said as he marched to the center of the stage in an attempt to once again enjoy the full attention of the assembly. "After we've had a good look at the Arab's so-called evidence, I propose we announce to the public that the Earth is flat. In these enlightened times, what harm could there possibly be in that?"

"Precisely!" Wordsmouth shouted from the plafond.

Lord Edmund shook his head in disgust. "Are you serious? You can't see how dangerous that would be? How our enemies would exploit such a foolhardy move?"

Bilbury shook his head, but his face hinted at his uncertainty.

The chancellor stepped in front of Bilbury and addressed his audience as a primary teacher might speak to a class of dimwits.

"Are you all so naïve that you don't appreciate how perilous the Academy's circumstances have become? Need I remind you of the Academy's less than stellar performances: at the Biddeford Witch Trial in 1641 for example, where our chemical test for witchcraft scalded twenty-three people and burned down a hops barn, or the Academy's infamous endorsement of the South Sea Trading Company which—when its bubble burst in 1720—cost the nation hundreds of millions of pounds, or our erroneous announcement in 1814 that Napoleon had died, which triggered the worst stock market crash the Realm has ever known, not to mention the horrifying outcome of our recent attempt to breed mermaids from dolphins or the farcical results of our armaments program in the last war? With each misstep, our enemies multiply. And today, those who would take away our mandate are abroad in every counting house, lurk in every impracticum, and even stalk the halls of Westminster. The very last thing we dare do is hand our enemies even more ammunition with which to challenge our authority."

Edmund paused, pulled a stained rag from his vest and wiped the sweat from his face. He then glared at Bilbury, turned back to the thousand dumbstruck greybeards, and bellowed, "Remember our mandate! To decree what is true! For a thousand years, the Academy alone has certified truth! The facts be damned. *We* have said what is true! And when has that responsibility ever been more crucial to the Realm than today? For more than four hundred years, we have been telling everyone the Earth was round when we knew the mathematics said otherwise. Do you think the rabble will continue to accept our certifications of truth when they're told this new truth? We shall—every one of us—we shall become a laughingstock. 'Which are you telling us now,' they will forever ask, 'the real truth or the other truth?' "

Toft Hall fell silent as each scholar weighed what this revelation might mean for his own career and circumstance.

"Now let me ask *you*, if we no longer decree what is true, if our mandate is taken from us because of this … this creature and his trivial discovery about the shape of the Earth, then who in our place will decide what is true and what is not? Without a credible and respected institution tasked to decree the truth, no society can survive, no society! Order will not hold!"

The worry written on every face in Toft Hall told Edmund his argument was hitting its mark.

"Without the official, established, binding truths that we alone ordain, I assure you, anarchy will o'ertake our Realm. People will bicker over everything. Vast amounts of time and treasure will be wasted in debate over the most trivial issues like the plight of the ill, the needs of the poor, the capabilities of women, and the admittance of the stateless to our Realm." He then pointed accusingly at every greybeard in the theater. "Everything will be called into question: the self-evident, the moral, the honorable, the deserving, *you*, and all your privileges!"

Edmund paused to let his words sink in before saying very solemnly, "But I do have a thought on how the Academy might salvage its credibility from this debacle."

The chamber exploded with shouts of "How?" "You must tell us!" and "There has to be a way!"

Lord Edmund turned to Bilbury and pointed to the man's velvet armchair, an unmistakable gesture of dismissal, before he marched to the front of the stage and began his exposition.

"This is what we will do. We shall not let this man's new facts—and its proof be damned—obscure the accepted, official truth about the shape of the Earth."

Lord Edmund's barely suppressed rage was obvious. Not a soul in Toft Hall would have dared cough, never mind challenge the chancellor, at that moment.

"First, we shall release the cannonaut's sketches, all of them, and we shall credit him with uncovering new information about the shape of the Earth. We shall praise the cannonaut's courage effusively and express immense gratitude for his discovery that the Earth is not quite as perfectly round as we'd once thought. Rather than the perfect sphere we'd believed the Earth to be, our cannonaut has revealed to us that it is shaped more like a grapefruit which has been left in the pantry too long.

"Some will ask why the Earth is so pie-shaped in his drawings. Well, we shall explain, his distortions were due to the immense pressures on his brain during space flight. The sketches must be adjusted for the projectile's speed and force and bad air and weak phlogiston and any other nonsense we can cook up.

"We shall assure the public that Academy greybeards are busy reviewing every navigational calculation and airship route and timetable and so forth to ensure their accuracy in light of this new, albeit minor, detail. In due course, we shall even release a slightly modified globe of the Earth which will change precisely nothing, and then we shall carry on as ever before."

"You fatuous bloody ass, Lord bloody Edmund, I'm right here!" Wordsmouth bellowed from the plafond. "I've heard every word you've just said, and if you think I'm not going to tell the whole world what you and your idiot friends are up to, you're sadly mistaken. Binding truths, what nonsense! No one can be allowed to pass off a grotesque scientific error as some sort of official truth. The drawing and most of my own calculations are already on their way to *The Times* and *The Mirror*. And from now on, I shall use every interview I give to expose your cover-up."

"No, you won't," Lord Edmund replied.

"I bloody well will!"

"You won't because you don't want harm to come to your family, and neither do we."

"Don't you dare threaten my family!" Wordsmouth shouted in a tone of horrified surprise.

The chancellor merely smiled at Wordsmouth's outburst, then called out, "Natterer, are you present?"

"Yes, Chancellor, up here," the smartypants replied from a gangway high above the stage.

"Wordsmouth's wife and son, you have them in confinement?"

"My colleague does, sir, up in Boggshead, sir, dockside."

"What?" shrieked Wordsmouth. "What have you done to my family?"

"And do you have Wordsmouth's tickets, Natterer?"

"I do indeed, sir."

"If you harm a hair …!" screamed Wordsmouth, but Lord Edmund paid him no mind.

"Then, will you kindly swing the golden stairs back in and disarm this interloper? You shall then accompany him to the Marble Arch Wind Wagon Station for his journey to Boggshead."

Lord Edmund turned his attention back to Wordsmouth. "Your wife and child, Mr. Wordsmouth, await you at the Boggshead ferry. From there, you three shall sail to Iceland. Now, let me be absolutely clear on this next point. You will cause our smartypants no bother. Mr. Natterer will accompany you to Iceland, so don't even think about jumping overboard on the way because, in a heartbeat, your wife and child will follow you over the side."

Lord Edmund then turned to his dumbfounded audience.

"This man and his progeny shall forever remain enemies of the Royal Academy, and we want them as far away from our Realm as is possible on our slightly deflated planet. Iceland, my dear colleagues, is where our former chancellor, Sir Samuel Rowbotham, estimated the Earth's magnetic waves might be their weakest.[10] There, he theorized, one might be able to push through the hypno-gravitational distortions to enter the barren lands he believed must encircle the habitable Earth. And once in those barrens, we can only hope Mr. Wordsmouth and family find their way to the rim because, Mr. Wordsmouth, that is where we expect you to go."

For an instant, Lord Edmund's rage got the better of him. He suddenly shrieked, "I began this day prepared to crack open your damned skull because you vex me, you ridiculous slug, you mealy turd, you stinking heap of—"

He stopped mid-rant, took a moment to recover his composure, breathed deeply for several seconds, and finished his earlier remarks.

"But as everyone knows, I am a sensitive and forgiving soul not given to murder."

Not when there'd be a thousand lily-livered witnesses....

---

[10] Samuel Birley Rowbotham, who dropped out of school at age nine, became very rich by developing and selling secret potions for prolonging human life and for curing every disease imaginable. Under an assumed name, he also wrote *Zetetic Astronomy: Earth Not a Globe*.

"So, banished you will be and banished you shall remain. Forever! At the very edge of your flat *irumbado* Earth!"

Pandemonium broke out across the theater.

"But," Lord Edmund shouted for all to hear, "if I ever set eyes on you again, I swear, next time, I *will* kill you."

Cannonaut's sketch circulated at the
Royal and Ancient Academy Conclave

Chapter Two

Earthedge 1967

Lord Edmund might have hoped that banishing Grimly Wordsmouth to the edge of the Earth would have put an end to the threat he'd posed to the Academy. But that's not how things turned out.

Wordsmouth did indeed discover a portal in Iceland where one could push through the veil of confusion to the barrens beyond. And after a year-long trek across a thousand miles of lifeless, fractured rock, he'd succeeded in reaching the rim of the Earth. There, in the company of two dozen like-minded adventurers whom he'd invited to join him, Grimly Wordsmouth established the village of Earthedge and lived to see the little community thrive. His deportation, trek, and hardships at the edge took a grave toll on him, however, and Grimly Wordsmouth passed away six months before my eighteenth birthday.

My name is Stalwart Wordsmouth. Grimly Wordsmouth was my father. I was eight when Father confronted the Royal Academy—and not yet nineteen when I was compelled to do the same. I am tall for my age, consider myself skinny (although my guardian insisted I was merely trim), have longish blond hair which was usually dirty, more than my share of pimples, and largish feet. And I live in Earthedge.

As my final bookylearn assignment before I am diplomatized, I am required to assemble this account of our second struggle with Father's nemesis, Lord Edmund of Muckyheath. Why? Because, as Dr. Tulip our teacher explained, our stories shape who we are, and recounting mine might help me heal. More importantly, I have to tell this story because I made a deathbed promise to a dear friend that I would.

***

Father often said how much Earthedge resembled the village of his birth, the tiny Devon fishing port of Cretchum. Cretchum's stone cottages clung to the rocky Devon coast in defiance of violent Atlantic storms, which ofttimes battered the village. Waves rolled endlessly across its shingle beach, the sound of their lapping audible in every dwelling. Each day, its fishing boats sailed before sunrise and returned by moonlight, and its sailors dreamt of adventure on far distant seas that they knew only in their imaginings. Such, Father said, is equally true of Earthedge.

The stone cottages of Earthedge cling to the rim of the Earth in defiance of solar storms, which sometimes sweep across space to batter the edge of the world. Gravity waves filled with ice crystals and dust perpetually wash our shore, jingling like a thousand tiny wind chimes. In our barren landscape, there is naught but stone—no soil, no water, no trees—only stone. Gravity at the edge is weak, but fortunately, strong enough to float the vessels we carve from rock.

We fishers of Earthedge sail in search of hydrogen. Hydrogen sustains us. Its particles become our water, energy, and even food. We set sail in darkness, troll copper nets for bursts of the elusive particle, and then return to port in darkness. All the while, we dream of sailing to the stars, or more daunting still, of descending into the unknown beneath the edge. The only difference between we stellar navigators of Earthedge and our counterparts in Devon? In the hours between departure and return, the sun never rises over Earthedge. The people of Earthedge dwell in perpetual twilight.

The great blue dome of air soars over the Earth like a giant soap bubble on bathwater. Earthedge exists in perpetual twilight because the dome is thinnest at its rim. Mere shades of the deepest blue distinguish day from night. Daylight does not deserve the name in Earthedge. The sun is never more than a dim, tarnished splinter, barely visible above the barrens.

Ah, but we have stars. Earthedge is bathed in starlight. Every star blazes like an arc lamp in a coal mine. Looking out across the vast rings of dust and ice crystals and beyond into the realm of perpetual night, Earthedgers see stars more numerous than all the sea glass on all the beaches in the world.

Like Cretchum by moonlight.

I was not witness to a number of the events in this account, so while I have tried to gather as many facts as possible, I have also had to take some poetic license in recounting them. I'd like to think I was the hero of this tale, but I know that wasn't true. Who the real heroes were, the reader will have to decide.

Chapter Three

Dinnerplate

In the ten years following Father's expulsion from Dinnerplate,[11] how conditions there had deteriorated. London had grown ever filthier. The Thames had become so choked with waste one could practically walk on the current from Kew to Greenwich. Poison fogs rolled in almost every afternoon. Some said the fogs were a blessing since they helped control the number of rural poor being driven into London by increasingly frequent crop failures. Pulpits and politicians decried eroding social mores. Men let their hair grow over their ears, and women wore skirts above their ankles. Music had acquired a decidedly aggressive beat. And inexplicably, the weather was changing. Summers were becoming intolerably hot, winters more damp and miserable, and midwinter snows but a distant memory.

Lord Edmund's efforts to limit the damage attending Father's exposé had had limited success. The public seemed to accept Academy assurances the Earth was only slightly less round than previously believed rather than totally flat as Father had tried to reveal. As a result, the Royal Academy's authority over the nation's scientific agenda remained largely unaffected. Its image, however, had suffered mightily, and music hall comedians had a field day.

"I hear tell Academy footballers was caught trying to sneak a deflated ball into a match. Well ain't that just like them! Always letting the wind out of people's balls."

"What else that's gone flabby at the Royal Academy d'ya s'pose them boffins is keepin' secret?"

"So, I read in *The Times* the only thing not deflated at the Royal Academy these days is its chancellor's pay packet."

---

[11] The Earthedger term for the populous center of the Earth

Earthedge

Oblivious to the ridicule, the Academy carried on with its most pressing projects. Could Lord Edmund's computing machine, now the size of a bathtub, be made to run entirely on wind instead of its backup rubber bands? Could Bilbury's tricycle be fitted into a flying machine? Would the Academy candle, the Realm's favorite method of illumination—which when burned down became a popular face cream—be produced in great enough quantity to satisfy female demand? The Academy's agenda was, however, changed in one very significant respect: it did not escape the disastrous consequences of the fourth American war.

A scant six months after Father's expulsion, Britain was again at war with America, and once again over coal. The fourth American war ended just as the third had done, in a stalemate. An armistice, signed in Come-by-Chance, Newfoundland, stipulated that global coal supplies would be apportioned to Britain and America by an international commission under the chairmanship of the Tsar of Russia, since everyone assumed Russia's reliance on peat rather than coal would assure the tsar's neutrality.

While the outcome of the war was not altogether ghastly, the performance of British forces during conflict was appalling. English arms proved laughable. Vaunted British research had yielded such ludicrous weaponry as guns that shot gum Arabic, cannons that fired string, gas that gave hives, and bombs that blew up unexpectedly whenever it rained. Only the ferocity of the Realm's colonial troops and the ludicrous state of America's own forces prevented the United Kingdom's defeat. Following the war, an inquiry chaired by Lord Edmund found some fault with British armaments research—but not much—and made several recommendations for improvement—but not many. The broadsheets were far less forgiving and called for the removal of arms' development from the Academy's purview. But of course, that hadn't happened.

The stress on Lord Edmund over the decade had been horrific, as his deteriorating health made manifest. He'd lost both feet to poor circulation in his legs, the use of his right arm to a stroke, the vision in one eye to diabetes, most of his teeth to decay, and the rest of his hair to something or other. Even so, he clung to his chancellorship with a ferocity that terrified everyone in his circle, many members of the Order of the Garter, and even the king himself.

Immediately following the American war and the Come-by-Chance Armistice, Lord Edmund swore to King Edward that Britain would soon regain its primacy in arms research. Edmund had ordered Academy members to bring him proposals for the most fearsome weapons they could conceive. But that was nearly seven years ago, and the king was becoming impatient for results. So secretly, Lord Edmund, in desperation, dispatched his most trustworthy dogsbody, Hobby Natterer, upon a ghastly mission.

In Earthedge, we knew little and cared even less about conditions in Dinnerplate. Nor did we have any inkling of Lord Edmund's predicament. Our thoughts for the moment were entirely on the three Earthedge fishing vessels that had gone missing during a recent solar storm and had only now struggled back to port.

Chapter Four

Rocksplitters Pub, Earthedge

Cepheus had set, twelve bells had rung, evening meals had been consumed, and now the Rocksplitters Pub was filled to bursting.[12] Publican Melody Fullbottle had turned on the electronical illumination for the occasion. She kept the lighting dim since no one living in Earthedge's constant twilight could cope with the kind of intense coal oil illumination they'd known back in Dinnerplate. Mothers, fathers, kiddies, crafters, and fishers of every age and gender, all eighty-three residents of Earthedge—save for two infirmed, one on a supply run across the barrens, and one on-duty essential at the mechanicals plant—had turned out to hear Captain Codkiss's tale.[13]

I squeezed onto a bench alongside Marigold Springpeeper. She smiled and took my hand. In her eyes, I saw excitement and anticipation. I, on the other hand, was very uneasy. Rumors of the captain's story sounded too much like one of Father's fantasies, and I instinctively resented anything associated with Father and his wild imaginings.

---

[12] Earthedgers marked their days and nights by the rise and fall of the constellation Cepheus, which appears above the edge of the Earth for twelve hours each day. The twelve hours were marked by the burning of the village candles. Made from fish oil scented with pyrargillite, the village's official timekeeping candle burned in Melody Fullbottle's pub. She lit a new candle each Cepheus rise, and it burned at a rate of an inch an hour. Hence, dawn or 7:00 a.m. was one bell, and 6:00 p.m., twelve bells. As the wick burn passed each inch marker, a clockwork device triggered by the candle's heat rang a bell in the spire above the pub's entrance. The bell, called the Melody Bell, could be heard all over the village. Villagers set their own hour candles by the Melody Bell. No bells were associated with the evening hours since no one in their right mind would ever need to know the hour while they slept.

[13] Seventeen singles, twenty-four couples, and eighteen children ranging from babes to older teens.

Earlier that afternoon, three of our fishing boats had limped home after having been missing for two days. The nine sailors were shaken and bruised, but alive. It seemed recent ferocious solar gales had swept their ships far from Earthedge and into the unknown. Word was they'd been carried several leagues downward, beneath the edge of the Earth. Miraculously, they'd returned and were now about to relate their adventure.

We had no way of knowing how thick our flat Earth might be or how its underside might appear. All we could see from up on the Earth's jagged edge were forbidding cliffs that dropped deep beneath its rings of dust and ice, and down into utter darkness. How far down the cliffs extended or how far our three ships might have fallen, no one in the Rocksplitters had any idea. Never before had an Earthedge vessel dared slip from the relative certainty of the edge and down toward the underbelly. Of course, every Earthedger who had sailed away and looked back at the Earth had wondered what might be down there, in that vast darkness, but no one had ever chanced a voyage. Not before now.

Captain Codkiss drew deeply on his onyx pipe and blew a ring of sweet potato smoke into the warm, close air of the crowded room. He wiped a line of perspiration from his cheek and began:

"We was coasting past Ariel Head at four bells, nets out for a burst of hydrogen, when our watchycallit[14] tells us it's near. And that's when Burpee shouts he's just seen an explosion on the Sun.

"None of the rest of us had noticed anything, but then our eyes are not clouded like Burpee's. He sees changes in the light we miss. But an hour later, these great streaks of green fire began dancing and darting across the sky.

---

[14] Detecting schools of hydrogen particles became possible when Middley Porter discovered quantities of a rare and lustrous silvery-white metal in the barrens. Called palladium, it has the curious capability of generating a small electrical charge in the presence of hydrogen. As a result, each fishing vessel in our fleet was equipped with a perforated obsidian box containing a fragment of palladium. When the palladium detected the presence of hydrogen gas, its charge ignited a moss thread, and the box glowed. Cogsy Eyebeam, a former chemist, named the device a watchycallit because he got tired of explaining the real chemical process.

Earthedge

"With those waves of green fire, there came these howling solar winds. They might have shredded our sails had we not been using that new mesh Covert Millrace devised. Even so, the sails crackled and glowed with the millions of excited electricons which swept over us. Sails flapped and twisted as if some giant creature had seized them. Our ships were tossed this way and that. The air popped and fizzed. Ice crystals and dust, which usually lap at our stone hulls, were driven like birdshot from a blunderbuss, lashing our flesh like scraping paper.

"The winds then hurled our ships toward a dark and unfamiliar coastline. We were terrified. Would our hulls be smashed against diamond-hard rocks and then ground to sand? But as we drew closer to the dark and forbidding shore, our ships were suddenly carried upward, higher and higher still, far above the edge. We was so high up I remember thinking, that's Farstation out there on the barrens, got to be a hundred leagues away. But then, as suddenly as we'd begun to climb, we dropped.

"Down, down we fell. Past the rim, through the rings, and into the darkness we sank. By the light of the radium lanterns on our masts, we could just make out jagged cliffs, mere fathoms off our bow as we plunged past. Falling a hundred, two hundred, three hundred leagues, we imagined our descent might never end, but then as precipitously as our fall had begun, it suddenly stopped. We were crushed to the decks by the violence of its end. At first, we lay dazed, breathless, barely able to rise. But then, as if a great weight was being lifted from us, we gently rose without effort. Indeed, we floated several thous[15] above our decks, bobbing about like autumn leaves on a puddle.

"I have sailed the ice crystal waves and the gentle gravity of our coast for near on seven years and I promise you, I have never known such an incredible sensation as that moment of weightlessness. Each of us rejoiced in our salvation. We called out to one another, laughing, tossing about in the air like

---

[15] In Earthedge, a thou equals 1/100 of an inch, 1200 thous equal one foot. Six feet equals a fathom (or four cubits). Sixty-six feet equals ten fathoms or a chain and 300 fathoms equals a league.

dandelion silk. But then the reality of our situation struck us, and we were terrified once again.

"Our ships were becalmed, listless as if the weakened gravity below the edge was barely sufficient to grasp the great weight of our stone hulls. At that moment, we were seized with the horrifying thought that our ships might at any moment break the hold of the weakened gravity beneath the Earth to then slip away into the limitless void with no hope of return.

"Entirely devoid of solar winds, our sails drooped. The air was thin. We gasped for breath. We felt weak and tired. Some crew like Burpee here even slept."

Everyone chuckled.

"By our radium lamps, we could make out a few dark shapes and contours above us. And that is when the import of our locale sank in—we were below the Earth. We were where no stone sailors had ever been. We were sailing the underside."

Everyone gasped.

"We had no time to dwell on this realization, however, because at that moment, there commenced a deep rumbling sound that rattled even the teeth in our heads. The rumble became a roar, and then grew ever more intense until it near deafened us. Even Burpee awoke. Then a deluge of dust like fine glass and razor-sharp, white-hot pebbles fell upon us from the underside, tearing our flesh and inflicting many terrible burns.

"In the distance we saw it—the source of the ear-shattering sounds and the downpour of lacerating stone fragments. A massive plume of fire and smoke shooting downward from a fissure in the underside, an inverted volcano!

"After several terrifying minutes, the plume of fire receded into the fissure, and a river of molten rock spewed from it. The lava snaked across the underside, moving ever nearer to the edge. We realized if we did nothing, the river of fire would soon consume us. It took but minutes for the first fingers of lava to begin sliding into the void. The white-hot liquid cooled and became glowing boulders that bobbed and careened about in the ephemeral gravity, crashing into one another in enormous explosions of embers and flame."

Children clutched their mothers. Men slid forward in their seats.

"At that moment, Burpee, who could barely see the dangers we faced, piped up with a miraculous thought. 'What if,' he said in a voice as calm as a mother putting her infant to bed, 'what if each ship tosses a net up the face of the edge? If we're lucky, the nets will catch on sharp outcroppings. Then we can use our winches to pull our ships up a few fathoms. Dangling there, we can then toss up another net and repeat the process. We only have to get high enough above the edge of the underside before the fiery flow has a chance to surround us in them flaming boulders. Is that not right?'

"And so that is what we did."

There were sighs of relief from every corner of the pub.

"Once we'd clawed our way high enough up the edge of the underside, the familiar tug of our gravity returned. Then our sails filled with gentle solar breezes and we were away home."

The pub exploded in cheers and applause.

"To the first Earthedgers ever to sail the underside," cried Publican Melody.

"To our heroes," everyone echoed, clinking goblets, clapping hands, patting the backs of the nine crew members, and bringing them innumerable refills of mushroom ale.

"Stalwart!" Melody shouted over the din, "Stalwart, what would your father have said about this achievement?"

"Yes, Stalwart, what would Grimly have said?" others called out. "Stalwart! Stalwart!" several even began to chant.

Marigold squeezed my hand. "Go on, say something," she whispered.

Marigold's was the voice that most immediately stirred my heart, just as it had done out on the barrens a decade ago, during the founders' historic trek to the edge.

But I didn't want to speak; I hated speaking. I most especially hated speaking for my father. Those last days with Father were still so raw in my memory. They'd been filled with bickering and disagreement over everything from mathematography to Father's hopes for my future. Few in the village knew of our quarrels, but I knew. I still felt their sting.

"Oh Marigold, this is Captain Codkiss's night," I replied.

Then Captain Codkiss said, "Go ahead, young Stalwart, remind us of your father's dreams."

There was no escape. I had to spout words I'd parroted on many other occasions, so many times I could not imagine how anyone might find them inspiring, but it seemed they did.

I waved to the captain and whispered to Marigold, "All right. For you," and rose to speak.

The room fell silent.

"Well, of course, my father would have been so proud of what the stone sailors of Earthedge have accomplished."

Deafening applause.

"It was always Father's dream to one day sail the underside himself."

"It was, he said that," people muttered.

"Father had so many dreams."

Loud applause followed by shouts of "More, Stalwart, tell us more of your father's dreams."

"You know better than I do how my father and mother, in coming to this barren place, dreamed of creating a community of curious minds. A place where we might be free to examine whatever we wish, create whatever we can, express whatever we believe, and go wherever our imaginations might take us. I was just a boy of eight when Father slipped his letter for the editors of *The Times* to the conductor on the Boggshead Wind Wagon, inviting other like-minded dreamers to follow us to the edge of the Earth. He couldn't have imagined how many brilliant and creative individuals would join his search for the portal in Iceland and the edge of the Earth.[16]

---

[16] Before departing Dinnerplate, Earthedgers had been physicists, engineers, calculators, geographers, archaeologists, and artists, but they now contributed to life in our village in whatever capacity they considered essential and which suited them best. All had come to the edge of the Earth in search of creative liberty and the freedom to contribute however they chose.

"Yet here we are, a mere decade on, and what wonders we have created!" I pointed at Melody's light. "Electronical illumination, amazing! When the rest of the world languishes in darkness," I exclaimed to loud applause.[17] I waved my hand around the room and tipped an imaginary hat to Melody, who curtsied in response.

"We fish for hydrogen particles and transform them into—well, everything. We sail on stellar winds in boats sculpted from stone, make music with granite chimes, build our homes from boulders, grow mushrooms in fields of cast-off clothing, and make our clothes from moss. What a wonder we are. Everyone here has contributed so much to the success of Earthedge. We feed everyone, educate everyone in a cornucopia of disciplines, set no limits on discourse or creativity, and empower every child. And now we have even done what my father always hoped we might. We have begun to explore the underside."

"Hurrah," bellowed the room.

"Well said, young Stalwart," called Captain Codkiss. "You're a credit to your father."

"Hear, hear!"

If the captain had only known how much his remark stung. The last thing I wanted was to be a credit to my father.

"I'm moved by young Stalwart's remarks," said Amirgo Gistring, rising from his bench, "I truly am, and I'm as thrilled by your accomplishment as everyone else, Captain, but from your description of its volcanoes and

---

[17] In Dinnerplate, research on all forms of artificial illumination had ended decades earlier when the Royal and Ancient Academy voted to protect the British coal industry by mandating a single British form of lighting—the coal gas lantern. In America, the fate of electronical illumination was decided by accident when former burlesque entertainer and junior senator from California, Charlie Chaplin, moved to ban all evening illumination brighter than a candle. "God turns off the Sun for a reason. Evening illumination serves only to enable sinful conduct," Chaplin said. "The brighter the light, the darker the depravity." The motion passed the US Congress by an overwhelming margin. "I was only joking," Chaplin later tried to explain, but the damage had been done. *Prohiblumination* became the *cause célèbre* of the Faith-Aflamers.

darkness, the underside doesn't sound like a place worth exploring any further. Sounds like venturing there a second time might be a perilous waste of resources. Is that right, Captain?"

"Yes, Captain, what's your opinion?" Melody called out. "Would another voyage to the underside be a perilous waste?"

"That was how I felt upon re-acquiring our familiar coastline," replied the captain, "but then, as we were sweeping the dust and stones from our decks, I came across these."

In the palm of his hand, Captain Codkiss held out a small shiny disk and a chunk of white stone which he then passed to old Bedazzles Middlefinger, formerly academiker of archaeology at Oriel Impracticum, Oxford.

"What do you make of these, Beedy?" he asked.

"Well," said Bedazzles as he accepted the objects and then fell silent for a long while.

Everyone waited. No point rushing the old gentleman.

"… if I'm not mistaken … Could I have a candle here, please?"

Melody passed a candle from the bar to Middley Porter, sitting next to the archaeologist. Middley held the candle over Beedy's shoulder.

"Thank you, Middley," said Bedazzles and returned to his examination. "… if I'm not mistaken …" he repeated and then paused once again.

At last, he looked up from the objects.

"Well, I'd have to conduct a great many tests to be certain, but it appears this medallion … it's a medallion, you see … it may have belonged to Emperor Charlemagne. It's his medal of office, one of several at least. Charlemagne was not only King of the Franks but also crowned Emperor of the Romans on Christmas Day in the year 800, and this piece might at some point have hung around his neck. At least that's what the Latin inscription on the obverse seems to indicate."

There were gasps from every corner of the pub.

"And this piece of marble … well, it could be … and I stress it could be … from Michelangelo's missing masterpiece, *Androcles and the Lion*. You see there?" He held the fragment high. Of course, no one in the dim light could make out what the old academiker was pointing at, but no matter, as long as he could see it. "Michelangelo never signed his work, but that's very definitely his mark, there, you see? And the fragment is most likely from *Androcles* since it's from a lion's claw. I know of no other missing Michelangelo work, and no other known work is missing a fragment of this size. So, there you have it."

"And these treasures simply fell on your vessels from the underside, Captain?" asked Melody.

The captain nodded. "If you think about it, everything created in Dinnerplate eventually—whether accidentally or intentionally—ends up in the trash. So, doesn't it stand to reason everything might also, in time, sift down through the Earth's many layers to emerge from the underside? There, an object might hover for eternity or perhaps be knocked away into the void by some other piece of detritus floating by."

"So ... you're suggesting every sort of treasure might be hovering down there ... dropping from the underside and then floating about?" Amirgo Gistring asked. As a former pennymarker, it appeared Amirgo was making a quick cost-benefit analysis of another voyage.

"And likely everything else before humans as well," said Bedazzles with uncharacteristic excitement in his voice. "Just imagine! Bones of the monsters which preceded us, even the remnants of Creation itself, if it comes to that. Who knows what might have sifted through the Earth and be waiting for us to simply sail by?"

"Good gracious, what we could learn," muttered Melody Fullbottle.

"And what an adventure another voyage to the underside would be," shouted Burpee.

"An adventure I think Earthedge should most assuredly undertake," Captain Codkiss cried out. "What say you?"

In one voice, the room bellowed "We sail for the underside!!"

Chapter Five

The Boggshead Ferry, off Minisculevik Harbor, Iceland

Hobby Natterer could recall few moments in his violent career when he'd genuinely feared for his life. He'd battled drunks in pubs all over Cambridge, stomped football fans in France, disarmed knife-wielding young ladies in alleyways, and on behalf of Lord Edmund, thumped far too many greybeards to count. But he had never elsewhere known the terrifying imminence of death he'd known right here, aboard a ship just such as this, off Thorfinger Rocks, in sight of Iceland's Minisculevik Harbor, and in the sweep of the Dunder Light.

A decade ago, a great wall of water had inexplicably arisen somewhere out in the North Atlantic and then raced hundreds of leagues across the open ocean at an unimaginable speed and smashed headlong into Iceland. The wave drove dozens of fishing vessels to the bottom, scraped tiny coastal islands to their bedrock, and crashed into the Boggshead ferry with the power of a dozen shipsticky bombs. The ferry was smashed to bits, its cargo scattered to the winds and waves, a herd of cattle impaled by splintered decking, and many of its passengers crushed against jagged rocks. Few survived the disaster. Nor would have Hobby, if that damnable man, Grimly Wordsmouth, hadn't pulled him to safety.

Trapped below deck in a tiny air pocket rapidly filling with water, Hobby had screamed like an infant, knowing that saltwater at any moment would most assuredly fill his nostrils, then his mouth, and finally his lungs. He would have been compelled to relive his entire pathetic existence before succumbing to the hand of death and slipping away into oblivion. But suddenly that damned Wordsmouth had appeared, grabbed him by his coat, and dragged him up through the tangle of rigging and wreckage to the surface.

Splayed on the beach like a gaffed fish, gagging, spitting up seawater, and gasping for breath, he'd looked up into the eyes of the man who'd saved him. Wordsmouth was standing there, shivering, dripping with seawater and bunker oil, and clutching his wife and son with obvious relief. Over the tempest, Wordsmouth had shouted, "Don't worry, Mr. Natterer, we'll find our way to the edge just as you wish. You needn't follow us. Please don't follow us."

What could have brought that night to mind? This place, of course—the temperature, the sound of the sea beneath the ship, the crash of the waves on Thorfinger Rocks to port, the reek of the shoreline, the shriek of the gulls—all of it, every damned detail. All of it had made him recall that night, and most especially, his latest assignment from Lord Edmund. Hobby was to somehow pursue Wordsmouth to the edge of the Earth, where he was to kidnap the man who'd saved his life—and kill everyone the man had ever loved.

***

A few questions around town and Hobby had identified his target, one Bloordrag Lorgeld, a ship chandler who, rumor had it, regularly dealt with visitors from the edge. Hobby spotted Lorgeld near the docks and trailed him to a house on the outskirts of Minisculevik. He suspected Lorgeld might have spotted him so he backed off for a few hours, time enough to compose a message to the chancellor.

Have located the key to Wordsmouth's lair. About to enter. Expect success in three weeks.

"Might take several days to reach London," said the clerk at the Royal Danish Semaphore Shoppe. "Recent storms displaced many of our signal ships from anchor."

"No matter," Hobby replied.

"And more storms to come. Them cloudwatchers is saying we're in for three horrible days. Just that time of the year, I guess."

Hobby returned to the ship chandler's house. Lorgeld was in his shed, doors wide open, examining a pile of timber. His wife was nowhere to be seen. Thunder rumbled in the distance as the sky darkened by the moment.

No time like the present.

Hobby broke from his hiding place, raced full tilt up the lane and charged into the shed. Lorgeld looked up to see Hobby approaching but didn't react, probably too shocked by the stranger's headlong advance. Hobby ran straight at Lorgeld and cracked him on the head before the man had a chance to defend himself. He then heaved the unconscious man over his shoulder and headed up into the hills.

In a cave high up on the treeless slope of an ancient volcano, Hobby broke a few of the man's toes and ripped out several of his fingernails. It didn't take much more than a night and a day of such treatment to get what Hobby required from the Icelander.

"An Earthedger's coming," Bloordrag screamed, "to collect my wood!" After that, he slumped forward, muttering, "Please, no more, no more. I don't know when. He just shows up."

"Alright then. I'll just have to watch your house until he arrives. If he does, I'll release you. But if he doesn't—"

"He will. I swear."

And sure enough, by the time Hobby got back to Lorgeld's home, an Earthedger was already at the Icelander's front door talking to his wife. Hobby guessed the stranger to be an Earthedger by his peculiar clothing and brass-ringed goggles with smoked lenses. Clearly troubled by her husband's absence, the woman sobbed, wiped away tears, and snuffled as she spoke. She must have previously confided her concerns to friends because, as she was talking to the Earthedger, several ladies arrived. It appeared they'd come to comfort her. The Earthedger followed the ladies inside.

The cracks of thunder were louder now. Lightning flashed over the distant hills. Winds were picking up. Dust from the lane was swept into the air to swirl about in great clouds. Darkness descended. After some time, the Earthedger emerged from the house and hurried to Lorgeld's shed. There he lit a coal oil lantern, briefly examined the stack of wood, and then shut the shed's double doors against the coming storm.

Hobby raced from his hiding place, across the front garden, to the side of Lorgeld's shed. Through a small window, he watched the Earthedger open his back sack and pull out a box-shaped piece of equipment. The fellow set it on the stack of wood, stretched a long wire from it up into the rafters, and then pressed a button on the device. From several points around its rim, the box glowed a pale green, dimly at first but then ever brighter. A ball in the center of the box flickered several times before shining with a steady bluish light. Standing over the box, the Earthedger grasped the ball and then released it, grasped it again, and released it. He repeated this motion over and over, the duration of his grasp varying each time as if according to some sort of predetermined pattern.

The wind howled. Lightning flashes were closer now. If Hobby was going to make it back to the cave before the worst of the storm struck, he was going to have to act fast. He burst into the shed, lay the Earthedger out cold with a single blow, gathered the unconscious man and his machine up onto his shoulder, and headed back to the mountain cave.

Lorgeld was not there. He'd escaped somehow. How long he'd been free Natterer had no way of knowing, but in this storm and with broken toes, the Icelander probably wouldn't have been able to make it down the mountain quite yet. Nevertheless, Hobby had to press the Earthedger for urgent answers. He slapped the man repeatedly until he came around, then Hobby screamed over and over into the man's stupefied face, "The gate, where's the gate?"

Dazed and confused, the Earthedger had no chance to gather his wits.

"I ... I don't under ... who are you?" he whimpered. "All right, all right, I ... I'll show you the gate."

They clambered up the rocky terrain, battling the elements for every thou of elevation. With each step, they risked plummeting over a precipice or tumbling down a jagged slope. The winds railed and howled, whipping up clouds of volcanic dust, choking them, lacerating their flesh. Thunder cracked and then echoed without end across the many crags and valleys carved by the ages into the sides of the ancient volcano.

"There," the Earthedger grunted at last.

"Where?"

"That cliff, there, that's the portal ... the gate."

"It can't be, you fool. There's nothing there."

"No, it *is* the portal."

"It's a damned cliff!"

Hobby crept as near as he dared to the precipice. A lightning flash illuminated the edge and the void beyond, a thousand-foot sheer drop into the mouth of the volcano. Despite the wailing winds, the stink of sulfur was almost overpowering.

"Where? Where's the gate, damn you?"

The Earthedger walked right to the edge of the crater. "Here. We jump right here."

"Into the volcano? You're mad."

"It's the veil of confusion, the magnetic forces. You can't see the other side. But it's right here. We don't fall more than half a fathom before we're on the other side."

"Okay, so you jump first."

"All right," said the Earthedger.

And let you run off? No way!

"No ... no, we jump together ... no, you jump ... no," Hobby babbled.

The Earthedger grabbed Hobby's hand and shouted, "Then we'll jump together." Before Hobby could react, he was yanked off his feet and into the abyss.

Chapter Six

Estate of the Royal and Ancient Academy of Knowledge

Lord Edmund had been overjoyed to receive this latest summons to appear before the Garter council.[18] At last, he thought, his appointment to the Order of the Garter might be at hand. After all, every other chancellor before him had been invested in the order. Now in the thirty-eighth year of his chancellorship, his investiture was long overdue. He'd often overheard Bilbury and others whisper that an Academy chancellor without Garter status in these perilous times might be a liability. Edmund had departed the Academy in a jolly state but from the moment he arrived at the Palace of Westminster, he began to suspect his hopes of a rewarding Garter appearance might have been misplaced.[19]

---

[18] The Most Noble Order of the Garter was founded by King Edward III in 1348 and ranked as Britain's highest civil and military honor. One theory was that Edward III, in creating the order, wished to revive the Round Table of Arthurian legend. Until 1969, the Order of the Garter exercised almost absolute authority in the United Kingdom. Members meeting to advise the king were referred to as the Garter council.

[19] The Palace of Westminster, as the Realm's seat of governance, housed three assembly halls. The grandest meeting chamber was reserved for the House of Lords, the titled nobility of the Realm. The lords assembled twice a year: first, just before Cowes week, when yachts raced between Southampton and the Isle of Wight, and second, on Ascot weekend, when members gathered to discuss the state of British horse breeding. The second chamber was for the one hundred members of the Order of the Garter. The monarch appointed Garter members for life from among the Realm's finest families and most accomplished entrepreneurs. Members met in council at the behest of the monarch to advise on pressing matters of state. The King's Lord Chamberlain, Sir Harold Liverwort, managed their meetings. The palace's third chamber, known as Talkyhall, had been the lords' former tennis court and was in imminent danger of collapse. There, a rabble of popularly elected nobodies met to advise the Garter council and give consent to its policies—if ever asked to do so,

Visits to Westminster were always an ordeal, what with the hideous stink of the Thames river so close by, and the off-key, almost comical, clattering of Big Ben's bells, which peeled at entirely unpredictable intervals. Judging by the utter absence of ceremony upon his arrival, however, this visit was likely to be worse than usual.

No one of any note was there to greet him. No one offered congratulations. No one ushered him through the dignitaries' door. A single Scots Guard, in the purple and pink combat fatigues designed by the Academy, attended his arrival.[20] The guardsman unloaded Lord Edmund's Bilbury Super Trike from the carriage and then heaved the chancellor up the steps to the main door. There, the guardsman simply plopped Edmund on the trike and marched away. Edmund was left to wrestle his legs into the artificial feet, which had been bolted to the trike's pedals. Ostensibly a gift from Bilbury, the contraption was a source of constant humiliation for Edmund, not to mention pain.

"Oy, I likes yer trike, Mister," a child shouted from the street below.

---

which they rarely were. Members of Talkyhall (MTs) selected the Primus Speaker (PS) from among their number to speak on their behalf to the Garter council and Crown. Few PSs ever served more than a single four-year term since most found the job frustrating and thankless. Talkyhall members were required to be present for 80 percent of their scheduled meeting time or lose their stipend. Many members were obligated to conduct their private business affairs from their Talkyhall desks. One member even built and sold furniture from his bench in Talkyhall. The King's Lord Chamberlain drew up Talkyhall's weekly agenda. The chamberlain's favorite lark was to see how many times he could have MTs debate laws prohibiting French postcards from entering the Realm without ever actually bringing the matter to a vote.

[20] A ground-breaking opinion survey conducted by Academiker Broadly Wellington-Ashpit had determined that the British public preferred flower gardens to underbrush. On the premise that more battles were fought in meadows than forests, he'd devised the distinctive new, wildflower-inspired army fatigues. To the accusation he had no evidence most battles were fought in meadows, Academiker Ashpit replied, "Well, they should be." Academiker Ashpit's *Dianthus, Darling Jeremy*, won the Westminster Flower Show blue ribbon for Pinks three years in a row.

Half a dozen street urchins emerged from the fog, laughing and chasing and shoving one another as they pushed an old barrow along the filthy cobbled lane. A curious figure made of rags and straw was perched in the barrow and bore a hand-lettered placard that read "Penneez fer Charlie Darwin."

Oh, stercus, it's Darwin Day. Can matters get any worse? [21]

"Hey, Mister, penny fer our apples? Bonfire's tonight up Threadneedle Street. Penny for some apples, Mister?"

"Go away," Lord Edmund muttered as he hammered on the palace door.

"Here, he looks like one o' them boffins up Snapthrottle Hill. Hey Mister, you one o' them boffins?"

"Hey, yeah, like he's one o' them eedjits what said the world was round."

"I told you, go away," Edmund grumbled.

"What-yer!" they shouted as they disappeared back into the fog. "Thick old toff." As a final sign of disrespect, one of their number let fly a rotten apple before he too faded from view.

The apple struck the palace door, splattering the chancellor with juice and brown pulp. He was trying frantically to wipe the mess from his coat when the door opened, and a footman muttered, "Oh, it's you."

Inside, Lord Edmund was instructed to park his trike in the Garter Chamber anteroom and await his turn. An hour ticked by. He desperately needed to relieve himself but dared not leave his post. And anyway, without someone to unshackle him from the ridiculous Super Trike, he'd need a chamber pot, and looking about the gilt and scarlet anteroom, there was no such pot to hand. Edmund was eyeing a Ming Dynasty vase when the enormous doors of the Garter Chamber opened and a footman gestured him inside.

---

[21] Named for Charles Darwin, who posited that humans are descended from apes, Darwin Day celebrated English eccentrics. Children marked the day by tossing rotten food at Darwin's effigy then throwing their soiled dummy onto a bonfire. Following my father's revelations, Academy members themselves reported being insulted and pelted with rotten food on Darwin Day.

Lord Edmund had never noticed his gears' high-pitched squeal before, but as he pedaled into the cavernous room, several Garter members winced in pain and covered their ears.

"To that table, Chancellor, if you please," said the king from his seat at the head of the U-shaped Assembly. A small wobbly table had been placed at the opposite end of the assemblage from the king. One hundred Garter members, representatives of the oldest, the wealthiest, and the most influential families in the Realm, watched in silence as Lord Edmund pedaled to the table. Their faces told the tale. Edmund was in for a rum go.

"Thank you for coming, Chancellor," said the king. "Busy Darwin Day, I expect, eh what? Lots of questions from the public about that fool Darwin, eh what? Oh, I've always wondered, do your members get much ribbing on Darwin Day?"

A decade ago, even the king would not have dared ask such a stupid question.

"No ... not really, Your Majesty," but that was a lie.

"Ah, well, I suppose that's good."

Is the damned fool disappointed?

"Of course, we do hate to take you away from your important work on behalf of the Realm," the king continued, this time in a far more earnest tone. "However, several of our counselors here present have expressed concern for the well-being of our armed forces and asked us to secure an urgent briefing from you. With the news that coal resources, which were supposed to be managed under the terms of the Come-by-Chance Armistice, are being diverted by my cousin, the Tsar of Russia, to the needs of his own nation, you can imagine that the state of our arsenal is of pressing importance. So, we have asked you here today to update us on the progress of the Academy's weapons' program and let us be very clear: we expect your accounting to be as precise and factual, and realistic as it can be. We are not interested in any 'explorations' or 'possibilities' or 'testings' or 'could bes.' We only want to hear about your 'soons,' your 'readies,' your 'next weeks'." The king gestured with each parenthesis. "Do we make ourselves clear, Lord Edmund?"

"Yes, Your Majesty," Edmund replied.

Stercus!

"But uh, before I proceed, might I have a moment to collect my thoughts so I can, as you say, be as precise as possible?" Edmund pulled a piece of rag paper and a charcoalizer from his breast pocket and began to scribble. "It's just that if I'd been advised in advance of the Garter's interest," he spoke as he wrote, "I'd have been able to prepare a more comprehensive—"

"Yes, of course," the king interjected, "but you see, sometimes comprehensive is the enemy of fact. Length is so often used to conceal reality. Not to suggest for an instant, dear friend, that you would ever stoop to such trickery. Of course not."

"Uh, of course not, Your Majesty. So, may I have a minute more?"

The king nodded and then folded his arms across the royal chest in a gesture of barely concealed impatience.

Garter members moved not a hair. Every eye remained fixed on Edmund. This was the moment he'd dreaded for years. Academy members had failed him utterly and their uselessness was about to be exposed. He had learned, to his disgust, that one simply cannot demand new ideas from old men. Nobody has a new idea after the age of thirty. In their dotage, the only thing any old man can do is elaborate, in increasingly nauseating detail, the few original ideas he had in his youth.

But Edmund had to report something and it had to be good. There was no avoiding it. It would have to be his plans for the space cannon.

Edmund hadn't planned on revealing his scheme until his dogsbody, Natterer, had Grimly Wordsmouth in custody because without Wordsmouth, there would be no plan.

"Well, Your Majesty, I could report fascinating developments regarding Lord Bilbury's flying machine, which will have its first test flight off Tilbury Hill in a matter of weeks."

That's it. Put Bilbury in their crosshairs for a change.

"And I would be proud to describe the progress I'm making with my computing machine, which just last week was used to calculate the new Wessex Wind Wagon's schedule for the southeast."

Oh, stercus, here goes.

"But what I'd most like to tell you about, since it is perhaps our greatest breakthrough in weapons research in decades, is the work we're doing to transform our space cannon into an Intercontinental Bomb Delivery System, what we scientists like to call an IBDS."

"A what?" the king asked.

"An IBDS, a system capable of delivering a bomb halfway round the world."

"But you tried that years ago. Your arithmetic never worked because of the ... the wonkiness of the Earth or the curves you couldn't figure out or those damnable magnetic fields or whatever. Bloody projectiles went up as intended but then kept coming down all over the place. You never knew where they'd land. Killed dozens, as we recall."

"That is so, Your Majesty, but now we've got the mathematography right."

Or we will have when Natterer delivers Wordsmouth.

The king sat forward in his chair. "Well, this is exciting," he said. "An intercontinental bomb would certainly shift the balance of power, I can tell you,"

Lord Trolleysmash, First Sealord of the Admiralty, noisily cleared his throat. "May it please Your Majesty, this is exciting indeed." He cleared his throat a second time, wiped his mouth with a badly soiled hanky, and glared at the chancellor. "So, Edmund, old friend, feet to the fire and all that. Tell us, when will we see a test of this new bomb thingy of yours?"

Damned fellow. Noggin full of seawater.

"Well, very soon, very soon indeed. Just doing the final theoretical validations, testing our algorithms, and ... and focus checking our field theories. Have to get the windjiggle compensators and the leveling cogs just right, as I'm sure you know, Admiral. And of course, we need programming cards that are fireproof this time. We're still working on those. But no, it shouldn't be long now."

"So, can you commit to a date?" the king asked.

"Uh, may I consult with my colleagues and get back to you?"

"Of course. But let's see," muttered the king, as an aide placed a red leather-bound date book on the table before him. "There's a meeting of the International Armistice Oversight Committee on the third of April." He slammed the book. "What say we plan on making an announcement of our system there, which means you will need to test fire your system in three months. Is that fair, Chancellor?"

Oh, stercus, stercus, stercus!

"Uh, I'm sure that will work. Thank you, Your Majesty."

"No, thank you, Lord Edmund. And we needn't tell you how grateful we shall be if your system succeeds."

The king's meaning could not have been more apparent: *... or how vengeful we'll be if your system fails.*

***

Lord Edmund returned from his meeting with the Garter council in the very blackest of moods, a mixture of profound disappointment, red-hot rage, and terror. And to cap his utterly hideous morning, his carriage was struck by two tomatoes and a muddy boot as it rumbled back through the Academy gates.

Every damned day ... more of the placard-waving fools shouting obscenities, demanding the Academy be dismantled. How stupid can they be? Have they no idea how quickly the Realm would flounder without the Academy? And now it seems, among such fools, I must count the king himself.

No sooner was he back at his desk than Lord Edmund summoned to his conference room knobfiddlers from every department.

Knobfiddlers lived a precarious existence. They were neither robust enough to be smartypants nor old enough to become Academy members. They did all the Academy's actual science and received no credit for it. A knobfiddler's scientific curiosity was his undoing. No sooner did he make a breakthrough than he was terminated, so his greybeard could take credit for the accomplishment. Never before had a greybeard's knobfiddler been summoned by a chancellor directly. Under normal circumstances, the very idea would have been appalling, but Lord Edmund had no time to be concerned with hurt pride and protocol. If the task required knobfiddlers, then knobfiddlers he'd use.

Within fifteen minutes of his return, thirteen young people, eight males and five females, were seated about his enormous mahogany conference table. All, Edmund suspected, had arrived with one thought between them: they were being terminated!

Everyone was sweating profusely, both from nerves and from the stifling heat of the afternoon sun streaming through the chancellor's massive leaded windows.

Windows formed the entire south-facing wall of Lord Edmund's chambers. On his appointment as chancellor, he'd chosen this wing for his suite precisely because of its windows. They had once afforded magnificent views out over Middlesex farmland. Now a Bilbury mill dominated the view.

Bilbury Enterprises processed solid material from the Thames into an inexpensive canned food marketed with the slogan "Enjoy Bilbury Dumplings. Good for You and Good for the Thames!" On days when raw river effluent was being pumped into the plant, a nauseating stench blanketed the countryside. Thankfully, the plant wasn't pumping that day. Even so, gases streaming from its stacks tinted the afternoon sunlight green.

Wasting no time on pleasantries or greetings, the chancellor launched straight in. "We have a national emergency and I need your absolute and undivided dedication to the task I'm about to set you."

Audible sighs of relief around the table.

"But Chancellor, what will our greybeards say?" asked a small voice from somewhere.

"They will say nothing. Nothing, nothing, nothing!" He was practically screaming. "They've had every indulgence the Academy can afford!" He drew a deep breath, paused to calm himself, and then continued.

"You lot from rocketry, you've been working on the fuel mix and making the projectile more comfortable for a cannonaut, is that correct?"

"Uh, yes, Chancellor," replied a pimply young man with red hair.

"Could the capsule be filled with explosives?"

"Whatever for?" blurted out one young woman. "Oh, excuse me, Chancellor."

"Because I need a weapon," Lord Edmund shouted, "the biggest, most spectacular *irumbado* weapon we can come up with, and I needed it yesterday, that's why!"

"So, you … you want us to turn the space cannon into that weapon?" the young woman asked.

"Does that offend your delicate feminine sensibilities, young lady?" Lord Edmund couldn't help the obvious sneer in his voice.

He'd always felt uneasy about hiring female knobfiddlers. He suspected they lacked the focus and attention to detail of their male colleagues, the creativity and stamina for the hard work and suffering that science demands, and worst, they distracted the greybeards. He himself had never had much time for females. Still, he'd been persuaded by Bilbury in a moment of weakness to employ a handful, if for no other reason than they might bring some color into the drab world of Academy science.

"No, Lord Edmund. My sensibilities are not offended." The mere slip of a girl showed no hint of unease. "On the contrary, my scientific curiosity is piqued. Abandoning our space exploration program is, in my estimation, a ludicrous waste of an exciting new dimension in science. I am nevertheless intrigued by the challenge of calculating how we shall adjust our targeting parameters to incorporate our new understanding of terrestrial magnetic fields and a flattened atmosphere."

Edmund was gobsmacked by her words. "Yes, that's it precisely!" he shouted. "That's the task I am setting you. And I want you to do nothing else until you've cracked it."

The young woman's candor impressed Edmund. Sitting there, back straight, amber hair pulled up in some sort of a ball thing, smartly dressed in a grey suit jacket and floor-length pleated skirt, and, perhaps most remarkably, full of the self-confidence one so rarely sees in a female of such tender years, his own curiosity about this strange creature was aroused.

"From which department are you, young lady?" he asked.

"I'm a calculator in the mathematography department, sir."

The few female knobfiddlers who'd preceded this current lot had enjoyed a fruitless tenure. Recognized for nothing, accommodated nowhere, abused by everyone, and with absolutely no hope of ever becoming Academy members, they'd inevitably transferred either to the kitchens or to Social Events or married some lonely old greybeard and left science behind.

"Miss—"

"Crossingguard, Lollipop Crossingguard, your Lordship."

"Well, Miss Crossingguard, I want you to head up our work on a trajectory, and you may pick your own team from among the knobfiddlers here present."

With no hint of gratitude for the honor he'd bestowed and as bold as you please, she leaned forward and announced, "I have several conditions, Lord Edmund."

"Conditions? I'm giving you the chance of a lifetime and you talk of conditions?"

"Yes."

Lord Edmund remained silent for a moment. He glared straight into the young woman's eyes and detected no hint of uncertainty. She neither flinched, nor bowed her head, nor turned away.

"What are your conditions?"

"That in the immediate future, women be eligible for Academy membership."

Lord Edmund smiled. "Succeed in your calculations, and I think I might be able to do something about membership after that."

"No, you will not do something after that. You will guarantee membership eligibility to women now."

He almost laughed out loud. Even so, he relented. "All right, I shall guarantee eligibility."

"And a privy for females somewhere on the estate," she added.

"You don't have one already?"

"No."

"Hmm. Well, right then. I accept your conditions. So, will you lead our team?"

"I will."

Lord Edmund never smiled at anyone, but in this most remarkable moment he smiled, if ever so briefly, at the young woman with the amber hair.

"Now, who's here from the calculating engine division?" he asked. "Ah yes, Giddyford, you will put aside our efforts to downsize my calculating engine for the time being and place it and your entire team at Miss Crossingguard's disposal.

"The rest of you will dedicate your energies to creating the most effective explosive for intercontinental delivery you can concoct and then to preparing our projectile for launch. Oh, and you have two months."

First, there was shocked silence and then a buzz of nervous chatter.

"Do we have a target, Chancellor," Miss Crossingguard asked, "if only a theoretical one, for purposes of testing our calculations, I mean?"

"Oh, a target, yes. Mmm, some insignificant spot that won't immediately ignite hostilities when we erase it from the Earth, but will most assuredly convey to our enemies the Realm's frustrations and our ferocious new capability. Ah, of course, Come-by-Chance, Newfoundland."

Lord Edmund looked around the table. Inconceivable mere hours earlier, the team which might yet save the Academy in its hour of peril was to be led by a young woman. Who could have imagined?

"So then, get to work, and if any greybeards object to your new assignments, send them to me. Oh, and Miss Crossingguard, remain please."

The knobfiddlers filed from the room chattering excitedly at this sudden, remarkable turn in their fortunes. When the last knobfiddler had left, Miss Crossingguard marched up to the chancellor's trike.

"Yes?" she asked with no hint of courtesy or gratitude, or deference.

Probably expects I'll make some sort of inappropriate demand in exchange for this opportunity.

Of course, he'd heard rumors of greybeards using their position to extort inappropriate favors from their underlings, but not him, and certainly not now. Edmund needed the young woman's utter loyalty and undivided attention if his chancellorship was to be saved. He wasn't going to let anything interfere with her work; not a single thing.

"Miss Crossingguard, I have some calculations which might be useful. I've reviewed them many times and I suspect they might lead to, if not already contain, the solution to our trajectory problem."

"If you already have the answer, Lord Edmund, then why do you require my help?"

"The calculations were done, not by a qualified calculator like yourself, but by a dilettante whose methods were ... let us say ... peculiar."

Lord Edmund pedaled over to the massive iron strongbox that stood alongside his bookshelf. He unlocked the box and withdrew a thick stack of crinkled, yellowing pages tied up in a frayed and filthy scarlet ribbon. He pedaled back to the conference table, placed the bundle before the young woman, and untied the bow. "These were prepared by—"

"Grimly Wordsmouth!" the young woman exclaimed.

A decade since his disappearance, few beyond the Academy could recall Wordsmouth's name, or would admit to doing so, because Edmund had done such an effective job obfuscating Wordsmouth's accomplishment. Apparently, Miss Crossingguard was among that few.

"How could you possibly know this is the work of ... that man?"

"I was just a child at the time, but I studied everything reported in *The Times*. I recognize his curious use of the omega and the epsilon in his equations. There, see?" She ran her delicate fingers across the pages. "Right in the first line, you can tell it's Wordsmouth's own work! How thrilling!"

It made Lord Edmund nauseous to hear the interloper's name spoken aloud and, worse still, with such obvious admiration, but circumstances precluded squeamishness.

"As I understand it," Edmund began, "Wordsmouth conducted numerous tests to determine the degree of distortion in light waves caused by the intersection of the Earth's concave gravitational force and its parabolic magnetic fields. Of course, he wasn't trying to calculate the trajectory of a projectile but the degree of distortion in light through space. Even so, the effect of the one force upon the other should be a mathematical constant, should it not?"

"Exactly!" Miss Crossingguard's excitement was palpable. "And when we figure out that constant ... well, its application to the flight of objects, to the way we perceive light, to ... to everything ... it will lift the veil from our eyes. We shall be able to see our curiously distorted world as it actually is for the very first time ever!"

To hear this snippet speak of seeing the world as it actually is gave Edmund such dyspepsia, it was all he could do to stop from stabbing the lass with a quill pen. But business first. "So," he said, "Wordsmouth's calculations might help us get that constant, correct? Trouble is, he did many of his sums in some sort of code. See here ... and here. Why, he doesn't explain, but I want you to review his work as quickly as you can and tell me what you make of it."

"Why don't we ask Wordsmouth himself for help?"

Only surviving Academy members who'd been present at the infamous conclave a decade earlier had any inkling of Grimly Wordsmouth's banishment, and Lord Edmund wasn't about to tell this girl.

"I have asked an associate to locate Wordsmouth ... but let's not spread that around just yet."

Chapter Seven

Earthedge

Cepheus had set and Melody's bell was peeling the twelfth hour. After a quick bite of dinner, my guardian, Raindrop Macintosh, and I had set off on our way to the Rocksplitters. The path from Raindrop's cottage took us past the lichen farm, the fishponds, and the mushroom meadows. At Dubbley Junction, the route connected with the trail from the Maidstone Cliffs and became the principal laneway into the village.

Down the trail from the cliffs marched the Junior Form, hooting with laughter and singing at the tops of their lungs:

Gosh, my galoshes are smelly,
they're so stinky they sicken my belly,
Still have to wear them for Mummy,
even though they both curdle my tummy.

The children were returning from an afternoon outing and picnic dinner at the cliffs, where they'd been star-spotting and practicing celestial navigation.

"What do we say, children?" asked Dr. Tulip, who strode at the head of her cohort like a drum major in a gunmen's' parade. Her trusty second, Opal Amethyst, brought up the rear.

"Good evening, Madam Mayor," the children shouted in unison. "Good evening, Stalwart Wordsmouth."

"And good evening to you," Raindrop and I replied as we fell in behind the little army.

All eleven children in the Junior Form were Earthedge-born. Persia Magenta, the youngest in the form at three years old, had cat's eyes, an adaptation seen in several newborns recently. The sight of their iridescent green eyes was so disarmingly beautiful that villagers called them kiddens.

Thanks to Dr. Tulip, Earthedge youngsters were remarkably accomplished. By four, they could read and write. By six, they were conducting

Earthedge

inquiries and experiments of their own. In Senior Form, they were doing original research or artworks or performance pieces. Indeed, there were two doctoral candidates, including Marigold, among my Senior Form classmates. Of course, I wasn't one of them. Despite my father's fervent wish that I diplomatize in mathematography, I was merely a fisher and fancied myself a poet like my mother.

We were entering the village now. Beneath a potato lamp dangling from a pole and a couple of fathoms from the Rocksplitters' front step, Dr. Tulip held up her hand, and the children came to a crisp halt. She turned, quieted her charges with a glance, and said, "Now when we reach the Rocksplitters, what will we do? We…"

They bellowed their response in unison.

"Wee first, watch, and then white!" They burst into gales of laughter at their silly joke.

"Write, yes," Dr. Tulip said with a feigned look of disapproval and then a grin. "Everyone has their slate and chalk? Good. I expect questions from each of you at the end of the meeting. So, now, why are we here?"

"To see our elders plan," the children shouted.

"And why must we plan?"

"Without a plan, we merely wander."

"And what are our elders planning?"

"To go under the Earth!"

"Wonderful, children. Now, what can you tell me about the Earth?"

A cacophony of answers.

"We live at the edge of a big flat circle of stone."

"Earth's made from a disc of swirling stardust."

"The early Earth formed into a plate."

"There was a layer of molten stone trapped inside the plate."

"Grimly Wordsmouth called the earth's molten middle its cream filling."

Hoots of laughter from the children.

"That's right, well done," said Dr. Tulip. "And what has become of the cream filling?"

"As the Earth cooled, we think it became lots of little molten puddles," said one child.

"Like mushroom chips in a cookie," shouted another. Again, gales of laughter.

"Good, very good. And now, what have we learned from Captain Codkiss's recent adventure?"

"That stuff moves from Dinnerplate down through the Earth."

"Well done, so now it's time you go to the privies, young ladies and gentlemen. Then we meet inside."

***

A single cucumber lamp illuminated the first meeting of the Underside Odyssey Planning Committee.[22] The atmosphere in the pub was a mix of excitement and trepidation. Villagers had crowded every seat. Dr. Tulip's Junior Form slipped in quietly to sit on the floor with their backs to the bar. Many villagers were present to witness this historic meeting but were content to defer to the wisdom of the ten-person volunteer committee. Pressed together around a long narrow table in the center of the room, the committee members sipped mushroom ale, smoked potato-peeling tobacco, and chatted amiably as they waited for Mayor Raindrop to call the meeting to order.

Raindrop, our mayor, was an astronomer by training and our pre-eminent moss weaver, and since Father had died, my guardian. She was sweet and kind in a grandmotherly fashion and very, very persuasive. She was the reason why, against every instinct in my body, I found myself on the Odyssey committee.

The two of them, Raindrop and publican Melody Fullbottle, would not let up on me. They pushed me into everything. The story was that before he died,

---

[22] Inspired by the unapproved research of chemist Jonathan Swift and his notorious Lagado Institute (which had attempted to extract sunbeams from cucumbers), our biologists, Lilly Seedling and Potted Edelweiss, determined that the high water and low salt content of cucumber juice made it an excellent medium for generating electrical current.

Father implored them to do everything in their power to ready me for a leadership role in the community, a role which I was equally determined I would never play. They and everybody else in Earthedge seemed to believe a Wordsmouth would always lead. I thought the last thing Earthedge needed was another Wordsmouth in charge.

That said, I adored both women. Raindrop was awe-inspiring in her limitless understanding of the universe. Melody Fullbottle was simply the community's most beloved citizen.

For almost a decade, Melody Fullbottle had supplied the ale, dried and flavored potato peelings for the pipes in town, and even crafted the table around which met every committee engaged in village governance. A notable medicator in another life, Melody constructed the village's unofficial parley-table from a bakery door. She'd single-handedly dragged the door across the barrens on that inaugural trek to the edge. The door had belonged to her parents' bake shop in Killarney.

Although not a member of any village committee, Melody's wisdom, not to mention her warmth and hospitality, accorded her *ex officio* membership on them all. Every decision of importance in Earthedge was made around Melody's table over a jug of her mushroom ale.[23]

"So," said Mayor Raindrop as she rose from her chair. The room fell silent. "If we're going to attempt this voyage, there's a long list of issues we must think about."

"Right," Amirgo Gistring interjected, "like who's going to net hydrogen while our ships are away?" The tone of the question might have seemed confrontational if Amirgo had not been its source.

Amirgo took a bit of getting used to. As a former biggybiz pennymarker, his manner could seem abrasive and impatient when the village's resources

---

[23] In her youth, Melody had drifted away from her family in an aggressive pursuit of prominence in the business of Harley Street medicating. Then at forty, after two failed relationships and a botched appendix transplant, she'd had an epiphany and determined to never again lose sight of her parents' example of service and simple dedication to craft.

were at issue. In truth, he was the most selfless individual in the community. Amirgo had arrived in Earthedge with the second group of settlers the year after the founders' great trek. Still, he hadn't been in the village more than a week before he'd been designated the Village Pennymarker-Prelate. Everyone adored Amirgo for his unswerving dedication to the task. Where many others who'd come to Earthedge had slipped quickly into alternate roles—physicist to fisher, bicycle repair to shipwright, medicator to publican—Amirgo could not escape his cast: a pennymarker once, a pennymarker forever.[24]

"True, Amirgo," echoed Paddler Upcreek, village astrophysicist and sailmaker. "And more generally, how many skills dare we release from the community for this voyage? If Raindrop sails, who will make fibers from her moss?"

"Or tend our fish ponds if Morgood goes," Middley Porter added, "or make our boots from fish leather?"

"Okay, so we can't simply accept all volunteers," Raindrop replied. "We have to think about the skills we'll need on the voyage and the skills we must leave behind."

"And it's not just folks we'll need. We'll need lots of gear, like illumination, ropes and nets for climbing back up the edge on our return," said Burpee, "and food because I doubt we'll find much to eat down under."

Captain Codkiss rose and said, "Even before we gather people and gear, I think we'll be needing a new ship, a thinner-hulled ship than any we have in

---

[24] Amirgo did have one other interest, however—an interest that made him a favorite of every woman in the village. He designed ladies' clothing, clothes of such subtle line and delicate craft that every woman was willing to wait weeks and months for an Amirgo creation. Into Raindrop Macintosh's lustrous moss fibers, Amirgo weaved glistening oxblood strands of fish leather, vermillion patches of dried potato fiber, and fragments of opal and lapis lazuli. Pennymarker *par excellence* and purveyor of Earthedge high fashion, who would have believed ... but then again, this was Earthedge.

our fleet. I know my ship was almost too much for the Earth's weakened grasp down under."

Melody Fullbottle called from behind her bar, "Raindrop, before we go any farther, may I ask a question?"

"Certainly, Melody."

"Well, doesn't it seem a little coincidental that the things we found on our very first venture beneath the Earth were those two extraordinary treasures? Not American tin cans or Chinese fans or African rands, but true treasures of civilization."

"Raindrop," Gemeny Farcryer spoke from the end of the parleytable, "I might have an answer for Melody."

Gemeny was a geographer who'd worked closely with Father. They'd been attempting to map the world as Earthedgers knew it. Along with Paddler Upcreek, they'd mapped the constellations visible from the edge and compared them with sky charts from Dinnerplate. They'd also mapped the Earth's magnetic fields as they wrapped around the edge of the world and measured the distortions of light waves across the barrens. Their goal had been to one day produce a map that positioned known features in Dinnerplate in their precise relation to Earthedge. Since Father's death, Gemeny had continued their effort without pause.

"Okay, good," Raindrop replied. "It's fair to say we're still a might uncertain whether this voyage will be worth the risks. So please, Gemeny, go on."

Gemeny Farcryer, whose tangle of red hair, freckles more numerous than stars, and voice like an Irish lullaby belied her distinguished academic accomplishments and middle years, rose to her full five-foot-two inches and cleared her throat.

"So, we know our village sits at the very edge of an unimaginably wide, rocky rim we call the barrens. And now, after Captain Codkiss's adventure, it seems things discarded in Dinnerplate sift down through the Earth. But I think they may move outward, spreading below the barrens at the same time, before falling free from the earth."

Gemeny emphasized the word *outward*.

"Their spread is a sort of guide to their origin. If we factor out distortions and draw lines—lines of alignment as Grimly called them—from our village across the barrens to the locations in Dinnerplate, which I've now done, we find that the closest corresponding point is not Iceland but Rome. So, treasures once held in Rome, in the Vatican archives perhaps, when they were lost or discarded, moved downward and outward ... toward the underside directly below us."

"Are you suggesting the Vatican archive might have tossed both Charlemagne's medal of office and Michelangelo's Androcles in the dustbin?" Melody asked. "It's possible," Gemeny replied. "Neither was popular with the Papacy. Charlemagne claimed supremacy over the Church in Gaul and Androcles is a classical rather than a Christian myth."

There was something in what Gemeny had just said that set off alarm bells in my memory. As a small boy, I'd been required to spend hours doing mathematical computations, algorithms, and fractals with Father. "Mathematography is the language of the universe," he'd say—which didn't make the subject any more interesting. Even so, some part of his instruction must have stuck.

I couldn't help myself. I jumped up and asked, "Gemeny, did I understand you correctly? Did you just say you've finished Father's lines of alignment?"

She grinned and nodded in response. "Yes, Stalwart, with Marigold's help, I have."

I glanced in amazement at Marigold. She grinned in response. For some reason which I couldn't immediately comprehend, I was actually excited by one of Father's schemes. However, everyone else in the pub appeared to be flummoxed by my exchange with Gemeny. But I was too excited to stop. "Then that means ... if you can now align Earthedge with communities across Dinnerplate . . . that you have a way for us to navigate across the underside using . . . using these lines of alignment of yours! You could actually navigate the underside!"

"That's right, Stalwart."

A collective gasp from everyone.

Over the hubbub that followed, Gemeny continued. "When Marigold and I finished charting the magnetic fields, we realized they correspond precisely to the concentric topographical features of our Earth, and well, we can plot them . . . and navigate by them. We've worked out a set of coordinates . . . kind of like the degrees of latitude and longitude sailors use to navigate the oceans despite winds and waves, and day and night."

Laughter and congratulations swept across the crowded pub.

"Gemeny, that would be ama—" Captain Codkiss started to say.

Suddenly, Cogsy Eyebeam, who'd been on twelve-bells duty at the mechanicals shed, rushed into the Rocksplitters, stumbled to the bar, and gasped, "It's terrible."

"Cogsy, are you all right? What's terrible?" Melody Fullbottle asked as she handed him a beaker of ale.

Cogsy knocked back the ale and blurted out, "It's Covert, Covert Millrace."

"Covert?" exclaimed Melody. "But he's not here. You know he's on a run to see Bloordrag about timber. He won't be back for weeks."

"Sure, sure. But Covert spoke to Bloordrag's wife and she was really upset. Apparently, Bloordrag had disappeared a couple of days earlier. Folks told her an Academy smartypants arrived on the Boggshead ferry just before Bloordrag went missing. The smartypants was asking all over town about the barrens and the edge and someone told him to talk to Bloordrag Lorgeld. And then ... Bloordrag vanished."

"Wait, slow down, Cogsy. How do you know this?" Raindrop MacIntosh asked. "Covert's been away almost a month. And even with his skipscooter, he won't get back for weeks, not with the load of lumber he's bringing."

"I know that, but he sent a message."

"Sent a message how?"

Cogsy accepted a second beaker from Melody and took another long gulp, after which he wiped his mouth on his sleeve and began.

"Okay, you remember Covert and Amos Uply had an idea for sending magnetic pulses through the ether by bouncing them off clouds. Well, after Amos passed away, Covert kept working on the idea. He came up with a system of bursts to represent letters. Anyway, I helped him build a prototype sender and receiver on our shifts together in the mechanicals shed. We tested his system a couple of times. It worked over short distances but not much farther than a league. Then he set off for his supply run to Minisculevik. I guess he must have taken the sender machine with him to do some more tinkering, only I didn't know it. That's why I never looked at the receiving device, not before tonight."

"But," I interjected, "I thought you said his sender machine didn't work."

"No, I said it kinda worked, just not very far. Then we had the solar windstorm that carried our ships beneath the earth, and I figure that storm must also have carried Covert's signal all the way from Minisculevik to Earthedge."

"So, he sent this message about Bloordrag some time ago?" asked Captain Codkiss.

"Yes, and when Covert sent it, he was worried. Not just because Bloordrag was missing and his missus was upset, but because Covert wondered if someone might be following him too."

"Following him?" I ask. "Did he say who?"

"Yes, the smartypants that arrived on the Boggshead ferry."

"And there's been no more messages?"

"No."

"What would a smartypants want with Covert?" Paddler Upcreek wondered aloud.

"Maybe this guy was just curious," Gemeny suggested. "Maybe he just wanted to ask Covert some questions."

"But then why is Bloordrag missing?" said Cogsy.

Captain Codkiss shook his head and grumbled, "Oh, I remember them smartypants. Chased me out of my impracticum after I tried doin' research without the permission of Academy greybeards. Smartypants could be very intimidating."

"That chancellor of theirs, he certainly hated your father, Stalwart," Burpee said. "Could he be behind this?"

Earthedge

"I guess so." My stomach heaved at the memory of the brutal smartypants who'd taken Mother and me prisoner. "But why would the Academy be interested in Earthedge now? Father said the chancellor wanted to ban any mention of our flat Earth."

"So," Melody asked, "do we think this smartypants means Covert harm?"

"And if he does, what should we do?" Amirgo added. "Do we wait to see if Covert comes back safely or do we go get him?"

There was a hush in the room as people digested the options.

To my surprise, I found myself caught up in the moment. I stood up and said, "We should send a couple of people across the barrens."

"To do what?" asked Burpee.

"If they cross paths with Covert and he's okay, they can go on to Minisculevik and pick up more wood, or they can keep Covert company on his trek back here."

"And if he's not okay?" asked Marigold. "What then?"

I had no idea where this sudden burst of bravado came from but I replied without hesitation, "Well, then we should send people with weapons ... people armed with Gilgilly's new shockshooters."[25]

There were nods of agreement all around the pub.

---

[25] Gilgilly Kneecap, once an anatomy academiker and now a village fisher, hadn't intended to create a weapon when he set out to generate and fire a bolt of electricity from a modified potato battery at a moving target. He'd been searching for a way to push boulders from the path of his stone ship, but he succeeded beyond his wildest dreams. A single charge from the first incarnation of his blaster shattered a boulder a dozen feet across at a range of fifty fathoms. However, the charge from the shooter, like any bolt of lightning, danced a jagged course as it leaped from the barrel of the shooter. It was quite apparent that the shooter had to be modified to make it less devastating for fear an errant discharge on its madcap trajectory to an intended mark might also unintentionally shatter some nearby boat hull. As a result, a shot from Gilgilly's Shockshooter Mark 2 could be cranked up and down according to the mass of its intended target. Someone might have conjectured the shockshooter could be used as a weapon but no one had ever imagined it would happen so soon.

"And so what does this development mean?" Amirgo wondered. "Do we forget about going back to the underside, for now anyway?" He was looking at me for an answer. Everybody was.

Why I felt such a sudden urge to champion Father's pipedream about exploring the underside I didn't know, but before I realized what I was doing, I opened my big mouth yet again.

"We should not forget about the underside," I said. "We won't know what's happened to Covert for several weeks. In the meantime, we should ready for the voyage. We need a crew and we have a boat to carve, Gemeny's new navigation system to learn, and all sorts of food and rigging and lights to prepare. So I say we carry on with preparations for our voyage until any new information we receive about Covert or the smartypants requires that we reconsider."

I sat back down to loud applause. Marigold, seated beside me, squeezed my hand and mouthed the words, *Proud of you.* My head was spinning. I couldn't for the life of me understand why I'd done what I had. And my confusion was compounded when Captain Codkiss rose to move that we sail to the underside in Grimly Wordsmouth's memory, "since Grimly's vision has always inspired everything we do."

***

I walked Marigold home from the Rocksplitters. We said very little. She knew me too well to press. There was no point in asking why I was still rattled from the meeting. I probably couldn't have explained anyway. Her mothers were already home when we got there, their faces pressed together, peering through the second-floor starlight (the Earthedge term for window) as we approached.

"See you tomorrow?" I asked.

She shook her head. "Gemeny needs my help with some calculations," she replied. Ever since Father died, Marigold had been indispensable to Gemeny.

"Okay."

She grasped the door handle but then turned back to me. "Are you okay?"

"Sure. I'm just thinking about the meeting and the voyage."

She gave me a peck on the cheek and went inside.

But I wasn't okay. I was confused. I didn't understand why I'd become so excited over one of Father's schemes. Ever since Mother died, I'd tried not to get caught up in any of Father's fancies. In fact, I'd tried to ignore them altogether. And yet, there I was during the meeting, arguing in favor of his wildest fancy of all.

Instead of heading straight back to Mayor Raindrop's cottage, I wandered up Fish Tannery Lane, past the hazelnut barn, and turned into Ruthie's Way. Wordsmouth Cottage was up ahead, its grey mass silhouetted against a star-filled sky. The place had been sitting empty for nearly eleven months now. After Father died, I couldn't remain there alone. I couldn't even cross its threshold without reliving those final bitter months.

Dark and squat, Wordsmouth Cottage sat atop a slight elevation that afforded a dazzling prospect over the twinkling lights of our village and on beyond to the very edge of the Earth. The cottage's four starlights stared like the sightless eyes of a corpse. I sat on the stone bench by the front door and peered into the void.

We'd been in Earthedge no more than eighteen months when Mother died. She passed away from pleurisy after many months abed. Turned out she'd been suffering from the illness since childhood. I was ten when I learned this, and when I realized how our journey to the edge must have broken her, I was furious at Father. I couldn't forgive him for putting Mother through our expulsion, the shipwreck, and that year-long trek across the barrens. I began to blame Father for everything, for antagonizing the Academy, for bringing us to this dark and unforgiving wasteland, for robbing me of a normal childhood, and for trying to inflict his maddening dreams on me.

It was especially painful to realize that the bone-chilling damp and icy gales of the Scottish Highlands had most likely inflamed Mother's condition because I'd actually enjoyed our year there. I'd loved walking with her, writing poems together. I'd even liked doing mathematography with Father back then, like the blustery afternoon we spent in the lea of a sheepcote as Father first explained fractals to me.

"You remember Uncle Bernie from the deli?" Father had asked. "Well, fractals were his idea. Walking home by the river one day, he'd realized there is a geometry behind the apparent chaos of nature, what he regarded as a form of geometric repetition. 'Fractals,' Bernie said, 'are smaller and smaller copies of a pattern successively nested inside each other, so that the same intricate shapes appear no matter how much you zoom in closer and closer.' Bernie loved to cite fern leaves and Romanesco broccoli as two examples of fractals from nature. Indeed, he came to believe all reality from the tiniest fragment of mass to the greatest agglomerations of stars might be one enormous fractal. 'Fractals,' Bernie was fond of saying, 'might be our way of seeing infinity.'"

After that, Father and I often spent hours doing fractals together. I remembered one particular afternoon we'd spent calculating fractals for petals and flocks of birds and the branches of an old oak. We'd remained on the hillside long past dinner and then watched the stars appear as the sun set before we'd started down the shepherd's trail to our croft. Mists rose from the bogs. Sheep bleated in the looming dark. A shooting star crossed the heavens and I remarked to Father how exciting it would be to see infinity. That was probably the last time I shared Father's passion for fractals or for anything else.

It wasn't long afterwards that we were driven out onto the barrens by the Academy. And then when Mother died, I blamed Father for her death and swore I'd never again have anything more to do with his schemes. So then why had I allowed myself to become swept up in a momentary excitement and to speak in favor of Father's most hairbrained dream of all—of actually sailing beneath the Earth?

Chapter Eight

Royal and Ancient Academy

"Come!" Lord Edmund shouted.

Scribben, the chancellor's aide, pushed open the massive door and Lollipop Crossingguard stepped inside. The cavernous office was once again bathed in green light. The countryside beyond the room's vast windows was lost in a sickly swirling mist. Lord Edmund was seated at an enormous desk that resembled a giant's coffin, right down to its ornate brass fittings. As Lollipop entered, Lord Edmund put aside his papers, smiled, and said very warmly, "You asked to see me, young lady?"

"Yes, sir. But oh, that's awful!" She pulled a hanky from the wrist of her blouse and held it over her nose. "Sir, excuse me, but that smell!"

"Oh yes, I suppose it is bad. I visited our chemical works earlier today to see their progress on the explosive. A lot of sulfur. If the bomb doesn't work, at least its stink will be deadly."

With Edmund's one working limb, he pushed his voluminous velvet chair back from the desk, struggled out of his frock coat and waist jacket, and struck a triangle dangling from an iron hook on the corner of his desk. Scribben appeared immediately. "Have these aired out," Edmund ordered. "And you might try some of Bilbury's latest inventions to get rid of the smell. What is it? Stinkykill? Yes, try some of that."

The chancellor sucked in his belly but then exhaled explosively and allowed it to sag back over his belt. "Am I right in thinking you've made progress?" he asked as he sank back into his chair once again. "Sit, please."

"Well, yes, sir." She dragged a small iron chair up to the desk. "I've been through Wordsmouth's numerations front to back and back to front. While there are some mystifying gaps where his very peculiar code is simply too perplexing, I think I've reconstructed the logic model he used in deriving his constant."

"Now that is encouraging news."

"Yes, sort of." Lollipop was nervous. She had no idea how much latitude for frankness the chancellor afforded her. Her role in the projectile project could evaporate in the next few moments if she crossed a line.

"Sort of?"

Lollipop's skin crawled at the chancellor's chilly tone.

"You see," she started nervously, "his logic model was one thing, but his precise inputs were another. Unless I can figure out the exact combination of integers he used, his logic model is as useless as Lord Bilbury's flying machine without its elastiky bandolas."

Edmund grinned at the implied slight of Lord Bilbury's ridiculous attempts to fly. "And so how do you propose we identify these integers? Are you making use of my calculating engine?"

"Uh yes ... but ...."

"But?"

"Well, it keeps producing nonsense."

"Nonsense, ah." The chancellor's tone was stern, icy even.

"Not nonsense exactly. It's just the new fireproof coating on the punch cards is sticky and it's gumming up the cogs. So I'm doing the sums myself."

"Admirable. But don't give up on the calculating engine just yet, please. I'll have a word with the engine team."

"No, sir, of course not. Oh, and another thing."

"Yes?"

"You see, as I run different sets of integers, I'm seeing a pattern. Wordsmouth wasn't just trying to find the constant for the curvature of light over a flattened Earth. He was also trying to calculate the topography of the world beyond."

"Beyond what?"

"Beyond this, what we see. Wordsmouth was trying to calculate how we might see the outside, beyond what he called the veil of confusion, what there is at the edge, the edge of the Earth I mean."

"Ah. Mmm, interesting." Lord Edmund fell silent for a moment, then asked, "Tell me, young lady, what impracticum did you attend?"

"I never attended an impracticum."

"No?"

"I ... I was invited here by one of the resident greybeards right out of my upper bookylearn. Arthur Conan Doyle recruited me."[26] The sudden change of subject was disconcerting.

Lord Edmund puzzled for a moment then said, "Conan Doyle, ah, mm. Medicator, isn't he? Doing work on spiritualism and the fairy phenomenon. He proved those little girls' sightings of fairies in their garden were real, as I recall."

"Yes."

"How did you come to his attention?"

"My parents are fishmongers in Wimpole Street. They do business with students at the nearby privy bookylearn, Saint Bunion's Enscripted, but the older boys were always trying to trick my parents with nonsense calculations of price and change. And so, from a very young age, I learned to calculate far faster than any student. One day, Conan Doyle overheard me correcting someone. After that, he came by almost daily until one morning, he asked to speak to my father. Conan Doyle had been offered a post here at the Academy and needed my help with his statistical calculations. He offered to support me and pay my parents a small stipend in exchange for my work. And so, I came."

"Well, the next time I see him, I must thank Conan Doyle for his perspicacity in spotting your talent," said Lord Edmund with a tiny smile.

---

[26] Arthur Conan Doyle was born in Edinburgh and became a medicator there. He went on to study eyeballology in Vienna and returned to Britain to establish a practice in London at 2 Dribblepot Street. Since his real passion was spiritualism, Doyle became a fellow of the National Laboratory of Psychical Research, where he came to fame for authenticating the claims of two young Cottingley girls who reported seeing numerous fairies in their back garden. Doyle published his results in the ground-breaking work, *The Coming of the Fairies*. Doyle went on to prove beyond question that many cases of diagnosed mental illness were actually the result of spiritual possession.

"Unfortunately," I interjected, "he's disappeared. Two years ago, we found a note saying he wanted to try his hand at writing novels before he grew too old, and we've heard nothing from him since."

"So, who is paying your keep?"

"The mathematography department. The department head is impressed with my work."

"Good to hear." The chancellor paused. "However...." His amiable gaze evaporated, to be replaced by a mean, cold glare. "However, young lady, you will never again speak of this so-called veil of confusion or the beyond or waste my time with speculation about any edge of the Earth." There was ice in his words. "Never speak of a flat earth again. The earth is curved in a somewhat curious fashion ... but it is not flat. Do I make myself clear?"

She nodded as the blood in her veins congealed.

"Good, because if ever you mention a flat Earth again, you'll find yourself back selling fish. And next time, you'll be missing a finger or two."

Lord Edmund grinned as the color in Lollipop's cheeks vanished.

"You have one task to perform, one only. And you most certainly will not waste another precious second on any damned veil."

"No, sir." A frightful chasm had suddenly opened before her. Howling winds threatened to topple her into the void.

"Fine," continued the chancellor. "Glad we had this chat. And remember, you have one more week. No more."

Lord Edmund returned to his papers but then glanced up just as Lollipop was closing the door behind her.

"Oh, and Miss Crossingguard, please tell the calculating engine team I want to see them ... this instant. Thank you."

"The entire team, sir?"

"Oh yes, every one of them."

Chapter Nine

The Barrens

Hobby and the Earthedger had landed amid a heap of jagged rocks in a landscape of unrelenting grey. Hobby had lain bruised and dazed for a moment as his heart rate returned to normal, but then he'd jumped to his feet in a panic at the thought his prisoner might already have run away. Fortunately, the Earthedger had also been dazed by his fall. And so even before the fellow had had time to regain his senses, Hobby beat him to within an inch of his life for no better reason than Hobby'd needed a release from the lingering terror of their leap through the portal.

Hobby had intended to get rid of the Earthedger once they were through the portal. However, the fellow's curious machine, called a skipscooter for traveling over the barrens' rocky terrain, proved far too complicated for Hobby to handle alone, so he'd been forced to bring the Earthedger along.[27]

Their leap had been two weeks earlier, and the Earthedger was still with him.

---

[27] Early in the development of our tiny community, our geologists determined the barrens between the edge and Dinnerplate to be highly magnetic. The barrens' intense magnetic field had confounded Dinnerplate technology and masked the barrens' existence for millennia. That same intense magnetic field, however, enabled Earthedgers to travel across the great emptiness at remarkable speeds. Where once the trek from Iceland had taken more than a year, with our skipscooters, we were able to make the journey in weeks. We constructed a skipscooter by first crafting a toboggan of pure iron and then turning the iron into a ferromagnet by pushing the toboggan far out into the intense cold of space at the end of a league-long tether. To the magnetized iron toboggan, we then attached a pair of slender clockwork stilts. The craft slid on its magnetic cushion at an unimaginable speed poled forward like a punt on the Avon River.

"Why must you scream every time you pull on your poles?" an exasperated Hobby asked. "No one can hear you for a thousand miles."

After endless rowing, the leather straps binding the Earthedger's arms and legs to the skipscooter's poling mechanism had sliced deeply into his wrists and ankles. He hadn't been permitted more than an hour out of his harness since they'd begun their race across the barrens, and then only to answer the call of nature. When they were racing along, the Earthedger could neither sit nor lie down. He was fed, watered, and even made to nap standing at the mechanism. But Hobby never permitted the Earthedger more than an hour's sleep. Getting to the rim of the world and finding Grimly Wordsmouth as fast as possible were the only concerns that mattered.

The skipscooter was the fastest device Hobby had ever witnessed. Not even the steam machine called the Catch Me Who Can, that he'd once seen thundering around a circular rail track in Bloomsbury, could have caught this sled.

Neither the cold nor shortage of food posed a serious danger to their progress over the broken terrain. Inattention, that was the real danger. It was almost impossible to remain alert with nothing to see—no animals, no trees, no ponds or lakes, not even spiders or lizards or moss, absolutely nothing except unending broken stone. At the speed they were traveling, if Hobby's focus had wavered for even an instant, a large boulder might have suddenly loomed up and the sled would have smashed into it before he'd had any time to adjust the elevation of their slide over the fractured plain. Hobby spent twenty-two hours a day staring ahead into the grey landscape with only Covert's screams to keep him awake.

Guess I shouldn't try to shut him up just yet.

Each day, the sun grew weaker and the sky an ever-deeper blue. After two weeks of almost constant use, the Earthedger's remarkable electrical lamp was on its last legs, which meant they would soon have no choice but to travel in darkness. Then they'd have to slow the craft. Fortunately, however, they were getting close to their destination.

At some point during their journey, Hobby had demanded to know the purpose of the mechanism in the Earthedger's sack. As soon as he'd grasped that it was a signaling machine that the Earthedger might use to warn others, Hobby had tortured his prisoner into sending a message telling his friends that everything was fine. Hobby had then smashed the device to prevent the Earthedger from sending another.

So here they were, within striking distance of his quarry; another week perhaps, ten days tops—if his companion was to be believed. There were moments, as waves of green light danced across the deep purple sky and the stars shone more brilliantly than cats' eyes in an alley, when Hobby imagined he could hear wind chimes out there in the black, across the limitless landscape of stone.

It'll soon be time to dump this fool and what a relief it will be to put an end to his screams. Wait. That's not chimes. That's voices!

Chapter Ten

Earthedge Quarry

The Odyssey Planning Committee's search for the ideal vessel was brief. Village quarrymen had already been sculpting a hull exquisitely suited to the purpose. Annadeena Guesswhich had commissioned an extraordinary craft, and it was going to be an absolute beauty. To be christened the Beatrice, the vessel was being carved from alabaster, and as such she was going to be significantly lighter than other crafts in the Earthedge fleet. Village quarrymen had only recently exposed the seam of gleaming white alabaster amid the unending landscape of dark grey granite. Sitting on the sculpting plinth, its alabaster flecked with golden mica, the Beatrice's unfinished hull both gleamed and sparkled in the moonlight. Also, at a chain from stem to stern and a slender three fathoms of beam, the Beatrice was to be the largest and nimblest vessel ever to sail the rings of the Earth.

Annadeena, a former physicist from the Kenya National Impracticum and our village watermaker, had designed her ship for both fishing and research. She intended to take her craft out beyond Earth's rings to map the intersection of gravity waves as they rolled across space from one celestial object and crashed into waves from another. In the same manner that ancient navigators illustrated the collision of winds and currents on their portolan charts with windroses, so Annadeena dreamt of mapping gravity roses across the realm of infinite darkness.

As soon as Annadeena had realized the forthcoming odyssey would require a very special ship, she'd offered hers—on condition she be permitted to crew. The opportunities for discovery on the voyage promised to be extraordinary. Even so, there was much dismay at the prospect of losing the village's senior watermaker. Annadeena's commitment to accelerate the training of her junior watermaker and to take on a second junior before her departure did ease some of the Odyssey committee's concern.

Electronical illumination had been installed in the quarry to hasten completion of the ghostly ship. Up on deck, a dozen villagers carved and drilled and fitted and tightened. Opal, as thin as a human hair, was fitted into portholes. Pumice planked the deck. Obsidian became cleats and blocks, and moss became shrouds and stays.

Given the uncertain strength of gravity beneath the Earth, the weight of the Beatrice was a serious concern. The planning committee had decided the hull of the Beatrice needed to be trimmed a further fifty thous to provide an extra margin of safety. Beneath the hull, Marigold Springpeeper and I worked our way along the keel line, chipping and polishing each segment.

In the golden light of her chipping candle, Marigold's cheeks sparkled with alabaster dust. She was unquestionably the most engaging person in Earthedge. The daughter of two teachers who had died on the Founders' March, that first horrendous trek across the barrens a decade ago, Marigold was only six when she was given into the care of three single women making the trek together. Her parents could not have loved her more or nurtured her remarkable talents more skillfully than her three new mothers.

Librarians all, the women imparted to Marigold three gifts: self-confidence, courage, and most engagingly, an unquenchable love of storytelling. With a dearth of books in Earthedge, the Three Pages, as the three women called themselves, had become the village's premier source of enrichment and entertainment. Twice a week, everyone gathered in the Rocksplitters to hear one of the pages retell a classic tale. Their example had made storytelling a shared passion for the entire village. On nights when the Three Pages were not performing, someone else was always willing to tell a story. From the moment she became their ward, the pages schooled Marigold in the art of telling a compelling tale, and her nights on stage were among the most popular. She was even writing her doctoral dissertation on the role of storytelling in creating community cohesion.

Marigold's beauty was easy, neglected, frivolous, her pale gold hair a tangle, her tall, slender figure as graceful as a cornflower in a gentle breeze, her clothes as disheveled as lane-side grasses, her lips ever-smiling and her midnight blue eyes ever-glistening and intense. To hear Marigold retell a tale was to be utterly swept away by the lilt of her Dorset accent.

I was momentarily captivated by the sparkle of her cheeks and realized I'd stopped polishing.

"What are you gawking at, Wordsmouth?" she chided me with a grin.

I felt a warmth in my cheeks. "Sorry, I didn't mean to stare. It's just you look like a...."

"Like a what? And you'd better be careful how you answer, young Wordsmouth."

"Well, when I was a child, I had this picture book about dragons and knights and wizards—"

"I look like a wizard?"

"No, but with the flecks of mica on your cheeks and the alabaster dust in your hair ... well, you look just like ... like the queen of the fairies ... the first girl I ever loved."

Marigold smiled and brushed dust from my shoulder. "So, are you saying I'm not the first girl you've loved?"

"No, you're just ... like ... the sixth or seventh." She punched my arm, and we both laughed.

At that moment, Cogsy Eyebeam raced into the quarry, breathless, sweating. "Stalwart! You here? Stalwart!"

"Down here, Cogsy. What's wrong?"

Cogsy scrabbled under the hull. "We just got another message from Covert!"

"How? There's been no storm."

"Dunno how. Maybe he's close," said Cogsy.

"Okay, so what's he say?" asked Marigold.

"Uh, not much, just that he's fine. He never saw the smartypants again, he's making good time, and everything's right as rain."

"That's good, isn't it?" I asked.

"I guess," replied Cogsy. "I mean, if he is close, I guess he'll soon meet up with Pewter and Deem, right?"

Earthedge

"We couldn't have sent two better fellows," I said. "They'll make sure he gets back safely. So, it seems we've nothing to worry about."

"I guess not, except . . . ." Cogsy looked down at his feet as his voice trailed off.

"Except what?"

"Well, why would he say 'right as rain'?"

"What's wrong with that?"

"Nothing . . . except . . . you ever hear anyone else say 'right as rain' here in Earthedge, I mean? Because it just doesn't rain in Earthedge. Here, rain wouldn't be right. It would be very, very wrong."

Chapter Eleven

London's East End

The Lord Mayor of London chose the test site for the new explosive but the suggestion had come from Lord Edmund. East of the Roman walls of the city, the area was sometimes called East of Aldgate Pump. Londoners knew it as the East End, notorious for crushing poverty, overcrowding, and moral depravity. The area was also a magnet for the rural dispossessed and waves of the Empire's colonial cast-offs, a veritable cesspool of expendables, at least in the estimation of the Garter Council.[28]

During the last American war, the East End had suffered the lion's share of the damage inflicted on London by American airships. Since then, the area had descended still further into chaos. Gangs ruled its ruins. National Police robbies dared not step foot beyond the River Lea. Gun battles raged through the night. Time and again, automata stationed on many lanes entering the area were pelted with excrement, scrawled with slogans, and stripped of their

---

[28] In his classic 1923 treatise on economichaos, *The Deserving Deserve More*, Archway Handlever—Medal for Cleverness recipient and Oxford *blatherdon emeritus*—set out the tenets according to which most business leaders and policymakers perceived the poor and the laboring classes in the UK. First, argued Handlever, those who *do*, deserve what they acquire, and those who *mooch*, deserve far less. Second, by rewarding the deserving generously, the nation created both incentive and opportunity for the deserving-to-be, since their fulsome spending stimulated production and set an example of the satisfactions attending accomplishment. And third, to assist or support the laboring class and the indigent in any manner was to incentivize lassitude, diminish opportunity, and disincentivize initiative. "Only by dint of my own strength of character and genteel determination," wrote Handlever in his autobiography, *You Don't Deserve Me*, "did I overcome the humiliation I endured at Eton for the modesty of my family's country estate and my paltry million-pound inheritance. Had I not transcended such hurdles and found the courage to invest in Mrs. Beaton's remarkable onion peeler, I shudder to think where I might be today. Living in Liverpool, I suppose."

armament. Steam wagons attempting deliveries were routinely set on fire. Every morning at dawn, bodies of the most recently maimed and murdered were discovered outside the East End's barricaded Spitalfields Gate. Decent women dared not walk within a league of the East End. And on one of its test flights, Lord Bilbury's unmanned flying machine drifted off course and disappeared over the East End. The following day from a robbie barge, its twisted wreckage had been spotted washed up on the river bank with a sign reading, "Com an' git yer toy, toffs!" As far as the Royal Academy was concerned, such an affront to the Academy sealed the fate of the East End.

"The perfect target," said Lord Edmund.

For years, London's property developers had implored the Lord Mayor to level the area so they might begin its reconstruction. Flattening the East End was likely to be simple; evicting its denizens was more complicated. Even determining how many residents there might be to evict was going to be difficult. Once again, Lord Edmund piped up. "Shall we let my calculating engine have a go?" he suggested to the Lord Mayor.

Allowing for the estimated consumption of available water in the area, for the number of dwellings observed from the river, the apparent murder rate based on the number of bodies abandoned at Spitalfields Gate, the smell, the volume of waste discharged into the Thames, and so forth, Lord Edmund's calculating engine estimated a total population of seven thousand.

In the three days before detonation, a hundred automata were dispatched to roust denizens of the East End from their hovels and march them to waiting craft docked along the Thames. Sweep after sweep through the East End expelled more than five thousand with a loss of no more than thirty automata.

"Good enough," said Lord Edmund.

On the day of detonation, dignitaries from the Academy, every ministry of government, the Order of the Garter, and the Royal Family gathered on Shooter's Hill, Greenwich. The celebrations began with a light breakfast of Scotch eggs, Yorkshire bacon, and mulled mead. Lord Edmund then spoke of the triumphs of British science; the lord mayor, of the new day about to dawn for London; and the king, of the message this new explosive would send to the enemies of the Realm.

Queen Wallis then hobbled to the podium—the years had not been kind to her—and waved a red flag. A line of flagmen relayed her signal across the city to the Spitalsfield Gate, where an army of automata immediately sprang into action. Hauling an enormous oak barrel on a brewery wagon, the automata marched through the gate and into the East End. They'd been programmed to proceed as deep into the area as possible and immediately ignite the explosive if they encountered any resistance. The procession reached the junction of Bethnal Green Road and Horedich, where a gang of street urchins began pelting the automata with cans of Lord Bilbury's dumplings.

***

The explosion leveled three square miles. Windows across London and as far away as Windsor Castle were shattered. The bells in Saint Paul's Cathedral tumbled to the ground, killing three elderly worshippers. Outside Camden Market, a crate of mackerel fell from a dray wagon and crushed a busker. Horses dropped dead from fright. A wave of filthy Thames water rushed up the river as far as Hampton Court, where it flooded the palace. The telescope at Greenwich collapsed, killing the Astronomer Royal. Children would not sleep alone for months. Mothers delivered babies weeks early—their milk soured. Queen Wallis was knocked off her feet and suffered a broken hip. And the lord mayor had to let pubs remain open till dawn to help men calm their nerves.

In the months that followed, it was determined the East End had housed not seven thousand as Lord Edmund's calculating machine had estimated, but seventeen thousand souls. It seemed a punch card had stuck and dropped a decimal from the calculation.

"Ah, but they'd ignored our warnings and damaged thirty automata," the king was to explain during his Christmas address. "What did they expect would happen?"

Needless to say, the Academy was delighted with the outcome of the demonstration, the most powerful explosion ever accomplished by science. A banner day indeed. Lord Edmund was awarded the King's Medal for Cleverness, but not, alas, his appointment to the Order of the Garter.

"Not yet," said the king, "not until you deliver your new projectile."

"Soon, Your Majesty, very soon."

Chapter Twelve

Dockside at Earthedge

Eve of departure festivities were nearing an end. The last of Melody's Odyssey punch had been quaffed, the dozen pans of Mackerel Raspberry Buckle had been scraped clean, and the crew of the Beatrice had been toasted more times than mushrooms in a mulberry wood.

"Bright and early, everyone," Melody called out, "we assemble dockside, so don't stay up too late!"

Marigold and I slipped away as the children were bustled out of the Rocksplitters and off to bed. My insides were aflutter with excitement. Ever since Cepheus rise, I'd been practicing what I was about to say.

Earth's rings lapped the village beach languidly. Moonlight refracted through their ice crystals like a million silver pinpoints. Solar breezes fluttered the burnished copper sails of the dozen ships made fast in the harbor. The Beatrice bobbed at its mooring lines, its lustrous alabaster hull and golden sails so breathtakingly beautiful against the ebony sky.

"What a wondrous vessel she is. I'm so excited for you," said Marigold as we sat together on the Founders' Stone and stared out across the harbor.

The Founders' Stone was engraved with the names of the first 23 people to arrive in Earthedge. Both Marigold's name and mine were among them. The stone was often the site of village ceremonials, but I'd never considered it any more special than a public bench, probably because Father's name appeared first on its list. I couldn't help but remember how painful had been those final days with Father.

***

Following Mother's death, Father had become ever more absorbed in his work and I in my bitterness. No one outside our cottage knew of our fights, but we'd argued over everything: his fanciful visions for Earthedge, his efforts to rekindle my interest in mathematography, his notions of my future. I resisted at every turn. I called him a coward for bending to the will of the Academy, a murderer for inflicting the Scottish Highlands on Mother, and a tyrant for trying to impose his passions on me.

"I'm not trying to impose anything," he'd protested. "I only want you to be all that you can be, and to become the leader you could be."

"I don't want to be a leader. I don't want to be you. I'm not you. If we have to be here, then I only want to sail a stone ship and to write poems like Mother."

The previous year, after uncovering a seam of an unknown and highly electrified mineral, Father had fallen ill. His fingertips had turned black and a painful, remorseless cough had tortured him. I remained oblivious to his condition, but he must have realized his end was near. That last afternoon, he'd lectured me about not closing any doors to my future. I'd shot back that he'd closed all my doors when he brought us to this terrible place. Afterward, I regretted saying such a hateful thing, but not for thinking it.

Then, just as I was about to storm from the cottage, and entirely out of the blue, Father called after me, "You know, Mother will always be with you. I will always be with you."

"No," I'd shouted in reply, "no, you won't. You have never been with me," and I'd left. I heard him shout to me once or twice more, but then a raucous coughing fit overwhelmed him and I heard nothing further.

When I returned home that evening, he'd already passed away. He was seated in his armchair like an icy statue, clutching his chest with one hand and a note to me with the other.

My beloved son, it read, *all I've ever wanted is that you strive to be the man you are, to do the best you can, and perhaps, one day, to see infinity.*

I'd torn the note to pieces and run to Marigold's cottage. She'd held me as I sobbed. "Now all I have is you," I'd whimpered. She'd been my anchor ever since.

***

And so, the time had come to repay Marigold's years of grace and kindness. I took her hand and whispered, "I ... I want to make you a promise. Before I sail, I mean."

"You needn't promise me anything," she responded, "not now ... not yet, anyway." She shifted uneasily and moved away slightly.

"I don't have to but I want to. You mean everything to me."

She shook her head and said, "Look, Stalwart, before you go any further, I know how limited are your choices here in Earthedge. Of course, I've adored you since I was a child...."

That's not quite how I remembered it. Marigold's parents had died from a terrible accident on the Founders' March. Some days after their passing, I'd seen her, a solemn and soulful six-year-old, sitting alone some distance from our camp. A bold and precocious seven-year-old myself, I'd assumed I could help, so I'd walked over to her and asked, "Are you all right? Are you sad?" And she'd said, "How stupid can you be? My Mummy and Daddy are dead. Of course, I'm sad." I think I'd loved her ever since.

"... and, I'm over the moon that you think you love me," Marigold continued, "but I wouldn't have stood a chance with you if you'd had other girls to pick from."

"That's not true." I was flustered. This wasn't going as I'd planned.

"Of course it's true," she replied. "There are only four girls in the village between sixteen and twenty-one."

"And what if you'd had other boys to pick from?"

"Oh, then I'd have dumped you in a heartbeat." Her cheeky smile was bewitching.

"We mustn't joke about this." I was rattled now, but I wanted to get this out. "Look, we live here, and we always will. We have each other, and I don't want anyone else."

"But that's not true," Marigold said as she released my hand. "That you'll always live here, I mean, because I don't think you will. This life is not what you want, to be stuck here in our twilight world forever."

How could she have known that? I might have mentioned I resented Father confronting the Academy and forcing this life upon us without even asking. But I'd never once said to anyone that I might one day want to leave. "Why... why do you think I won't stay?"

"Stalwart, we've known each other forever. I know you. You aren't happy here."

I stared at her, this beauty who knew me better than I knew myself. "Earthedge killed my mother and father." The words were no sooner out of my mouth than I realized how whiny I must have sounded.

"Mine too," she whispered.

How horribly selfish of me! I felt like such an ass. "Of course, I'm sorry."

"Besides, it's not just Earthedge," she continued. "You're never truly happy, not ever, are you?"

Never happy? I was thunderstruck by the thought. Was it true?

"Maybe because people think of me as Father's—I don't know—as his successor perhaps, and that makes me sick. That's the last thing I want. I want a different life, my own life, not his. I want to be me, not him."

"Stalwart, you aren't your father. No one expects you to be. You're you, sweet, smart, kind. You're you."

"But here, I'm my father. That's how people see me, and I have to live every day with the choices he made for me, and I hate that."

"You think you're the only young person who ever resented your parents, who wanted nothing to do with the life they'd imagined for you? Every kid feels that way."

"I guess maybe it's this voyage. It's like everybody thinks it's my duty to go."

"You don't want to go?"

"I do, but not because I have to fulfill the great Grimly Wordsmouth's dreams."

"Nobody is making you go." Marigold retook my hand. "And if you're not happy in Earthedge, then no one will make you stay."

No one will make me stay?

A cold hand gripped my heart. "It seems so unsettling when you say that out loud."

I wiped my face on my sleeve. Nothing about our conversation was as I'd imagined it, but I was still determined to say what I'd planned. "Whether I stay or go is not important. What is important is that whatever I do, I want to do it with you." I wrapped my arms around her. "With all my heart, at the Passing Comet Festival, I'd love to announce we'll wed on your eighteenth birthday."

Marigold smiled, touched my cheek, and said, "No."

I could not have heard her right. "No?"

"No, not yet. You're not the only one trying to figure out your future. I'm not making any commitments, not until I know what *I* want. I have my studies to finish, then maybe I'll know."

I was thrown. It had never occurred to me Marigold might say no. "Okay, okay," I mumbled, trying to find some solid ground. "Okay, then when I return, we'll work out our goals together, okay?"

She hesitated, dropped her eyes to her lap, and said softly, "Okay."

***

A calm Cepheus rise and gentle ripples of ice crystals across the beach foretold a fine day for departure. The fishing fleet would usually have sailed by that hour, but not that day. That day was a day to remember, the day we sailed for the underside. The entire village had turned out for the occasion. Everyone was bubbling with excitement.

First, Mayor Raindrop delivered a brief speech about curiosity and dreams. Then, a dozen schoolchildren sang Dr. Tulip's composition for the occasion, *Let Not the Dark Dissuade You*. Their voices—sweet and pure as ice wine—rose from the shingle beach to the stars.

What you'll see we cannot know, none has gone before,
Down to realms of darkest night, you'll breach a daunting door.
While cold may bind your heart, and black may shroud your eyes
Dread may stay your hand. You'll fear you cannot rise,
But be assured your way ahead is brightened by our love
And we shall hold your hearts in ours until you're back above.

As applause for the school children faded, Annadeena Guesswhich stepped to the bow of her vessel and said proudly, "I name this ship, the Beatrice," and broke a clay cup of mushroom ale across its bow.

The rest of the crew gathered on the dock, where we waited before boarding. Annadeena said a few words about each crew member in turn.

"Armature Codkiss shall captain our vessel," she began.

The harbor rang with cheers and hearty applause as the slender gentleman with the deeply wrinkled face, ragged whiskers, and enormous mane of silver hair marched aboard.

"As we know, Captain Codkiss was the Distinguished Academiker of American Literature at Magdalene Impracticum before he trekked to Earthedge with our founders. Why Armature insists on talking like a pirate is anybody's guess—"

Loud laughter. Armature grinned and lowered his eyes.

"—except to recall in his earlier life, he'd written many scholarly articles on Robert Louis Stevenson, so if Armature fancies himself our Long John Silver, then who are we to criticize. No matter. Here in Earthedge, he is indisputably our finest sailing master."

Warm applause once again. Captain Codkiss smiled broadly and waved to the crowd.

"Next, our first officer shall be Burpee Kettle."

Again, thunderous applause. Burpee, bald, broad-faced, and squat like the stump of a fallen tree, exuded strength as he marched aboard and came to a crisp halt alongside Captain Codkiss.

"It's no secret Burpee has limited vision, but there are times when he sees more clearly than any of us. As a former squaddie and firefighter, Burpee possesses an uncanny capacity to think clearly and recognize the right course under the most extreme circumstances."

Cheers and shouts of "Show them how it's done, Burpee!"

"Gemeny Farcryer shall be our navigator. Gemeny has trained the rest of us in her remarkable new system of navigation and devised our route. I'm excited to announce we sail for the underside of Rome!"

Shouts of approval and loud applause. Gemeny's red hair fluttered in the gentle stellar breeze as she waved at the crowd and marched to Burpee's side. Even Burpee seemed tall alongside the elfin navigator.

"Hopeful Wayward here has been selected for his extraordinary strength, quiet confidence ... oh, and for his cooking. No one can do more with potatoes, fish, and mushrooms than our Fully."

Shouts of "Going to miss you, Fully!"

Hopeful, a former art historian and gymnast, whose closely cropped blond hair glowed like gold dust in the light of the radium lanterns, looked down at the deck boards modestly as he towered over Gemeny and Burpee.

"We shall be joined by Stalwart Wordsmouth." Loud applause as I took my place alongside Hopeful. I glanced at my crewmates and felt like such a fraud. "At his young age, Stalwart is already an accomplished stone sailor, and of course, he carries on his father's legacy of unconstrained curiosity and exploration."

Please stop. Please.

"Now, if you will help me persuade Marigold Springpeeper that taking Stalwart away is for the best...."

Good-hearted laughter. Marigold, standing beside her three mothers, blushed deeply and grinned like a child.

"And finally, I shall be our science officer," concluded Annadeena. Her salt and pepper hair was pulled back in a tight bun, her slender figure sheathed in an iridescent Amirgo creation of ocher and burgundy, and her refined mahogany features glowed in the silvery harbor lighting. The crowd cheered wildly.

The Beatrice was stocked with provisions for two weeks. Sacks of potatoes and mushrooms, greens, salt fish, and ale filled one hold, and Annadeena had installed a portable watermaker in a second. The ship was armed with three shockshooter guns, and most extraordinarily, a culverin crafted by Bedazzles Middlefinger. It amused Bedazzles to think the Beatrice would be sailing with a medieval cannon aboard. There was no expectation of ever using our armaments. Even so, to humor the beloved antiquarian, we'd installed the culverin on the foredeck along with the dozen cannonballs he'd also forged.[29]

For fear the weight of debris raining down from the underside might push the vessel out of reach of the Earth's gravity, the deck had been roofed over with several blankets of thick moss stiffened in potato water.

Annadeena and her fellow physicists had also developed an exciting new power source for the voyage. Earthedgers used potato-based batteries to produce electrical current for lighting their homes. Annadeena had the idea of running the electrical current from a potato battery through an exagifier.[30] The result was a dramatic multiplication of electricity and heat from the new power cell. With a new lantern filament developed by Melody Fullbottle from moss thread steeped in a suspension of tantalum and osmium, we expected to have all the light and warmth we required.

The plan was to return in time for the Passing Comet festival. Comet Porter-Guesswhich was a sunscraper predicted to make a month-long perihelion passage across the sky in March. The village was to celebrate its passage, and someone might even attempt a voyage of encounter if its course passed close enough. We, the crew of the Beatrice, were determined—and indeed we had promised the village—to be home in time for the festival no matter what temptations to extend the voyage we might encounter.

---

[29] A culverin was a relatively simple ancestor of the musket. It was later adapted as a cannon by the French in the fifteenth century and renamed the *couleverine*. The English navy in the late sixteenth century employed the *couleverine* for bombarding targets from a distance.

[30] Invented by Amos Uply, an exagifier's function was to turn a small electric current into a larger one. As such, it was perhaps the single most crucial invention any Earthedger concocted. The exagifier was the basis of so many Earthedge devices, from potato-based lamps to shockshooters, from watchycallits to skipscooters. All contained an exagifier of one kind or another, a relay in which electromagnets coupled two electric circuits together so that when a small current flowed through one of the circuits, a much larger current flowed through the other.

Earthedge

Burpee cast off the mooring lines. As I stood at the gunwale, I couldn't help but kick myself. I should have declined this adventure. I had no right to be here. Among the faces ashore were so many others more worthy. But it was too late now.

The Beatrice slipped slowly away from the dock. Solar breezes fluttered her golden sails. Gradually they filled, and she began to heel over and pick up speed. We stood at the marble gunwales waving and shouting our goodbyes. Our cheers and waves were returned from the thronging shore. My eyes were glued to one face in the crowd. She smiled, waved, and dabbed her eyes with a hanky.

The Beatrice was now running like a racehorse. Farther and farther she glided from shore till the village was but a smudge of tiny lights on the dark grey edge of the Earth.

Chapter Thirteen

The Barrens

Deem Worthy heard the screams first.

"Stop, stop!" he shouted, then grabbed an anchor and tossed it out onto the wasteland of jagged, tumbled stone. Pewter immediately released the skip-scooter's propulsion poles and the sled came to an abrupt halt. Deem and Pewter were both thrown to the deck of their craft.

"What is it?" Pewter shouted, rubbing a badly bruised knee. "You scared me half to death."

"Sssh. Listen." The sled bobbed on its magnetic cushion.

Nothing.

Pewter whispered, "What am I listening for?"

"I was sure I heard a scream."

"A scream out here?"

Crack! Clang!

The shot echoed across the barrens. The shell ricocheted off the iron sled inches from Deem's feet.

"Jump," shouted Pewter. They threw themselves from the sled and down into the rocky chaos. There they concealed themselves behind a huge boulder.

Another shot smashed into the boulder, sending shards of granite flying in every direction. One fragment nicked Deem's cheek.

"Shooter's over there," Pewter said.

"Think you can circle round?" Deem asked as he wiped the stream of blood from his mouth and chin.

"Oh yeah."

"I'll keep him busy." Deem tugged a shockshooter from his back sling, pulled the charging lever, and waited. The barrel glowed, the chamber crackled, and the grip pulsed in his hand. As Pewter leapt and danced from boulder to boulder, Deem clambered to the top of his hiding place, wound the shockshooter gear to the max, and aimed.

There was motion a hundred feet away. Gesturing, Deem shouted to Pewter, "The stone with the silica, there, yes that one," and pressed his shockshooter's fire button.

A white-hot bolt of lightning lanced from its barrel, splitting the air, crackling and sparking as it crossed the sea of stone and smashed into the silica-striped rock, breaking it into a thousand pieces. A blinded, terrified figure tumbled away from the shattered rock and fell backward into a narrow crevice between two boulders. Stunned, bloodied, and winded, the man began firing his pistol wildly until he'd emptied its clip.

Pewter stepped onto a rock above the trapped man and aimed his own shockshooter down into the crevice. Below him, pressed tightly between the two huge boulders, a stubby man in a filthy yellow shirt and tattered plaid trousers wriggled frantically to extricate himself from the crevice.

Rubbing his eyes as he struggled, the shooter bellowed angrily, "Lightning! That was lightning! Where the *stercus* did that come from?" But as his eyesight cleared, the man saw the strange weapon pointed at him, and his belligerent tone gave way to pleading, "Whoa, hey wait! I ... I'm trapped! And I'm wounded. You wouldn't shoot a wounded man."

"Oh, wouldn't I?" Pewter replied. "Deem, this guy must be that smartypants Cogsy was talking about, the one that was trailing Covert back in Minisculevik!"

"How'd he get out here?"

"Guess we'll never know," Pewter said as he cranked the charger on his gun. "Never shot a smartypants before, but there's always a first time."

"Please no! My leg!" the smartypants squealed. "I think it's broken. I never meant to hurt you. I thought, I thought you were robbers. Yes, robbers, that's it. I was just defending—"

"Pew!" Deem shouted, "it's Covert's skipscooter. Oh *stercus*, and here's Covert."

Covert Millrace dangled from the skipscooter poles like a marionette from a hook. His sleeves were soaked in blood from the terrible injuries to his wrists. His face was the color of wet clay and smeared with blood, drool and vomit. His trousers were soiled, he dangled in a pool of his own waste, and his labored breathing rattled in his chest like Deathwatch Beetle in an abandoned chapel.

"Is he okay?" Pewter called, not taking his eyes off the smartypants for a second.

"I ... I don't think so."

With his shockshooter crackling and popping again, Pewter aimed at the trapped man. "If he dies ... so do you."

The smartypants was shouting loud enough to beat rain from blue sky. "Who the maggots are you?" he screamed. "Blasting your hellish lightning guns at an innocent man like that. What kind of monsters are you?"

"You saying it wasn't you that fired at us?"

Deem called out, "Covert's coming round. He's got some horrific injuries. We've got to get him back to Earthedge."

"I have never seen that fella before," the Smartypants protested. "Must have been his captor what fired at you. I ... I just happened to come along when he ran off."

Pewter looked at the smartypants, laughed, and called to Deem, "I think I should shoot this guy first."

"No, wait!" the smartypants cried, then shrugged his shoulders in resignation and said, "Okay, so maybe I did shoot at you, but there's lots I can tell you. Stuff you need to know."

"No, Pew, don't shoot him, not yet anyway," Deem muttered. "We'll get Covert home first, then we'll execute the fishrot proper-like, in front of the whole village."

"Hey, we should let Covert's wife fire the shot," Pew replied.

"I've an even better idea," Deem said, "how about we suggest his missus cook this fellow for the Passing Comet Festival? We never have enough of her Outsider Chutney."

The smartypants, who'd tried until now to appear unshaken by his captors, looked gobsmacked at the prospect of being pickled. "You do that? You eat ...?"

"Of course," replied Pew. "Out here, we spare nothing. Everything goes in the pot."

"But ... but you need me, you do, you need me," the smartypants babbled. "You got enemies. They sent me. I'll tell you everything."

"Oh, we know that," said Deem, "we never doubted for a moment you'd spill your guts."

Chapter Fourteen

Wimpole Street

A week after the East End blast, horse-drawn omnibuses and steam-powered charabancs were still having an almost impossible time navigating the heaps of rubble-clogging streets all across London. In every borough, so many structures had suffered irreparable damage that hundreds of shops and thousands of families were forced into makeshift shelters in the raw March weather. To get people off the streets, the Lord Mayor had issued temporary habitation permits for structures that otherwise would have been condemned. "If they want a roof," said the lord mayor, "who am I to deny them?" The death toll from buildings that had collapsed since the blast had now topped ninety-three.

Lollipop Crossingguard's Number 27 omnibus couldn't make it through to the end of Wimpole Street. Automata had erected a wicker barrier across the road one block from her parents' business and were searching everyone. An enormous crowd awaited their passage through the checkpoint.

"Have your bags and Handifax ready for the automata," bellowed a robbie standing on a barrel.[31] "No need for alarm. Reports of marauding East End corpse robbers remain unconfirmed. Move along, quickly now. No tricycles beyond this point. Everybody walks."

An automaton snatched Lollipop's bag and ripped the stitching when it peered inside with unseeing eyes. The purposeless gesture was made in imitation of an actual inspection but fooled no one. An automaton couldn't recognize a gun or bomb if it was painted red and labeled "Deadly."

---

[31] The *National Robbies Act* required all citizens to carry booklets called Handifax, containing essential information including birthdate, birthplace, address, occupation, current income, religious affiliation, emotional commitment index, frequency of intimate engagement—the intimacy quotient—within the past ninety days, a signed pledge of fealty to the Crown, and one's most significant genealogical connections.

"Thank you for you ... you ... erp ... erp ... acton ... erp ... copper-acting," said the automaton in a strangely falsetto voice, tossing Lollipop's bag into the street.

Lollipop eventually made it through the bottleneck and hurried on to her parents' shop. There, she struggled to control her emotions. "It's terrible, so much worse than I expected," she muttered to herself. "Oh, what if Mother and Father...."

To her immense relief, home—a three-story building at the corner of Wimpole Street and Noddingvicar Lane—was still standing, but its windows were boarded over and much of its roof torn away. Lollipop recognized portions of her childhood bedstead among the splintered pieces of wood covering the ground-floor shop window. On the second floor, a door and part of a bench covered her old bedroom window, and on the third, soot around the windows of Mrs. Gupptlesauce's bed-sitting flat indicated she'd had a fire. Hopefully, the old dear had escaped.

The shop door to Crossingguard Fish Mongers stood open. The smell of rotting fish emanating from the shop was overpowering.

"Mother," Lollipop called as she stepped inside. A single candle on the shop counter dimly lit the room. "Mother, it's me."

A slender woman of indeterminate age appeared from a darkened back room. She was wearing a filthy house dress and headscarf, her hands were covered in slime, and her cheeks were streaked with soot. "Ah, my dear," she said. "How lovely you're here. Oh, I must look a fright."

"You look great, Mum." Lollipop lied. "I'm so relieved you're safe." They fell into each other's arms, both struggling to be strong for each other.

When at last they separated, Lollipop asked, "Where's Dad? Is he ... is he all right?"

"He's fine, but he's been helping everyone in the lane. Right now, he's helping Mrs. Pickle next door. They're looking for her two boys. Do you remember Wobbly and Nobbly? They had good jobs digging the Thames tunnel. But they were trying to save the tuition for an impracticum somewhere, so they took very cheap digs down Bethnal Green. Mrs. Pickle hasn't heard from her boys since the ... well...."

Earthedge

"Oh, the poor dear."

"You know your father. He offered to help the deary search for her boys. They set off to look for them right after breakfast." Mother brought a stool from behind the counter, then dragged a chair into the middle of the room so both could sit.

"And what about Mrs. Gupptlesauce upstairs? Did she have a fire? Is she okay?"

"Yes, she's gone to live with her son in Greenwich. She was cooking some potatoes on a new-fangled coal-gas burner her son gave her when the blast knocked the contraption off its stand and set her clockwork armchair on fire. Your father rescued Mrs. Gupptlesauce and put out the blaze. They couldn't save her husband, though. You did know she'd had him tinned. She kept him on her sideboard, she did."

"Yes, I remember."

"Well, in the heat, his tin exploded. Poor Mr. Gupptlesauce. All over the walls, he is."

"And you, Mum? How are you?"

"Getting by, dear. It's just the fish. With so much rubbish in the streets, the iceman can't get into the city and all the fish in the shop have spoiled. We tried burning them, but they're so wet and slimy they only smoldered and smelled even worse. Now I'm trying to wrap them to cut the smell, but no one is taking the rubbish away, so that won't help for long."

There was a great crash in the street outside. A cloud of dust and soot billowed past the shop door, followed by several people caked in ash and plaster who staggered past like automata.

"Dear dearie me," muttered Mrs. Crossingguard, "that'll be The Squatting Dog. For days they've been saying it was going to collapse. Hope everyone got out in time."

"The pub was open? None of the other shops in the lane is open," said Lollipop.

"Ah, but pubs have to open, don't they. T'would be the end of times if the pubs didn't open."

"But even the tobacconist, Mr. Rivet is closed," Lollipop muttered with a shake of her head. "He's never closed. He always said selling tobacco is a public duty."

"Oh, Rivet did try to open, but the robbies took him away. Seems he had an illegal lamp in his parlor for his poor wife and her bad eyes. Some electronical device it was. Since Mrs. Rivet can't see well enough to open the place, no one can have a nice pipe of an evening."

"How are you eating?" Lollipop asked as she caressed her mother's cheek. "Do you have any food or water?"

"Well, we have some tinned goods. Two days back, a Bilbury dray wagon came through the borough giving out cans of dumplings. Said they'd be back in a few days with some new sort of biscuit they're making. And we do have tea."

"So you have water?"

"Oh yes. We're very fortunate. There's a cracked city pipe in our cellar that's dripping, so we can fill a pot at least. Dearie me, I should put the kettle on for a nice cuppa."

"No, Mum, don't bother. I just wanted to find out how you're doing. When Lord Edmund admitted the explosion was much larger than planned, I got worried about you. I had to know how you were. Oh, and I wanted to drop off a few things, some butter, and bread and a few cans of mushy peas." She unpacked the shopping sack she'd carried from the Academy.

But then, Lollipop's brave front weakened, and she began to weep. "Oh, Mummy, I had no idea how horrible …."

"That's all right, dear. Chin up, or as your father would say, the next net's bound to be a full one."

"That's Dad alright," she said with a chuckle and a smile as she mopped away her tears. "Oh, look at the time. I really must be getting back to the Academy."

"Lollipop, darling, why must you work there? You're just seventeen. You could go to an impracticum."

"I thought you were proud I work there."

"Well, we were ... when the Academy was doing things to help the people. Now, the Academy only seems to be doing wrong."

"Wrong?"

"Things that don't help at all ... things that hurt people."

"Like what?" Stupid question.

"Like the blast."

"But we're building a bomb to defend the Realm," Lollipop said with precious little conviction.

"From what?" exclaimed her mother. "I've been through three wars, and no enemy has ever done more damage to our city than that damned Academy blast. Oh dear, forgive my language."

***

From the upper deck of the horse-drawn omnibus, Lollipop saw people in lane after lane picking through the rubble of their lives, and once again, she wept.

We've broken our city.

The day Lollipop moved out of her tiny childhood bedroom above the fish shop and into her bedsitting cubby at the Academy, she'd cried like a toddler. Today she wept the tears of the angels. "So shattered are they by the graceless sins and unforgivable venalities of Man," she muttered to herself as the omnibus rumbled past devastated lane after ruined mews.[32]

And now there was talk at the Academy of a second explosives test. Lollipop's grief at the prospect choked the breath from her chest. The whopping error in calculating the population of the East End had apparently been forgotten by the palace, or at least forgiven, in the afterglow of the blast's supposed success. But then, after much uncharacteristic public grumbling about the shocking extent of the damage, the palace put out a story that the blast was more powerful than expected because Russian and American saboteurs had manipulated Academy calculations. Fortunately, the palace claimed, the

---

[32] From Strophe 9, Canto 17 of the *Apocrypha* of the *Mycenaean Troglodytic Brethren*.

culprits had been caught, made to confess, and been punished. Lord Edmund's miscalculation of the East End population, however, was a personal black eye and he appeared frantic to avoid another.

He'd taken to visiting the calculating engine department every day. Its tests were going badly. The machine cranked out error after error, and even though the machine's design was entirely Edmund's own, he lashed out at the engine team for its many failures. Inevitably, the head of the team paid the price. Lollipop was horrified the day Knobfiddler Giddyford was expelled from Academy grounds. She watched from the MacPherson Tower as the hapless Giddyford staggered down the long lane to the gate and an awaiting steam carriage, clutching his bloody hand the whole way.

Oh God, I'm on the wrong side!

The realization was devastating. She was so close to finding the concave curvature constant, and the mathematical challenge had been wonderfully stimulating. Reading Grimly's work had been more thrilling than she could ever have imagined. And delivering the constant was going to earn her an Academy appointment and a lifetime of rewarding scientific study.

But the thought of providing the curvature constant to Lord Edmund was deeply troubling if it meant another community might be blown to chips and peas. The chancellor had said he'd selected Come-by-Chance merely for purposes of perfecting her targeting math. But what if he had a more savage fate in mind for the unsuspecting village?

Lollipop had done a little research on Come-by-Chance. After Newfoundland voted in its 1949 referendum to remain a British dependency, its inhabitants had labored in abject poverty. The monstrous Icelandic fishing fleet had ravaged the cod fishery, which had sustained Newfoundlanders for centuries. Only the production of whale oil and seal skins along with an annual dole from Great Britain provided the colony with any income at all. Even so, Brits who would happily have given the "freeloading Newfies" the boot, would probably have stopped short of blasting them out of existence.

The tiny sealing port of Come-by-Chance had no more than three hundred inhabitants. It had languished in utter obscurity until 1958, when a late autumn nor'easter brought the village to prominence. The dreadnought USS *Mae*

West, carrying the leaders of the UK, America, and Russia, had been blown from its course to Havana, where the leaders had planned on negotiating a treaty to end their latest conflict. Instead, the *Mae West* anchored in Come-by-Chance harbor where the three leaders got blind drunk on Newfoundland screech and concluded a deal at 3:00 a.m. while retching into a four-seater in the men's outhouse.

Admittedly, obliterating Come-by-Chance would have entailed a tiny loss of life, and there was no denying the gesture would have sent a powerful message to the Realm's enemies. Still, even the sacrifice of one life was so obviously barbaric. Was it conceivable that obliterating Come-by-Chance was truly what the chancellor intended? And if it was, then Lollipop would be complicit! Perhaps Edmund planned to warn the villagers before the launch, but that notion presumed a degree of compassion the chancellor had never before displayed. No, without knowing Lord Edmund's true intentions, she couldn't possibly give him her targeting calculations. But how could she not?

Perhaps she could quit the Academy, walk away, close this chapter of her life. Her mother would be pleased. But would the chancellor let her go? Not likely, not without extracting an excruciating price.

Or perhaps she could simply disappear, head off in search of this edge place Grimly's writings suggested might exist through a veil somewhere beyond Iceland. But what chance would she have of getting to Iceland, never mind through Grimly's veil, on the run, alone, with nothing more than her paltry savings to sustain her? Heavens, she'd never even been out of London before.

Then, perhaps, her best course might be to provide a set of targeting calculations which would successfully carry the Academy projectile across the sea to a target near, but not on, Come-by-Chance. The flight and the blast would probably accomplish the chancellor's ends without needlessly sacrificing lives. And if the chancellor was not happy with the first firing, then she would have warned the people of Come-by-Chance of Britain's treachery and bought herself time to figure out her escape.

As the omnibus rolled to a stop outside the Academy gates, its horses snorted in the acrid air. Lollipop's tears had dried and her courage was steeled.

The smartypants on duty examined her Handifax, made some lecherous comment about her intimacy quotient, and rolled away the high wrought-iron barrier across the entrance. In the dim light of the late afternoon, she began the long walk up the gravel lane. Trees lining the way were leafless, lifeless, their branches clattering in the chill breeze like the bones of a skeleton dangling from a gibbet. Through the green mist, the lights of the estate flickered like the signal lanterns of ships at sea, urgently warning one another of treacherous shoals ahead.

Standing on the Palladian steps between two automata, the main door porter greeted her with a sneer.

"Ah, Miss Crossingguard, finally returned, have we? Well, the chancellor has been waiting most of the day to speak with you."

"I … I'll just freshen up before…."

"No. You'll see the chancellor now."

Chapter Fifteen

Aboard the *Beatrice*

Descending the ragged edge of the Earth wasn't as perilous as I'd feared. Far enough out from the edge, at the very rim of the Earth's icy rings, the Beatrice simply settled in the extremity's weakened gravity. Down, down she sank like a child's rubber toy, slowly filling with bathwater. Then, when Captain Codkiss adjudged her descent to be deep enough, he swung the ship back toward the edge. The Beatrice caught a chill solar wind from some distant star, and we tacked lower still, down toward the looming void. As easy as the descent was, however, entry into the shadow realm below the Earth was a heart-stopping, hellish transit.

A swirling, chaotic field of debris hung below the Earth, rolling and waving about violently like the mourning weeds of some maddened widow caught in a gale. I stared from the gunwale in horrified wonder at a maelstrom of dust and stones. The whirling black mass made entry into the darkness beneath the Earth both terrifying and perilous. The solar storm, which in weeks past had carried Captain Codkiss and his companions beneath the Earth, must have opened a temporary channel through the curtain of debris. Now we could find no such channel.

We had no choice but to coast alongside the debris field hour after hour, searching for some new way through. The writhing sea of rock, gravel, pieces of marble columns, petrified timbers, swirling mud, and myriad fragments of pottery, bone, and metal was seemingly without end. The skull of some great beast swung suddenly out of the churn of detritus and shattered against our mast. Fine crystalline dust caked everything aboard the Beatrice. For fear of what it might contain, we donned masks of moss and cord and the brass-rimmed darkened glasses which all Earthedgers wore whenever we visited Minisculevik.

"Helmets as well," ordered the captain. From gunwale boxes, Gemeny hurriedly distributed helmets crafted from sheets of fish leather with thick moss padding sandwiched between each layer.

Through the veil of debris, I glimpsed the volcano that had so terrified our colleagues on their earlier voyage. Although it still rumbled and spewed fire, its lava flow had ceased. "Is that your volcano, Captain?" I called.

"Be grateful she's taking a breather, lad," Captain Codkiss replied.

At last, we spotted a gap in the veil. Several great marble columns, tumbling and twisting in the light gravity, had crashed and battered away the largest of the debris and cleared a passage of sorts through the worst of the rubble.

"Columns on each side ... like a gate," Burpee muttered. "Abandon hope all ye—"

"Batten down!" cried Captain Codkiss as he swung the Beatrice into the opening.

To call it a passage was an overstatement. Of erratically fluctuating width, the channel was little more than a thinning of the roiling debris. The rocks and stones still in the passage were smaller and less threatening but a danger still. The moment the Beatrice entered the channel, we were assailed from every direction by mud and rocks, fragments of iron, and shards of marble and alabaster. We raced to stow most of Annadeena's lights so they'd not be smashed, and then galloped about the deck like dervishes, closing hatches, lashing sails, and securing cargo.

Stone dust and rubble quickly began to accumulate on the ship.

"Weight's building fast," shouted the captain. "Gonna carry us down. We gotta clear the mess from our decks. All hands to the sweepers."

With my crewmates, I swept and wiped and shoveled and tossed heaps of debris overboard until my arms could lift no more, and then I swept and shoveled and tossed some more. All the while, Captain Codkiss struggled to avoid collision and maintain a steady keel against the shifting and changing weight of the vessel.

"Break ahead!" Hopeful Wayward shouted from the bow, and within an hour, the Beatrice cleared the veil at last. We were now sailing through calmer circumstances, a debris field still, but its objects were generally small and tumbling and bouncing about more languidly, less perilous to our alabaster hull. Even so, objects struck the hull incessantly, maddeningly, like boys endlessly kicking a ball against the side of a house on an empty afternoon.

The captain ordered Annadeena's lights back on and sent Hopeful aloft to watch at the extremity of their illumination for any imminent changes in the ship's prospect. We re-erected the stiffened canvas roofs over the deck to give ourselves some respite from the unending shower of flotsam falling from the underside. Then, at last, we collapsed exhausted.

"We're here," I whispered. "We're below." What would Father have made of me, the youngest member of the first crew to journey beneath the Earth? "Just a deckhand? Why aren't you in command?" he probably would have said. "That's the trouble with you, Son, no ambition."

"Anybody watching for relics?" Annadeena called out.

"I did see a marble torso go by," Burpee replied, "and there, look, an iron flywheel."

"Good thing it didn't strike us," Captain Codkiss muttered. "Ahoy Fully, did you see that flywheel? What are you doing up there?"

"Watching, sir," Fully shouted back. "It was safely off our starboard."

"Okay then how about you shout if you see something big, even if it's safely off."

"I'd be shouting all the time."

"Okay so maybe you sing it, like 'Maaarble Coluuuumn, Captainnnn,' " sang the captain in a rich baritone.

"Ayeeeee Captainnnn," Fully responded like a tenor.

The captain's easy humor helped calm us all.

"Still believe we're doing the right thing?" Burpee wondered aloud. "Nothing useful so far. Just broken pots, and bones, and chunks of iron."

"It is unsettling," said Gemeny Farcryer,

"Whirlpool," Fully suddenly shouted, "Captain! Whirlpool!"

Too late to avoid it, the Beatrice was swept into the swirling mass of rubble nearly a league across. We were tossed and thrown about as the ship whirled faster and faster in the current like a paper boat around a drain. With each circuit, the Beatrice drew closer to the eye of the pool and our speed grew exponentially. I could barely breathe, never mind hang on to the gunwale. And when the ship entered the eye, it shuddered, pitched to port, and was plunged ever deeper into the nether realm beneath the Earth.

"We're falling too far, Captain!" Annadeena cried. "We'll soon be beyond the Earth's grasp!"

As we dropped farther and farther away from the Earth, the morass of debris thinned like a morning mist lifting from a lake. The sky beneath the vessel was a limitless black and filled with innumerable stars. I gasped for breath in the thinning air.

Just as it seemed the voyage of the Beatrice might end before it had truly begun, she slowed, and then, without rhyme or reason, began to roll.

"She's going over!" shouted Captain Codkiss. "We're turning turtle! Hang on!"

Every lashing strained and creaked. In the diminished gravity, all loose objects floated into the air, and each crew member was lifted thous away from the deck to float like specks of dust in an empty room. The hull groaned, the mast bowed, the sails twisted and tangled, and then slowly, the Beatrice came gently to rest.

The ship had rolled one hundred eighty degrees. Up was down, down was up, and the Beatrice now bobbed asea on a roiling mass of water droplets and mud. An ebony star-filled sky, which just moments earlier had been the depth down into which we'd plunged, now arched over us like a seam of diamonds in the ceiling of a coal mine.

For a moment I lay motionless, exhausted, sprawled on the deck, staring breathlessly up into the firmament. First, one of my crewmates, and then another, rose from the deck to make their way to the gunwales. There we peered down into the moiling sea of detritus through which we'd fallen and over which we now drifted.

Suddenly the sails rose from the deck and billowed, caught in some stellar breeze from a distant star. The captain's cry awakened everyone to a horrifying new reality. "We're still falling," he cried. "I mean rising, oh, you know what I mean! We're moving too far away from the underside!" The Beatrice continued to rise ever farther from the reach of the Earth's gravity. The debris field was now leagues below us. We were rising into the void.

"We've got to get back to that muddy current!" Codkiss shouted. "Burpee to the tiller! Everybody, windbags over the side! We have to catch a bailing breeze to haul us back down!"

I and my crewmates rushed to the gunwales and dragged several great copper-wire sacks with hoops at their mouths from the gunwale boxes. Then we affixed ropes and lowered the baskets from the vessel toward the heaving sea of roiling debris. The baskets immediately caught gravity currents and their ropes went taut.

For the next twenty torturous minutes, we struggled to bring the Beatrice back down into the tumbling current of detritus. And when the Beatrice was once again awash in the swirling mess of mud and stone, Captain Codkiss shouted, "Stand down. We'll let her drift for a bit, catch our breathings an' do some figuring a 'fore we set a course."

Back in Earthedge, I part-time crewed the fishing vessel Argon along with Raglan Bookbinder and Gilgilly Kneecap. Captain Kneecap was as accomplished a stone sailor as I might have imagined, until now, that is, until I'd seen Captain Codkiss in action these past many hours.

At the limit of the ship's illumination, across the mass of droplets and mud and stone, churning and heaving like a sleeping beast, we periodically glimpsed a boulder, a piece of masonry, or a tangle of metal. They rose from the heaving mass and drifted in the weak gravity across the passage of our vessel to then glance off its hull and tumble away into the firmament.

Occasionally, the sea of debris swirled outward in a great circle, away from some unseen point as if propelled by an invisible force, much as a pebble tossed into a pond sends swells outward. Only the mysterious power that created this circle in the sea of rubble was beyond our understanding, and the void it created was vast.

As the Beatrice sailed across these circles of emptiness, I glimpsed far below us —with the ship's most powerful lanterns—the actual, roiling underside of the Earth itself. I saw fissures and geysers, mountains and plains, ruins of stone, and structures of angled iron, all rolling and tumbling in the turbulent landscape.

From time to time, great chasms sliced the underside, crevasses leagues wide, their walls hard and jagged, the minerals in their sides shimmering in the light of the ship's lanterns, and their emptiness incomprehensibly vast. Each time the Beatrice crossed a crevasse, our curiosity and the temptation to descend into its darkness both grew.

"Gemeny, any idea where we are?" I asked.

"I've taken magnetic readings and used my algorithm, and I believe we're somewhere below the steppes of Ukraine and heading for Poland."

"Amazing! And you can figure this out from the magnetic fields?"

"Uh-huh, and from the Cyrillic script on the gravestones we've just passed." She chuckled at her little joke.

"And there's another thing," she continued, "I've been taking readings each time we sail across a crevasse, and the numbers shift in some very peculiar ways."

Captain Codkiss approached Gemeny. "Peculiar? Peculiar how?" he asked.

"Well, as Grimly discovered, the Earth's magnetic fields and its gravity waves swirl across its surface both horizontally and clockwise, and they do the same both above and below the Earth."

Indeed, I recalled Father's excitement at his discovery. At the time, I couldn't grasp its significance. It seemed like just another of Father's many distractions and an excuse to inflict yet another math lesson on me.

"But when we sail over one of these crevasses," continued Gemeny, "it's like their numbers drop off a cliff, like their gravity patterns tumble into some sort of vortex. Their magnetic readings make no sense, and then, just as suddenly as the fields fall apart, they form this new pattern."

Burpee joined the group as well. "What pattern?" Burpee asked.

"Down. The magnetic fields align downward, down deeper and deeper into the Earth."

"What do you think it means?" I questioned. Would that I could remember what Father had said.

"I think it might mean each crevasse skirts one of your father's cream-filled centers," replied Gemeny, "And…."

"And what?" I blurted out, taken aback by my own excitement.

"And maybe some of the crevasses go right through."

"Through?" Annadeena practically shouted.

"Through the Earth … to Dinnerplate, to the surface of the Earth. I think each crevasse might be the entrance to some sort of tunnel."

At that moment, I don't think any of us quite grasped the significance of what Gemeny was telling us.

"It's like when we build comet shields for our boats," Gemeny continued, "you know, how we put tubes between the two plates of armor—pressure vents we call them—to strengthen the plates. Well, these crevasses might serve the same purpose, binding the Earth's roiling underside to its hardened upper surface."

Suddenly, from the crow's nest, Fully cried, "Wall!"

All thought of Gemeny's crevasses evaporated as we rushed to the gunwales.

"Wall?" Captain Codkiss shouted back to Fully.

"Yes sir, dead ahead," came the reply.

"I knew we should have turned back," Burpee muttered.

"Is it too late, Captain?" Annadeena whispered as we peered into the darkness, "to turn back, I mean?"

Before the captain could answer, the beam of light running before the Beatrice touched the wall, and we all gasped in unison. The wall, cliff of heaving mud and stone, rose hundreds of fathoms above us before being absorbed in the darkness.

"Come about," shouted Captain Codkiss. "Come about!"

Annadeena threw the tiller to starboard as we scrambled for our whisker poles. The Beatrice heeled over and planed away from the wall. Annadeena then swung the ship in a great arc to have the ship stand off the wall at a safe distance.

"We'll have to get higher before we run at that barrier again," said the captain.

"But how, Captain?" questioned Burpee. "Besides, we have no idea how high it is. There may be no getting over it."

From my post on the starboard side, I spotted a curious motion at the wall, different somehow from the chaotic swirling about elsewhere. "Captain," I called, "Look there, the debris near the wall. It's flowing up the side, upwards like a waterfall in reverse."

"Gravity currents," cried Gemeny. "They might give us a way up, Captain."

"Captain has the helm," Captain Codkiss shouted.

Annadeena stepped away as Captain Codkiss spun the tiller. "Hang on!" he hollered. The Beatrice was again charging directly at the wall.

"Burpee to the bowsprit! And the rest of you, stand by your whisker poles. If we don't catch that upward current, we'll need to push away hard to break our course and keep us off those rocks."

Heart pounding in my chest, I held my breath as the Beatrice careened toward the wall. Then, just thirty fathoms out, she began to rise.

Chapter Sixteen

Chancellor's Suite

When Lollipop got to the chancellor's suite, the door was ajar. She peeped through the gap. Edmund was seated at his desk, with Scribben standing to one side.

"Nothing? Still nothing from Natterer?" Lord Edmund roared as he sifted through the late afternoon signals spread across his desk. "What is that fool up to? He promised success in three weeks, and what has it been? More than three weeks and still nothing! Do something! Send another signal. Dispatch more smartypants to Iceland. I have to know if Natterer succeeded or not."

Lollipop summoned her courage and knocked.

"Come!" Lord Edmund barked.

She stepped around the edge of the enormous door. "You wanted to see me, sir?"

Edmund looked up and glared. "Where the *stercus* have you been? I've had automata tramping the grounds since mid-morning looking for you."

"I had no idea, sir, it's ... it's my day off, and I wanted to see how my parents are doing in the city. They ... they live close to the blast area."

"Ahh," responded Lord Edmund, and for a moment, the contorted look of anger on his face softened, "And so are they well?"

"I ... I think so." At first, Edmund's look of concern was disquieting, but then his cold indifference returned.

"Of course they are. There was never anything to worry about. Don't believe all the lies about the blast." Lord Edmund's face reddened. "Those damnable broadsheet scribblers, stirring up trouble with their *postiche* purporting. Evil enemies of responsible citizenry, that's what they are."

Lollipop knew better than to engage the chancellor. "Well, I'm here now, sir."

"So you are, and what is it you want?" Lord Edmund's tone brightened.

"I want?"

"No? Oh yes, it's me." He chuckled, smiled, then turned decidedly more severe. "I want a ... you know ... an accounting of your work." The chancellor was obviously still flustered by whatever had prompted his earlier outrage.

"If you're asking about my progress, sir, well I ... I do have a set of candidate constants."

The chancellor jumped on her answer. "You do? That's wonderful news."

"But I was hoping to review my numerating with Grimly Wordsmouth. You did say you were attempting to contact him."

Lord Edmund's jaw tightened as he growled, "Ah, yes, I did." He shifted uncomfortably. "But the search is not going well." The chancellor scowled at Scribben. "However," he said as his mood appeared to brighten. "I'm delighted to hear you're making progress. And I'm confident you'll provide what I require without the help of that ... of that Wordsmouth fellow." Lord Edmund visibly grimaced as he said Wordsmouth's name. "So, let's set up a meeting to review your constants."

"Yes, certainly, but before we do that," Lollipop screwed up courage, "could I ... could I ask you a question?" She had to know. How else could she complete her work in good conscience?

Lord Edmund's face hardened, his eyes narrowed, and he nodded almost imperceptibly.

Lollipop swallowed, and then said, "I ... I wanted to ask whether we now have our actual target. We've been using Come-by-Chance for purposes of testing our targeting parameters, but I think we're now ready for the real target."

Lord Edmund's response was barely above a whisper. "If you've done your work using Come-by-Chance, why would we need a new target?"

Icy fingers ran down Lollipop's spine. "Because Come-by-Chance is inhabited, and ... and it's part of the Realm, sir. They're our fellow subjects."

"Barely," responded the Chancellor with a dismissive shake of his head. "They haven't paid for the privilege in decades."

Lollipop had feared just such a response. Even so, in that moment, the chancellor's cavalier tone and his implied indifference to the loss of so many lives were more appalling than she could have imagined.

"But we could target somewhere else," she managed to say, "some uninhabited place, I mean. There's no real need to kill anybody merely to demonstrate the power of our projectile."

Edmund drew a long breath. "Studied statecraft, have you?" he asked with a feigned smile.

For an instant, Lollipop was caught off guard by Lord Edmund's pleasant tone and apparent calm. "No ... no sir, I haven't."

"No, you haven't. You're a little strip of a thing who knows nothing except numeration." Any hint of calm or compassion vanished from Lord Edmund's demeanor. His voice grew angrier by the second. "You know nothing of the hearts of men, their wicked imaginings, their merciless intentions. I do ... too well, and I can assure you, a miss by our cannon will be dismissed, discounted. We categorically must hit what we intend to hit, and we intend to hit the site of our last humiliation. Destroying Come-by-Chance will signal to our enemies we shall never be humiliated again."

Near breathless with horror, Lollipop could only whisper, "But the loss of lives—"

"Nothing compared to the lives we'll save." Edmund waved his hand in a gesture of utter dismissal. "Leadership is making hard choices, young lady. I don't expect one such as yourself to grasp the brutal truth about statecraft. You must accept that my decisions are only ever intended to serve the greater good. One day you may glimpse the truth of what I'm saying, but in the meantime, you must serve the greater good in the menial role I've given you and be satisfied with that." His glare was murderous, demonic. Then he smiled and asked, "So, what is the next step in finalizing your constant?"

Lollipop's heart was pounding in her chest. The blood had drained from her face. It took some time to get her breathing back under control. "Well ... well, of course, I must use the constant to work out the projectile's flight path, but . . . that shouldn't take too long."

"How long, precisely?"

Commit to nothing... commit to nothing!

"Well . . . if Wordsmouth is not available to confirm my work, uh . . . then I expect I'll have to use the calculating engine to test and confirm the numeration before . . . before I . . . before I can finally uh, um, be confident in the constant and the um, the targeting coordinates."

"Of course. But if . . . and I'm not saying there's anything to be concerned about . . . but if the calculating engine gives you any trouble, then you must trust your own numbers. After all, you're a capable young lady, and I have complete confidence in you ... and of course, I am holding you accountable for the constant."

Despite his obsequious tone, the look in Lord Edmund's eyes was as hard, as hateful and accusatory, as she could ever have conjured in her most horrifying nightmare.

"Of course, Chancellor."

For an instant, the chancellor squinted in suspicion. "You ... you're not trying to play me for a fool, are you, Miss Crossingguard?"

A cold sweat moistened her skin. She shuddered as if someone had just walked across her grave. "No ... no, sir," she replied.

"No, of course not." The chancellor smiled. "Well then, we must fire our projectile as soon as we can. Let's say in seven days. So, let's meet again in two days to review your candidate constants." Edmund smiled, chuckled even. "I may be old, but it will give me pleasure to strap on the old cinder shields again. I might even spot errors in your numerating that you've overlooked. Never know, but I still might be the one to find the correct constant."

"I don't doubt that for an instant, Chancellor."

Chapter Seventeen

Earthedge

Hobby Natterer was trussed like a pickled piglet on Grateful Day, his thighs drawn up and lashed to his chest, his hands tied behind his back, and his knees, nose, and forehead pressed against the tabletop. The only thing missing was a jellied pear in his maw. Every joint in his body ached, but he'd known worse. When it came to intimidation and terror, the denizens of this twilight world in their gossamer garments and silvery leather boots were amateurs. All right, so they had strange weapons and artificial lighting and weird vehicles, but many of them were old and academicky and obviously perplexed by his presence. Despite his humiliating situation, every advantage was his, and in time he'd make them pay for trussing him up this way.

"I know him," said some old saggybits, barely visible at the edge of the pool of light around him. "Melody, don't you see it? Around his nose and mouth? That twist to the right?"

What twist to the right? What are they talking about?

From somewhere over his right shoulder, another saggybits replied, "Yes, Tulip, it's him."

"Him? Who's him?" asked one of the other shadowy figures in the room.

"The smartypants who escorted Grimly and Ruthy from London to Minisculevik. Ruthy told us the story many times, how she and Stalwart had been taken hostage by a smartypants with a strangely twisted grimace, how they'd been forced onto the Boggshead ferry which had then been swept onto the rocks, how everyone had been tossed into the sea, how she'd managed to save Stalwart while Grimly saved the smartypants with the twisted face. A twisted face just like the catch we have here now."

"Is that true?" asked a male voice from the darkness. "Are you the smartypants Grimly Wordsmouth saved?" It was the gravelly voice of a man who'd smoked too many pipes and seen too many sunsets.

"Grimly Wordsmouth was a fool," Hobby sneered. With his abdomen crushed and chin pressed forward on his chest, it hurt to speak, but Hobby Natterer was not to be cowed. "I cannot abide fools," he grunted.

"Grimly Wordsmouth could have let you die and yet he saved you, and now you have almost killed his friend … our friend. What kind of a monster are you?"

"I'm just doing my job."

"What job is that?"

"Piddle off," Natterer grunted.

"Who are you working for?" asked another voice.

"The Girly Campers! *Stercus*! Are you blind? Who do you think I'm working for?"

"Okay, for the Academy," replied the male with the time-worn voice. "But why has the Academy sent you here? It did everything possible to wipe out all knowledge of our flat earth. So why this sudden interest in Earthedge?"

"Earthedge, is that what you call this dump? The Academy isn't interested in you or your village." He tried to laugh in derision, but it sounded more like the angry snort of an old boar. "You're as inconsequential as this place."

"Then why are you here?"

"I'm looking for Grimly Wordsmouth, of course."

"What does the Academy want with Grimly?"

"Not talking," Hobby gasped. A stitch in his side constricted his lungs.

"Well, it might help you to know that Grimly died a year ago," said the gravelly-voiced old man.

"The chancellor …" Hobby struggled to draw a breath, "is not going to be happy to hear that."

"The chancellor sent Grimly away, said he'd personally kill Grimly if they ever met again, and now your chancellor needs him? You'd better tell us what's going on." The old man with the gravelly voice was now doing most of the talking.

"What ye-er," Hobby sneered.

"I've had enough experience with smartypants to know this one isn't going to tell us anything willingly," said another old gentleman. "We'll need to be more persuasive."

Bah, many's a time I've endured more pain than these wrinkly dimthinkies could ever cook up.

"The Passing Comet meteor shower," someone called out of the shadows.

"Yes. Brilliant, the meteor shower," replied the old man. There followed a babble of assent from around the darkened room.

Three candle-inches later, Hobby lay on his back, blindfolded, stripped to his underbaggies, and strapped to a wooden platform. He'd overheard the gravelly-voiced individual whom someone called Bedazzles volunteer his door for the purpose.

"This is how things are going to work," said one of the young men who'd taken him prisoner out on the barrens. Hobby knew the voice immediately.

You'll be the first to suffer.

"The comet Porter-Guesswhich is on route for a flyby of the Earth. Escorting the comet is a great cloud of debris, dust, ice crystals, small fragments of rock. Many will enter Earth's atmosphere and burn up in seconds. Shooting stars, you'll call them. But out here at the edge, in our thin atmosphere, they do not burn up. We must take shelter for the duration of the comet's passing and its debris cloud continues its merry dance across the universe.

"We're going to lift the door to which you're tied over the side of one of our fishing vessels to let it float amid the rings encircling our world. We'll let the door drift away, far out beyond the rings, at the end of a long tether. And then we'll wait for the approaching meteor shower. If you're lucky, the many little meteors will whiz past and not strike you. But if you're unlucky and a tiny fragment does strike you, it will burn right through you so fast the wound will be cauterized before you even know what's happened."

Hobby gasped at the image of a hole burned right through him.

"And if you're especially unlucky, you will be Swiss cheese in the blink of an eye."

"Do you remember," said another voice, "that time a meteor took off Nestor's leg and cauterized the stump at the same time? He didn't even know he'd lost his pin until he toppled sideways."

Lose a leg? Become a wonkywalker, or worse? Wait, no, that's not fair. The pain would be okay ... but to take away my livelihood?

"Now regrettably, Mr. Smartypants, out there amid the shooting stars, if you do decide to talk, we shan't be able to hear your cries because you'll be so far from our boats. Instead, you'll have to press that button there, by your right hand. Feel it? A tiny light will tell us to pull you out of the shower. Of course, we'll have to wait until we think it's clear to come out of hiding, and then we'll do our best to pull you clear of the shower before you suffer too much damage, but we can't make any promises."

"Hope the light will actually work, Bedazzles," uttered another. "The potato battery is getting a little moldy."

The sensation was so unfamiliar. Hobby was terrified! He had never before known such a shattering sensation of utter helplessness. The imminence of pain would have been one thing, but the prospect of losing everything in the blink of an eye—a limb, his independence, his identity, his life—on the meaningless trajectory of a tiny particle of dust. The very idea was shattering.

He sensed himself being lifted aboard some sort of vessel.

"Cast off," someone said in a dark, funereal tone.

"Aye, Captain," said another.

"Set a course for Ariel Head. Methinks the shower will be its most intense out past the Head."

Several women's voices shrieked, "Oh please stop, this is far too cruel, you can't do this."

"Not our doing, ladies. It's his choice," answered the deepest, darkest voice.

The vessel tossed and rolled. The wailing receded into the distance.

Candle inches burned by.

"We're three leagues off Ariel Head, Captain," someone shouted.

"Right. Lower away our guest."

Earthedge

Hobby sensed the door rise and then drop down into an icy cold. He felt small stones and ice fragments collide with the board as it bobbed in the weakened gravity. He felt a hand pat his leg and then push him away, away from the ship, away into the void.

The voices receded. "Now remember, Mr. Smartypants," someone called out, "the button is by your right hand. When the pain becomes too great, when you want to talk, just push the...."

He could hear no more. Only an occasional bump from a passing stone broke the silence. Never had he known such utter isolation, afloat off the edge of the world, waiting ... for what? Then it happened, an instant, a millisecond of excruciating pain shot across his arm. Oh *stercus*, had he lost a limb already? Had it been obliterated by some tiny crystal whirling past the Earth? First his arm, and then what? A leg? Would he need a trike like Lord Edmund? Trikes were okay for greybeards, but no smartypants had ever used a trike.

Then another searing pain, more prolonged this time, tore across his cheek. Had the right side of his face been burned away? Then another flash of pain struck, and another! The jolts grew more frequent. Every limb had by now been scored, sliced, and raked by the merciless rain of microscopic projectiles.

What if one perforates my heart ... or my skull? I'll be a babbler, a dribbler, a dullard!

A glancing blow lacerated the side of his head. He felt blood trickle down his temple and cheek; he tasted its saltiness at the corner of his mouth.

Someone nearby let out a bloodcurdling shriek of terror, but then Hobby realized it had been him. He was screaming in mindless panic. Screaming and screaming.

The button! Oh please, please, where's the button? There! There it is.

"Help me," he cried out, "come now!"

There were more flashes of pain, more blows, more mindless panic until he heard voices approaching.

"Oh my God, the damage," someone shouted. "We might be too late."

"Any point in even trying?" said another.

"I'm alive," Hobby screamed, "you've got to get me away from here."

"Are you ready to talk?"

"Yes, yes, but get me away from here first, please, I beg you!"

Moments passed as he sensed the door being jostled and jerked about.

"Okay, so you're out of the meteor shower. What have you to say?"

"Get me off this door, let me aboard," Hobby begged.

"Not until you talk. We'll return you to the meteor shower if you don't."

"All right, yes, there's going to be another war," Hobby squawked.

"With whom? America again?"

"Yes, but also with the Russians. Please, my injuries, you've got to tend them!"

"Not until you've told us everything, then we'll do what we can."

The disembodied voices were terrifying.

"Oh, *stercus*, the pain! Okay, okay, so the Academy wants to scare the Americans and Russians into giving up before a war begins. The chancellor wants a bomb that can fly over the ocean, and he needs Wordsmouth to figure out the math for the flight."

"Grimly would never have helped you calculate the flight of a bomb," replied one of the women.

"After I'd killed everyone close to him," muttered Hobby, "I think he might have."

"You'd do that?" someone asked. "What sort of monster...."

"I'm a monster?" Hobby screamed. "You people put me in the path of a meteor shower!"

"When does the chancellor plan to fire this projectile?"

"How would I know? Now, please, my injuries!"

"Get him down from there," someone said.

Down?

"Wait, down from where?" Hobby shouted.

Someone pulled the blindfold from his eyes. As his vision returned, Hobby discovered he was not afloat on waves of ice crystals but slung from the ceiling of a smokey pub.

"What is this place?"

Earthedge

"Welcome to my pub," a woman behind the bar shouted joyfully. She drew a long iron poker with a needle-like tip from the fireplace, held it aloft, and said, "And here are your meteorites."

The pub rang with laughter.

Someone else, holding up a coal scuttle filled with small stones and grit, yelled, "And here we have Earth's rings of ice and stone!"

"You mealworms, you muling dozen dibbies of a floppy soppy sow!" Hobby Natterer shrieked with rage. "I'll make you pay!"

The laughter only grew louder with each new threat Hobby uttered. They clearly didn't believe he'd ever make good on them.

"We don't need to be concerned over a war back in Dinnerplate, do we?" one villager wondered aloud. "Their last one didn't affect us. What danger to us are any of their fiddle-faddles?"

"Amirgo's right," said the publican. "We came here to be free of Dinnerplate's madness."

"Yes," another young woman chimed in, "but if the Academy ever does develop a weapon that can fly across our flat Earth, how long do you think it will be before their chancellor decides to fire it at Earthedge?"

"I fear Marigold's also right," added an old man. "We're unfinished business as far as their chancellor is concerned."

"You're not suggesting we try to stop their war?" asked another.

In spite of his bindings, his injuries, and his ignominious situation, Hobby couldn't help grinning at the notion of the Earthedgers interfering with the chancellor's plans.

They won't stop the chancellor. They won't stop his war. And when the time comes, they won't stop me.

"I'm not sure what I'm suggesting," replied the young woman, "but I do think we should let the crew of the Beatrice know what's happening."

The Beatrice? What's the Beatrice?

"And how do we do that?"

"I think we should go after them."

Chapter Eighteen

Washington, Bureau of Official Stories and Alternative Facts

Recliner Broadbutt—Ol'wreck to his friends—one-time football star, retired marine colonel, founder and CEO of the Wrecking Balls donut chain, was currently Undersecretary of Official Stories. He stood with his shirt unbuttoned in the open window of his third-floor office of the Dennis Day Building, trying to catch the slightest breath of a cooling breeze across his mammoth gut. It was the hottest Lana Turner Day on record.[33] Washington was not the place to be on any warm day when the midges and the stinking mists rose from the Potomac to plague the productive and the purposeless alike. But on a national holiday when the mercury soared into the 90s Fahrenheit before noon, the city was a nightmare, fit only for northerners and sewernewers.

There was a knock at his door. "Come, Shoppingcart," Ol'wreck shouted as he attempted to fasten the shirt buttons across his belly. He only managed to get the top two closed before the door opened.

"You sent for me, Undersecretary." First Deputy Assistant Filer Hebert Shoppingcart was a career public servant and a skeleton of a man in an ill-fitting double-breasted suit of teal-tinted worsted tweed.

---

[33] Lana Turner Day commemorated the outstanding contribution of Lana Turner, actress and entrepreneur-owner of the highly successful Shake Shoppes chain, to the study and treatment of spousal abuse. Following the death of her second husband at the hands of her sixteen-year-old daughter, Turner withdrew from her life on the stage to devote her fortune to research. "Would that more celebrities could model equitable, caring companionship instead of marrying merely for egotistical display or attractive breeding stock," she was reported to have once said to a flamboyant New York property developer on the occasion of his third marriage.

"What do ya know about this explosion in London? The semaphore bulletins from our embassy tell of many dead, and of roving animals feeding on the corpses. They say buildings are still collapsing days after the blast."

"Just got a briefing from State, sir. At first, the UK government said the explosion was part of an experiment in urban clearance. Now they're saying the blast was far larger than intended because Russian saboteurs with American assistance monkeyed with the device."

"The Brits are blaming us? Why?" Goosebumps rose on his arms. "Does State think they know about our Mexican coal deal?"

"No, the Brits don't know, not yet anyway. But they have got wind of the Ruskies' Greenland coal."

"We gotta keep it that way till we're ready to tear up the Come-by-Chance Armistice on our own terms. Hey, you suppose the explosion was really some sort of weapon?"

"Not sure, sir, but I was speaking to an old acquaintance with the British Consulate, a fella I met on my Ditheryear at Cambridge. He's posted here now. Anyway, he's heard through an old academiker of his who's at the Royal Academy—you remember Lord Edmund's crowd—that a team there is attempting to put a bomb atop some sort of super projectile and that building this weapon has something to do with Come-by-Chance."

"Then maybe the Brits do know about our new coal source," muttered the undersecretary, his irritable bowel rumbling to life.

"Pretty sure it's just the Russians and their Greenland coal that's upset Brits."

"So, do you think we need to be concerned about this projectile business? Besides, they couldn't shoot any projectile at us, could they? It wouldn't be possible, not across the ocean. The Earth's magnetic fields are too unpredictable over that kind of distance."

"Well," Shoppingcart began hesitantly, "not unless the flat-Earthers are right ... and the Brits have worked out some new kind of math."

Ol'wreck gave Shoppingcart a puzzled look. "What flat-earthers? What new math are you talking about?"

"Well, for a few years now, there've been these rumors some Brit had proved the world is actually flat. Anyway, your predecessor ordered our skunkworks unit out at Roswell to look into the matter," replied Shoppingcart. "And, well, word is they think it might be true."[34]

"You're not serious. That has to be the biggest cartful of cowpies I've heard of. And the Roswell crowd thinks it might be true? Roswell is our most respected research center. If anyone gets wind that bunch thinks the world is flat, the institute will become an ass's hind end and us, its tail."

"Not gonna hear it from me."

"But we gotta find out more about the Brits' plans. Maybe even order a navy ship to Come-by-Chance. Show of force couldn't hurt."

---

[34] Roswell Institute. The institute was established at the site of a crash of a mysterious aerial vehicle, purportedly of extraterrestrial origin. Initially, the institute operated under the control of the US Army. It was transferred to the Department of Agriculture when seeds were discovered amid the wreckage. None of the seeds has yet sprouted, but cattle in the area are reported to have developed curious mutations, including wings, flippers, and large grey eyes.

Chapter Nineteen

Calculating Engine Steam Conversion Project, Royal Academy

Following her morning tea in the knobfiddler tuckhall, Lollipop was surprised to find an automaton waiting at her cubbynook with a hastynote. Her first reaction was panic. In her two years at the Academy, she had never received a hastynote from anyone. Regular posts, yes, but never a hastynote. Someone was so anxious for her to receive their information, they'd paid a schlepper to carry it across the city and up Snapthrottle Hill to the Academy—an increasingly dangerous and challenging trip given London's worsening conditions. Or, more alarmingly, they'd paid a tuppenny-tricycler—notorious for their exorbitant fees, reckless peddling, and obscene hand gestures—to deliver it.

Lollipop's panic turned to dread when she recognized the handwriting on the envelope.

Oh no, Mother, what's happened?

She tore open the note and read.

> My darling daughter, please excuse this note, but I simply have to let you know that our plans are changing by the minute. Father returned safely from the East End, but sorry to say, he'd found Mrs. Pickle's boys, Wobbley and Nobbley, both dead. Your father was badly shaken by the conditions he witnessed, and our own situation is deteriorating quickly. We still have a trickle of running water, but the stench from our fish, from the rotting food everywhere, and far worse, from the many bodies still unburied beneath the wreckage of the East End, is too much to endure. Father says he cannot, in good conscience, reopen our shop. He wants nothing more to do with this city and spends every hour examining options for our immediate departure. He's talking about booking passage to Canada or perhaps to Iceland. I gather several mates of your father have heard

intriguing rumors about the Danish province. Irrespective, your father has asked me to start packing. I wanted to get this note to you as soon as possible because we may not be here the next time you try to visit. If, by some miracle, you could come with us, we'd be overjoyed. I'll try to persuade your father to delay our departure to give you time to free yourself from the Academy. But if you cannot, we shall write as soon as we have managed to settle somewhere. Your loving mother.

Lollipop wept quietly for several minutes.

So that's it. I can't dither any longer. There it is, either I filet or I flog, as Father would say.

Her choices couldn't have been more glaring. Either she left with her mother and father immediately and carried some of the blame for the loss of hundreds of lives for the rest of her life, or she mistargeted the projectile and accepted whatever punishment Edmund inflicted—including her own demise.

Lollipop wiped away her tears and headed for the calculating engine laboratory.

Basenote Bugspray, interim head of the engine team since the sudden and alarming departure of Abated Giddyford, greeted Lollipop with a strained smile. "Numbers are coming out of the engine, Miss Crossingguard."

As soon as she saw the machine's display, Lollipop knew its calculations were wrong. Even so, she said, "Looking good," to the half-dozen members of the engine team gathered about the brass and glass display table to watch the numbers pop up on their silver pins.

For the most part, team members grinned in response, but then, after a moment of silence, one of their number said very softly, "Except...."

"Except what?" Lollipop asked.

"Except," the junior algorythy said again but then hesitated a second time. "No, I'm sorry, I should be quiet."

"No, you shouldn't. You most definitely should not be quiet."

Earthedge

The young algorythy looked around sheepishly, swallowed hard, and began. "Well, I was going to say … the numbers can't look good because … because … the machine got stuck twice. The numbers have to be wrong."

At first, Lollipop was silent, but then she nodded and said, "Yes, I saw the error. There, on line 83, the engine should not have tried to divide the coefficient by zero."

The calculating engine team looked devastated, disconsolate, even desperate. No one could forget the sight of Giddyford's bloody hand as he'd staggered out of the Academy gate.

Whispered panic swept over the team.

"What can we do?"

"We're lost."

"The damned engine will never work."

"It was flawed from the moment the chancellor conceived it."

"But we can't tell him that."

"Our fingers will be on the chopping block if we do."

Lollipop signaled for quiet. "You mustn't despair," she said. "We still have time. If you can solve the problem of the machine sticking, then I have some candidate constants for you to test. We might need a slight delay from the chancellor, but I think he'll grant it once he sees how close we are."

Some of the team smiled weakly.

Basenote touched Lollipop's arm and whispered, "Can I have a quick word?"

They stepped to one side of the room.

"I realize, Miss Crossingguard," Basenote Bugspray said very softly, "that as our team leader, you're trying to be encouraging. But the simple fact is we can't make the chancellor's calculating engine work, not with all the time in the world."

Despite his youth and slender build, Basenote Bugspray already sported a prominent belly, prodigious jowls, and a web of fine red veins across his cheeks. The thinning spot at the back of his skull grew by the day, and his left eye wandered with a will of its own. Even so, knobfiddlers knew Basenote to be kind, bright, and grateful for their companionship, which his lonely childhood as one of two home-schooled offspring of an embittered, ascetic novelist had denied him.[35]

Lollipop looked deep into Basenote's eyes, or at least into the one which wasn't wobbling about, and asked, "How do you feel about the projectile? I mean, is it a good thing or a bad thing?"

Basenote appeared to be taken aback, but after several seconds, he responded, "I guess I have no opinion on the projectile."

Lollipop stared hard at her colleague. "Even if the chancellor intends to use the projectile to destroy Come-by-Chance solely to frighten our enemies?" Lollipop's tone was almost accusatory. "You'd still feel that way?"

This time Basenote didn't hesitate. "Then I'd try to stop him."

"Even though you're just one person? Even if you'd almost certainly fail?"

"I'd still have to try, wouldn't I." Basenote's resolve was inspiring. "Lord Edmund is a scary fellow, but if something is wrong, well, then it's wrong."

There it is; the answer. It's so clear, so obvious. If something is wrong, it's wrong.

Was this the ally she'd been looking for, this gawky fellow with the wobbly eye? "Well, I do have a plan to stop the chancellor," Lollipop said, "but I'll need your help."

"Wait. Are you saying it's true? That Lord Edmund intends to destroy Come-by-Chance?"

"Yes."

Basenote's face hardened. "So, what's your plan?"

---

[35] Widowed at a young age, Absinthe Bugspray was the reclusive author of many popular dark and erotic tales including *Tear Away My Nightie, Rip Away My Bodice, Slash Away My Chemise,* and her acclaimed literary work of historical fiction, *Cleaveth Away Mine Chastity Belt.* In a stroke of bitter irony, she herself fell prey to the attentions of an itinerant Irish minstrel. Shortly thereafter, the musician moved in with Bugspray and her two children and it wasn't long before he'd swindled the poor woman out of her life's savings. Before he could run off, however, the musician died quite suddenly of a violent intestinal disorder. But his death came too late to save Absinthe's money, and she died a pauper two years later.

Of course, Basenote might have been setting her up, tempting her to reveal her scheme so he could run straight to Edmund. But sometimes, one just has to go with one's instinct.

"I have already identified the curvature constant and used it to calculate targeting parameters—not for Come-by-Chance, however, but for a spot in the North Atlantic just off Come-by-Chance."

"Gosh. You have the constant? You realize you'd get a permanent appointment for your achievement. You'd be the first woman ever to get an Academy appointment."

"Don't remind me. But that's not going to happen because saving Come-by-Chance is what truly matters . . . because it's the right thing to do," she added with a smile.

Basenote grinned in response. "How can I help?"

"We need to buy time, time enough to arrange our escape."

"Do we keep this to ourselves?"

"No, I want to tell the whole team."

"Really? That's a huge risk. You won't know whether someone might betray us. Someone might even think you're only revealing your plan to implicate them as well if things go wrong."

Lollipop realized how sensible Basenote was being, but she knew in her heart how she had to proceed. "They're all knobfiddlers like us. I have to believe they'll want to do the right thing too."

Lollipop touched Basenote's arm, turned, and walked back to the center of the laboratory.

"Everyone? I need your attention."

After a few moments of shuffling and shifting about, the team was once again gathered around her.

"Look, I have to be truthful with you. I did lie a moment ago. We're never going to make the calculating engine work, but that's okay because we don't actually need it to work. We only need it to buy us time."

"Time for what?" someone asked.

"Time enough to devise an escape plan."

The team reacted with silence, then confusion, and finally with a host of frantic questions.

"Escape, why?"

"From the Academy, you mean?"

"What have we done?"

"Are we being punished?"

"But I thought we were getting a new privy?" asked a young lady in a heavy tweed skirt.

"I doubt we're getting anything," replied Lollipop. "The chancellor is not a man of his word. Far worse, he's a butcher. You do know what he did to the East End."

"The explosion, yes, but it was a success," exclaimed a gangly young man with a prominent Adam's apple. "Everyone says so."

Wavey Marshgas, yes, that's him, a denominator.

"Have you visited the East End?" Lollipop responded. "Have you even left the Academy recently? The dead are everywhere. The living are abandoning the city in droves. The blast was not a success. It was a travesty."

"But that's not the Academy's fault," Wavey protested. "Foreign agents tampered with our mixtures."

"Foreign agents tampered with nothing," Lollipop said dismissively. "We … no, I mean you, the engine team, you all got the number of East Enders wrong. The explosives team got their formulas wrong. The chancellor, the lord mayor, and the entire Garter council chose a target that was horribly wrong. And our fellow citizens suffered the consequences. And I will not help the chancellor with his next harebrained scheme if it means more lives will be lost."

"You mean the projectile?" Wavey asked in a tone of disbelief. "What's so harebrained about the projectile?"

"Edmund means to fire it at Come-by-Chance."

"No, that's not true," Wavey protested. "He only chose Come-by-Chance for practice, for testing our calculations."

"Sorry, but you're a fool if you believe that." Lollipop couldn't help the cutting tone of her response. "Lord Edmund intends to blow Come-by-Chance off the face of the Earth simply to make a point."

Engine team members were ashen, speechless.

Lollipop continued, "He means to signal to our enemies the Realm's new might and its ruthless determination to rewrite the Come-by-Chance Armistice. And I know this because he told me so."

At this news, hubbub broke out among the knobfiddlers.

Marshgas still wasn't convinced of Edmund's evil intent. "Okay, let's say you prevent the projectile's launch and save the lives of a couple of hundred people," he posited. "Word is already out regarding the Academy's new explosive. You don't think delaying the projectile will actually give our enemies more time to prepare for war?" Wavey's tone was snide, almost condescending.

Clearly not on my side. And Marshgas may have some influence among the others.

"Wavey's right," echoed the young woman in tweed.

Meadowlark something, yes, that's it, Meadowlark Morningsong, been here six months.

"Isn't it possible the more time we give our enemies to prepare, the more of our own people they'll kill?"

Wavey was emboldened by his acolyte. "The better choice for the Realm might be to hit Come-by-Chance, just as the chancellor intends," said Wavey. "Wouldn't that send the strongest imaginable message to our enemies? It's not like Come-by-Chance would be a big loss."

Lollipop looked about the laboratory and sighed audibly. Then she crossed her arms and remarked in an icy tone, "Setting aside the question of strategy for the moment, let's suppose you continue to do as the chancellor demands. You do your best to get the calculating machine to work. But answer me this, has it worked yet? Do you think it ever will?"

"No," admitted the Meadowlark girl.

"So then you must have the chancellor's targeting parameters?" Lollipop looked directly at Wavey and his prominent Adam's apple.

"No," he replied sheepishly.

"Surely you've worked out the curvature constant by now, right?"

"No," said Basenote Bugspray, glancing into the faces of his team members.

"Which all means what?" Lollipop walked among the calculating engine knobfiddlers, looking each team member in the eye as she spoke. "Which means, you can admit to the chancellor you have failed on every count and pray he is a forgiving man. Or you can help me save Come-by-Chance."

"But how?" asked the young algorythy who'd dared to speak up in the first place. "We're not politicians. There's nothing we can do. We don't have the curvature constant and the machine will never give it to us."

"In fact, I have already calculated the constant," Lollipop announced. The team chattered in amazement. "I just need you to create a realistic-looking engine display of the constant so I can tell the chancellor his engine is working. I'll tell him we only need a few more days to complete our targeting parameters. He'll be so tickled to hear his ridiculous machine is working that he's bound to give us more time."

"I don't understand what you're proposing," Wavey Marshgas challenged. "Are you going to aim the projectile at Come-by-Chance or not?"

"I intend that we miss it."

Basenote was listening intently, weighing everything. "Won't the chancellor know immediately we'd deliberately mistargeted the projectile? Won't we be punished anyway?"

"If my targeting is correct, the projectile will have a successful flight across the ocean and splash down in the sea, missing Come-by-Chance by only a few leagues," explained Lollipop. "I think our success in sending a projectile over the ocean will frighten our enemies even if we don't actually sacrifice the lives of our compatriots."

"So then maybe we won't lose our positions here?" asked the Meadowlark girl.

Lollipop hesitated before answering. The team was skittish enough, but Lollipop couldn't deny the obvious. "Perhaps not, but we'll still have to be ready to run if things go badly."

The team members looked at one another as the reality of their predicament sank in.

"I've been entirely truthful with you," continued Lollipop. "Now I have to trust you. Even though you know the projectile will not strike Come-by-Chance, I have to believe you're not going to tell the chancellor what I plan to do. In return, you have to trust me. If I'm successful, I shall vouchsafe you blameless for my sabotage, and if I'm not, I'll help you escape."

"But if we ask for more time, won't the chancellor just tell us to work harder?" said Basenote. "We probably won't get more than a day at best, and I doubt a day will be enough time to make arrangements for an escape.

That's when a miracle happened.

A knobfiddler from rocketry raced into the calculating engine workroom. He shouted, "The chancellor's going to kill us! There's something wrong with the rocket fuel. We need more time!"

"What's happened?"

"The new fuel is too volatile for the old housing," replied the rocketeer. "We need a safer fuel or stronger tanks or a new trajectory to get the projectile higher. Whichever, we'll need weeks to make the adjustment."

A wave of desperate optimism swept over the engine team. But then an automaton arrived.

"Chancel Lord Edmu ... Edmmm ... in his beedrom ... now wants yup in boardroom ... now."

Chapter Twenty

Below the Second Tier

Wailing solar winds, wild and whirling gravity waves, and an unending stream of stones and mud so battered the Beatrice that we couldn't be sure we'd ascended high enough to clear the wall.

"Gad man, are we above or not?" Captain Codkiss shouted from the tiller, his voice barely audible over the howling gale, the crackling electricons ablaze in our golden sails, and the crash of debris against the hull. "Fully, for gad's sake, man, have we cleared the wall?"

From high above came Fully's faint reply, "Not sure, can't … can't make anything out … need more light…."

"Stalwart, Gemeny," Codkiss called over the cacophony, "the radium lantern a'farud, smartly now."

I rolled and stumbled forward, was tossed up and down, to and fro, this way and that by the maelstrom. In spite of the heaving vessel and assault of debris, Gemeny and I managed to lash the lantern to the bowsprit and connect its batteries. Its greenish beam sprang forward into the torrent.

"Hell's boils!" Fully shrieked from above, "Up! For God's sake, take her up now!"

Agonizing minutes later, the ship, at last, cleared the edge of the second tier and bobbed mere thous above the underside. The ship's keel, indeed its entire hull, was at risk of being shorn away by the jagged rocks and boulders tumbling about in the tier's roiling surface. The surface of the second tier tossed and bubbled like a pot of thick stew on a rolling boil.

"We've got to get higher still, get clear of this mess," Captain Codkiss exclaimed.

"Can't rise any further, Captain," said Burpee in reply, "the stream is weakening. It's pulling us back over the edge and downward."

"Annadeena to the tiller!" Codkiss ordered. "Hard to larboard. All hands, windbags over the side. We'll try to snag some other upward currents."

I was terrified, but my fear abated as I joined my crewmates in lashing the windbags to the gunwales. With our windbags strained to near breaking and ropes taut as fiddle strings, the Beatrice was again being dragged upward by the solar gale and away from the sea of mud and stones.

"We're clear, Cap'n," Fully hollered at last.

"Right, Annadeena, bring her about. Tack into that stream of smaller stones."

I was tempted to ask for a watch at the tiller. Then again, I would probably have made a fool of myself. The captain would have been an idiot to allow me to take the tiller. But I had to do something useful. Rubble was again accumulating on the deck. I grabbed a scrapespade from the gunwale and began heaving mud and marble chips over the side.

Just as the currents had behaved above the first tier, so here too, they layered according to the mass of the material they carried. Heavy debris like stone and marble immediately made up the first layer above the underside. Then finer material like trinkets, splinters, and soil formed a second, calmer current. Lastly, the finer dust, water droplets, and ice crystals comprised the surface layer of this sea of detritus.

"We'll try to remain in this current for as long as we can," ordered the captain.

"Should we stow the windbags, Captain?" Burpee asked. "At this speed, a collision with anything could fracture our hull."

"Don't stow 'um just yet. We'll maintain this speed … get as far from the edge as possible and beyond this slush and mud." He then called up the mast, "Eyes peeled, Fully. Can't afford a smashy bollocks."

In an unending rain of slush and mud and small stones, a heavy crust—almost like mortar—was quickly accumulating on the roof sheets slung over the deck and on the deck itself. I was doing my best to knock the debris from the sheets, but it was piling up thicker and faster than I could break it free.

"Weight's building, Captain," Annadeena observed. "Tiller's resisting."

"Right. All hands join Stalwart. We'll jettison the roof sheets. It'll be faster to scrape this muck directly from the deck."

"Without the sheets for protection, Captain, someone might get crowned," replied Annadeena.

"Aye. Hear that, everyone?" Codkiss shouted. "Don't no one remove your helmets just yet."

"Look, see there, Captain," Fully yelled from the crow's nest. "Off the starboard bow, one of them pools of ... of nothing."

Through the rain of muck and at the very limit of our illumination, we could just make out a wide pool of black, a void, a vast circle of emptiness. As the ship approached its rim, I peered down into the depths, and there, hundreds of feet below, was a crevasse slicing deep into the underside of the Earth.

"Artifacts, I'm seeing artifacts, Captain!" Gemeny exclaimed. "They're gathering around the circle's rim. Whatever force is clearing the void is drawing the artifacts inward as well. Look to port. There's armor, and swords, every kind of sword."

"Captain, Captain, massive statue to starboard," yelled Fully. "Huge thing. Looks to be bronze."

"Draw nigh to it, Annadeena," ordered the captain. "Stalwart, get a rope around it. Standby to haul it in, lad."

"Some Roman statesman, sir," I ventured. Suddenly, a piece of flint careened across the ship, struck my shoulder and clipped my neck. I was thrown to the deck.

"Gad a' mighty! Someone, see to the lad! You still with us, boy?" Codkiss roared.

"It's nothing ... it's just a ...," I mumbled, as I tried to get back to my feet. But as I touched the gash on my neck and saw the blood on my fingers, hot bile rose in my throat, and I pitched forward onto my face like some silly child. "What ... what happened?" I muttered, my cheek pressed to the ship's pumice planking.

"Get him below, somebody," I heard the captain order. "Burpee, see to the boy. And release that statue a 'fore it strikes the hull!"

"No, please, Burpee, I'm ok ... say, do you hear those birds? Geez, their singing's lovely!"

Earthedge

Annadeena shouted to the captain from the tiller, "Could we stand to, sir? See to Stalwart and maybe collect some of these artifacts?"

"Aye, lassie," he answered.

Below deck, Burpee got me onto my berth. "Please, you don't need...," I burbled. "I'm okay, really. Just a scratch."

Burpee poured a bowl of water to wash my wound but I insisted on taking the cloth from him. Try as I might, however, with my shaky hands, all I was able to do was splash water everywhere, everywhere except on my wound. I felt utterly useless—or worse, a burden—as I caught snippets of the muffled activity up on deck.

"We'll descend into the crevasse," the captain ordered, "moor there before the debris field washes back into the void." Then he yelled up the mast. "Fully, get down here, lad. We'll set a wind brace."

"Aye, Captain."

Minutes passed, with only the wail of the wind and the crash of flotsam against the ship. Then the sounds of impact ceased, and Captain Codkiss shouted, "That's it, well done. We're clear of that mess. So now, take her down into the crevasse."

"It's huge," Gemeny exclaimed.

"We'll moor to that stalagmite, that big one," Annadeena called to the captain.

"Good, excellent."

A sudden jolt ran through the ship. The hull had nudged the stalagmite.

"Champion, lass," Captain Codkiss yelled. "Right, Fully, let go the wind brace."

Even with all the colors and stars swirling in my brain, I could picture Captain Codkiss at one end of the ship and Fully at the other, unrolling the long narrow sheet over the side. A Codkiss innovation, a wind brace was deployed alongside a vessel's hull to act as a wind vane. Its curvature captured and stabilized solar currents along the length of a hull.

"Right, now we'll lash our whisker poles in a triangle around the stalagmite," said the captain. "The ship'll rotate with the currents but we won't be in any danger of getting pushed onto any rocks."

Burpee asked me if I was feeling any better. I didn't quite catch the question but nodded anyway, so Burpee headed up on deck.

"How's the lad?" I heard the captain ask.

"Bad gash across the neck and his shoulder's dislocated," answered Burpee. "I've closed the cut but we gotta reset the shoulder before all the swelling starts."

"I can do that, Captain," said Annadeena.

"Right, Burpee, you take the tiller."

"Captain! Below us!" yelled Fully. "Look there!"

"Swivel that light," Codkiss ordered and then he must have peered over the side because he exclaimed, "Heaven a' mercy."

"Oh, oh my," said Burpee.

Annadeena had not yet come below. Whatever my crewmates were seeing, it had totally captivated them.

I could not remain in my berth. I had to see what had so transfixed everyone. In spite of a cold sweat and a spinning head, I stumbled up the steps to the deck and across to the gunwale. In their awe, my crewmates didn't notice my arrival. I too peered over the side.

The golden finger from the ship's radium lamp probed downward into the enormous cavern. There, it played across the many jagged and twisted surfaces before exhausting the limit of its illumination in the coal-black nothingness far, far below.

"It's vast," whispered Gemeny, "so much bigger than I'd imagined."

The crevasse extended hundreds of fathoms down into the darkness. The crystals and minerals embedded in its walls sparkled and glistened like specks of fire in the beam of the ship's lamp.

"How far d'ya s'pose it goes?" asked the captain.

"My instruments say leagues," Gemeny replied.

"Leagues? Gad a' mercy!"

"And the magnetic fields in the area suggest there may be many more such chasms nearby."

"The void above us is filling in, Captain," said Burpee. "Our ascent is gonna be messy."

"Tis so," answered the captain. "We'll lay by for a while, see to the lad, gather up some of these relics on deck, and get a few bells' rest before we head back up into the storm."

Annadeena discovered me standing nearby and shouted angrily, "Stalwart, what the blazes?" She immediately hustled me to the steps. "Somebody, anybody, I'll need help!"

Brrrr! Ca ... can't stop shivering....

"Burpee, give Annadeena a hand," ordered the captain, "and Fully, you go below as well, maybe get some grub started. Gemeny and I will chip and sweep as much of this debris from the deck as we can."

"And then I'll take first watch, Captain," added Gemeny.

"Thanks, lass."

"No problem. I want to study this chasm."

In my berth again, with Annadeena holding my arm at a curious angle, my eyes were shut against the violent reeling of the lounge. "Wish someone'd stop the ship spinning," I gabbled.

"This may hurt," Annadeena said.

Wait, what will hur—

Chapter Twenty-One

Royal and Ancient Academy

Edmund surveyed the group gathered around his enormous table in disbelief. Lollipop Crossingguard, the entire team from the calculating engine division, and two or three knobfiddlers from rocketry all looked as terrified as toddlers at a clown convention.

How dare they ask for more time? How dare they?

"No delay!" Lord Edmund screamed, "d'you hear me? No delay!" His face was the color of strawberries, and the very prominent veins in his temples were beating time to the *Flight of the Bumble Bee*. Spittle flew in every direction while the chancellor's pisspants appeared to have failed in their one and only function. "No delay!" he bellowed as he pounded the table.

"But Chancellor, it's not just the parameters we need," said the engine team captain Bugspray with a pronounced tremor in his voice. "Unless we can strengthen the fuel housing—"

"No *irumbado* delay! I don't care what you have to do to strengthen the housing, double the sheeting, paint the outside with cow dung, hell, line the tanks with Bilbury's dumplings, whatever! But you will have that projectile ready to fly in seven days or you will each forfeit a finger. In fact, you'll lose a finger for every day of delay, no matter whose responsibility the delay might be."

The chancellor suddenly turned up his nose. "What's that smell?" Then he noticed the spreading stain in his lap and muttered. "Oh, *stercus*!" His screaming recommenced, "Damn you! Look what you've made me do! Get out! *Stercus*! Get out! Get out!"

The knobfiddlers scrambled for the door like scared mice, everyone that is, except the skinny knobfiddler with an Adam's apple the size of a damson plum. He stood, coughed loudly, and said, "Uh Chancellor, uh, could I ask…."

The other knobfiddlers froze, spun about, and several very audibly gasped.

"What?" demanded Lord Edmund.

"Marshgas, sir, Wavey Marshgas."

"What is it, Marshgas?"

"Well sir, uh, if one of us has information that the uh others don't wish … uh…."

The chancellor's good hand shot up into the air. The Marshgas fellow fell silent. Lord Edmund glared at him and growled, "Are you turning on your team?"

The worm of a knobfiddler looked confused and terrified. He murmured, "Uh … no?"

"Good, because I already have enough rats around me that need squishing and I certainly don't have time to settle petty squabbles among you lot. One of you is as worthless to me as the next. All that matters is that I've given you all a job to do and you will succeed together, or you will suffer your failure together. No exceptions. So if you value your fingers, you'll get the job done without another word. Now get out!"

"Thu … thank you, Chancellor," whispered Marshgas as he scrambled after his colleagues.

Before the door could close behind the last knobfiddler, Lord Bilbury stepped into the chancellor's office.

"Ah Edmund, I've been meaning to see you."

"What? What?" Edmund blustered as he tried to cover his lap. "Can't you see I'm—"

"Oh, going to the privy, were you? Well, I hate to break it to you but…."

"I know! I know!" the chancellor howled as he blotted the spreading stain with some correspondence from his desk. "What do you want, Bilbury?"

Bilbury dropped into a chair and smiled. "Coincidentally, dear friend, my visit does have to do with your … uh… your timing."

"My timing? What are you on about?"

"I've just come from the palace." The smirk on Bilbury's face was maddening.

"The palace?" An icy hand seized Edmund's entrails.

"Yes, I was chatting with the king, and he—"

"You were chatting with the king ... about me?" Lord Edmund's voice was icy.

"Only in passing, dear boy. He expressed concern for your health and I assured him you had, shall we say, everything under control." Bilbury chuckled at his own humor.

Edmund would have ripped the face off Bilbury if he could have gotten off his damned trike. "Why were you meeting with the king? You know Academy policy. I'm to be notified whenever—"

"Relax, dear fellow, our meeting had nothing to do with the Academy," said Bilbury with a dismissive wave of the hand. "The king merely wished to congratulate me on my new book and kindly offered to write a foreword. Have you read it yet? *Recognizing Inner Greatness*. I did send a draft to Scribben."

"No, I haven't seen it." A lie. Edmund had read every self-serving word. Bilbury had taken three hundred pages to argue that inner greatness is discernible in one's outward aspect, in one's bearing, one's comportment, and one's associates. Hell, he might just as well have said in one's blue eyes, grey hair, and canned dumplings. More to the point, Bilbury argued inner greatness is most apparent by its conspicuous absence in any of the chancellor's own externalities.

"The king also asked me to give you this."

Bilbury drew a piece of stationery bearing the king's seal from his waistcoat pocket and slid it along the table toward Edmund. The note didn't slide far enough, but Bilbury made no effort to retrieve it. The two merely stared at each other until Edmund weakened and pedaled down the table to retrieve the note.

"Thank you, Bilbury." Edmund made no move to open the correspondence.

Bilbury then shrugged, stood up, and left without another word.

Once he was alone, the chancellor tore open the note and read.

"My dear Edmund, we have several pressing engagements next week, so we require that you launch the new projectile earlier rather than later. Please schedule the launch for this week."

The warm pool in Edmund's lap widened. The scarlet on his face drained away like the last rays of a sunset.

"Scribben!" he screamed, "Scribben!"

The door opened, and Scribben's gaunt face appeared. "Yes, your Lordship?"

"Go to Miss Crossingguard and tell her we shall launch in five days, not seven." His voice rose to a thin whine, almost a whimper. "Not seven, oh *stercus*, in five."

Chapter Twenty-Two

Fish Leather Shed, Earthedge

The nauseating smell in the shed was overpowering. By the tiny potato lamp perched on a mound of dirt at Hobby's bedside, he could just make out the principal source of the stink: the many fish skins dangling overhead from the dozen rusty rods. Sometimes, a tiny breeze slipped between unmortared stones of the shed's walls and rustled the drying skins. Then they reflected the light from his lamp and glimmered blood red, rust orange, burnished silver, and iridescent gold.

The damp dirt floor didn't help the stench, nor did Hobby's own filthy state. He'd been days in this horrid cell with nothing but dried fish and mushroom bread to eat. Earthedgers had furnished his cell with a bench and blanket for a bed, and a potato lamp. His chamber pot was emptied and his washbasin refilled each time a keeper called. The iron chain from Hobby's wrist to the spike in the wall prevented him moving more than a few feet from his bed. He was left alone for twenty-three hours at a time with nothing to occupy him except his many imagined scenarios for getting revenge. Clearly, the Earthedgers didn't see him as a danger; not yet, anyway.

How wrong they are.

Hobby couldn't figure out what the Earthedgers were up to. They seemed far more concerned with preparing for some stupid adventure chasing something called a Beatrice than they were with him. Time and again, he overheard Earthedgers outside his cell discussing this mysterious trip of theirs and only the odd mention of his own fate. It was apparent they had no clear plan for him. He'd heard one person suggest that he be abandoned somewhere to fend for himself. Another had proposed returning him to Iceland and turning him over to the local robbies. But there'd been no talk of killing him, so at least that was good. One or two proposals would have had the same effect, however. And besides, if he didn't deliver something of value to the chancellor and soon, then the Earthedgers might just as well kill him. But whatever the

Earthedgers might have been thinking about doing to him, one thing was clear. It was best he not give them time to decide. No, he needed to take control of the situation, starting with getting out of the shed.

The pebbles wedged around the pin fastening Hobby's chain to the wall were surprisingly loose. He shattered his chamber pot and used a long shard of porcelain to pop the stones out and pulled the pin from the wall. Then he wrestled an iron rod loose from the drying rack overhead and used it to pry open the chain link nearest his wrist.

Next, he tackled the shed door. Its hinges were made of many layers of fish leather stitched together and anchored to the door frame with granite pins. He listened for voices outside. Villagers fed and watered him to the clang of a village bell. It hadn't been long since his keeper's last visit so there shouldn't be anyone around the shed for some time. Even so, he listened intently. He made out the sounds of a large gathering in the distance, but nothing close by. So, it was time to make a move. It didn't take more than a tap from the iron rod to shatter the door's pins and knock it to the ground.

Hobby crept outside. His cell was some distance from the village. Tiny lights burned in the windows—or starlights, as he'd heard villagers call them—of several buildings along the trail into the settlement. The brightest emanated from the village pub. Loud voices singing and laughing rang from inside. Hobby's skin crawled to think some of the laughter was probably at his expense. No one had ever laughed at him before and lived. How he would have loved to burst in on their celebrations, swinging an ax with deadly precision. But this wasn't the time for pleasure.

He needed a plan. Perhaps he could steal food and then head out across the barrens back to Minisculevik. Or maybe, he could kidnap a guide and steal one of the Earthedgers' magnetic sleds. But how could he take some villager prisoner without bringing everyone else in Earthedge down upon him?

So, what about this trip of theirs? Perhaps it would be easier to take over one of their weird stone ships than to take on an entire village. With a ship under his control, he'd have hostages. He could demand the gear and the guidance he needed to cross the barrens back to Iceland. Maybe he could even demand Grimly Wordsmouth's notes and calculations.

So, where's this ship of theirs?

Hobby slipped through the village and down to the Earth's edge. There, waves of ice crystals and dust lapped the rude stone wharves. A dozen vessels were moored out in the tiny harbor. One ship in particular clearly had pride of place. It was tied alongside the village's main jetty, with barrels and caskets crowding its deck and tiny flags fluttering from its rigging. It had apparently been provisioned for a long voyage.

Chapter Twenty-Three

Aboard the Sunstone

The lightest craft in the Earthedge fleet, the Sunstone, with its sails of gold and tiller of oak, was wonderfully elegant, remarkably responsive, and a delight to sail. Every Earthedger knew her owner, Pullover Shears. Pullover had expected to captain his vessel on this urgent voyage, but when Amendment Hardknock volunteered, he'd deferred and with good reason.

Captain Hardknock had risen from an ignominious birth in the dirt beneath a Jamaican market stall to become an immensely wealthy speckylender and then to own, design, and captain a fabled America's Cup winner. Amendment had sailed every type of ship at sea, and he'd conceived and designed the very first stone vessel for Earthedge. Ever hungry for knowledge, in his spare time, he'd even become an amateur scientist back in Boston. When approached by Grimly Wordsmouth, he'd been only too pleased to fund the second trek, the Trek of the Many, across the barrens to the infant settlement of Earthedge, and upon the death of his beloved wife, Amendment had sold his vast holdings and joined the third trek himself. Once in Earthedge, he'd studied the solar winds and clouds of hydrogen atoms and realized his compatriots could sail on the Earth's rings in vessels of stone. And so if Amendment Hardknock was willing to captain the Sunstone in pursuit of the Beatrice, then no one was going to deny him.

With Captain Hardknock would sail Deem Worthy. Deem was coming along not just to provide his muscle, but also because he had some notion of what they'd encounter. He'd been aboard one of the three vessels that had been swept beneath the underside during the great solar storm.

And the Sunstone's third crew member? Marigold herself. Having often fished with Pullover Shears, she knew the Sunstone well, and she'd asked for the privilege. Of course, everyone assumed she wanted to go because she was concerned about Stalwart, but this was only part of the reason.

Saying goodbye to her guardians Mildew, Cobweb, and Anemone, the three ladies who'd raised her, had been heartrending.

"When you came into our care, my darling," said Anemone Bellpull, the largest of the three ladies at near fifteen stone, "we were determined you would never feel subservient to anyone, least of all, us. We wanted you to be self-confident enough to chart your own course, to be the heroine of your own story."

"We wanted you to always be brave, determined, and wise in your choices," said her second mother, Mildew Fogbank. In contrast to her powerful voice, Mildew was as pale and fragile as a spider's thread. "Now you are and we're so very proud." Mildew paused, drew herself up, placed her hand on Marigold's cheek, and said, "So please understand when I say this. We don't want to stop you, but we do want to be sure you're going on this voyage for the right reasons."

"What would be a wrong reason?"

Her three mothers glanced at each other before Mildew continued somewhat apologetically. "If . . . let us say . . . just as an example . . . if you wanted to embark on this dangerous voyage . . . merely . . . merely to pursue your young man . . . ."

Marigold smiled at each of her three mothers in turn.

"Please, dear," said Anemone, "please don't misunderstand. We think Stalwart's a charming and well-intentioned boy, but he is just a boy. He doesn't have a clue where his future lies. He's dithering. He's a ditherer."

Then it was her third mother's turn. Cobweb Linenchest was as disheveled and wind tossed as a patch of meadow flowers and as quick to weep as a willow tree in a breeze. She snuffled, and her voice cracked as she spoke. "Oh, we know Stalwart wants the best for you, and you for him, but an infatuation is never a good enough reason to put one's life in jeopardy."

Marigold looked into the faces of her mothers and then embraced all three. "My darlings," she said, "if it will give you peace, I promise you, I've thought long and hard about joining this voyage." Again they hugged. This time they found it difficult to part. When at last they did, Marigold continued. "First, I'm going because I think it's important the crew of the Beatrice understand the new danger we've learned the Royal Academy now poses to our village."

"Good, that's a good reason," her mothers muttered.

"Second, I'm going because I want to help Gemeny with the navigation system if she needs me."

"Another good reason. Nobody could be more helpful than our Marigold," the mothers said.

"Third, yes, I admit I'm concerned about Stalwart, and I want to be there for him. You're right. He is searching for a purpose and I'd like to help him find it."

"All right, we can understand that."

"But I realized the other evening after Stalwart and I talked about our futures that I do know what I want . . . for me. I don't just want to collect other people's stories. I want to write my own stories one day, starting with the story of this voyage."

They were silent for several seconds before all three mothers blurted out, "Oh, that's our girl!"

The Melody bell above the Rocksplitters chimed three times. Embarkation was at hand.

***

If the Sunstone was to catch the Beatrice, then speed was going to be of the essence, and Captain Hardknock knew better than anyone how to coax speed from a stone vessel asea in a vast ocean of ice crystals. Its lines cast off, the Sunstone's golden sails filled to bursting with a trillion sizzling electricons. The Sunstone immediately heeled over and practically flew out of the tiny port of Earthedge. In minutes, she was several leagues from shore.

"Areal Head three leagues to starboard, Captain," called Deem Worthy.

"Aye, lad. Comin' about," Captain Hardknock replied as he swung the tiller. "Hard over," he shouted. The boom flew across the deck. Sails fell slack and then quickly refilled with solar winds as the Sunstone planed away, off toward Areal Head and its harrowing currents that dove down to the underside.

***

"Raindrop, Mayor Raindrop!" Amirgo shouted, "he's gone!"

The mayor and many others were still gathered dockside to catch their last glimpse of the Sunstone. "Gone? Who's gone?"

"The smartypants. I was late taking the prisoner food and water this morning. But when I got to the fish-leather shed, it was empty."

The crowd drew in around the mayor. "Where can he have got to? Has anyone seen him?" asked Raindrop.

The villagers babbled various responses.

"Right. Scour the town, post guards," Mayor Raindrop ordered. "Who knows what he might try,"

Amirgo turned and looked out across the vast plane of dust and ice crystals at the last glimmer of the Sunstone's golden sails. "You don't suppose he's aboard the Sunstone, do you?"

Chapter Twenty-Four

Aboard the Beatrice

I woke to the captain's voice. "Get us underway, me lads and lassies."

As someone detached the brace from the stalagmite, I felt the Beatrice rise from the crevasse. She lurched upward into the mass of debris as solar winds filled her sails. From the thunderous crashes up on deck, I knew we were being assailed by a whirling torrent of mud and water and marble fragments.

"Windbags, everyone!" bellowed the captain. He could barely be heard over the crash of debris against the hull, the crackle of electricons in the golden sails, and the wail of the winds around the fractured marble columns and granite plinths which nudged and tumbled against our bow. "We've got to get through this as quickly as we can!"

"Can't clean my goggles fast enough," growled Burpee, who was at the tiller. "Too much mud! Can't see!"

"Keep swinging your whisker poles, everyone!" yelled the captain. "We're holding the worst of the debris at bay."

"Think it's getting thinner!" Fully shouted from the bow.

"Right. Ascend to the current of finer particles, Burpee. Then turn abaft to the solar wind."

"Aye, Cap'n."

"Okay, Fully, time to get aloft," the captain ordered. "Shout the moment you spot a bergy bit or a growler on a course to strike us."

I sensed the ship's rise through the current of heavier material into the layer of finer debris, there to resume its heading.

"Still think this expedition is worthwhile, Captain?" Fully called down from the rigging.

"We'll let our experts make that call."

I was ashamed to hear crewmates near thrice my age struggling against the bottom side of the Earth to get our vessel underway, and fighting off boulders which at any second might have shattered our hull. Meanwhile, I sat in my berth like some grand pooh-bah, treasures arrayed around me, with two serving women at my beck and call. I felt like such a useless ass.

Never, I never should have come on this voyage. I'm a complete waste of a berth.

"It's a Frankish sword," Gemeny mused. "I'm sure of it. And this little reliquary, the engraving on its hasp, it's a Cathar cross."

"And these objects are why you think we're somewhere beneath France, most likely the Pays d'Oc?" Annadeena asked.

"And my calculations, yes," replied Gemeny as she unrolled her map of alignment and pointed to a spot in southern France. She then traced the closest line of alignment to a point on the underside. "Here, I think we're just here."

"But what of the walls and the levels we've encountered. How have they affected your calculations?"

"And who's to say we won't come across more walls," I piped in.

Gemeny hesitated before she answered. "Well, I'm kind of counting on it."

"You are?" I was shocked. Gemeny had known we'd encounter walls . . . and hadn't warned us?

Apparently, Annadeena was also troubled by Gemeny's response. "Wait! You knew there'd be walls? You knew we'd discover some kind of upside-down wedding cake beneath the Earth? How could you possibly have known that?"

"It's the only way the numbers worked," Gemeny answered.

"And you said nothing?" Annadeena's tone was reproachful.

Gemeny lowered her gaze, fell silent for a moment, but then spoke sheepishly. "Until now, all this," her hand swept over the map of alignments, "it was all just so much theorizing, the gravity waves, the magnetic fields, and ... the alignment lines . . . and, well . . . ."

"Well what?" I asked.

"And the levels to come," Gemeny practically whispered.

"So for sure there will be more?"

"Oh yes."

"How many more, do you know?"

"Seven."

"So that makes nine. Nine levels in total. Really?" I was genuinely rattled. Why had Gemeny kept her suspicions about these fearsome tiers a secret from us?

"Dante's nine circles of hell," Captain Codkiss muttered over Annadeena's shoulder. The captain and Burpee had joined us below decks.

"Who?" I asked.

"Dante Alighieri."

All trace of the captain's seafaring accent had vanished. He was once again the distinguished Magdalene academiker of old. "Dante was an Italian geographer back in the fifteenth century. He wrote *A Topographical Survey of the Realms Beneath the Blessed Landscape.* He claimed to have been guided through several layers of the earth by a mysterious woman. Dante managed to get his book published, but the work was mocked mercilessly by priests and scholars as a farce and a joke."[36]

"How do you know this guy, Captain?" Burpee asked.

"I once studied Robert Louis Stevenson and since he'd read Dante, I did too."

"You're right about Dante, Captain," said Gemeny. "The layers, they're just as he foretold."

"So if you suspected these levels would be down here, why didn't you say so sooner?" Annadeena asked.

---

[36] After all the ridicule and humiliation Dante endured over his *Topographical Survey*, even his publisher disowned the work. He later republished the manuscript under the title *Comedy*, which he advertised as comic literature to recoup some of his earlier costs. After that, Dante gave up writing about geography and turned instead to writing travel guides for the wealthy, including his very successful *Guide to the Trattoria of Venice*. Dante introduced the three chili peppers symbol to indicate which cafes sold the spiciest pasta *all'arrabbiata*.

"Because I've been dismissed before for suggesting Dante's account might be real. Back at my impracticum, I proposed we might be able to find Dante's passage through the earth, and I was … I was terminated."

I could understand her unwillingness to broadcast her theories about some Italian geographer but not her reluctance to trust us. "I don't know why you couldn't tell us. We're your shipmates."

"I guess I was afraid you might not want to attempt this voyage if you knew we'd be sailing into Dante's nine circles, that you'd also think me crazy."

"Did my father know about these layers?"

"Yes. Grimly agreed the layers had to be here. They're the only way our alignment calculations can work."

"So Marigold must have known about these layers as well," I ventured, not sure how I felt about her keeping such a secret from me.

"Probably," replied Gemeny.

"Anyway, we're here now," Captain Codkiss pronounced. "But what do we do about the layers still to come? Do we keep climbing?"

"Well, I hoped at some point we might try climbing through to Dinnerplate," replied Gemeny.

The crew sat in stunned silence until the captain pointed at Gemeny's map of alignment and mused, "We did say we might try to climb through the Earth to Rome."

"But that was before we knew there'd be nine more layers of the Earth to climb through," observed Annadeena.

"So, how far would the journey be?" Burpee inquired.

"Well, we'd have to ascend to the last level, the bottom of the Earth, I mean. Let's see," said Gemeny as she started scribbling figures in the margin of her alignment map. "The radius of the Earth is about 4000 leagues. At the Earth's edge I estimate we sank about two hundred leagues, and with each layer we've descended another 200. Which means with nine layers, the Earth is about 2000 leagues at its thickest point."

"The ninth ring, where Satan resides," muttered Captain Codkiss.

Earthedge

"You're saying we've already ascended … or … descended maybe 600 leagues," said Burpee as he peered over the map, "and now we're on this level? And that's Rome there, right?"

"Yes," Gemeny answered.

"If we're here and this is the route to Rome," observed the captain, clearly deep in thought, "then we'd have to transect seven more layers to get to a point immediately below Rome."

"And then climb all the way back through the earth to get to the Eternal City," said Burpee.

"Yes, but we don't have to go to Rome," Gemeny declared. "We only picked Rome as our target because the artifacts Captain Codkiss found on his first voyage were from Rome."

Just then, Fully cried from the rigging, "Wall! Another wall!"

Everyone raced up on deck, me included. I wasn't going to remain an idlesop any longer.

As we peered through the swirling debris and fearsome darkness, Gemeny shouted, "Do we ascend this wall, Captain, or steer away?"

"Until we have a different destination, I say we go on," the captain shouted back. "Yes, sir, we go on. To your whisker poles everyone."

"So," I asked Gemeny, as we raced to the gunwales and prepared to push away from the wall, "what does Dante say we'll find above the next tier?"

"Freezing slush, lots of slush, and in that slush … the remains of the dead … many, many dead."

Chapter Twenty-Five

Winter Palace St. Petersburg

Even at a full sprint, Footman Frisbinovich took more than twenty minutes to carry the ambassador's message from the Imperial Eagle Semaphore Station atop the Rasputin Tower, across the Winter Palace to Tsar Alexei II's antechamber. The footman galloped, breathless, sweating, and shouting, "For the tsar, for the tsar!" from one end of the gargantuan palace to the other. When at last he arrived at the gilt-encrusted door of the tsar's study, he struggled to catch his breath, used the sleeve of his moss green livery to wipe some of the perspiration from his face, straightened his astrakhan, and then knocked.

A Cossack officer in sweat-stained dress uniform opened the door, eyed the footman up and down, and snatched the blood-red leather pouch from his hands. He then disappeared back into the study, slamming the door in the footman's face.

"Der'mo vysshego klassa," Frisbinovich muttered, spun about, and returned to his duties on the Catherine Gate.

Polkovnik Sergei Horseizset had a quick glance inside the leather pouch and then announced, "Ahem, Your Imperial Majesty, communiqué marked urgent from Ambassador Popover at the Court of Westminster."

The tsar was oblivious. At that moment, he was entirely preoccupied with coal.

Coal was rarely ever out of Tsar Alexei's thoughts. The matter of coal divided his court like no other. "Black death" in the minds of the landed aristocracy, coal had in a decade already become the poppilirium of the new oligarchy. The Romanov Empire's tentative efforts at industrialization had almost overnight spawned an impatient class of bizzybuilders, too gauche to host at court but too wealthy to ignore. Their demand for cheap resources—coal foremost among them—grew by the minute.

In the company of his Minister of Riches, Baron Needlesovich, and Marshall of the Army, Prince Pockmarkoff, the tsar was engrossed in maps of the Empire's coal-carrying canals, searching for ways to expand their transport capacity on the cheap.

The Cossack colonel cleared his throat a second time.

The tsar glanced up. "What did you say?"

"Urgent communiqué from our ambassador in Lond—"

"Well, read it, man!" the tsar snapped.

"Of course."

> "Greetings, etcetera, British broadsheets this morning carried Garter council announcement blaming Russian agitators for the excessive damage done during the recent slum clearance project in the East End—"

"Slum clearance project?" exclaimed the tsar. "What interest do we have in British slum clearance projects?"

"None, Your Imperial Majesty," replied Prince Pockmarkoff with a dismissive gesture.

Prince Pockmarkoff was bearded, barrel-chested, as windburned as a grassland peasant, and as resplendent in his multicolored, food-stained cavalry tunic as the ringmaster of an itinerant Siberian circus. Safety pins clasped myriad medals to his threadbare tunic. They dangled at odd angles and tinkled as he walked. [37]

"I'm told the East End explosion," Pockmarkoff continued, "was a test of a new explosive that went very badly wrong. I expect the Royal and Ancient

---

[37] At the insistence of the tsarina, full military attire was the dress code at court. Even civilians were obliged to frequent one of a gaggle of fancy dress and uniforms-for-hire shops just outside the palace's gate before entering its precinct. Rumor had it the tsarina received a percentage of their hire trade.

Academy responsible for the blast is simply trying to shift the blame for its catastrophic miscalculations."

"And you're sure we had nothing to do with it?" asked the tsar as he walked to the giant samovar. It leaned precariously against a stained and singed tapestry of Peter the Great in full battle regalia. There he poured a demitasse of thick black coffee and sipped it gingerly.

"I'm certain, Your Imperial Majesty."

"Then why has their Garter council swallowed the Academy's line?" the tsar asked. "Is the Council deliberately looking to pick a fight with us?" The tsar shifted his tunic collar in an attempt to relieve the irritation of a persistent rash around his neck. The drab field officer's jacket dangled from his spare frame, and the trousers bagged about his soiled boots. The years had not been kind to His Imperial Majesty, and winter conditions in the palace did little to slow his deteriorating health. Even so, after decades of simmering tensions among the Empire's many fractious classes, he wasn't prepared to spend a ruble to improve the palace's crumbling amenities.

"Ahem," interjected the Cossack colonel.

"Yes?" answered the Marshall of the Army.

"The ambassador does address the issue."

"Read it then," Pockmarkoff ordered.

> "This morning, received a formal protest from UK Lord Chamberlain over coal shipments through Murmansk. King Edward accusing Your Imperial Majesty of violating terms of the Come-by-Chance Armistice by importing coal from Greenland for Russia's own use."

"So they know about the Greenland shipments," said Baron Needlesovich, the Minister of Riches. Needlesovich was as round as he was tall, teetered atop legs as thin as pipe cleaners, and was uniformed as an artillery Komandarm although the baron wouldn't have known a whizbang from a Ouija board.

Earthedge

The baron lit a French cigarette. Its acrid smoke tussled with the roasted aroma from the samovar and the tang from three heavy, unwashed serge uniforms. In winter, palace plumbing, which was fragile at the best of times, was for all practical purposes non-existent. Until spring, the only way for mere mortals beneath the tsar to wash or launder was in horse troughs in the cavalry stables. Walls behind the many huge tapestries hung throughout the palace become makeshift privies. The Winter Palace was the last royal residence in Europe to install Crapper's new water closets. The tsar had consented to have only two, neither of which were currently functional since the water in their pipes was frozen.

"I thought you told me Greenland coal isn't covered by the Come-by-Chance Armistice," the tsar said angrily, "that it's ours for the taking." The last thing the tsar needed was a conflict with his English cousin when he had so many contentious parties to contend with at home.

"The British position is that every source of coal on Earth is covered by the Armistice," interjected the Marshall of the Army. "Of course, that's not our position."

"And that's why the Garter council wants to stir up anti-Russian sentiment? Because they resent us taking our own share of coal from the global supply."

"Our ambassador reports the Brits are making similar charges against the Americans," said the Cossack.

"But the Americans aren't importing Greenland coal. And the Americans have known we're doing it since we leased some of their coal ships."

"I was in the UK recently," said the Minister of Riches. "I attended a vaudeville performance. The humor, which was decidedly anti-Russian, must have been approved by the Garter council. It occurred to me the council might be fostering war fever to distract from worsening domestic conditions. The country's becoming a cesspool."

The Marshall of the Army scratched the flea bites in his groin and pondered the matter for a moment. "Let's suppose the Garter council believes another war is desirable for domestic purposes. They might be thinking they can deal with the Yanks and us at the same time ... especially if they have some new weapon."

"We can't let the Brits or anyone else interfere with our coal shipments," said the riches minister. "We've only just begun to meet demand. The oligarchs would never stand for an interruption of supply now."

"I could ask for a new round of talks to clarify the status of Greenland coal," the tsar suggested. "I could propose a conference on coal to our cousin Edward."

"Russia has no room to maneuver on the Greenland issue, Sire," the riches minister warned. "The oligarchs would never be satisfied with less coal."

"What if we take pre-emptive action?" the marshall suggested. "Might be best to strike the Brits first if there's any truth to the rumor they're building a new superweapon."

"New weapon? And you believe it? Their weapons have always been laughable," said the tsar.

"Until the London explosion, Sire. It destroyed half the city even if it was an accident," the Marshall of the Army replied. "If they're finally getting some better weaponry, then the sooner we strike, the better."

"All right," the tsar says, "prepare some options for my consideration. But also have a letter to Cousin Edward drafted proposing we chat. Oh. and let's reach out to the Yanks. See what they make of British warmongering."

Chapter Twenty-Six

Palace of Westminster

The Garter council restaurant was full to bursting. Wednesday fare in the vaulted fifth-floor dining hall was steak and kidney pie with strawberry trifle for sweet. Garter members always turned out for the Wednesday menu. Well before dawn, aromas of the flaky pastry, roasted rabbit, and rich gravy wafted through the labyrinthine halls of Westminster Palace.[38]

Bilbury usually found dining with Dingaling a treat. The man appreciated a good pie. Today, however, Bilbury's focus was not on food. Today he was stalking Dingaling like quail in a copse.

First Sea Lord of the Admiralty, Lord Trolleysmash—Dingaling to his friends—was from a glorious and ancient family. His ancestral estate in the Midlands, the sprawling and picturesque Duckdrooping, was now open on alternate weekends to steam-carriage tours and to the annual National Homing Pigeon Trials on Pickalilly Weekend. As a boy, Lord Trolleysmash had owned a sleek little sailing dingy, which the future King Edward—his school chum—had enjoyed over extended weekend visits away from school. Never one to forget a courtesy when awarding honors, Edward had appointed his old friend the First Sea Lord after the humiliating performance of the previous incumbent in the last American war.

---

[38] In contrast to the opulent dining arrangements of Garter members, elected members of Talkyhall were not permitted above the first floor of Westminster Palace. They had to be content with the keddigree and spotted dick served in their basement Gnoshcrypt. Nothing aggravated Talkyhall members more regarding the lowly status of the People's Chamber than the paucity of their dining options. Primus speakers regularly condemned the Talkyhall Gnoshcrypt. Predictably, their comments were as ineffectual on matters of cuisine as they were on anything else having to do with affairs of state.

"To your good health, Dingaling," toasted Lord Bilbury, leaning back from the table to unbutton his waistcoat and drain his Oban and rainwater. "And I do hope our new Bilbury Liver Pills will ease your dyspepsia."

"And to you, Bilbury," replied the admiral as he popped the last sliver of Manchego into his mouth and then sipped his Fino sherry. "So, Bilbury, what is it you wanted to talk about?"

No rush. Ease into this. Enjoy the hunt.

"I'm worried about poor Edmund. After so many years of service, it's such a shame to see him suffer."

"Ahh, right to it then," muttered Trolleysmash. "So, you want to make your move now."

"Heavens, no," Bilbury protested. He twisted about and waved at a factotum lurking nearby. "Ah, there you are, Marrow, another Oban for me and one for my dear friend." He then turned back to the sea lord and continued, "As I was saying, heavens no, I'm not planning any sort of a move, most especially not against my dear friend, Edmund."

"Best not. Stirring a hornet's nest, eh what?" muttered the portly sea lord. "Whenever Edmond's challenged, the man's a cornered rat."

Easy now. Let the beaters do their work. Not your job to frighten the prey.

"One must admire Edmund for being so ... resolute ... after all these years in the saddle," said Bilbury. "Any normal person would have hung up his jodhpurs before now, if not for the good of the Realm, then at least for his own well-being."

"Edmund will never willingly give up his authority," the sea lord observed, the phlegm in his chest rattling and rumbling like the seas upon which he had never sailed.

"No," Bilbury said as the factotum placed two whiskeys on the table between them. "But perhaps we, his dear friends, we need to do what is best for Edmund—ah thank you, Marrow."

The Admiral took a sip and asked, "So what are you suggesting, Bilbury?"

And the prey rises from the underbrush.

"Only that perhaps the time has come to help our dear friend see what is in everybody's interest, most especially his own."

"And?"

Now swing the barrel ahead of the bird ... and pull.

"Suggest the king order Edmund to retire."

"At this critical moment?" rumbled Admiral Trolleysmash. "His projectile project is essential. Fate of the Realm, and all that."

A miss. The beaters are off again. And another bird rises into the air.

"Ah, but I've heard the project is not going well. There's much talk that the fuel containment system is nobbled and that Edmund's calculating engine is ... well ... not as reliable as it needs to be. Oh, I'm sure Edmund can fix such problems given enough time, but time is something we simply don't have."

Admiral Trolleysmash drained his glass. "Let's assume I agree Edmund must go. What would you have me do?"

Swiftly now, swing the barrel, precede the bird's flight ... and fire.

Bilbury smiled and leaned forward. In a hushed tone, he said, "Nothing much. Simply have a word with the king. Suggest it might be best if Edmund retired now—before the next war begins. If enough of Edmund's friends make the same suggestion, I'm sure the king will take our advice before conditions at the Academy get any worse."

"Perhaps you're right, old man. Perhaps it's best."

And the hounds are away, off through the underbrush in search of our felled bird.

***

Marrow never took his eyes off the two lardy nobs seated by the Henry VII window.

Fancy that. Lord Bilbury and the First Sea Lord in cahoots!

Marrow knew only too well which side of his bread was buttered. The monthly retainer Lord Edmund paid him for information dwarfed his paltry restaurant wages. And there was bound to be something extra to be earned for a titbit as juicy as this one.

Chapter Twenty-Seven

Aboard the Sunstone

The fog began to lift from Hobby's brain. He winced at the pounding in his temples. He let out a groan but then choked and sobbed at the searing pain in his throat. As sere as seaweed on a scorching sandy beach, the lining of Hobby's throat cracked and tore with each breath.

Stercus, the pain! Water! Please, someone, I need water! Stercus, how long have I been out?

His head throbbed and one eye was crusted over with something, blood most likely, given the long gash his fingers felt across his forehead. Every joint ached and he had too many bruises to count.

What the stercus happened?

He remembered escaping from the fish leather shed and making his way to the docks. There, he'd crept aboard the one ship most obviously provisioned for a long voyage. Aboard, he'd found a hiding spot in the ship's hold among the barrels and sacks of supplies and awaited some unsuspecting crewmember. His intention had been to take the crewmember prisoner and use him to bargain a way back to Iceland. Hobby vaguely recalled the sound of boots up on deck and then many shouts as the ship got underway.

"Jibe ho."

"Set course for Ariel Head."

"Windbags to the ready. We'll be descendin' fast!"

"Steady lass, winds be shiftin'. Dat's right, girl, catch de current."

"Speed, everyone, dat be our goal, speed,"

"Ariel Head three leagues to starboard, Captain."

"Current down the edge, sir."

"Right all, we be takin' de edge full-on, so here we go!"

Hobby'd been poised to pounce on some unsuspecting crewmember. But hours had passed and no one had come down into the hold. He remembered thinking, *We're getting too far from that damned village!*

Earthedge

He hadn't dared venture up on deck for fear of losing the element of surprise. But if he didn't act soon, the vessel would soon be too far from Earthedge for him to control a prisoner for long. Holding a prisoner alone, against the rest of the crew, and for hours on end would simply be too dangerous. The crew would have the advantage.

Hobby had finally decided there was no course but to leave his hiding place and tackle someone out on the open deck. As he'd tried to stand, however, the ship suddenly lurched violently to one side. Hobby'd been tossed across the hold and cracked his head against a bulkhead. The last thing he remembered as he'd slipped away into darkness was collapsing behind several enormous sacks and curling up in a ball.

So now here he was, barely conscious and in a state of utter confusion.

Even with the incessant pounding against the hull of the ship, he could just make out voices up on deck.

"Another wall, Captain!"

"Right, approach on the starboard side! We're going to slide over this edge, the way we did the last one. Deem, boyo, if you need supplies for our meal, best get them now. We goin' ta be very busy for the next few hours."

Hobby heard footsteps crossing the lounge above.

A figure appeared silhouetted in the hatchway. Grasping a rope alongside the ladder to steady himself against the violent roll and tumble of the vessel, the figure descended into the hold. The crewman shone a tiny lantern over the ship's provisions stacked at the far side of the hold. He took a couple of dried fish from a small barrel, and then used a marlinspike from his belt to tear open a sack of potatoes.

The figure didn't see Hobby concealed across the hold, not until Hobby leapt out, dove for the crew member, jerked the marlinspike from the man's hand, and got an arm around the fellow's throat. With the crewman in a headlock, Hobby pressed the point of the spike against his temple and whispered, "One sound from you and I'll drive this spike into your grey stuff, get me?"

The stunned crewman could do naught but nod.

"How many aboard?" hissed Hobby.

"Three," the Earthedger gasped.

"I want you to call your captain. Tell him to come. Say anything else, and you're a dead man." Hobby released the Earthedger's head ever so slightly.

"Captain, Captain!" shouted his prisoner. "Captain, can you come below, sir?"

"Not now, Deem," replied a muffled voice, "we're comin' up on another wall. Need you up here, smart-like!"

"No, sir, you must come here. Now," shouted Hobby's prisoner in reply.

Hobby heard the sounds of heavy footsteps crossing the lounge above as the silhouette of a frighteningly large man appeared in the hatchway.

The crewman had dropped his potato lamp in their brief scuffle. By its tiny beam, Hobby could make out the look of surprise on the captain's face. Hobby must have looked a sight—desperate, with a bloody forehead, his arm around the neck of a crewman and holding a marlinspike to the man's temple.

"I'll drive this home if you make any sudden moves," Hobby growled.

"Where did you come from?" exclaimed the giant of a man, his coffee-colored skin aglow and his silver hair sparkling in the beam of Deem's tiny lamp. "Wait, you're that smartypants we locked up back in Earthedge."

"He was hiding behind the potato stacks, Captain," Hobby's prisoner managed to croak.

"I want you to take me back to Earthedge now," Hobby demanded. "I want one of those sleds of yours and a guide to get me back to Iceland. I'll let this fella go the moment we clear your village."

"You're mad, we're more than a day away from Earthedge. There's no way you could keep a grip on my mate for that length of time. An' there's no way we can sail this ship without him. For bilges-britches, man, we're under the earth, not on some fishpond."

From up on deck, a girl cried out in apparent desperation, "Need help here, Captain! We're going over. I need you up here now, sir!"

Hobby ignored the girl's pleas. "You're going to have to get us back to Earthedge or this man dies." Hobby could taste the blood from his shredded throat. He felt it dribble from the corner of his mouth.

"Captain, please!" cried the girl, "we've got to set the windbags now, sir. Please!"

Earthedge

Whether from dehydration or the ship's lurching about, or the constant clatter of debris against the hull, Hobby's head was spinning faster and faster. He was trying to steady himself against a barrel when it suddenly shifted. He toppled to his left. The point of the marlinspike scraped deeply across his prisoner's cheek. The man's shriek caught Hobby off guard just as the ship heaved to starboard. There was a moment of weightlessness as the vessel rolled to one side. The heavy barrel against which Hobby had been leaning first rocked away from him, then back again, and crashed itself against his leg. He buckled at the knee, and in that instant, the Earthedge captain was upon him.

The captain pulled a cudgel from his belt and smacked Hobby across the skull. Hobby slumped to the deck, dazed, as stars filled his vision.

Standing over Hobby, the huge Earthedger said, "We's saved you once, then captured you, and now we've captured you a second time. You're an abiding nuisance, Mr. Smartypants. I think it's time you found a new career."

The captain then turned to his crewmate and ordered, "Secure him, Deem. Chains are in the mechanicals chest. Then join us on deck." The captain then galloped up the ladder. "Coming, girl!" he shouted as he clambered out through the hatch.

The last thing Hobby remembered before he succumbed to darkness was the girl's desperate cry.

"Captain, Captain, I can't hold—

Chapter Twenty-Eight

Royal and Ancient Academy

Basenote Bugspray slipped Lollipop a note during morning tea break asking her to meet him in the rocketry laboratory immediately after biscuits.

"The rocketry team are out on the blasting pad," Basenote explained as Lollipop entered the laboratory. "They're testing a new liner for the fuel containment tanks." Lollipop reflexively covered her nose against the appalling smell. "I thought the smell might discourage visitors," Basenote explained.

"Clever," gasped Lollipop.

Basenote grinned. "Really, you think so?"

"Certainly working. Nobody's here," Lollipop said with a smile. "So, what do we know about the team? Are they going to help?"

"Okay, so three members are prepared to mock up a display of your constant and the other three won't obstruct us in any way. They'd like to hang on to their positions at the Academy, however. I've made a couple of commitments in order to buy their silence. First, I said we'd create a paper trail that exonerates them from any knowledge of our plan to sabotage the projectile. And second, I said we'd assign them tasks for which Lord Edmund is sure to be grateful even if the rest of us have fled."

"That's very good, Basenote," Lollipop said as she patted his hand.

Basenote grinned in response. "And third, I've generated new Handifax for everyone," he said as he handed Lollipop a stack of booklets. "I've included references, recommendations, qualifications, everything. I did it in case we all have to run. With these, some of us might actually be able to get better appointments away from here. When he saw his new Handifax, Wavey Marshgas said he might want to help us after all."

"This is amazing," marveled Lollipop as she flipped through the many pages. "Gracious, you've made Marshgas the former housemaster of a prestigious public bookylearn and an Oxford gowny to boot! He'll be able to get a headmastership at any bookylearn he fancies with his new Handifax!"

Earthedge

"It should keep him quiet, anyway," Basenote whispered with a giggle.

"But how did you do this? They look so real, even the National Police encryptions. And how have you had the time?"

"Oh," Basenote replied, looking sheepishly at his feet, "I … I have free evenings. And as for how … well, the Handifax was invented for the National Police by an Academy greybeard named Amos Uply, and we still have his original coding equipment down in the second crypt. The story goes he was so disgusted by what he'd done for the police that he promptly fled the Academy to join Grimly Wordsmouth at the edge of the Earth."

She stared warmly at a very self-conscious Basenote. What was it about this lovely man? Lollipop wasn't sure whether she dared ask the obvious question, but then she felt she had to, what with so much at stake. "Basenote, forgive me for prying, but … well, you've been at the Academy so long, and you've obviously been happy here.…"

"Yeah," he said, "I was. I've made some wonderful friends and it breaks my heart to lose this position. I only ever wanted to do science. But hey, there's talk that a person can do whatever science one wants at the edge of the Earth. I think I might try to go there."

"But if you'd prefer to stay here, then why are you helping me? I know stopping Edmund from killing people is the right thing, but what is Come-by-Chance to you?"

"Could I ask you first?"

"Okay. I guess it's because my parents are no longer proud of me," Lollipop answered as she stared out the window at the rails for the projectile and the launch pad a league away.

"They're not?"

"Not after the East End … not after the deaths of eleven thousand Londoners."

Basenote's eyes filled with tears. "The eleven thousand included my sister."

"Oh you poor dear." Lollipop sighed.

"Growing up, it was only the three of us. My mum was a writer. We lived in the middle of nowhere. My sister was my best friend, my only friend. Then mum needed money or something and she took up with a musician, a real piece of *stercus*. He tried it on with my sister. My sister was so horrified she put belladonna in his gravy—it grew everywhere around our place—and then she ran away. I only found out she'd been hiding in the East End when some of her new friends who'd survived the blast brought me her remains."

"I'm so sorry."

"Yeah, thanks. So anyway, to answer your question, what's saving Come-by-Chance to me? I wasn't able to save my sister, but maybe I can save the folks there."

"We can't let the chancellor take any more lives."

"No." He wiped away his tears, blew his nose loudly, and sat to attention. "Okay, so after the chancellor realizes you've rerouted the projectile, he'll likely come after the whole team and you for sure. You're okay with that?"

"No, but what choice do we have?"

"If he does want to punish us, at least we'll have the documents we'll need on the outside. But first, we'll need a way out of the Academy … and I think I might have that too."

"Go on."

"The excavations for the new women's privy … we can go out through the dig," he said excitedly. "The loo's being built well out of sight of the greybeards, beyond the old piggery. The tunnel to get there runs from the old mechanicals building so the old men won't be distressed by the sight of young women attending to their bodily functions. And around the dig, there's not an automaton to be found."

Lollipop smiled warmly, leaned forward, and kissed Basenote on the cheek. "What a wonder you are, my friend."

Basenote fell silent, turned scarlet, and grinned the biggest grin imaginable.

Chapter Twenty-Nine

Aboard the Beatrice

After ascending for what seemed like days, the turbulent trip up the third wall eventually ended. The Beatrice slipped languidly over the rim onto the third tier ... and out onto a nightmarish new sea.

By the greenish light of the ship's lanterns, we beheld a gruesome prospect too horrifying for the mind to comprehend. A limitless tangle of skeletons, limbs, and skulls all sloshed about in a thick stew of icy slush and mud. Shattered coffins and crumbled tombs, headstones and plinths, bronze plaques and cracked and broken busts all rolled and heaved like the surface of a fetid bog in a windstorm.

"For gad's sake, Burpee, steer us higher," cried Captain Codkiss, "get us away from this travesty."

Under Burpee's hand, the Beatrice rose through a steady rain of bone fragments and slush until the morass thinned, and we could peer some way across the roiling funereal gruel.

I was nauseated. "They're ... they're human remains sure enough," I whispered to Gemeny. "It's just as you said."

"Dante wrote that he'd seen vast numbers of bones inside his third circle," she replied. "I guess we're seeing remains that have leached through its walls and out into this void."

"There are ... millions of dead ... millions upon millions," I muttered as skulls and spines and ribs clattered and shattered against our hull.

"Growlers ahead!" Fully shouted from the crow's nest.

"Hands to the gunwales," ordered Captain Codkiss.

We took up our whisker poles again, this time to push away the many huge agglomerations of ice and bone rolling past the Beatrice. From each great icy globe protruded contorted limbs and glaring skulls. The accumulations crashed into one another and formed even more ghastly orbs of ice and death.

"Fully, can you see where these huge frozen chunks are coming from?" I called up to the crow's nest.

"There," he shouted as he pointed off the starboard side. Through the chilling mist, we glimpsed vents in the roiling Earth, geysers spewing slush and human remains hundreds of fathoms up into the void.

"And that wailing?"

"Probably the winds whistling around the mountains of ice," replied the captain.

Despite our best efforts with the whisker poles, skeletons and skulls and limbs of every description collided with our vessel from all directions, clattering and shattering as they did.

"Gemeny, any idea why so many remains are gathered here?" asked the captain.

"I'm guessing the Earth acts like a sieve, separating the different weights of debris into layers. As detritus passes through the Earth, metal is sifted from bone . . . ."

"Sail!" Fully suddenly shouted. "Sail abaft!"

"A sail, here?" cried the captain in reply.

We galloped to the stern and from there we glimpsed a dark shape at the very limit of our pool of illumination. Bearing no lights and sorely tipped to starboard, its gunwales awash in the icy debris, a vessel loomed out of the darkness like the spectral Flying Dutchman of lore.

"Ahoy!" shouted Captain Codkiss. No reply. "Ahoy!" he repeatedly called as the Beatrice turned into the wind and crept alongside the ghostly vessel.

"The Sunstone! It's the Sunstone," Fully yelled. Her mast was snapped and her sails were tumbled across the deck. There was no sign of life aboard the ravaged vessel.

"The Sunstone!" Burpee echoed as he lashed the vessels' two broadricks together. "What in sweet Dilly's boudoir is she doing down here?"

Suddenly. from beneath the Sunstone's sails, there came a voice, weak, little more than a whisper, "Help me, please."

I instantly recognized the voice. "Marigold! Marigold!" I cried out as I clambered aboard the derelict ship.

Captain Codkiss and Burpee followed, and together we heaved away the golden sails. Beneath, we discovered the vessel's three crew. Two did not move, seemingly lifeless where they'd collapsed. From their injuries, it appeared both had been felled by some sort of sudden blow, most likely from the broken mast. When I reached Marigold's side, however, she was already attempting to free herself from a tangle of rigging.

A second crew member stirred. Lashed to the tiller and flopped over like a rag doll, the figure raised an arm and opened his eyes.

"It's Captain Hardknock!" shouted Burpee as he helped the skipper to his feet. "Captain, sir, how badly are you hurt?"

"My arm." Amendment Hardknock winced as he spoke. "Thinks it might be broken. How's my crew? How's Marigold?"

"I'm okay," Marigold replied, "just winded. Bit dizzy. Spar struck me as it fell, but not badly."

"Good, my girl," replied Hardknock as Burpee unknotted the captain's lashings.

"Yes, she is," I whispered. I was confused and elated in the same moment. I took Marigold's hand and helped her across the deck to the gunwale to sit and regain her bearings. She might think the blow she suffered had been a minor one, but she was going to have an awful bruise on her face.

"And Deem?" Captain Hardknock asked as he attempted to stand.

Captain Codkiss knelt by Deem, who appeared to have been driven against the cabin door by a section of the shattered mast. It still lay across his legs. "Took a mighty blow to the chest, I think," he replied. "There's some blood around his mouth like he has a broken rib or two. And his right leg might be broken as well, but he's still breathing. He hasn't come around yet, though," the captain explained. Then he started shouting, "Deem, Deem, can you hear me? Deem!"

The young man groaned, shook his head, and suddenly shrieked, "Growler, Captain!"

"Well done, me lad," Captain Hardknock called in response.

"It's so great to see you," I said to Marigold as I dabbed blood from her cheek, "but why are you here?" She gave me a weak smile.

"There'll be time enough for questions," said Captain Codkiss, "once we've seen to their injuries."

Annadeena and Gemeny joined us aboard the Sunstone. "Let's get them back to the Beatrice," Annadeena said. "Treat them there."

"There's one more," said Amendment Hardknock as he stepped free of his lashings.

"One more what?" Captain Codkiss asked.

"One more man aboard."

"Where?"

"In irons below."

***

After having moored the Sunstone and the Beatrice, Captain Codkiss climbed down into the Beatrice's lounge. I followed, and moments later, we were joined by Burpee and Fully. Below, Captain Hardknock and Marigold were already seated at the dining table, both extensively bandaged and nursing mugs of steaming lichen tea. Annadeena and Gemeny were mopping the wounds of a groggy Deem Worthy who was stretched out on my berth.

"Okay, so we're larded to stalagmites in a small crevasse, and we've lashed the Sunstone alongside," said Captain Codkiss. "Should be safe here while we assess her damage and make repairs. How are you feeling, Amendment?'

"Much better, thank you, Armature."

"And you, Marigold?"

"A little bruised and battered, but I'll be okay," she replied and smiled at me as I slipped onto the bench beside her and took her hand.

"Well, so now," began Captain Codkiss, "perhaps you can tell us how … and why … you come to be here?"

"Certainly, well, as for how, when everyone at home decided we had to catch you, speed was of the essence," began Captain Hardknock in his wonderfully rhythmic Jamaican accent.

"We threw caution to the wind and sailed at breakneck speed. Miraculously, our passage was without incident until this last terrible descent. We had a ... a commotion let's say ... below decks, which was distracting. And before we sorted matters, we tumbled down the wall and careened out into this current of slush and bones. We turned turtle, and as we were struggling to get the vessel back under control, our mast collided with a growler. The mast was fractured and then toppled across the deck. I'm guessing a piece struck poor Deem. Marigold and I were both pinned to the deck by the weight of our sails. After that, we drifted helplessly until young Fully spotted our ship. If he hadn't glanced back when he did, we would most likely have floated away into the darkness never to be seen again. We're in your debt, young Fully."

Captain Hardknock nodded to Fully, who grinned in reply.

"But why did you come after us in the first place, and who is the fellow in irons aboard your ship?" asked Captain Codkiss.

"Well, he's the reason we were distracted on this last descent. Damned stowaway, he'd been hiding down in our hold. Seems he'd taken a blow to the head and been lying there amidst our stores for some time. When he came to, he sprang at Deem. We wrestled his weapon away and put him in irons, but poor Marigold, she'd been left at the tiller alone on our descent down the last wall. She did her best but by the time Deem and I got back up on deck, the ship was already turning turtle."

"So who is this stowaway?" Captain Codkiss asked.

"He's a Royal Academy smartypants," replied Hardknock. "His name is Hobby Natterer, and he's the Academy escort your father pulled from the ferry wreck ten year ago, young Stalwart."

My flesh rose in goosebumps. "What? Really?" I exclaimed. "So, what's he doing here?"

For the next fifteen minutes, we sat enthralled as Captain Hardknock and Marigold related the entire ghastly tale: Covert's kidnapping; his rescue from Natterer's clutches; and Natterer's own story about how he'd been dispatched to seize Grimly Wordsmouth, return him to London, and kill everyone else in Earthedge.

"Apparently, the king wants another war with the Americans," explained Captain Hardknock. "And he wants the Royal Academy to create a new super projectile that can cross the ocean. But to do that, the Academy needs Grimly's calculations for the trajectory across a flat Earth."

"But Father's ... gone," I replied.

"The point is," Captain Hardknock said, "if the Royal Academy needs this new weapon, then they'll get the required calculations from somebody or other."

"So what if they do?" Annadeena asked. "Who cares? The Realm's wars with America have never been our concern."

"That's why the village insisted we follow you," Captain Hardknock replied. "We know how the Academy resented its humiliation and how much the chancellor loathed Grimly. Our village is afraid that once the Academy figures out how to fire its projectile at America, it won't be long before the chancellor decides to fire a projectile at Earthedge. Our village is Grimly's legacy. It's virtually certain the chancellor will want Earthedge to disappear too."

"But what can we possibly do?" Captain Codkiss asked. "Go back? And then what? Okay, say we try to cross the barrens at an unprecedented speed, say ten days. Then we set out for London, maybe take another ten days? And after nearly three weeks of travel, what do we do then? Beg the Academy not to shoot at us?"

"The war, if there is to be one, might have already begun by the time we get there," added Annadeena with a shake of her head. "So now you've told us about the Academy's plans, what are the others back home expecting us to do about them? Return to Earthedge? And then what?"

And that was when I opened my big mouth. "Or maybe we could go forward."

The truth is, I'm not sure why I spoke. Maybe because until that moment, I'd felt like dead weight on this voyage. I'd done nothing except sweep debris, push boulders away from the hull, get injured, and require care like some helpless child.

"Forward?" asked Captain Codkiss.

I sat upright, suddenly excited for some reason. "Like Gemeny was saying earlier, we set a new course … only for London this time. We find a crevasse through the Earth to England and then make our way to the city … and on to the Royal Academy. Going forward might save us a week or more."

"Okay, good," said Gemeny, who was already rolling out her map of alignment, "I like what Stalwart is saying."

"But even if a voyage through the Earth is possible, what can a handful of Earthedgers do if the Academy is bent on building its projectile?" Burpee asked.

Burpee was looking directly at me like I was suddenly the one with all the ideas. I didn't have an answer, not immediately. But then it came to me. "We will employ our one great strength, the one quality that has always set Earthedgers apart: our unfettered imagination."

Chapter Thirty

Royal and Ancient Academy

The Academy echoed with the chatter of countless greybeards. They wandered about its halls, congregating, complaining, and commiserating. Then, like flotsam in a stream, they drifted away again, each back into his own aimless current. Every knobfiddler in the Academy's employ had been appropriated by the chancellor for his projectile project. Greybeards, as a consequence, had no work of their own to concoct, confound, diddle, criticize or cast away.

Shortly after mid-morning tea break, the chancellor came rolling down the corridor toward his suite, waving away gaggles of greybeards entreating him for a moment of his time.

Not Lord Bilbury, however. He wasted not a syllable in supplication. Stepping directly in the chancellor's path, Bilbury bellowed for the milling throng to hear, "Ah Edmund, I must tell you, you're not looking well."

"I'm fine, never better, now out of my way," muttered the chancellor as his trike smacked into Bilbury's shins, "I'm late for a meeting."

Bilbury didn't move. "Ah yes, with our knobfiddlers, I know. But I hear rumors the fuel canisters for your cannon are giving you grief. Is it true? Will this mean another delay? Such a shame."

Edmund sneered at Bilbury and asked, "So is your flying machine going to get off the ground any time soon, Bilbury? How long's it been since you said you'd take to the skies? Years, isn't it?"

"Ah, but the king isn't watching me," Bilbury replied.

"No, he's not! And that's because your work counts for nothing, nothing!" Edmund screamed and began peddling, forcing Bilbury to hop aside. "And don't you forget that," Edmund shouted over his shoulder, "He's watching me! Not you, the king is watching me!"

Edmund's aide, Scribben, pushed open the giant door of the chancellor's office and hissed, "He's coming!"

Earthedge

Lollipop and Basenote sat forward in their chairs as Edmund pedaled into the room. "Out!" he shouted at Scribben, who scooted from the room, pulling the giant door closed behind him.

Edmund rolled to the head of the long table, spun, and faced the two knob-fiddlers seated some twenty feet away. "And so?"

A sickly pea-green light streamed through the office's enormous windows. It was all too apparent Bilbury Enterprises had chosen that day to pump effluent to its nearby plant. Bilbury Industries was working around the clock to fulfill its commitment to supply the East End with Thames dumplings. As a result, the Middlesex countryside was blanketed in a yellowish-green fog, and the factory's stench pervaded every corner of the chancellor's cavernous office.

The acrid smell burned Lollipop's throat as she began to speak.

"Well, your Lordship—" She swallowed painfully. "We do have a set of working coordinates."

"And was the calculating engine useful?" Edmund asked. "I'd like to tell the king it helped." The chancellor looked like a child hoping against hope for a gold star on his coloring.

"Yes and no," replied Basenote, "it confirmed Miss Lollipop's flight co-ordinates. We'd like to show you the display if you have the time. However, we had to override the engine's targeting parameters."

Edmund's face hardened. "And why was that?"

"It kept targeting Paris," said Basenote. Knowing how Edmund loathed the French, Lollipop suggested he use this response to deflect the chancellor's wrath.

"Hmm, interesting. What does my engine see that we do not?" muttered the chancellor. "I'll have to tell the king my engine's calculations raise suspicions of the French."

While Edmund scribbled a note to himself, Lollipop continued.

"Also, the rocketry team say they have a partial solution for the fuel containment problem."

"So, if Miss Lollipop has managed to calculate the flight coordinates, then we're ready to fire," Edmund said excitedly.

"Well—" Basenote tried to respond.

"We could fire tomorrow!" In his excitement, Lord Edmund's spittle flew the length of the table.

Lollipop's jaw drops. "No sir, we couldn't possibly—"

Edmund exploded. He pounded his one functioning hand on the conference table. "Listen, young woman," he bellowed, "I've had it up to here with your obfuscating and equivocating. You're a guttersnipe from a fish stall. Do you know to whom you're speaking? I'm in charge here, not you, and I'm telling you that you shall make the launch happen tomorrow. Tomorrow or else!"

Lollipop sighed in a fashion she knew would further aggravate the chancellor, then smiled condescendingly and said, "I meant no disrespect, Your Lordship. I only meant to say you will need at least a day to inform the king and the Garter council of the impending launch."

"And of course, they will expect snacks," added Basenote.

The scarlet color in Edmund's cheeks gave way to a cadaverous pallor. He glared at Lollipop, did not speak for several seconds, and then muttered, "We shall launch the day after tomorrow."

Chapter Thirty-One

Wimpole Street

Lollipop was seated on a bench in the fish shop's back parlor, her mother's arm around her shoulders. Her father was slouched in his heavily soiled armchair alongside a cast-iron grate, its small coal providing the only illumination in the tiny room.

"Your tea is getting cold, dear," Mother whispered. "Last of the biscuits, I'm afraid. I've scraped off the green spots."

"Please, Mother, we have to agree on this. You must leave tonight, right now, this instant. You have to believe me when I say you're not safe here."

"And we've told you, my darling," Father said with a weary smile, "we are leaving. We want to leave, but we're not going before we've arranged for Mrs. Pickle. She's alone, what with her boys gone and such."

"Why don't you take her with you, at least as far as Treaklesbury, then put her on a wind carriage to somewhere like Barndoor. I'll go help her pack then bring her back here, and we can put you all on a carriage out of the city tonight."

"The poor dear will be asleep by now," Mother said. "Tomorrow, we'll get her tomorrow."

"I don't understand this panic, love," said Father. "Things have been bad for days. What's changed?"

Lollipop sighed, caressed her mother's hand, and said, "Remember how you said you wished I would leave the Academy?"

"We both feel that would be best, dear," Father replied.

"Well, I'm doing that. But my leaving might come at a cost."

Father was shocked. "The Academy wants money to let you go?"

"No." How could she have explained the terrible risk she was about to take without frightening her parents to death? Then again, perhaps it was too late for subtlety.

"So then, what kind of a cost?" Mother asked.

"I'm not telling anyone there that I'm leaving, and . . . and I expect the Academy will come looking for me when they discover I'm gone."

Father was horrified. He jumped forward in his chair and asked, "Will they want to hurt you? Oh no, dear, you stay where you are. We'll stay too. Tell them we're all staying."

"No, it's too late for that, but don't worry about me. I'm taken care of. But I'm frightened when the Academy can't find me, they'll come looking for you. And since I'm leaving tomorrow, you have to leave now . . . right now!"

***

Lollipop managed to catch the last omnibus of the evening from Wimpole Street back to the Academy. The noise of the horses' hooves clattering on the cobblestones echoed through the dank and lifeless alleys. She sat by the window of the near-empty vehicle and wept softly. Earlier, as she'd helped her parents and Mrs. Pickle board the midnight wind wagon for Treaklesbury, she'd wondered whether she'd ever see them again. Elderly and naive as they were, what chance did they possibly have of reaching Iceland, never mind the edge of the Earth? For that matter, what chance did she? To put her grief out of her mind, she ran over the knobfiddlers' escape plan time and again in her mind ... such as it was.

Right before ignition, when Lord Edmund was preoccupied with entertaining his royal guests, she would excuse herself from the launch shed on the pretext that the calculating engine team required help with some last-minute technical matter. Once out of the launch shed, she, along with Basenote and his sympathetic colleagues, would make their way to the old mechanicals building, then through the new ladies' privy, to the back lawn and under the fence. But then where?

***

"Chancellor's been wanting you, Miss," growled the smartypants on duty at the gate.

"What's he want now?" she muttered as she moved quietly through the Academy's darkened halls.

***

"I'm sorry, Lord Edmund, but I did leave word with Scribben that my mother is ill."

"Why would I care about your mother? I wouldn't care if she turned to a pillar of salt. You don't leave the Academy again until Come-by-Chance has been blown from the Earth, is that clear?"

Lollipop glared at the chancellor.

Edmund had never been able to withstand her gaze for very long. He turned back to the paperwork on his desk and said, "I've just heard from the palace. The king will not be coming to the Academy for the launch."

"So . . ." Her heart almost stopped. "Does this mean the launch is canceled?"

"No. His Majesty wants us to launch from Hyde Park. Two dozen automata are moving the cannon and projectile right now."

"Hyde Park?" There went her escape plans. "But won't that be dangerous? I mean moving the space cannon and the projectile across the city . . . and then launching so close to the palace?"

Edmund's sudden alarm was obvious. "Will it? Will the launch be dangerous?"

Oh, gracious, do we proceed or do I frighten him into postponing?

"Oh no, not dangerous, no, I don't think so."

Delay will give Edmund the chance to discover my altered targeting. We can't postpone.

"You don't *think* so?" shouted the chancellor. "What are you telling me? What have you done? Will the launch be dangerous or not?"

"I mean, no, it won't be . . . but what if uh . . . what if it rains?"

"Then you'd best arrange for brollies and tents, hadn't you."

Incredulous, she tried to object, "But it's two in the morning."

This is a nightmare. Move everything to Hyde Park by dawn? It's madness. But what choice do we have?

"And the catering must be moved as well," muttered Edmund. "Oh, and you will ride with me to the launch."

"But what if I'm needed here?"

"I need you! You work for me! And after the launch, I expect we'll be asked back to the palace. So do something about that smell of fish on you, Miss Crossingguard."

If you do something about that smell of desperation on you, Lord Edmund.

Chapter Thirty-Two

Aboard the Beatrice

The Sunstone decoupled its broadricks from alongside the Beatrice, released her moorings, and began to rise up through the crevasse. As she slowly disappeared into the darkness above, we waved one last time to our departing friends and then drifted away to our respective duties. Fully started up into the rigging while Gemeny, Burpee, and Captain Codkiss headed down to the galley for a final mug of hot broth before we took up our new course for the UK. Marigold and I were the last on deck.

"The Sunstone's a nimble ship," I said. "Captain Hardknock and Annadeena should be able to handle her while Deem recuperates."

"Are you pleased with how our discussion turned out?" Marigold asked.

The two crews had taken many hours of wrangling to settle upon a plan.

"I guess so," I replied.

"I'm very proud of you," Marigold said with a pat on my hand.

"Truth is, I only spoke up because I'm tired of feeling useless."

"Useless?"

"Yeah, useless."

"I'm sure that's nonsense." She wrapped an arm around my shoulder. "Besides, it's not important why you spoke. What matters is that you did. And your proposal got us going."

"But if things go wrong, I'll be to blame."

"Not true. You gave us a vision, but we all own the plan."

Plan? It was hard to consider our hare-brained scheme, with all its unknowns and mad assumptions, a plan. We were asking that our friends back in Earthedge immediately dispatch another team across the barrens to meet up with us in London within three weeks. We were also asking the second team to bring along every piece of gadgetry they could muster: shockshooters, electrical lights, methane gas bobbles, and even Covert's new message machine. In whatever confrontations were to come, we'd have to rely on our superior technipacity to compensate for the Royal Academy's superior numbers.

But what if the Sunstone came a cropper on her way back to Earthedge and our request didn't get through? What if our fellow Earthedgers took us to be mad for thinking it possible to climb through the Earth? What if they refused to send the resources we'd need in a confrontation with the Academy? And most worrying of all, what if Gemeny was wrong and there was no passage through the Earth?

The most contentious question during our planning had been what to do with the smartypants, Hobby Natterer. Sending him back aboard the Sunstone seemed too risky for just two able-bodied crew to manage. Abandoning him in a cavern was adjudged too heartless even if a case could be made for doing so. After much wrangling, we'd decided to bring the Academy dogsbody along and pry what information about the Academy that we could out of him as we climbed. Then at the surface, we'd planned to turn him over to authorities for the kidnappings of Covert Millrace and Bloordrag Lorgeld.

I slipped my arm around Marigold's waist and whispered, "Why did you sail with the Sunstone?"

"Now that's a silly question," she replied. "Because Earthedge is in danger."

"No, I mean, why did *you* sail and not a dozen others in your place?"

"Why not me?" she asked as she wriggled out of my embrace.

"Because I love you and I'm scared for you, and I want you to be safe," I answered.

"And I love you and I'm scared for you and I want you to be safe as well, and that's one of the reasons I came." There was a note of impatience in Marigold's voice.

"You look...."

She blushed and turned away. "Like I've sailed through storms and wreckage and slush and bones and half my face is purple?"

"Like you're the most beautiful creature on the planet."

"Under it, anyway," she said with a dismissive huff.

"But the risks you've taken...."

"The risks we're all taking, and . . . and that's why I've come. Because, one day I intend to tell our story."

I was about to ask, *So not just for me then?* when Captain Codkiss appeared on deck and shouted, "All hands, ready to cast off!"

"Debris field is still clear aloft, Captain," Fully called down from the crow's nest.

Gemeny came up on deck, followed closely by Burpee. "Is the next wall very far?" he asked.

"Half a day maybe."

"And it'll be the last tier we have to climb?"

"Think so," Gemeny replied, patting Burpee on the shoulder. His nervousness was quite apparent.

We began to rise from the crevasse. The debris field was clear for the moment, the solar winds light.

"Dante described the next ring as the realm of the miserly," Captain Codkiss said.

"So, what are we in for then, according to your Dante feller?" Burpee asked.

"Won't be easy," replied Gemeny with a smile. "Huge boulders rolling about, crashing into each other. But we've been through worse."

"Growl—," Fully started to shout but then fell silent. All eyes turned to port. "Okay, not a growler," we heard Fully say.

At that moment, the badly charred hull of a Viking longship drifted past the Beatrice, its lone occupant, a blackened, leathery figure lashed amidship to the scorched frame of an oversized chair. The figure's carbonized skull dangled at the end of a tarry sinew and bobbed from side to side with the current.

"How in gad's name did an entire ship sift down through…," muttered the captain, as the hideous vessel drifted on and disappeared once again into the darkness and the mortifying rain.

"Okay, boulders it is," Burpee whispered.

Chapter Thirty-Three

Royal and Ancient Academy

As the chancellor's steam carriage rumbled away from the Academy steps, knobfiddlers' faces crammed the many small windows in their cellar living quarters. Each face was etched with fear. Everyone knew they would receive no credit if the launch went well, but if it went wrong, not one knobfiddler's fingers would escape the chancellor's wrath. Furthermore, they wouldn't be told a word, not until their fate was already cast. They were in for many hours of terrifying uncertainty and every kind of imagined horror.

Only two of their number were required to attend the launch: one from rocketry, who would attempt to light the fuse without getting himself blown up in the process, and Lollipop Crossingguard.

Already in a highly agitated state, Lord Edmund had become apoplectic at the news the king had invited Lord Bilbury to attend the launch. When Bilbury then had the audacity to request a ride to the launch site in the chancellor's steam carriage, Edmund, of course, refused. He had to depart very early, he said, and could not in good conscience make Bilbury rise so early. Besides, the carriage had to transport essential equipment and a menial member of the projectile team, a certain Miss Crossingguard. She was required to minister to Edmund's unique needs. "You understand, I'm sure," said Edmund and feigned a leery grin. Lollipop was standing right beside both men throughout this exchange, but neither acknowledged her presence.

"Say no more, my dear friend," Bilbury responded with an equally lascivious look and then a lengthy leer at Lollipop before he wandered away.

In Lollipop's imagination, the carriage rumbling out of the Academy gate sounded like a trundle rolling through the cobbled streets of Paris carrying aristocrats to the guillotine.

Lord Edmund was dressed in his scarlet gown of office and outsized top hat symbolizing his royal appointment. The hem of his gown was snagged in his girdle, leaving his pallid backside bare for the world to witness. And with no hair to hold his top hat of office above his lordly ears, it had slipped down to his earlobes and eyebrows. And then there was his smell, a most appalling combination of Stinkykill and corruption. The greenish color and black lines on the back of his right hand suggested his useless limb was deteriorating in a very ghastly and rapid fashion. Lord Edmund's eyes were closed, and he winced in pain with every rut in the road the steam carriage encountered.

"If the king addresses you," Edmund whispered to Lollipop, "you will say only that you are with the Academy Heir Conditioning Unit."

"The what?"

"The Heir Conditioning Unit."

"Is that the secret laboratory in the old tool shed beyond the pond?"

"That's not for you to know," snapped Edmund. "Just repeat what I've told you."

"I gather they've been trying for years to help the king perform his husbandly—"

"Did I not make myself clear?" Edmund opened his eyes and glared at Lollipop. "You will simply mention Heir Conditioning, and the king will move along immediately. Say nothing else."

"And that's what you want, for me to be invisible."

"I want you close and no one to notice you." Edmund shut his eyes again.

"Unless something goes wrong, and then you will want everyone to notice me," Lollipop muttered.

"Will anything go wrong?"

"We have hurried this launch. I'm concerned the space cannon might have been damaged during its transport across the city," Lollipop replied.

"But you're satisfied with the targeting calculations, right?"

"I am."

Although I doubt you will be, Lord Edmund.

***

"Here we are," Edmund said as the carriage rumbled to a stop beside a footpath to the launch site newly hewn through the Royal Wood.

To prevent the projectile's ignition from setting fire to the Royal Wood, trees had been felled in every direction around the site. The launchpad itself was a brick platform some five-by-five fathoms square and about three-fathoms high. The space cannon stood upon it, an iron tube four fathoms in diameter and rising nearly six fathoms into the sky. And from a steam crane high above the cannon's mouth, the projectile dangled like a bug in a bird's beak above a voracious fledgling.

Shaped like a football in a dunce's cap, the projectile was painted yellow and sported an orange stripe and tiny wings at its midriff. The upper half was marked "Explosives" in an elegant cursive script, while in an equally elegant hand, the lower half was labeled "Fuel."

The paint and calligraphy didn't conceal the rude manner of the projectile's construction, fabricated as it had been from hand-beaten iron sections riveted together. Lollipop couldn't help but recall that the last time this projectile design had been used, a hapless cannonaut had been riveted inside.

Some fifty fathoms from the launch pad, a temporary pavilion in an oriental style had been erected for the pleasure of the royals, Garter members, and their guests. All were gathered inside, out of the chill morning drizzle, enjoying a tipple and light refreshments of marmite on blood pudding, quails' eggs wrapped in strips of kipper, and keddigree on fried bread with Branston Pickle.

As she waited for the chancellor to be buckled into his trike, Lollipop glanced about the grounds and glimpsed Queen Wallis outside the pavilion, alone, and trying to hide behind a potted laurel. Lollipop caught the queen's eye just as the woman gagged into her napkin and then dropped it into an urn. The queen then stepped from behind the laurel and staggered with every ounce of dignity she could muster back into the pavilion.

The queen's hip had apparently healed since the East End explosion, although according to *The Daily Trumpery*, it had had to be replaced with an experimental iron hinge. The quite audible squeal of the hinge might explain why she was having difficulty slipping back into the pavilion without attracting attention.

"Let's go," muttered the chancellor as he rolled away across the grass. He didn't get far before his trike became mired in the soft earth.

"Help me, damn you," he hissed at Lollipop. Their tugging and pushing to free the trike caught the king's eye.

"Ah, Man of the Hour," the king called from the royal pavilion, his hand extended toward the chancellor.

"No ... no, Your Majesty," Edmund responded as he grunted and heaved the trike forward. The king made no move to narrow the gap. "I'm ... I'm merely a functionary ... I'm merely enacting your wishes."

Edmund eventually reached the king and was about to take His Majesty's hand when the monarch spun about and walked away. "Well, that is true," the king said as he moved to a small dais next to the canapés.

"Me lords and ladies," bellowed a functionary in puce livery, "His Majesty the King."

The king ascended the dais. Several coughs, one or two spits, a gurgle or two, and the king began.

"My wife and I are so very pleased to be here today to witness the United Kingdom's return to its rightful ascendancy in weapons development. This day comes none too soon, I can tell you. Eh, what, Edmund? Neck on the line and all that?" The king chuckled, and his guests then did the same. Edmund tried to grin and wave off the king's remark.

Lollipop didn't believe for a moment that the king intended his remark to be a joke.

"But better late than never," the king continued. "And so, we're all here now, and I'm looking forward to seeing this ... this magnificent uh yellow and orange creation uh rise and fly across the ocean to strike its target. And what target is that, Edmund?"

"Uhm, Your Majesty, if you'll permit, I want to surprise you, but I can assure you, our target has been chosen to send a message." Edmund waved at the crane operator, who then slowly lowered the projectile into the mouth of the cannon.

"Good, good," the king replied, "just so long as our enemies get that message."

Admiral Trolleysmash coughed loudly and said, "If you'll forgive me, Your Majesty, but I have to ask. Since Edmund won't tell us the projectile's target, perhaps he might explain how precisely he shall control the projectile's flight."

Edmund glared at Trolleysmash. "Well, first we ignite an explosive charge at the base of the space cannon to lift the projectile out of the barrel and on its way. After that, explosives aboard the projectile propel it to its destination. The lower half of the projectile is packed with very special explosives ... huge firecrackers actually—"

"Oooh," squealed the queen, "I like firecrackers."

"All charges are connected to one single, very long fuse. As the fuse burns, it ignites different charges at different intervals during the projectile's flight. A clockwork mechanism will adjust flaps on the projectile's fins at the same timed intervals. In the course of its six-hour journey, the mechanism will make adjustments every ninety minutes as wind and gravity erode its flight path. If we've entered its initial settings correctly—and I'm confident we have—the projectile should land precisely where we intend."

There was much applause and cries of, "Here, here!"

"And we'll know in seven or eight hours. Allowing, of course, for sea conditions at the locations of each signal ship in the Royal Semaphore Network across the Atlantic."

Again, enthusiastic applause and much chatter.

The king spoke, "And following the launch, will you all join me for a spot of hunting? No Wallis, come back, dear, we haven't launched yet. And so now over to you, Edmund, for the grand event."

A mat of bulrushes and straw had been laid from the pavilion across the wet grass and over the bog, to the base of the space cannon. Along the mat, a rocketry knobfiddler had poured a trail of black powder.

"So now we light the fuse," Edmund announced, and he nodded to the rocketry knobfiddler, who was fidgeting like a frightened cat. The knobfiddler put the smoldering taper to the black powder, which sputtered and promptly went out.

There was some muttering among the crowd.

Earthedge

"Closer, go closer, fool," hissed Edmund.

The knobfiddler moved some ten fathoms nearer the cannon and again ignited the powder, and again it sputtered and went out. "It's the damp, sir," the knobfiddler called out.

More chattering, and this time there was a smattering of laughter from the crowd.

"Then go closer, man!" the chancellor bellowed.

Twice more, the knobfiddler crept nearer the cannon, and twice more the fuse failed to ignite.

The laughter from the crowd was now impossible to ignore.

Lord Edmund was shouting at the knobfiddler at the top of his lungs. The poor sod had no choice but to go right up to the foot of the launch platform to ignite the black powder and then run like the wind in an effort to escape the blast zone. He almost made it.

At first, there was a rush of flame, then an earth-shaking rumble, and finally an ear-shattering boom. The queen, who wasn't steady on her feet at the best of times, was knocked over into an arrangement of potted plants. The projectile rose from the cannon's mouth, slowly to begin with, then faster and still faster into the steel-grey sky. Over the terrible roar, the crowd cheered and applauded excitedly until, several thousand feet in the air, the projectile swerved to the west.

"It's coming down!" someone shouted. The crowd screamed and ran off in every direction. After the East End blast, every Londoner was understandably skittish around Academy explosives.

"No, no," cried the chancellor, "it's supposed to do that! It's heading out over the ocean! It is supposed to do that!" Then he whispered to Lollipop, "It is supposed to do that, isn't it?"

"Yes, of course," she replied.

"Ah, well, then that's fine," said the king, emerging from behind the trolley of black pudding canapés. "So, now let's go hunting, shall we?"

Chapter Thirty-Four

Aboard the Beatrice

Hobby stirred. His back ached, his throat burned, and his lips were parched and cracking. But he would not give his captors the satisfaction of glimpsing his discomfort. He opened his eyes and sneered. The Wordsmouth boy was staring down at him. Hobby had been shackled in this hole for days in complete darkness, battered and bruised by the ship's motion and with nothing more than the odd mug of water and hideous mushroom bread to sustain him. But with his first glimpse of the boy, he recalled those icy blue eyes from the wreck of the Boggshead ferry and the Icelandic beach. "What do you want?" he muttered at Wordsmouth the younger.

The boy was seated on a sack, his back to the alabaster hull. "You were never grateful to my father?" he asked.

"For what?"

"For saving your life?"

"I never asked him to," Hobby muttered.

"If he hadn't, you wouldn't be here."

"No ... but then I wouldn't care, would I?"

The captain clambered down the ladder into the hold. "May I join you?" he asked.

"Please," the Wordsmouth boy replied. He then faced Hobby and asked, "Is it true you were planning to kill everyone close to my father?"

"I had a job to do," Hobby replied as he shifted to ease the ache in his spine.

"I can't understand," the boy said with a shake of his head.

The sanctimonious prig. He's judging me.

"You can't understand that I'd do what I'm ordered to do?" said Hobby with an unmistakable sneer in his voice.

"That you could do something so wicked."

Hobby sighed and slouched back against the hull. "In life, we're given jobs to do." Hobby tasted the salty blood from his bleeding lips. "They're jobs and we do them, and when the next job comes along, we do it too. It's the way of things."

"You don't think you have some responsibility to choose jobs that improve life over jobs that diminish it?" the captain asked.

"From down here in the muck and not up there on some puffy white cloud, how would I ever know that? I do the job before me, like a fly landing on the nearest heap of dung. I don't dither over which heap to land on."

"When my father pulled you from that wreck," said the boy, "I expect he thought you might at least leave our family in peace."

Going to preach at me, are you, Wordsmouth?

"Then your father was a fool."

All right, let's goad this slurpy babby a might.

"Ah, but your mother, she was no fool," Hobby continued. "And what a beauty. How the *stercus* did she ever get stuck with a sniveling mouse like your old man?"

The Wordsmouth boy stared at him then suddenly lunged, swinging his fist as he did, and caught Hobby across the jaw. Hobby kicked out as he tumbled to one side. The heel of his boot connected with the boy's shoulder. The boy howled in pain. Hobby had already braced for another blow when the captain restrained the lad in a crushing embrace.

"You're an ass," shouted Hobby as he felt about his mouth for any loose teeth, "and a dead one when I get the chance!"

"And you're excess baggage," said the captain as he continued to restrain the Wordsmouth boy, "so show some sense and shut your yap or yer goin' over the side."

"Captain, please," said the boy as the captain slowly released him, "we can't let this monster climb with us. It makes no sense."

Hobby's heart lurched in his chest.

Climb? Climb where? Are we back at their village? Stercus, that's great!

"Climb where?" he shouted.

The Wordsmouth kid ignored him. "And there's no way he can climb in chains, not without slowing us to a crawl," the boy pleaded. "We have to leave him."

"Climb where, damn you?" Hobby cried out.

"Through the Earth," replied the old man.

"Through the what?" Hobby gasped. "You mean up, like through volcanoes and seas? No ... no, you're mad, all of you."

The old man squatted and stared into Hobby's eyes. "Listen carefully, Mr. Natterer. You have only one choice. Climb with us or remain below, and by below, I don't mean below decks."

Hobby's hope of an early escape dashed, he said nothing, and merely turned away from the old captain to stare into the darkness.

"Unchaining this maniac would be madness," muttered the Wordsmouth boy.

"Perhaps, but perhaps not. I think our guest understands what's at stake," replied the old man, still staring intently at Hobby. "At the first sign of trouble, we'll put him over the side. Mr. Natterer, we'll leave you on some ledge, there to rot. You do get that, don't you?"

Hobby huffed but said nothing.

"I'm going to give you the facts, Natterer. You're not stupid. The prospect of being left beneath the Earth should terrify you. Chained down here in the hold, you've not seen how truly ghastly is the underside of the Earth. I guarantee it's more horrifying than you can imagine."

Hobby twisted away from the captain's glare, but the old man drew even closer.

"If you force us to leave you here, you'll be utterly alone, awash in the debris and the bones that have been seeping through the Earth ever since the Big Spinning. In absolute darkness, without food or water, trapped until hunger and thirst and loneliness and horror drive you mad, you will throw yourself from the ledge, out into the void to drift away from the Earth and off into the infinite."

"I'm not afraid to die," muttered Hobby.

"No, I suppose not. But you are afraid to confront the truth about yourself, that much I know for certain. I've known many characters like you. You are terrified that in your final hours you'll be faced with the inescapable truth about yourself: that you're worthless, your life has been pointless, yours is a record of abject failure, and you've been a disappointment to everyone. I can assure you if we leave you here, there will be no escaping the miserable truth about yourself."

"You know nothing about me, NOTHING!" Hobby screamed.

The captain grinned, rose, turned, and nudged the young Wordsmouth toward the ladder.

Hobby's glare at the departing Earthedgers was filled with bloodlust.

Me? Worthless? Weak? A disappointment? No, not true, never, and at the first opportunity, I'll prove it, I swear. I'll have your guts on a griddle, Captain!

Chapter Thirty-Five

Royal and Ancient Academy

As the hours slipped by, Lollipop struggled to come to terms with the inevitability of her suffering. There would be no flight through the women's privy, no journey to Iceland, no reunion with her parents, and no escape from the wrath of the chancellor. He hadn't let her out of his sight since the projectile lifted from the space cannon, not during the excruciating hours spent watching the drunken spectacle at the king's hunting lodge in Green Park, and not since their return to the Academy.

"Do you suppose I might go to the mathematography lab and brief the calculating engine team on the launch?"

"No," replied Edmund.

"May I be excused to use the new privy?"

"Not finished yet."

"It's cold in here. May I go to my quarters for a cardigan?"

"No."

"I'm feeling a little nauseous. May I go to the dispensary for a dyspeptic?"

"No, and stop asking to leave. You're going to stay right here where I can watch you until we hear from—"

At that moment, Scribben heaved open the chancellor's office door and shouted, "Steam carriage from the palace, sir! Coming up the drive!"

"Push me, push me!" the chancellor shrieked at Scribben as he started pedaling his trike for the door. "Get me to the Pantheon!" He glowered over his shoulder at Lollipop, "With me, girl!"

They arrived at the Pantheon entrance just as a liveried palace footman entered. "Semaphore message from Signal Hill in Newfoundland," he announced, handing the chancellor a large envelope bearing the royal seal.

"Has the king seen it?" Edmund asked. Without his peepers to hand, he had to pass it to Scribben to read.

"Of course," replied the footman. "This is His Majesty's copy."

Earthedge

"What does it say, what does it say?" Edmund shouted at Scribben.

Still breathing heavily from their wild race through the Academy halls, Scribben broke the royal seal and read, "Projectile splashed down—"

"Splashed down? It missed? Oh, *stercus*! It missed!" shouted Edmund. "You shot it into the sea, you stupid, sniveling, crawly, creepy worm of a ... of a girl!"

Lollipop displayed no surprise or remorse, or fear. She wasn't about to give Lord Edmund the satisfaction. What would have been the point?

Edmund grasped Lollipop's arm and pulled her to one side. "You knew it was going to miss!" Edmund's face was contorted with rage. "You did this on purpose! I should never have trusted you! I shall have your—"

"—off Come-by-Chance," continued Scribben in a louder voice to catch the chancellor's attention.

"I was not about to let you sacrifice innocent lives," Lollipop replied with not a hint of apprehension in her voice.

"Well," growled the chancellor, "you've forfeited your own life, my girl. What did you think would happen? That you'd simply run away?"

"Yes, to the edge of the Earth, if you must know."

"Brilliant choice, my dear Edmund," Scribben practically shouted.

"What?" Edmund asked, "what did you just say?"

"It's the king," replied Scribben, "He's written 'Brilliant choice' in his own hand across the message, and there's more."

"More?" exclaimed a dumbfounded Chancellor.

"Yes, lots," replied Scribben. "The signal from Newfoundland, it goes on to say, '... massive swell from splashdown and explosion swamped an American naval ship, several crew lost. Americans livid. Demanding full accounting for this act of aggression, but villagers in Come-by-Chance say the vessel was well inside Newfoundland territorial waters. US mobilizing their reserves, but intel suggests they're petrified of our new weapon."

"But ... but...," stuttered the chancellor.

"And Admiral Trolleysmash has added a scribbled note of his own," Scribben said. "Congrats on targeting American vessel. Masterstroke. His

Majesty has sent message to Washington saying US ship had no business being in the area. The ship's loss is America's own fault."

"*Stercus*! *Stercus, stercus, stercus,*" Lord Edmund muttered. He then turned to Lollipop and whispered, "Did you know there would be an American ship in the area?"

Lollipop smiled and shook her head.

"You, young lady, are the luckiest knobfiddler there ever was. I would laugh if I didn't want to slice you into bloody little pieces."

"And there's a note from the Lord Chamberlain as well, sir," added Scribben. "The king wishes to meet with the chancellor at the earliest convenience to discuss next steps."

Edmund didn't take his eyes off Lollipop. "If you ever tell a soul what has happened...."

Neither moved nor spoke for several seconds. Scribben slid up alongside the chancellor. "If you don't need uh me, your Lordship, then I'll just uh...." and he crept away.

"But is it possible you've slipped up?" Edmund asked with a cruel smile. "Does the mathematography department now have your curvature constant, and can I now use my calculating engine to determine my own targeting parameters? Am I free of you after all?"

"You might think so, Lord Edmund," Lollipop responded with a slight nod, "but no. Mathematography doesn't have my constant. You've had no luck locating Grimly Wordsmouth. And that calculating engine of yours couldn't tally the bill on a bag of tuppeny-ha'penny gumballs. Oh, and you still need me, Lord Edmund."

Edmund sat stone-faced. "Well played, young lady. Perhaps I do need you for the time being. But let me be very clear on this point. The next time you disobey me, I shall burn away that pretty face of yours, whether I need you or not. And I shall do so merely for the pleasure of watching you suffer."

Chapter Thirty-Six

Aboard the Beatrice

Another tier and another nightmarish sea, hopefully the last before we located our passage to London. Hours on end, we sailed across a churning morass of gravel and ice. The stones were smaller near the churning surface where the Beatrice tacked to and fro in the erratic stellar gales, but in the depths beneath us we could see much larger stones careening about. We watched them roll and heave in every direction like billiards on a giant's snooker table after a most violent break. They crashed into one another, cracking and shattering, and then tumbling on.

For much of the day, we stood at the gunwales with whisker poles at the ready. We did our best to nudge the tumbling rocks away from the vessel and along in their mindless passage. Some boulders in the depths were so huge, we knew with certainty that a single glancing blow would most assuredly shatter our hull. From time to time, two such monsters collided down in the dark. One came hurtling upward, terrifying us with its sudden appearance and erratic and irreversible course. But we could only do what we could do, and so I focused not on my dread but on my task, while I silently implored the fates to deliver us from this hellish transit.

"Void, Captain," Fully called out. "Two thumbs to port, sir!"

"See it, Helm?" the captain shouted to Gemeny, who was on watch at the tiller.

"I ... I do, sir," she called back.

"Steer for it, my lass," Codkiss ordered. "The rest of you remain at your posts. Can't let our guard down now."

For ten harrowing minutes, we sailed through the worst of the sea of stones, the ship spinning ever faster around the dark void like bathwater rushing down a drain. At last, the Beatrice entered the circle and was momentarily becalmed.

"Your crevasse, Gemeny?" asked Captain Codkiss.

"Should be, sir," she replied.

"Lights on, then. Let's have a look," ordered the captain.

Burpee and I struggled the radium lights to the gunwales, pointed them down into the darkness, and turned them on.

The sight momentarily took my breath away. "Starry Night! Look at that!" I exclaimed.

The captain joined us at the gunwales. "Gad a 'mighty," he muttered, then shouted, "You put us right on it, lass."

Hundreds of feet below, the opening of an enormous crevasse yawned like the maw of some great beast.

"Stellar winds picking up, Captain," Fully called out.

"Right, windbags over the side," Captain Codkiss ordered. "We ready for this?"

"Aye," we all yelled in reply.

"Right, then take her down, lass. London, here we come."

As the Beatrice descended toward the mouth of the great canyon, its fantastic proportions became increasingly evident. The opening was bordered by a broad seam of marble speckled with mica. Its rough and ragged walls were embedded with crystals of every color. Its breadth was narrowed in places by jagged cliffs, and in others, was as gaping as the Khyber Pass.

"How shall we do this, Gemeny?" asked the captain. "Do we moor the ship and walk, or do we sail on?"

"I suggest we let these stellar winds carry us as far into the crevasses as they blow," she said. "Eventually, gravity will strengthen and we'll fall still faster. I'm hoping we might be able to remain aboard ship for a goodly distance."

"Got to navigate those narrows first," said Burpee.

"Right, Stalwart to the bow," shouted the captain. "You keep us off them rocks now, lad. We'll be in your keeping."

My heart stopped. Did the captain say me? "Me, sir?" I asked? "You want me?"

I raced to the bow, muttering, "Oh, *bowfing, bowfing.*" As we descended, the walls of the crevasse narrowed to within mere thous of our gunwales.

Earthedge

"Hard to port," I bellowed. "Good, now ease her to starboard five thumbs, that's it."

"Good lad," Captain Codkiss called out.

The ship edged past scraggy, toothy boulders the size of steam carriages. Our hull took several nasty blows and gouges as it did. A portion of the aft mast was fractured and tumbled overboard. Sharp stones fell from the ragged sides of the crevasse, tearing holes in our sails. With each scrape and splinter, I cursed and called out, "Sorry."

"You're doin' fine, lad," responded the captain. "Only, stop all yer sorryin'."

Once the ship cleared the scraggy narrows, the crevasse widened dramatically. With a chance to breathe, we realized that its walls were in fact roiling and churning mud cascading like a river over a weir.

"Artifacts," shouted Marigold, "the walls are filled with artifacts!" She'd joined me at the bow.

It dawned on everyone simultaneously that we were actually witnessing the process by which refuse from Dinnerplate sifted downward through the many layers of the convulsive Earth.

"Look there, that huge stone, like one of the standing stones at Stonehenge!" cried Gemeny.

"And that's a cathedral arch," I shouted. "And the mud around it is filled with fragments of stained glass."

For hours we sailed on, sinking ever deeper into the crevasse, past crumbling sections of castle walls, carved and blackened beams of oak, and unrecognizable tangles of rusted iron.

"We're accelerating," announced Gemeny, who had spent the last hour studying her instruments and maps. "I think we're approaching a gravity inversion, Captain."

"A what?"

"We'll roll just as we did when we climbed onto the third tier."

"So down will become up?" Burpee asked. "We'll be rising in this crevasse, right?"

"Right. We'll still be going in the same direction, up toward London, only now it'll actually feel like we're going up."

"Everyone got that?" yelled the captain. "Stand by to turn turtle."

"Getting mighty hot," I called out from the bow.

"Off starboard, look there!" Fully shouted.

Below the Beatrice in the crevasse wall, I spotted the mouth of a vast cave. It emitted an intense white light and blasts of heat like the scorching winds from a pig iron furnace.

"One of your father's soft centers," Gemeny said to me. "They're likely the sources of Earth's gravity and.... Oh, and here comes the inversion!"

The sails, which had been laggard for hours, suddenly filled with the scorching wind from the soft center. The skin of every crew member was near-fried from our bones, everything we touched branded the flesh, and our world tumbled head over heels.

Chapter Thirty-Seven

US Department of State

"You gotta give me whatever ya have!" the secretary shouted. "The president learned of the attack on the thirteenth tee. He's mad as a cow with a tick in her teat. Word is he was having his best round in months when he heard about this sinking. POTUS wants a full briefing the moment he's back in the White House, so give me everything. What the gall darn do we know? Admiral, you first."

Chairman of the *ScrambledEggs* Admiral Rainslicker moved forward in his chair, pulled a slate from his toitybag, and read.[39]

> Some kinda projectile splashed down and exploded about twenty yards off the port bow of the USS *Mae West*. Her masts were blown away, stern paddlewheel twisted beyond recognition, and iron cladding ripped from her stern. She's taken on a great deal of water and would have sunk altogether if the iron cladding had remained in place. Three crewmen are known dead and seven are missing. The ship is under tow to Portland.

Secretary of State Skip Blarneyson was new to international affairs. Only a month earlier, he'd been operating a large chain of steam carriage showrooms. His success in obtaining a business license from the Emperor of China for several dealerships in Peking had brought him to the attention of President Saddlesore. After attending a performance of *Madame Butterfly*, the first lady

---

[39] *ScrambledEggs* referred to the tangle of gold braid on the peak caps of senior naval personnel and on the shoulders of commanding generals of land forces. It was also used to designate the most senior committee of the American military. 'When the *ScrambledEggs* screw up,' went the saying among enlisted personnel, 'it's we what gets covered in ketchup.'

had nagged the president endlessly for a tour of the Orient, and Blarneyson had seemed just the man to arrange it.

"So, where the hell did this projectile come from?" Blarneyson asked.

"The British, sir, at least we think so," replied Admiral Rainslicker.

Blarneyson looked around the conference table and eyed Recliner Broadbutt.

"Hey, I know you, you're Ol'wreck Broadbutt. We met at one of my company retreats in the Poconos. Your people catered my speech and you came along to check on arrangements."

"We did, sir, yes."

"Love your Cinnamon Wrecking Balls, by the way. Oh, and your new slogan, 'No holes in our nuts', love it! Brilliant. Stick it to them Mainers with their ring-shaped donuts. Don't ya jes hate it when some guy reduces his product size and passes it off as new and improved?"

"No, sir. I mean, yes, sir."

"So, Ol'wreck, what's your piece of this crap show?"

"Well, I'm Head of the Bureau of Official Stories."

"Miserable job, is it? You should 'a donated more. I always say you can't scrimp if you want the big office."

"No, sir. I'll remember that."

"Okay, so what do you do at the Bureau of...."

"Official Stories, sir. We gather facts and observations and then sort them into stories we can work with."

"And you've gathered stuff on this ship thing? So what kinda story you got for me?"

"Well, we've confirmed it was the Brits, their Royal and Ancient Academy of Knowledge in fact. The Academy built and fired the projectile. Damn thing's an adaptation of the cannon they used a decade ago to send a man into orbit. It's taken them all these years to make … uh … adjustments to their projectile to be able to send it across the sea."

"That took ten years?" asked Blarneyson.

"Turns out it's one thing to send a projectile straight up. It's quite another to send it across our flat Earth," explained Ol'wreck, who'd had the matter explained to him not twenty minutes earlier. "The projectile never escapes the pull of gravity and until now, no one has known how to keep a projectile in the air and on target for more than an hour."

"Wait, did you say over our flat Earth?" asked Blarneyson, momentarily shaken by the possible implications of this revelation for the president's Faith-Aflame constituency.

"Yes, sir, it seems some Brit also figured that out ten years back," Ol'wreck said.

"And so now we believe it too? Sounds like phony broadsheet scribbling to me."

"No, Earth's flat, sir. We've had the national laboratory out in Roswell look into the matter, and they're saying it's true."

"Fill my britches with saguaro pricks. And you're saying the Limeys have now figured out how to fire their projectile across … a flat Earth."

"Looks that way."

"Okay, but flat Earth or not," asked the Secretary, "isn't shooting at one of our ships like an act of war or something?"

"Would be … but there's a hitch. The Brits are claiming our ship was inside their territorial waters. They say our ship should not have been where they were lawfully conducting target practice."

"Any truth to that, Admiral?" Blarneyson asked Rainslicker.

The admiral shifted in his chair, glanced at his aide-de-camp, coughed a couple of times, and then said, "It's complicated, Secretary."

"In other words, yes," Blarneyson said angrily. "I been selling carriages long enough to know crappola when I hear it. So who ordered our ship to Newfoundland in the first place?"

"I did, sir," Ol'wreck answered.

"Why the hell d'ya do that?"

Ol'wreck sat forward in his chair. "Because we had intelligence the UK wants to renegotiate the Come-by-Chance Armistice and that they were readying some kind of demonstration there. We wanted to have a look-see."

"I guess we got a closer look than we bargained for," muttered Blarneyson.

"Yes sir."

Blarneyson looked around the table and grunted. "Okay, so the guy who figured out all this flatness stuff, he some sorta military guy?" he asked.

"No, just a schoolysort," Ol'wreck replied.

"Is he for hire?"

"No idea where he is. Apparently, years ago, he was banished by the Royal Academy … to the edge of our flat Earth."

"Bust my buzzard's britches! There is such a place? How do we get there?"

"Through Iceland, we believe."

"So let's get assets to Iceland as fast as possible. See if we can dig up this teacher. And schedule me a briefing on this flat Earth crap. I'm gonna need to understand it. Meantime, get some calculations of our own started on shooting bombs over the ocean. President's not gonna be happy until we have projectiles of our own."

Chapter Thirty-Eight

Earthedge Quarry

Cogsy Eyebeam was visiting Farstation to test Covert's signaling system when he heard voices approaching. He climbed to the shieling's roof and peered out over the rocky barrens. Against the starlit sky, he spied shapes moving in his direction. As the figures drew closer, he recognized their curious attire.

Smartypants! Six of them. Judging by their torn and bloody condition and their stumbling gait, Cogsy guessed they'd had a catastrophic journey across the barrens. Likely starved and thirsty, they seemed to have long since forgotten the purpose of their mission. They staggered to the shieling's door, rattled it and then moved on, oblivious to Cogsy's skipscooter parked not ten fathoms away. Cogsy hurriedly sent a warning on Covert's device back to Earthedge, then boarded his skipscooter for the run back home.

Two Cepheus rises later, as the smartypants reached the outskirts of Earthedge, the villagers were waiting for them.

After a brief skirmish in the quarry, the six smartypants had been blindfolded, gagged, and tied to the base of a sculpting plinth. Three had suffered severe shockshooter burns, two had broken bones from tumbles they'd taken in the quarry, and one had been blinded by a sudden flash from a radium lamp. In return for medicaments and food, they were more than happy to spill their story.

Dispatched by the chancellor of the Royal Academy, their mission had been to locate Hobby Natterer as quickly as possible and return him to London along with Grimly Wordsmouth. They'd been given the liberty to take whatever measures necessary to ensure success. In Minisculevik, they'd found sealed notes left by Hobby at the office of a local courtjabber along with the name of an Icelander having knowledge of a portal into the barrens. They'd no sooner shown up at Bloordrag Lorgeld's home than he'd told them everything they'd wanted to know. With local police hot on their trail and without any notion of, or preparations for, the horrors they were about to endure, they'd crossed into the barrens and begun their trek to the Edge.

"How did you make it here so fast?" Cogsy asked.

"We'd been Royal Marines," replied one of their number. "We ran." He'd then coughed nonstop for five minutes, groaned, and passed out.

"What do we do with them?" Paddler Upcreek asked. "Return them to Minisculevik?"

"They'd just get properly equipped and try again," Middley Porter replied, "No, I think we should set them adrift on the rings or … or kill them."

"Middley!" exclaimed Melody Fullbottle, "we couldn't do that!"

"Why not? I can't imagine killing anybody myself, but that's what they'd planned for us. And you know this chancellor of theirs is going to keep sending more smartypants until we're beaten or until we teach them not to trifle with us."

Mayor Raindrop spoke up. "Nobody is going to kill anybody, but I do have a suggestion. What if we sail them down the coast, way, way down the coast, farther than we have ever sailed before, and we put them ashore. We give them a few supplies and then leave them to fend for themselves just as we have done."

"Might just as well kill them. They probably won't survive," Cogsy replied.

"Why not? We did," Melody chimed in.

Cogsy shook his head and said, "But what if they do survive and figure out how to sail, and one day they return to Earthedge to terrorize us?"

"Well then, in the future, we'll have to be prepared to defend ourselves at a moment's notice," said our mayor.

Morgood came running into the sculpture pit, shouting, "Sail! There's a sail approaching."

He was followed close behind by Tulip Wateringcan, who shouted, "It's the Sunstone! She's back!"

"Any sign of the Beatrice?"

"No, just the Sunstone."

Chapter Thirty-Nine

Winter Palace St. Petersburg

A late winter gale swept across the Baltic Sea and bound St. Petersburg in an icy shroud. Windows in the Winter Palace rattled. Chilling drafts probed every corridor. Candelabras flickered frantically. Tapestries flapped, shutters groaned, sparks jumped from fireplaces and singed carpets. Guards on every door warmed their frozen fingers over candle sconces. Only the poor serving girls, endlessly galloping here and there, carrying coal scuttles hither and yon, knew any warmth at all.

Bundled up in his greatcoat and mittens, the tsar burst unannounced into the office of the Head of the Imperial Department of Royal Inquiry. "So," he shouted, "the Brits sank an American naval vessel with a projectile they fired from London. You know about this?"

Head of Royal Inquiry, Baron Balletshutz von Tapdanzer, a Prussian on loan from the Westphalian Academy of War, jumped out of his armchair, spilled his hot schnapps and nearly singed his socks in the fireplace.[40]

"Your Imperial Majesty!"

"Well, do you?" demanded the tsar.

"Uh, yes, sir, it seems the Brits do indeed have a frightening new weapon."

---

[40] Baron von Tapdanzer was part of a military exchange between the German and the Russian courts. German schoolchildren had raised money to pay for the return of beloved children's author Vladimir Illich Ulyanov's remains to Russian soil. Lenin, as Ulyanov was better known to children everywhere, was the author of *Anna of Zelenyye Frontony*. His remains had been exhumed from a pauper's grave on Malta and returned aboard a Prussian dreadnaught for interment alongside his parents on the property of his childhood dacha. The Russian Royal Family expressed their nation's gratitude by entering into an exchange of military personnel and an annual gift of Greenland coal.

"So the rumor is true. And have the Americans declared war on the Brits?"

"No, apparently not, Imperial Majesty. It seems they're looking into the Brits' accusation that their vessel violated UK waters."

"In other words, the Yanks don't know what to do. If they were resolved to fight, they would have denied the accusation and thrown down the gauntlet. Have we heard anything from either the Yanks asking for our help or the Brits threatening to strike us next?"

"Nothing, Imperial Majesty. For the moment, I'm sure the Brits are happy just to let the implications of their new weapon sink in."

"It is intimidating," the tsar said as he slipped off his boots and warmed his bare feet by the fire. "And do we have work underway on a projectile of our own?"

"I understand the Marshall of the Army has asked Academiker Khrushchev of the Moscow Impracticum to nominate a committee. It will review Orthodox theology on flying things and Russian scholarship concerning explosives, and then the committee will develop a proposal for a rocketry research center."

"In other words, if the Brits start shooting their projectiles at us, we'll have no way to retaliate."

"My staff has developed several proposals for Your Imperial Majesty's consideration," said the baron. He got up and crossed to his very orderly desk, where he retrieved a sheet of paper and handed it to the tsar. "It's a combination of intimidating military maneuvers and punishing economic sanctions, Your Imperial Majesty."

The tsar glanced over the list and threw it into the fire. "You're seriously suggesting we cut off shipments of caviar and Russian dolls to the British?"

"And vodka, Your Imperial Majesty. The thing is, we don't actually send them very much."

"So why the hell would we threaten sanctions?" bellowed the tsar. "No, I must send another letter to Cousin Edward before he takes it into his head to fire a projectile at us! Tell him I'd like to meet face to face to discuss global coal supplies."

"But Your Imperial Majesty, you know the Englanders will demand a portion of your Greenland coal, and you simply can't spare it. Your oligarchs can't. And Germany certainly ca—"

"Methinks you may be more concerned about Germany's share of Greenland coal than Russia's, is that right, Baron? No, we cannot let the UK shoot one of their projectiles at us. Prepare another letter to Edward immediately."

"Certainly, Sire, but we mustn't be intimidated. I mean Russia mustn't be intimidated. Besides, we don't think the Englanders have any more projectiles, not yet anyway," said the baron. "And what damage could a few projectiles do anyway?"

"They won't be firing at your German castles, will they Baron?" the tsar asked as he pulled on his boots and buttoned his greatcoat. "The simple fact is Russia needs its own projectiles, and we need them now. So get this Academiker Khrushchev in here. And draft that damned letter."

Chapter Forty

Inside the Crevasse

We'd been forced to abandon the Beatrice. The crevasse had narrowed to such a degree that one could have touched both walls simultaneously. We'd had no option but to moor our beautiful vessel to a stalagmite some leagues back, but not before she'd carried us many hundreds of leagues upward toward Dinnerplate. Now traveling on foot, we climbed steadily up the jagged and treacherous sides of the crevasse with everything on our backs we thought we might need in our struggles to come.

The nightmarish ascent was taxing everyone's strength, not to mention nerves. Sometimes we found wide shelves and ledges that climbed upward for many leagues and allowed us to march onward with minimal effort. At other times, we had to clamber and scrabble up the sheer sides of the crevasse with picks and cords like mountaineers battling for every thou of ascent. The climb was made so much more treacherous by the constant roiling and tumbling of the crevasse's walls as the layers of the Earth sifted detritus from Dinnerplate ever downwards. We could never be sure whether a crampon hammered into a crack one minute would be there the next or whether a ledge upon which we paused wasn't going to tumble away into the darkness before we could continue on.

From time to time, we had to rest despite our uncertain perch. We lashed ourselves to stalagmites to avoid drifting out into the emptiness of the crevasse.

As the temperature in the crevasse rose, sleep became a painful impossibility. We struggled past one cream center after another. The walls simmered, smoked, crackled, and were excruciating to touch. Some crew members tore away strips of clothing to tie around their hands, which were already horribly blistered. Nails were shredded, shoes burned through, and faces were as red as the blood on our fingers. And we had to be doubly vigilant the scorching stones didn't burn through our ropes, thereby suddenly releasing us into the void from whence there would have been no possible return.

"Captain," Fully called out, his voice a tortured rasp for want of water, "I ... I'm sorry, sir, but I don't think I can continue like this, not without a chance to cool off somehow."

"Aye, Captain, this heat is driving me mad," Burpee muttered, "and I was a fireman!"

"Seems like the walls are getting hotter," I gasped.

"So far, we've been able to climb past these cream centers, but is it possible we're now heading right into the middle of one?" the captain asked. "The higher we go, the more numerous and closer together they seem to be coming."

"I don't think so," Gemeny replied as she consulted her instruments. She dangled away from the wall at the end of a single cord hundreds of fathoms above nothingness. "In fact, I think we may be getting beyond the greatest concentration of cream centers."

"So eventually we'll be okay," replied the captain, "but is there any way we can escape this heat, if only for a few minutes?"

"We could try one of the caverns running away from the crevasse, like that one there." Gemeny pointed to a crack in the wall a few fathoms above us and to the right. "Instruments suggest the cavern runs away from the nearest cream center rather than toward it. It might provide some relief from the heat."

We struggled up the wall for another fifteen minutes, then scrambled through the tiny crack and into a large chamber. In the beams of our potato lanterns, the chamber appeared to extend for many fathoms.

"Do you hear that?" shouted Fully. "It's dripping water." I shone my lantern back and forth across the cramped space.

"There, that dark shiny rock," cried Marigold, "that's ice!"

We crawled to the icy rock and caught the dripping meltwater in our hands. The refreshing chill ran down our parched throats. Some of us broke ice fragments from the rock's surface, wiped them across our faces, and tended to the many burns on our hands and feet. While most of us recuperated, Gemeny set off to explore our sanctuary.

"Captain," Burpee asked, "is there any point in hauling this useless smartypants any further?" He booted Hobby Natterer, who had his face planted in a tiny pool of meltwater. "Can't remember why we brought him in the first place."

Natterer bolted upright in alarm.

"We didn't have much choice, did we?" the captain replied. "Keep him alive or let him die?"

"But he's deliberately moving as slow as he can. And besides, we're only going to turn him over to the robbies when we reach the surface, so why not spare them the bother of paperfiling him?"

"I admit he's become a regal butt wart," admitted the captain.

"Then I move we leave him here," Burpee said.

"What if he moved a little faster?" Marigold asked.

I'd about had it with Hobby Natterer. "I'm with Burpee, Captain," I said. "Let's leave him here."

Marigold looked askance at me, then turned to the captain. "No, we can't leave anybody behind. That's not who we are. But, Captain, what if the smartypants makes an effort to climb faster? Do you suppose we might consider releasing him at the surface?"

"Uh, I...," Captain Codkiss started to say.

"I'll do it," Natterer jumped into the conversation with unbridled enthusiasm. "I will. I'll move faster if you'll release me at the surface."

At that moment, Gemeny reappeared and announced, "Along the cave that way about thirty fathoms or so, there's a chute, an ancient lava chute. It might be our most direct route to the surface."

We clambered to the edge of the chute and shone our potato lanterns down into the seemingly bottomless shaft and then up into the darkness. It quickly became apparent the tube with its glassy walls wouldn't aid our ascent in any way. It afforded no footholds, no hand holes, and only the occasional fracture in its surface with edges as sharp as a barber's razor.

Earthedge

Just then, a great howling commenced far below, down at the very bottom of the chute. "It's a draft," cried Gemeny, "rising through the shaft." And as the first wave of a screaming gale reached us, Gemeny called to Codkiss, "Captain, sir, you feel that? That's our ride to the surface!"

Chapter Forty-One

Garter Chamber

The king had picked up a nasty cold awaiting the projectile launch in the early morning drizzle. For the third time, he interrupted Admiral Trolleysmash with an explosive sneeze.

"Bless you again, Your Majesty," said Trolleysmash, "but I merely wished to ask Lord Edmund—"

An aide leaned over the monarch's shoulder to mop phlegm from the papers in front of him. The king snorted into a regal nose wipe and bid Trolleysmash continue.

"—to ask Edmund whether the American vessel was, in fact, our projectile's intended target?"

Lord Edmund shifted uncomfortably. He took a moment to collect his thoughts and smiled, before replying to a question he knew was intended to rattle the king's confidence in him.

Bilbury! The Bastard. Seeding his treachery in Trolleysmash. Well, now's the time to shut them both up.

"I'm so glad you asked me that question, Admiral, my dear friend," Edmund began with a smile that belied his murderous inclinations. "There is, of course, always an element of uncertainty when testing a new invention. In my very long and, might I add, distinguished career in science, I've known both disappointments and successes. But I don't think anyone would doubt that our transoceanic projectile was an outstanding success."

Warm applause from the entire council.

That should silence Bilbury and his perfidy.

"Yes, of course," replied Admiral Trolleysmash, "but I thought we wanted to frighten the Russians. After all, they're the ones violating the Come-by-Chance Armistice. I'm not quite clear why we struck an American vessel."

The king stopped mid-sneeze to listen to Lord Edmund's response.

Edmund was momentarily rattled by the question. "Well, that's true, but uh ... but we also want to keep the Americans out of the picture, do we not?"

"I didn't think the Americans were in the picture." Trolleysmash replied.

"They certainly are now," grumbled several members.

"Never trust the Yanks."

"Damn Yanks, always causing trouble."

"So, what are you doing about the Russians?" Trolleysmash asked. "Anything?"

"Speaking of the Russians," said the King, "I've received a second letter from my cousin, Tsar Alexei. Now he's asking to meet-face-to face to discuss Greenland coal."

Members glanced at one another for some sort of signal on how to react. There was nothing members disliked more than venturing an opinion before they knew the king's mind.

"My cousin is a worm," muttered the king.

Garter members took the bait.

"An idiot."

"A weakling."

"Ignore him, Your Majesty."

"Ah, but I suspect certain interests might be pressing my cousin to back his claim to Greenland coal with more than words," continued the king. "And your launch, Lord Edmund, might have helped make their case."

Members prattled on.

"The arrogance."

"He's playing with fire!"

"Something must be done."

The king raised his hand for silence and said, "We need to send Russia a stronger message, an absolutely unequivocal message this time, Lord Edmund. How soon can you be ready to fire another projectile?"

"Uh ... mmm ... uh a month, Your Majesty?"

Oh, stercus, no, it can't be done, it can't be done!

"Right, good, two weeks it is, and this time a Russian target. Got that, Lord Edmund? A Russian target. Now, you'll forgive me, gentlemen. On my medicator's orders, I must go and sit in the latrine for an hour to allow its fetor to drive away dangerous vapors."

***

Edmund spent the carriage journey back to the Academy doubled over in agony. As a consequence of the king's absurd new demand that the Academy launch another projectile in two weeks, both Edmund's acid stomach and his ulcers were reaping simultaneous havoc on his innards. But what choice did he have? If he was to make the launch happen, then never mind the sweat and pain; real blood would have to flow.

***

The Mary Toft Theater had never known the like. Greybeards filled the auditorium seats while a dozen knobfiddlers occupied the plush armchairs on stage. It was as though the women who remove London's night soil had suddenly been given charge of the city's kitchens.

Gaggles of greybeards waved their arms about, grumbled, and threatened to walk out of the theater at this affront. They fell into cowed silence, however, the moment Lord Edmund pedaled on stage. He rolled to the edge of the proscenium and wasted no time on pleasantries.

"I've just returned from the Garter council with orders from the King. He wants us to launch more transoceanic projectiles in two weeks."

Hubbub broke out everywhere, not least among the terrified knobfiddlers, who knew only too well how close they'd come to disaster with the first launch.

"Fulfilment of the king's command will require Herculean effort from the Academy, but fulfill the king's command we shall. Nothing else matters. Every resource we possess will be devoted to this purpose. Those engaged in the enterprise will spare no measure, take no time away from the cause, do nothing else until we launch. Those not engaged in the enterprise can dance, drink, go to the seaside, cavort with the fairer sex, or whichever sex they fancy. But no one will in any manner obstruct our work on the projectiles. Stay the hell out of our way! Do I make myself clear?"

Earthedge

Edmund glared at Lord Bilbury, who was shifting uncomfortably in his front row seat.

"I know too well what blabbermouths some of you can be," said Edmund directly to Bilbury. "This time, I don't give a cankered ass what you spill to the broadsheets or the music halls because the more people who know and fear what we are planning, the better."

From somewhere in the theater, a voice shouted out, "May we know the targets?"

"No, you may not, but speculate to your heart's content. Rumors will only heighten our enemies' dread."

The chancellor looked out across the theater at the blotched and pallid faces of his congregants. *Brightest minds in the kingdom, bah.* "Now clear out." There was a scramble for the exits. "No, not the knobfiddlers. Remain where you are."

When the theater was empty of greybeards and its doors had been barred, Edmund turned to the semicircle of knobfiddlers and said, "You will not leave the Academy for any reason until we have two projectiles dangling above space cannons at the Hyde Park launch site. Automata will be stationed at each end of your residence corridor day and night. They will accompany you to and from your place of work. To be clear, you have to cast a second cannon, two projectiles, and all their parts. You must manufacture sufficient fuel and explosives, construct two sets of clockwork flight controls, and compute the targeting parameters. You will work around the clock to do so, everyone, and you, Miss Crossingguard, will oversee the project once again. And this time no errors of any sort, no errors will be tolerated."

His glare should have left no doubt in the treacherous young woman's mind as to his meaning.

"We'll need to know our targets," said Lollipop.

"Everyone out, except you, Miss Crossingguard," ordered Edmund.

Alone on stage, the two stared at one another for several seconds.

The treasonous creature, she's looking for weakness! In me!

Edmund smiled and said softly, "The first target will be St. Petersburg."

Lollipop sighed. "Beautiful city, I'm told. And the second?"

"Earthedge."

The color disappeared from her face. "Earthedge? On the king's orders?" she whispered with a quiver in her voice.

"On my orders."

"But why? How? We don't know where it is,"

"Oh, we'll know. As for why, because I don't want anyone else getting the math from Wordsmouth's spawn. And also...."

"What?"

"As punishment."

Chapter Forty-Two

Druid's Cave, Montelordie Estate

The longer they climbed, the less inclined Hobby Natterer was to believe the Earthedgers would make good on their offer.

Set one's enemy free? Who would do such a thing? That would be foolish. They'd have to be bonkers.

Admittedly, for days now, they'd been treating him with a measure of decency, letting him rest, sharing their food and water, ghastly though it was. The young woman had, anyway. But at the same time, Hobby had a duty to the chancellor. And it was going to be such a pleasure to fix the Wordsmouth kid once and for all. Pity he hadn't done it a decade ago. And if there was collateral damage, so what? There was always collateral damage.

Hobby knew only too well how it felt to be collateral damage. Every time his dad beat his mum, his pa had never really intended to hurt Hobby as well. But when Ma was asking for it, sometimes Hobby just got in Pa's way. When someone gets beat, others sometimes get hurt as well. That was just the way of things.

Putting aside the matter of vengeance, he had to admit these Earthedgers were an intriguing lot. Their devices, extraordinary knowledge, and curiosity about everything brought back memories. He'd once wanted to study science, back when he thought he might get the chance. But then he'd seen the old greybeards supposedly doing their research and he'd realized what fakery their science really was.

Earthedger science was the real thing, however. How he would have loved to examine their weaponry. The shockshooters were astounding. Lightning! Earthedgers could shoot lightning, for *stercus* sake. And that the strength of their lightning strikes could be adjusted was breathtaking.

Hobby couldn't imagine what the Earthedgers might be planning to do when they reached the Academy, but one thing was sure, with a weapon like the shockshooter, it wasn't going to be good. The chancellor had to be warned.

Hobby wouldn't have Grimly to deliver, but he did have intelligence. And so his responsibility was clear. He had to reach the Academy ahead of the Earthedgers, which meant he had to escape as soon as possible. Secretly, he picked up a pointed crystal, hid it under his belt, and awaited escape.

As they'd passed each cavern of white-hot oozing iron, Hobby's head had spun, his eyes rolled back in his head, and every piece of shrapnel in his flesh had ached and squirmed. But no amount of suffering could have prepared him for the terrifying leap they were about to take into the volcanic shaft.

The Earthedgers weren't the least bit amazed to realize the walls of the tube were studded with diamonds.[41] Diamonds held no apparent interest for them. Their navigator, the little woman of indeterminate age, said something about volcanic pipes binding the Earth's layers together. But after that, Hobby had grasped not a word of her explanation until she'd shouted, "Fastest way to the surface!" and leapt out into the powerful updraft that rose like a tornado through the diamond tube.

One by one, her crewmates followed the woman into the updraft. Hobby'd hung back until suddenly, the old captain shoved him into the vortex. The force of the gale howling up the tube carried them all hundreds of leagues upward before its strength weakened. The walls of the diamond column widened out into a pool of warm air and Hobby found himself bobbing about in the weakened winds like a water baby on a bubble.

Hobby's captors then clambered from the chute and continued their climb. The route snaked through cave after cave, around dark pools of murky water and beneath iridescent ceilings, over mountains of collapsed stalagmites and stalactites and through tangles of marble, bones, metal, and slime. Sometimes, there was no obvious pathway forward, but the little lady navigator piped up and pointed to some ledge high above or to a crack in a wall, and up they went again. What was this strange navigation system she used?

---

[41] Diamonds originate in the Earth's mantle and are brought to the surface in a type of magma called kimberlite. They erupt at a rare form of volcanic vent called a diatreme or pipe.

Earthedge

At last, they began to see signs of a human presence: first, butchered animal bones and then wall paintings, then fragments of hewn stone, then metal tools, and finally, actual items of forgotten clothing and picnic lunches.

"Ocher," someone said. "This was an ocher mine. Might mean we're in Gloucestershire."

Suddenly, from the far side of the enormous chasm, they heard voices and spotted the flicker of several candles.

Someone called to them, "Oy, who are you? How'd you get down here? This is private property, you know."

An elderly gentleman in tweed was leading half a dozen ladies and gents dressed in knits and leather and oiled walking coats.

Captain Codkiss shouted back, "Sorry, we've come from another cave. Didn't mean to bother."

"Don't know no other caves," the old man leading the walking party replied.

"So this isn't Codkiss Cave then?" asked the Captain.

"No 'tisn't. T'is Druid Cave. Don't know no Codkiss Cave," said the old tour guide.

"Ah, well, we must have taken a wrong turn. Sorry to have disturbed your walk," said the captain. "We'll just be getting along." As the Earthedgers crossed the chasm, they drew nearer to the tour group. "This is the way out, is it?"

"Here! Ya have's ta pay, ya know. This here's the property of Sir Maltvinegar Tartarsauce, and ya gots ta pay ta be down here, like these here folks."

"Of course, certainly," replied the captain, "We'll pay at the surface. And how far's that now?"

This was the moment Hobby'd been waiting for. No one was paying him the slightest attention. He pulled out the shard of crystal he'd hidden under his belt and dove at the girl, Marigold. Seizing her hair, he yanked her head back and held the shard to her throat. She screamed in pain. Her cry echoed and re-echoed off every fractured surface. People covered their ears against the reverberations as they stumbled away from Hobby.

The boy, Wordsmouth's kid, shouted, "Marigold," and dove at Hobby, but he stumbled headlong across the boulders in his path, and suffered a good crack on his skull in the process.

"Get back, back everyone," Hobby shouted. "We're leaving and you're not going to follow, not until you can't see us anymore." He pointed in the direction from whence the old man and his party had appeared. "I'll let the girl go as soon as we clear this chamber, so long as nobody does anything stupid."

"Hurt her and I'll kill you!" yelled the Wordsmouth kid as he struggled to his feet.

"Nobody's killing anybody," ordered the captain, "so let's just calm down."

"What's this about," the old tour guide called out. "Who are you people? And who's this here bloggyfeller? What's with all this orderin' an' shoutin'?"

A large woman in a broadbrimmed hat, pea-green worsted suit, and leather boots stepped forward and said, "I'm not having this. I paid for a mineral tour, not some ridiculous pantomime. Do something, Waldorf, show them we're not to be addressed in this manner."

"But Lilly," the diminutive gentleman in jodhpurs and pith helmet remarked, "he's got a sharp thingy."

"Everybody!" pleaded Captain Codkiss. "Please! Just remain calm and stay right where you are."

Stalwart moved toward Hobby and shouted, "You're a dead man, I swear—"

"Stalwart," Marigold hissed. "Be quiet. Do as the captain says."

"We're going now," growled Hobby, "so nobody moves, right? Not until we've cleared the chamber."

But as Hobby backed away, the large woman, Lilly, barked, "Aren't you men going to do anything?" and picked up a jagged piece of flint. Her throw was remarkably accurate.

The flint's razor-sharp edge lacerated the side of Hobby Natterer's head. Blood gushed over his ear. As he shrieked in pain, Marigold attempted to pull away from his grasp. Instinctively, Hobby's arm tightened about Marigold's shoulders, and his hand grasping the crystal shard jerked and drove the shard into her throat.

Chapter Forty-Three

Minisculevik Harbor, Iceland

After a harrowing three-day flight in a winter gale from the airship station in Machias, Maine, the USAS *Fanny Brice* dropped its landing lines into a field on the outskirts of Minisculevik and moored to the barn of a local constable. A dozen Sears-Roebuck combat contractors (or robocons, as scribblers liked to call them, since so many were ex-convicts) rappelled to the ground, where they promptly collapsed in the mud from dehydration and fatigue, having spewed their guts for the entire crossing. Their contract with the State Department was to locate the edge of the Earth and detain some of its denizens, a truly mad assignment if ever there was one, but contractors weren't in the business of turning work down.[42]

After some minutes of lolling about in the mud, one of their number asked to use the constable's privy, and the twelve covered in dirt and vomitus trooped through the tiny cottage to its adjacent pit toilet. The filth was one thing, but when several robocons referred to the constable's Sámi wife as Nanook of the North, they were immediately ordered off the constable's property.[43] Things went from bad to worse after that.

---

[42] Sears-Roebuck, a catalogue company, stumbled into the mercenary business when one of its most valued suppliers urgently requested the assistance of several Roebuck wagon drivers in putting down a strike. Thereafter, Roebuck wagon drivers were only too pleased to take on the occasional and very lucrative combat contract. The new enterprise soon proved so popular that demand outstripped supply and Sears-Roebuck was forced to recruit from several unsavory sources like prisons and college fraternities. The American government found it convenient to contract robocons for missions where deniability was essential.

[43] Sámi are indigenous people inhabiting large parts of northern Norway, Sweden, Finland, and the Kola Peninsula within Russia. The Sámi have historically been known in English as Lapps or Laplanders. The terms "Lapp" and "Lapland" are

As they swaggered through town, the robocons drank to excess, started bar fights, insisted on paying their bills with American currency, harassed local girls, and browbeat every villager they encountered. They demanded information about the edge of the Earth from everyone and offered worthless Yankee dollars in exchange. No one was inclined to cooperate until a crew member off a visiting Norwegian fishing boat, even more drunk than the robocons, recalled hearing something about strangers from the edge of the Earth doing business with a local ship chandler.

After that, it didn't take the robocons long to locate Bloordrag Lorgeld. As they approached Lorgeld's house, they realized he was in the company of half a dozen people dressed in strange shimmering garb and wearing dark brass-ringed glasses. The crew from another visiting vessel, the Americans assumed. Since they were impatient for information, without so much as an apology, they butted straight into Lorgeld's conversation. Their intrusion was not well received. Insults became shoving matches and then fisticuffs. The dozen drunken robocons did not fare as well as they might have expected, and it wasn't long before weapons were drawn. That's when the robocons realized they were up against Earthedgers, and their situation turned very ugly.

Gunfire erupted and was returned by shockshooter blasts. Through town and all the way back to the constable's field, the robocons and the Earthedgers waged a running battle. At its end, five robocons required hospitalization for burns and four others medical attention for injuries from flying debris. The remaining robocons concealed themselves in the constable's barn. They were forced quite suddenly from their sanctuary and into the arms of the local police when an errant blast from a shockshooter ignited the USAS *Fanny Brice*. The airship exploded in a ball of flame and its burning remnants showered down on the barn.

The Earthedgers reimbursed the constable in gold for the loss of his barn and gathered up their equipment. They purchased Dinnerplate clothing from a local haberdashery to blend in with other passengers aboard the Boggshead

---

considered offensive by some Sami people, who prefer the name Sapmi for their homeland.

Earthedge

ferry. The six Earthedgers were escorted to the ferry dock by the constable and many cheering locals, and departed for England on the tide.

One robocon, who managed to evade local police, watched the Earthedgers depart, then made his way to the Royal Danish Semaphore Shop and sent word of the Minisculevik debacle to the American Consulate in Reykjavik.

Chapter Forty-Four

Royal and Ancient Academy of Knowledge

The chancellor's giant door swung open and Scribben stepped inside. "Excuse me, sir, but I have some—"

"Have you seen these police reports?" Lord Edmund shouted as he waved a fistful of papers in the air. "Mobs from the East End are now roaming across central London, breaking into businesses, looting."

"I understand they're breaking into greengrocers and stealing food, sir," Scribben said softly.

"Stealing is stealing," muttered the chancellor. "And twenty automata have been destroyed."

"Not a big loss, sir," he replied. "They don't actually do very much, do they, sir."

Lord Edmund glared at Scribben and shouted, "They're a symbol of authority, of the Realm's technological superiority, of our superiority! The Academy created them! When the rabble attack automata, they attack us."

"Of course, sir, I didn't mean to—"

"Why are you here?"

"Oh, uh, there's been an incident in Iceland I thought you should know about. We've just had a message delivered from the palace saying that a contingent of American mercenaries arrived in Minisculevik, Iceland, yesterday aboard an airship. Their assignment had been to find a way to the edge of the Earth and imprison anyone they found living there. They encountered an unidentified band of fighters, however, who taught the Americans a very costly lesson. The unidentified group also destroyed the airship."

"Do we know who they were, these fighters?"

"We have no information, but by all accounts, they were very well armed ... oh, and they caught the ferry for Boggshead."

Earthedgers, they have to be. And they're almost here.

"What are the Americans saying?"

"Nothing yet, but this is the second ship the American navy has lost in as many weeks," replied Scribben. "They're not going to take such losses kindly."

"We need to get ahead of this news before these strangers land in Boggshead," ordered Lord Edmund. "First, dispatch smartypants to Boggshead to intercept the strangers, and then send a message to the palace recommending the king issue a statement."

Scribben wrote with his charcoalizer as Edmund dictated.

"We recommend His Majesty announce that a contingent of American mercenaries attempted to invade Iceland but was repulsed. This confirms our suspicions that the American ship recently destroyed in our waters was there for no good purpose. It probably intended to put mercenaries ashore there as well, in order to terrorize our loyal and beloved Newfoundlanders. Furthermore, we suspect the Americans are colluding with the Russians to dictate the terms of a new Come-by-Chance armistice, which would most assuredly result in stealing coal supplies from the Realm. But our Academy of Ancient Knowledge stands ready to defend the Realm from enemies foreign and domestic with the finest science and the strongest weaponry on the planet."

"If we're concerned about violations of Icelandic sovereignty," Scribben said, "then it's probably a good thing the Icelanders didn't discover the Academy smartypants you dispatched there."

Lord Edmund glared at Scribben. Scribben lowered his eyes, turned, and hurriedly slipped away.

Chapter Forty-Five

Montelordie Hall

The bedchamber was magnificent: twelve-foot ceilings resplendent with gamboling nymphs and satyrs painted in the Baroque style, gilt moldings, mirrors everywhere, towering windows with gossamer curtains, and numerous portraits of lordly forebears in armor and courtly garb.

Marigold stirred in the enormous bed. I hadn't left her side since we carried her from Druid Cave, across the meadows and paddocks of Montelordie Estate, and up to this opulent room. Montelordie Hall's housekeeper, Mrs. Wideload, had washed and sutured Marigold's wound, but the bleeding continued. Someone had to sit at her side and apply as much pressure as Marigold could bear to staunch the flow. A stable boy had been dispatched to summon the medicator from a nearby village, but he'd not yet arrived.

Marigold's pallor was cadaverous, her lips almost purple. As I changed hands on the compress, she grimaced and opened her eyes. But then she smiled. "There you are," she whispered.

"Oh, Marigold, I'm so sorry," I murmured through my tears. "This is my fault. If I hadn't—"

"Stalwart, please stop," she responded with a tiny shake of her head. "You're not to blame."

"But if I—"

She looked at me reproachfully. "If you, nothing. This is not about you." And she turned away.

"But I was supposed to protect you."

"No, you weren't. I was careless. I was supposed to protect myself."

"I told your mothers I'd always be there for you."

"I know, and they thought it sweet," Marigold swallowed with difficulty and continued, "but they expected me to look after myself. *I* expected *me* to look after myself."

"It's just that everyone thinks I'm—"

Earthedge

Marigold's voice was firm, cold. "Stalwart, listen to me. Stop going on about what others expect of you. You only have to do what you can, that's it, just do what you can." She smiled, slid her hand across the sheet to touch mine, and turned away again. "Now I … I need to sleep." And she closed her eyes.

The ornate door opened and Gemeny came in. "Stalwart," she whispered, "let me sit with Marigold for a while. You get cleaned up and then have something to eat. The lord of this place has sandwiches in the parlor. He's chatting with the others."

"Any sign of Natterer?" I asked as we switched hands on Marigold's compress.

"No. Not yet. Sir somebody-or-other has his men out searching."

The parlor was as large as the arrivals hall at a wind wagon station. Captain Codkiss, Burpee, and Fully were seated in front of a grand fireplace at the far end of the cavernous room. They were sipping drinks and chatting with a slender, grey-haired gentleman in a deep blue smoking jacket. "That's Sir Maltvinegar Tartarsauce," whispered the menial holding the parlor door for me. "Owns the place. Likes to be called Sir Vinny."

"Ah, here's the young man," called Sir Vinny as he waved me to an oversized leather chair beside him. "So … I gather your father was the notorious Grimly Wordsmouth. After what I've just been hearing, let me say what an honor it is to welcome you to my home. Your friends here have been recounting your adventures."

I merely nodded. I was in no mood to think of anything except Marigold.

"So, Captain, let me get this straight," Sir Vinny said as he turned back to my crewmates. "Our world is not the partially deflated ball the Royal Academy insists but is instead as flat as a plate."

"Yes, well, with some smaller salad plates layered beneath it."

"And because the Academy was humiliated when Grimly Wordsmouth tried to reveal the truth a decade ago, the Academy's chancellor banished you to the edge of our … of our flat Earth. But now the Realm needs Grimly Wordsmouth's mathematography, so the chancellor sent an agent to kidnap him and murder the rest of you."

"That's right."

Sir Vinny sipped his whisky and then continued. "But you captured the chancellor's agent, extracted his story, and decided you'd go to London to confront the Academy. Then you dragged the Academy agent along with you and traveled right through the Earth."

"Seems a might foolhardy when you sum it up that way," Captain Codkiss said with a smile.

"It's a staggering tale that would make a terrific adventure story for children."

I found it hard to tell whether our host was impressed by our odyssey or merely humoring us. I was inclined to think the worst.

"And this Academy agent, he's the one who wounded the young lady upstairs, and for whom my men are now searching?" Sir Vinny asked.

We looked at one another and nodded.

"Her name is Marigold ... Marigold Springpeeper," I said. I couldn't help the break in my voice.

"Well, it's a whale of a tale. Indeed, I might be interested in publishing it."

"As it happens, that's part of our plan," said the captain. "We intend to contact broadsheets like *The Times* and *The Mirror* when we reach London."

"You have been away for some time," Sir Vinny said with a chuckle. "Both are no more. Collapsed. Too much discourse, not enough sensationalism, or as my father used to say, 'too many nitpicks, not enough naughty bits.' To survive today, broadsheets must simplify, simplify, simplify. Readers won't read anything that contradicts what they already believe."

"Then what about Westminster?" Burpee asked, "Aren't its chambers supposed to debate issues? What if we contacted some Westminster people?"

Sir Vinny smiled, his seeming condescension grating on my already red-raw nerves. "Before your flight to the edge, you can't have followed politics much."

He thinks we're a load of bumpkins.

Sir Vinney continued. "Westminster chambers have always debated. But Talkyhall's function has never been to air grievances. Rather, its purpose is to test the acquiescence of members in order to gauge whether they're suited for elevation to the Garter council. Make no trouble in Talkyhall for ten years, and you just might be appointed to the Order of the Garter."

"And if you are appointed to the Order of the Garter, do you then get to debate issues?" Fully asked.

"No, certainly not, but one does at least get to hear the king pontificate on them," Sir Vinny replied, "and that's as good as it gets."

"What a useless lot those Talkyhall toffs must be," I grumbled. "And to think people are stupid enough to let them get away with their pointless blather."

"But their blather isn't useless if the people find it reassuring," said Sir Vinny with a condescending smile. "Even if Talkyhall's debate is a sham, most people prefer the appearance of orderly discussion among their leaders to the messiness of real disagreement."

Does this poncy squire actually believe such lichenrot? Or perhaps he's expecting us to challenge his gibberish?

Sir Vinny continued. "Let me ask you this. If there is to be another war and you have the calculations that our nation needs to defend us from our enemies, then are you not traitors for withholding that knowledge?"

Captain Codkiss, any trace of his seafarer's brogue gone for the moment, answered for everyone. "If we thought for one minute the nation truly needed our knowledge, we'd give it, but this conflict with the Americans and the Russians is fabricated. It's obvious the Crown and the Academy have concocted it to deflect criticism from their own failings and to hang on to power."

"Forgive me," I interjected, "but someone with your ... pedigree ... you couldn't possibly understand." The sneer in my voice escaped no one's attention.

Sir Vinny looked into the fire for a minute, and then squarely at me. "My pedigree? To begin with, my family, we're not nobility, not by a country maunder. For forty years, my grandfather was a cooper for Biggles Brewery. When Gramps died, my father bought teams of dray horses from the Biggles Brewery and made a fortune in haulage during the French war. And me? When I sold the family's haulage business, I bought *The Tittle-Tattler*, the largest broadsheet in the Realm. Oh, and I'm also the Member of Talkyhall for Biddleford-Fordingreen."

"But what about the portraits of your ancestors?" Captain Codkiss asked. "They're on every wall."

Sir Vinny chuckled. "Purchased by my late wife from the *Pedigrees Are We* catalog."

"Okay, Talkyhall member, so do you approve of this concocted war or not?" I asked angrily.

"Stalwart!" Captain Codkiss exclaimed.

"Ah, the innocence of youth," Sir Vinny replied with that patronizing smile of his.

I'm not going to let this pompous ass dismiss us like that.

"If you had any backbone, you'd publish what we've told you about the Academy and their smartypants and this war," I muttered.

Again, Sir Vinny smiled that irksome smile. "I could if I thought anybody would read it. My broadsheet publishes what our readers want. For example, we've just published a half sheet on whether the short pants our footballers wear are too … revealing."

"Do you report on Garter debates?" the captain asked.

"Not their debates, no, but from time to time, we do publish exposés on Talkyhall members: those suffering gout, their favorite condiments and their preferences in ladies' swimming attire, that sort of thing."

"So you don't believe citizens worry about war and conflict?" pressed the captain.

"Far too complicated for our readers."

Captain Codkiss shook his head in disbelief. "But you're an elected representative. Wouldn't you like your debates in Talkyhall to be more meaningful?"

"I'm sorry, Captain," Sir Vinny replied, "but I live in the real world, not some twilight village on the edge of nowhere. Talkyhall debates are about demonstrating skillful obfuscation, patience, and acquiescence to the established order. They're not about airing complex issues."

I made no secret of my disgust at this ponce's low opinion of working men and women. "And you believe that, do you?" I practically shouted. I then slumped back in my chair.

Our host hesitated, sipped his whisky, and looked wistfully into the fire. "I suppose I would prefer to do more," murmured Sir Vinny. "I've always tried to achieve real things in my life. But I'd also like to be a Garter member."

"Imagine for a moment if Talkyhall discussion became the focus of public attention," argued the captain, "instead of the fashion tastes of the Garter chamber. Your broadsheet would have many more targets to pick from instead of the paltry few Garter members. Imagine the cases of gout in Talkyhall. Better yet, imagine the affairs and the drunkenness. And if you managed to nurture some public interest in the coming war with America, could you imagine the numbers of broadsheets you might then sell?"

"Besides, it's the laboring classes what get sent to war," Burpee grumbled. "Bet they'd like to know what's coming."

Sir Vinny appeared intrigued by the captain's argument. Then he said, "You have to understand, we publish for the middling classes, not for a wider readership. If the laboring classes started buying our broadsheet, we couldn't keep up."

"You could if you had an electronical press," Fully interjected.

"An electronical press?" Sir Vinny asked.

Just then, the door at the far end of the parlor opened and the housekeeper popped her head in. "Sir Vinny, the medicator has arrived, sir. I've shown him to the young lady's bedside. He says he needs to see her guardians ... urgently, he says."

Chapter Forty-Six

US Department of State

Secretary Blarneyson's morning began with word his son had been arrested overnight for silhouexting, and his day had been getting worse by the moment.[44] Before leaving home, he'd composed a note to his courtjabber, Paperbag Wrenchammer. Blarneyson had given the courtjabber instructions to do whatever he could to keep news of his son's arrest out of the broadsheets. First the flat Earth crap and now his son's escapades. The Prez would have his jigglers if word of this dungfest ever reached the Faith-Aflamers. And now the news of the Sears-Roebuck mercenaries' debacle in Iceland. *Our* mercenaries, for *irumbado* sakes!

"You can't be serious! They're in an Icelandic jail?" he bellowed at Admiral Rainslicker.

"Those that aren't in hospital," replied the Admiral. "Seems the contractors got drunk, caused fights everywhere, and then got into a ruckus with some strange guys making their way to the Boggshead ferry."

"A dozen Sears-Roebuck contractors and the crew of an airship, all of them?" Blarneyson could barely believe his ears.

"Well, eleven contractors actually, sir. One guy hid out and then semaphored us the details."

"And we lost the airship as well?" the Secretary exclaimed.

---

[44] Silhouexting was a reckless and immature practice among a particular element. One prepared a silhouette of one's naughty bits and then provided it to an *amour*. The crime arose when a recipient copied the silhouext and circulated it to innumerable others. Courtjabber Oilrag Oggleson won a landmark Supreme Jury case in which the father who'd emasculated his daughter's supposed boyfriend with a carving knife was set free on the grounds that the principles of natural justice and good taste had both been served by the father's actions, and the young man's suffering was well-deserved.

Earthedge

"Of course, we've denied the contractors had any connection with the American government or with our airship. Just a bunch of schoolteachers from Alabama on a walrus-hunting weekend that happened to be in the area when our airship got in trouble. Unfortunate coincidence," explained Rainslicker.

"Goldarn right it's unfortunate! The Prez is going to be grit-faced. Holy crap, who were these guys the contractors tangled with? Brits?"

"Can't rule that out, sir, but more likely they're folks from the edge of the Earth." The admiral spread the semaphore messages on the table. "Our fella describes guys in big goggles and shiny clothes carrying guns that shoot lightning."

"Shoot lightning!" exclaimed the Secretary as he examined the messages. "You sure our man wasn't still drunk when he sent this stuff?"

"He's been interviewed by our consul general in Reykjavik," replied the admiral. "Says the guy's serious and sober ... now, anyway."

The Secretary threw the messages back on the table and went to his chair. "And you say these strangers with the crazy weapons, they boarded the ferry for England. So what are they up to? What do we know?"

"Okay, well, we heard the Brits are looking for that schoolteacher, the one they banished to the edge years back, the same one our contractors were looking for" Rainslicker said. "They want his help with their projectile. So now these guys from the edge show up and they're heading for England with a bunch of new-fangled weapons."

"*Gorotz!*" cursed the secretary. "This is beginning to sound like some sort of alliance; the beginnings of one, anyway. If the Brits have this new transoceanic projectile and these edger guys have some kinda lightning gun and they get together.... Well, then we'll be up to our sweetcheeks in crawdads. I gotta brief the president."

"He'll ask what you suggest we do."

"I'm gonna recommend we go to Kickbutt Three," replied the Secretary.

"Every asset to—"

"Damned right," said the Secretary, "Every asset to battle stations."

Chapter Forty-Seven

Boggshead Ferry Terminal

Annadeena stood at the railing staring intently at the Boggshead pier as the ferry approached its berth. Crowds waved excitedly from the docks. Stevedores sat patiently, smoking, spitting, and sipping the last of their morning grog. Uniformed officials in their wickets prepared to examine tickets and Handifax. Beyond the gates and the barriers, cabbies waited to carry connecting passengers from the ferry to the wind wagon station across town. All the while, myriad ticket holders and vehicles streamed past the dock officer and into the boarding line to await the ferry's return voyage to Iceland.

Aboard the ferry, a crew member shouted through a megaphone. "Disembarkation from deck three. Have your tickets and Handifax ready for examination."

Near the gangplank, passengers pressed forward to disembark as quickly as possible. It had been a long and stormy crossing. On the carriage deck, steam lorries sputtered to life, their whistles frightening teams of haulage horses. The horses clattered their hooves and chomped at the bit for the feeling of steady purchase beneath them once again. The very few private vehicles aboard built their heads of steam as owners suited up in their cinder-shedders, gloves, and goggles.

A small company of acrobats had assembled alongside their colorful caravan to await the decision of the goggled strangers they'd encountered during the crossing.

"Yes, I count at least three smartypants and four automata, there, to the left of that ticket booth," Annadeena said to Paddler Upcreek, who stood several feet behind her. Annadeena spoke in hushed tones.

"So we'd best get those disguises," whispered Paddler.

"Seems the smart move," Annadeena replied.

Paddler turned, raced down a nearby ladder to the lower deck. There he found the rest of his companions, Pewter, Cogsy, Covert, and Bottomly, all gathered near a lifeboat, and said, "At least three smartypants on the dock. Don't think we've got a choice."

"Right," said Pewter Doubting, "I'll go make the deal." He turned and crossed the deck, squeezing between skittish horses, belching steam wagons and wobbly handcarts. His target: the caravan bedecked in colorful flags and a gaudy banner proclaiming "Barnacle's Renowned Funambulists."

"So, Mr. Barnacle," Pewter called out.

A portly, loudly dressed and very filthy older gentleman stood alongside the caravan. He was in the company of several ladies and gents all wearing equally soiled and tatty garb.

"Mr. Barnacle, my colleagues and I have decided to accept your terms," said Pewter. "Three hundred pounds for your horses and caravan. Oh, and we also require your clothes."

"Oy, what's that then?" exclaimed the gentleman.

"We want your clothes."

"What, all o' them?"

"No, certainly not, just the outer clothes you're wearing now."

Mr. Barnacle's colleagues had a good laugh. "You must be joking. You want us to go ashore starkers? Sure, we're performers, but not like them Frenchies what dances nudey-like." Barnacle shook his head and turned away.

"We'll give you our clothes and our Handifax in exchange for yours."

"You want our Handifax as well?" Mr. Barnacle exclaimed.

"Obviously, you can't go ashore wearing smart new attire with Handifax describing you as acrobats."

The old fellow's curiosity was piqued. "So what's your Handifax say then?"

"That I'm a teacher," Pewter replies. "We're all teachers. We've been on a walking holiday. With three hundred pounds, smart new clothes, and new identities, Mr. Barnacle, I daresay your little company could make a new beginning, an advantageous new beginning with a little imagination, if you understand my meaning."[45]

"I do, sir, I do indeed."

---

[45] In 1967, the average annual salary of a London laborer was 130 pounds, an engineer, 200 pounds, and a senior clerk in the Home Service, 250 pounds. The payment of 300 pounds would have provided three months' income to each of the six funambulists, more than enough to prepare for some new calling or enterprise.

Chapter Forty-Eight

Royal and Ancient Academy

Hobby Natterer's signal was delivered to Lord Edmund's office mid-morning, right after a pot of lukewarm tea and a new dung and dandelion poultice for his arm. Neither had helped his mood very much.

The buffoon is alive. Well, he might be now, but he'll be dead the moment I get hold of him. He's failed every assignment I gave him.

Natterer was returning with nothing, no Grimly Wordsmouth, no gravitational constant, no Earthedge prisoners, nothing. He claimed to have been captured and tortured—as if his suffering was any sort of excuse. However, he also claimed to have overheard the Earthedgers' plans, which he characterized as grave and alarming.

"They're coming," read Natterer's message, "to prevent your war. They have weapons beyond your imagination and are close behind me."

"Scribben, Scribben!" the chancellor bellowed, "send a rider to the palace at once. Tell the Lord Chamberlain I need to meet with the Garter council immediately. I have urgent news."

***

" 'Av' ta take a detour, Lard Edmund. Robbie automata blockin' the lane ahead," said the steam carriage driver. "Seems crowds is riotin' down Trafalgar Square, yer Lardship."

"Just get me to Westminster as fast as you can. I'm already—" A turnip smashed through the carriage window, sending shards of glass everywhere. One struck Lord Edmund's nose. Blood spurted across the carriage.

"Ya hurt, sir?" called the driver.

Edmund's hand flew to his face to staunch the gore. He glanced out the smashed window just in time to see a dozen toughs brandishing cudgels and burning torches suddenly appear from an alleyway abreast of the carriage. "Get us out of here! Go … Go!" Edmund screamed.

***

"Goodness, Lord Edmund," the king said, "you're an appalling sight."

"It's nothing, Majesty, just a flesh wound," Edmund replied. "Crowds near Trafalgar Square—"

"No, I mean it's unacceptable," responded the monarch, "to appear before the Garter council in such an unseemly state." Edward turned away in disgust. Council members took their cue. Faces were upturned, noses held.

"Forgive me, Majesty, but I—"

"Simply unacceptable," the king said. "Perhaps the council should adjourn while you tidy yourself up." His Majesty started to rise.

"Sire," Edmund shouted, "I ... I'm afraid my news cannot wait!"

"What?" The king turned in surprise at Edmund's affrontery. "Not wait for some common courtesy, sir?"

"Majesty, a short while ago, I received news you need to hear now."

Just as Lord Edmund had intended, the king appeared shaken by the urgency in Edmund's tone.

The king sat back down. "Well then, what is it?"

"Majesty, foreign agents are on route to London," Edmund said. "They have dangerous new weapons and are intent on interfering with the prosecution of the Realm's official policies."

"Interfere how?" the king asked.

"Majesty, they mean to attack," Edmund announced with every ounce of menace he could muster.

"Attack?" The king blanched, rose slightly, and looked about urgently.

Lord Edmund continued, "We must recruit more smartypants as quickly as possible and deploy them around the Academy. We must also activate as many new automata as we can."

"Wait," the king interrupted, "you said around the Academy? So not the palace?"

"The Academy, Majesty, they're planning to attack the Academy because they ... these agents ... they mean to interfere with our own weapons program. It's the Academy they will attack first."

"Oh well, that's fine then," said the king with evident relief. "No, but no, they shouldn't be attacking the Academy either. So, uh, yes, you can hire more of your smartypants and build more automata. But if there are foreign agents in our city, then I also want the palace guard doubled, no tripled, no fourbled, whatever."

"As you wish, Your Majesty," replied Lord Edmund. He could not conceal the look of satisfaction on his face.

The king then continued. "Oh, and while we're talking about spending money, can nothing be done about the awful smell arising from the East End?"

"It's the dead bodies, Majesty," said Reginald Sir Footplaster-Barnswallow.

"Heavens, man, we don't need to know the source," the king shouted. "If I said your breath smelled, would you feel the need to describe your rotten teeth to me? No, I simply want the smell gone. Is it any wonder there are mobs in the streets if they have to breathe that stink the day long?"

Opportunity!

"Your Majesty," Edmund called out, "Perhaps I could have Lord Bilbury draft a plan for spraying his Stinkykill across the East End. Spraying might serve two purposes: get rid of the awful odor and drive the rabble from the streets."

"Now that's the sort of creative thinking we need more of around here." The king clapped his hands together in glee. "The crowds will dissipate once the stink is gone."

"I think there's more to the rabble's displeasure, Your Majesty," said Harrold Liverwort, the Lord Chamberlain.

"Tish tosh!" the king said with a wave of his hand. "Lord Edmund, have Bilbury prepare his plan. No more stink, no more riots. It'll work, I'm sure."

Chapter Forty-Nine

Winter Palace, St. Petersburg

Tsar Alexei usually dreaded these diplomatic occasions. But the Americans had urgently requested the meeting, and besides, the Yanks were always so … so diverting. As a gesture of goodwill, the tsar had ordered that fires be lit in fireplaces throughout the palace to ward off the chill. However, it was hard to imagine Americans ever felt the cold, given their customary girth.

"Your Imperial Majesty, the American Plenipotentiary and his cortege have arrived."

"I'll greet them in the Great Hall. Refreshments ready?"

Americans always expect food.

The tsar's aide-de-camp passed him a menu. "As you instructed, Your Imperial Majesty."

"Ah good, yes, caviar, Veuve Cliquot, the Grand Dame, and the pickled mackerel, excellent, and the American delicacies, the hot … dog and the fried frenchies, and their fizzy beer from roots."

A valet helped the tsar dress: his scarlet tunic, a Cossack sash, numerous medals and awards, and the cowboy boots President Dewey had presented on a visit two decades earlier. How comfortable they'd remained all these many years. He'd had them polished for this occasion. It wouldn't hurt to have the raised heel since his guest would tower over the tsar like so many other Americans.

Alexei loved the click of his cowboy heels on the marble floors. At the sound of his approach, the Cossack guards swung open the great doors, and one announced, "Tsar Alexei II." The Americans rose from their armchairs and waited as His Imperial Majesty marched the length of the vast room.

No, of course, the Americans won't bow.

The tsar walked straight up to the tallest of the dozen guests, extended his hand, and said warmly, "Ronald, so nice to see you again. How is Nancy?"

Earthedge

"Very well, Your Imperial Majesty. She's in Biarritz at the moment, taking the waters. She sends her greetings and conveys her gratitude for the adorable bears you sent our grandchildren. The children will have to wait until they're a bit older before they can play with live bears, but it was a lovely gesture."

An aide entered the room carrying a large envelope and hurried to the tsar's side, where he waited to be acknowledged.

"Ah yes, children do love bears," said the tsar. "I was just three when I killed my first bear. Had him stuffed. I sleep with him still."

"It's good to see you looking so well, Your Imperial Majesty," the American said in his languid brogue. Midwestern, someone had described it.

"And you, Ronald, as handsome as ever. I remember our first meeting. In London, right after your last war with the British."

The American chuckled at the memory. "I was on a cultural exchange, first since the cessation of hostilities. Performing at the Old Vic."

"And I was in London for the peace conference. I went to your opening. *Ol' Something or other*. A gunfighter must shoot his beloved dog—"

"*Ol' Paint*. Yes, my beloved horse, Your Imperial Majesty."

"Yes, saved at the last minute by your dance-hall girlfriend who's a secret animal medicator. Not a dry eye...." Both the tsar and the American chuckled at the memory.

"We'd been expecting demonstrations but our play ran for six months, sold out every night. We've never had any trouble with the British people, just that damned government of theirs."

"And that's why we're here," the tsar said as he clapped Ronald on the shoulder and moved him to the sideboard. "So please, eat something, and then we'll talk."

"We ... we have eaten, Your Imperial Majesty."

"Hopefully to your satisfaction. Our chef did his best to interpret your foods. The fried frenchies we took to mean some sort of erotic pastry, as you can see. And we've assembled an array of hot dog dishes. The Pomeranian in mustard sauce is palatable. As for your jellied beans, well, they defeated us. Chef tried every sort of legume in gelatin but produced nothing edible."

"Very thoughtful all the same, Your Imperial Majesty, and how gracious of you to agree to meet so promptly."

"Imperial Majesty," whispered the footman.

The tsar turned to the man and hissed, "What is it?"

"An urgent semaphore message from London, Your Imperial Majesty," the footman replied as he handed the envelope to the tsar.

"Excuse me, Ronald," said the tsar. He quickly perused the message. "Mmm, uh, mm. Well, Ronald, it seems our meeting is timelier than I imagined."

Ronald drew an envelope of his own from the breast pocket of his frock coat. "I've also received an urgent signal from Washington," he said. "Seems relations with the Brits are deteriorating more rapidly than anticipated."

The tsar handed his message to the American, who in turn gave his to the tsar. "King Edward has just refused my request for a meeting to resolve misunderstandings. Seems he's threatening some sort of retaliation—for what, I'm unclear."

"And a mysterious armed group, likely in the employ of the UK, destroyed one of our airships and attacked a group of American contractors on a fact-finding mission in Iceland," replied Ronald.

"I'm advised by our ambassador that the United Kingdom is making accusations that our two nations might be colluding."

"Well," said the American as he took two glasses of the Veuve Cliquot from the table and passed one to the tsar. "Then perhaps it's time we put some meat on that bone, my friend."

Chapter Fifty

Montelordie Hall, Estate of Sir Maltvinegar Tartarsauce

The medicator from Fighelwhallop cauterized Marigold's wound with a red-hot poker. At her imploring, I reluctantly restrained Marigold's shoulders as she screamed. Afterward, as I wiped the perspiration from her ashen face, she kissed my hand, whispered, "Please, I . . . I can't . . . die yet." But then, as the *Opiusmoothum* took effect, her eyes closed, and she nodded off to sleep.

"I've done all that I can," the medicator pronounced as he rinsed his hands in a bowl of water the housekeeper held before him. "I'm afraid the shard that inflicted her wound also bore some unknown squirmything. It's now abroad in her system and taking a terrible toll. Her internal organs are failing and I can do nothing to prevent their eventual destruction."

I could barely get the words out. "Does Marigold know?"

The medicator looked at me with a sympathetic gaze. "She's . . . she's a bright young woman."

As Marigold slept, I escaped to the end of the Montelordie gardens and shrieked my sorrow at the stars.

***

After a bountiful breakfast spread, for which few had any appetite, my crewmates gathered in Montelordie's opulent entrance hall for a few last words with our host before he departed for London.

"I can't tell you how grateful we are for your hospitality and support, Sir Vinny," said Captain Codkiss. "And again, please forgive our young colleague for his discourtesy."

"I understand entirely," Sir Vinny replied, "and you must stay as long as his lady friend requires. But now that I've cast my lot with your cause, I must return to London immediately to set our next steps in motion. When you're ready to move on, I want you to use my canal barge. You'll be able to travel without stopping and reach London in two days. There's ample room aboard and you'll avoid prying eyes. I've no doubt the Academy already has spies out hunting for you. Oh, and tell my housekeeper to signal me when you're underway. I'll make arrangements for your arrival."

***

I sat by Marigold's bedside with no sense of the time. When her pain became intense, the medicator administered *Opiusmoothum*, after which she would be lucid for a short while before eventually dropping off.

For a day or two, she sobbed, lamented, and begged the medicator to do what he could to save her. But then, the pitiable Marigold passed, and another more reconciled Marigold emerged.

At first, we reminisced about our earliest memories of each other: I of her confusion and then stoicism in the wake of her parents' deaths out on the barrens, and she of my fussy and troublesome behavior with my father. I recalled her calm, poised demeanor in the company of her three new mothers, and she the time I ran away and hid in the moss meadow for several candle bells when Father wouldn't let me sail with the fleet. She chuckled painfully as she recounted the time I shaved my head bald because Mother wouldn't allow me to grow my hair over my ears. I blushed like a clown to recall the first time I noted Marigold's exquisite figure. And we both savored the memory of our first kiss, hiding in the fish shed, fumbling and giggling in the pale glow of an aquafarm lantern. Then she smiled and dozed off, and I was left inconsolable.

Another time, after I'd whimpered on and on about how much I loved and needed her, she'd lost her patience.

"Do you think I want this?" She wept as she struggled to speak. "I'm only seventeen. This isn't supposed to happen at seventeen."

I took her in my arms and eventually her weeping subsided.

"Do you remember when we talked about our futures?" she whispered.

"When I asked you to marry me?"

"And I ... I said I didn't know what I wanted?"

"All I've ever wanted is you," I muttered through my tears.

"That night, after we spoke, it came to me what I truly wanted. I wanted to write stories, stories I'd created, stories I'd lived. That's why I came after you. Because one day I wanted to be able to tell our story, the story of this voyage."

"And you will."

"No." Her voice was barely above a whisper, but her words wounded like a knife. "No, not now. But you must tell it, for me."

"I ... I—"

"Promise me, you'll tell our story." She gripped my hand. Her eyes were filled with desperation. Then she managed a tiny smile. "And if you make me sound weak or whiney, I won't forgive you."

For a moment I smiled back, but then I blurted out, "Oh, Marigold, you can't leave me."

She touched my hand. "Want to know something funny? All this time, I ... I've been afraid you'd be the one to leave *me*. After all, why would you stay? I knew you hated Earthedge. Perhaps that's why I ... I said no when you asked me to marry you, because . . . you wouldn't be able to leave me . . . if you were never mine to begin with."

"No," I blurted out, "I would never have left you!"

"I know that now," she said as tears spilled down her cheeks, "And yet, here I am, about to leave *you*." She swallowed hard and whispered, "And I need you . . . to help me go."

I sobbed uncontrollably, my cheek on her chest. I felt her breath rattle as it rose through her damaged throat, her faint heartbeat, her fingers stroking my hair. And then she slept.

***

Marigold's pain grew ever more intense, her doses of *Opiusmoothum* ever more powerful.

One time, her eyes flew open, and she said with a tiny chuckle, "Please, tell me, what have you loved about me? How wonderful was I? Will my memory bring you joy?" She fell silent for a moment, then sobbed, and said, "I . . . I need to know my being here . . . meant something."

"Everything! It meant everything! You meant everything . . . you mean everything . . . to me, to your mothers, to our village!"

"Oh, how I've loved our village." Marigold sighed. "Living beneath our canopy of stars, walking our paths by moonlight, filling our sparkling sails with stellar winds, sailing our sea of crystals, the close embrace of Melody's pub, and sharing our tales of passion and adventure." She grinned. "I want to be remembered as . . . as adventurous, grateful, strong . . . but most of all, as happy. Please, you must tell my mothers how happy I was." And again, she slept.

***

"She can't last much longer," the medicator whispered over my shoulder. Whether Marigold heard the medicator I didn't know, but her eyes slowly opened. Pain creased her face, her voice was weak, her skin almost translucent.

"Stalwart, will you be stronger for having known me?"

Taken aback, I could only mutter, "What? Stronger? How?"

"I don't want you to mope when I'm gone. Okay, maybe a little, but then, you must move on." She squeezed my hand as a piercing pain wracked her body. Even so, she struggled to continue. "And stop resenting people . . . for having high hopes of you. It's the promise in you they see."

She swallowed with difficulty. I touched a wet cloth to her lips. "Please, no more," I said softly, "This isn't the time to be helping me, not now—"

"But don't you see? Letting me help you . . . is how you . . . can help me go," she said with a transcendent smile. Both her hands enfolded mine.

Grief closed my throat. I couldn't swallow, couldn't manage a breath.

"Someday, when you're being tested," Marigold continued, "don't doubt yourself. Don't promise more than you're able . . . but you must do what you can." She drew a long breath. "Because you can accomplish miracles. I know you can. Just as long as you try." Her eyes closed. Her grip on my hand weakened. "Try as . . . as we might have tried . . . together." She fell still.

Minutes passed before she stirred again. She drew a shallow breath and whispered, "Thank you, my love . . . I can go now."

Earthedge

In her final moments, I lay on the bed and held her in my arms. And when she sighed and her chest rose for the last time, I watched the color drain from her flesh and felt the warmth slip from her body. I remained at her bedside as the birds in the garden ceased their song and the room darkened, as the gossamer curtains fluttered in the evening breeze and then fell still. Near midnight, three lady Dressers of the Dead arrived from the nearby village to prepare Marigold for a mid-morning meal of remembrance and her incremation. As the Dressers began their task, I fled to the gardens and wept till dawn.

Chapter Fifty-One

Royal and Ancient Academy

Looking like Tweedledum and Tweedledee, the two projectiles dangled at the ends of cables as the rocketry team members painted them black.

"Bringers of death," muttered Basenote.

"Nearly finished?" Lollipop asked.

"Fuel is still fermenting, and one of the canisters for the explosives is backordered from Marks and Spencer's, but it should arrive by the end of the day."

"Good," Lollipop replied, "we don't want to give Lord Edmund an excuse to dismiss anyone, not at this stage."

"I don't understand," Basenote said. "Days ago, you were prepared to do anything to sabotage the projectile aimed at Come-by-Chance. Now that the new targets are certain to bring death and provoke war, you want us to hurry?"

"I want no war," said Lollipop emphatically. "Nor do I want any of our team members to lose a finger. No, I want you to complete the projectiles on time and then leave it to me to ensure their targets cost no suffering and cause no war."

"You don't have to do this alone, you know," said Basenote softly.

"You're a dear friend, but I don't want anyone else to bear the blame for my actions." Lollipop gently stroked his cheek.

At her touch, Basenote's errant eye seemed to set off on a wild romp. "When the chancellor sprays the East End with Stinkykill" he said, "I'm sure many more will want to join us in bringing down the Academy."

"What?" Lollipop blurted out in astonishment, "What's he doing?"

"You hadn't heard?"

Lollipop shook her head.

"The king has asked to have the stench of rotting bodies in the East End masked, and Lord Edmund proposed that Lord Bilbury's Stinkykill be sprayed from his flying machine."

"He can't!" Lollipop reacted in horrified amazement. "Stinkykill might not burn fabric, but it certainly burns skin. It's made from … from acids of the most noxious kind."

"Edmund knows this," replied Basenote, "just as he knows Lord Bilbury's flying machine doesn't fly. He's promised the king that Bilbury will spray all the same. The chancellor is probably reveling in Bilbury's discomfort."

Lollipop was not reassured. "But if Bilbury does somehow manage to spread his poison, he'll heap calamity upon calamity."

Chapter Fifty-Two

Sir Vinny's London Townhouse

Sir Vinny arrived in London on the afternoon wind wagon from Middle Thumping. The journey had been exhausting, what with the wagon's wooden seats and the deteriorating state of countryside laneways. Even so, Sir Vinny promptly took a steam carriage from the Marble Arch station to his Talkyhall offices. There he met with Primus Speaker Sellers to inform him of his intentions. Sellers was unnerved by Sir Vinny's plans. Still, after an hour of intense discussion, the Primus Speaker agreed to endorse the proposals. Sir Vinny then retired to his townhouse in Belgravia to craft the Talkyhall speech of his career and to get some sleep.

An appalling smell enveloped the city like the slime on a dead fish. To keep it out, Sir Vinny's household staff had pushed rags under doors, covered windows with blankets, and filled fireplaces with onions. Their efforts were for naught.

After several hours of work and a light supper of Mowbray pie and Branston Pickle, Sir Vinny retired with balls of cotton soaked in oil of roses shoved up his nostrils. Well past midnight, he was awakened by a tap on the bedroom door.

"Sir Vinny," his valet whispered as he opened the door a crack, "the Lord Chamberlain's man is here with a message."

"I'll read it in the morning," murmured Sir Vinny.

"No sir, the Lord Chamberlain wants to see you now, sir, at his home, sir. His carriage is waiting outside."

***

The chamberlain's man would divulge nothing regarding his employer's invitation. The steam carriage rumbled through the dark and stinking streets like a belching war machine at the front. Gas lights glimmered through the drear and the drizzle. Shadowy figures materialized out of the mist and then disappeared once again into its chill embrace. A dog howled, a baby cried; from an alley, several angry voices arose, followed by the shrill alarm of a robbie's whistle. A gaggle of women in a lighted doorway laughed and pointed and shouted lewd propositions.

Since he had no royal eminence, Harrold Liverwort was not obliged to live within the precinct of Buckingham Palace. Who in their right mind would ever have lived there if they were not obliged by aristocratic duty to do so? The palace was forever freezing, its plumbing temperamental, and its furniture chipped, threadbare and uncomfortable after centuries of use. The Lord Chamberlain instead lived in a stylish new mews house in Downing Street. Sir Vinny disembarked at the end of the street and showed the robbie on duty his invitation from the Lord Chamberlain.

"Number 10, on your right, sir," said the robbie with a sloppy salute.

On the oversized door, a large brass plaque read "Sir Harrold Liverwort, Lord Chamberlain to His Majesty, King Edward VIII."

Like Sir Vinny, Sir Harrold Liverwort was the progeny of the middling classes. Son of a dancehall musician and a chorus girl, he'd studied pennymarking at the Upton Snodsbury Techyteach. He'd become a successful speckylender before being recruited by his future father-in-law, the Earl of Anklesox, to sort out the family's estate. The task had allowed Liverwort to court both the Anklesox daughter and the Anklesox fortune. His wife's royal connections had brought him into Queen Wallis's circle and, thereafter, into the king's employ.

A slender maid of continental extraction opened the enormous ebony door. She was dressed in the new French couture for domestics, with its knee-high black skirt and bodice too scant to constrain very much at all. The young woman showed Sir Vinny through the atrium, past the dining room and into the Lord Chamberlain's study. An extensive collection of etchings in a Grecian style adorned its walls.

There, for several minutes, Sir Vinny pondered this portentous invitation.

We're like two stray cats in a dark alley sniffing each other out, taking each other's measure.

The Lord Chamberlain arrived in a damask smoking jacket, cognac snifter in one hand and red-leather satchel in the other, and settled himself in a comfy armchair.

"Ah, Tartarsauce, good of you to come. Please sit. You will forgive the hour, but I wanted to have a chat away from the throng of courtiers and come-uponers at the palace."

"You have a nice home," said Sir Vinny.

"And so, I believe, do you. Far larger than mine, I gather. Oh, and I understand you've been out of town at your estate. Montelordie, isn't it?"

"Yes."

"You're fortunate, Sir Maltvinegar. Done very well for yourself."

How long will this chit-chat last?

"I expect you're grateful," said the Lord Chamberlain with a wry smile. "You've enjoyed many benefits, haven't you? Being a friend to the palace, I mean."

What does Liverwort know?

"Tell me, if you are indeed a friend to the palace, why then would you go straight to Talkyhall upon your return to the city?" Liverwort asked, his voice barely above a whisper.

There it is. He's spying on me.

"Why not? I have responsibilities there. I dropped by my office for a quick check on my team."

Liverwort sipped his cognac and cast a cold eye at Sir Vinny. "You were overheard talking to the PS." Once again, Liverwort scowled. "I'm told you intend to propose that Talkyhall debate on French postcards be terminated."

"Yes," Vinny replied. He displayed not a hint of doubt or uncertainty.

The Lord Chamberlain shook his head and snorted in derision. "Not something a friend to the palace would do." He picked up a charcoalizer and sheet of parchment from a small table beside his chair, scribbled a note to himself, folded it, and slipped it into his jacket.

An order for my arrest, perhaps? A death warrant?

Looking up at Sir Vinny once again, Liverwort's face hardened, "How stupid can you be?" he asked. "To throw away the good graces you've enjoyed, the political capital you've amassed. And you were so close to Garter membership."

Show no weakness, no doubt.

"I would be honored to serve on the Garter council," Sir Vinny replied.

"Of course you would," bellowed the chamberlain, "and so would every other Englishman with half a brain. So why are you tossing the opportunity away?"

"Because in recent days, I've come to realize the people's representatives ought to be free to debate the people's concerns."

"That notion is patently absurd," the chamberlain said with obvious derision. "The people don't care about public debate. They find it confusing, disconcerting. They already enjoy every freedom they desire. Freedom from troubled sleep. Freedom from fruitless arguing and unpleasant disagreement among their leaders over issues they don't understand or care about. The last thing the people need or want is to see their leaders quibbling and bickering, snuffling and snorting like pigs in a sty."

Sir Vinny returned Liverwort's glare with an icy glare of his own.

"Lord Chamberlain, you may believe freedom means freedom from the messiness of politics. I've come to realize true freedom must include the freedom to disagree openly, vigorously, passionately about public policy, messy though that disagreement might be."

The Lord Chamberlain was clearly baffled by Sir Vinny's position. "Why are you really doing this?" he asked. "Even if Talkyhall suddenly started blathering on about politics, surely you're not doing this for readership? You wouldn't be so stupid as to report Talkyhall debates in your broadsheet, would you?"

Sir Vinny didn't answer.

"You know that approach killed *The Times* and *The Mirror*."

Again, Sir Vinny did not reply.

"Your broadsheet has prospered under our current arrangement. His Majesty might have taken exception to the criticism in your last edition regarding the East End explosion. Still, he was pleased you carried the Academy's explanation. Drop your idea of covering policy matters in your broadsheet and

I will ensure the palace cooperates on whatever story you choose to cover next. Which Garter member is the best whist player? Who has the most dogs? What's Queen Wallis's favorite romance novel? You name it."

Sir Vinny smiled and said, "I want to examine our relations with Russia."

The Lord Chamberlain fell silent. He sipped his cognac and looked away pensively.

Sir Vinny seized the moment. "It appears we're picking this fight with Russia for no good reason."

The Lord Chamberlain turned to Vinny. There was hatred in his eyes. "The Russians are stealing our coal."

"No, they're importing Greenland coal," replied Sir Vinny.

"Illegally. The Come-by-Chance Armistice covers global coal resources. The Armistice states clearly that all coal shall be divided equally between the Realm and the Americans."

"That's absurd. No one knew Greenland had coal when the Armistice was signed. Besides, other nations must have some access to coal. And anyway, we only rely on coal because the Academy stifles research on alternative forms of energy. I myself have recently seen remarkable new possibilities."

"Be that as it may," the Lord Chamberlain responded, "Russian theft provides the pretext for war."

Sir Vinny was aghast at the chamberlain's cynicism. "War is a tragedy, a failure of statecraft," he exclaimed.

"You're a fool to think that. A good war unites a nation," the chamberlain growled, "and heaven knows the Realm needs uniting."

"There's no such thing as a good war."

"Of course there is," snorted Liverwort. "War clears out the gregarious, smothers dissent, makes heroes, stimulates demand and fosters innovation … and it makes fortunes."

"It kills the young and lines the pockets of the undeserving."

"Where has this naïveté suddenly come from?" exclaimed an exasperated Chamberlain. "May I remind you, your own father made his fortune … your fortune … from war?"

The Lord Chamberlain fell silent, stared at Sir Vinny, then suddenly leapt from his chair and took Sir Vinny's hand in a crushing grasp. Liverwort towered over Sir Vinny. "Thank you for coming. This has been most stimulating." Without releasing Vinny's hand, the chamberlain continued, "But let me tell you what is going to happen."

Sir Vinny tried not to wince at the chamberlain's grip.

"As soon as war is declared—and it will be declared, I assure you—His Majesty will proclaim the War Measures Act. We shall then suspend civil allowances, clear protesters from the streets of London, level the East End—this time to the ground—and rid Talkyhall of suspected enemy sympathizers. So be warned, my dear chap, be warned."

Chapter Fifty-Three

The Royal and Ancient Academy

Even before her morning ablutions, a folderfiler from the chancellor's suite arrived at Lollipop's cubby with a request that she join Lord Edmund in his boardroom forthwith.

As she climbed the narrow stone staircase from the calculating machine laboratory in the Academy's second cellar to the chancellor's wing on the ground floor, Lollipop ran over in her mind the terrifying news of Edmund's plan to spray Stinkykill. If he expected her to help, she would refuse. "No matter the price," she murmured. "No matter."

Lollipop approached Lord Edmund's meeting table as Scribben heaved the great door closed behind her. The smell, most likely from the chancellor's arm, grew more nauseating the closer she drew. Sitting on his trike, Edmund was chatting with an unfamiliar figure, a stubby man wearing the tartan trousers of a smartypants. The pants were worn and filthy and faded, and the man's face was grizzled and scarred.

"Ah, here she is," Lord Edmund said, "the young woman I was telling you about. Attractive isn't she, but don't be taken in by her petite stature or demure appearance. She's quite the handful, this one. You'll have your work cut out keeping an eye on her."

Edmund then spoke to her directly. "Miss Lollipop, I want you to meet Hobby Natterer. You recall I once mentioned I'd asked an acquaintance to locate Grimly Wordsmouth? Well, this is that acquaintance."

"He's found Grimly Wordsmouth?" Lollipop blurted out.

"Oh no," replied Lord Edmund with a chuckle, "not Grimly. Turns out Grimly's been dead for some time," the chancellor said with a smile. "And good riddance to him. No, Natterer here hasn't returned with Wordsmouth. He has, however, brought us some useful information, starting with the location of Earthedge."

Earthedge

Dread seized Lollipop's heart. "But ... but if Wordsmouth is dead, then isn't it likely he never made it to the edge? Isn't it likely no such place exists?"

"Ah, quite the contrary, Miss," said the smartypants. "I can assure you Earthedge is very real. I've been there and what wonders I've seen—boats of stone sailing on the Earth's rings, the actual underside of our flat Earth, and even its fiery innards."

"Enough! Enough *stercus* about a flat Earth," Edmund roared. "The important thing is we now have some idea where Wordsmouth's village is. We're an important step closer to blasting Wordsmouth's memory into oblivion. Miss Lollipop, you will work around the clock with Mr. Natterer to devise targeting coordinates for Earthedge. And Natterer, you will never let this woman out of your sight."

"A pleasure, sir. And may I say how attractive you are, young lady?" Natterer stepped directly before her, looked up into her eyes, and touched her arm.

Her skin crawled at his touch. She drew back in revulsion. The smartypants couldn't have missed her reaction.

"And may I say how utterly abhorrent you are, sir?" she replied.

"Yes, yes I am," Natterer said with a smile. His face oozed malevolence. "And don't you ever forget it."

Scribben opened the door. "Sir, it's Lord Bilbury. He'd like a wor—"

Bilbury burst past Scribben and charged at Edmund.

"What the hell are you playing at, you filthy cripple?" Bilbury shouted.

"Ah, Bilbury, I've been wanting to chat. I have some news from the palace."

Lord Edmund attempted to backpedal away from the towering Bilbury, but Bilbury pursued him.

"News, hah, I know you're trying to put my neck under the ax!" Bilbury shouted.

"No such thing, my dear chap, but let me just conclude this bit of business, and then we'll talk."

Edmund turned his back to Bilbury and said to Lollipop, "So you're clear on your task? Right after we've finished chatting with Bilbury, you'll meet with Natterer to map out next steps. Good. Now run along."

As the door closed behind her, Lollipop said softly to Scribben, "Lord Bilbury is livid."

"Come," Scribben whispered in reply and signaled her to follow. They slipped into a tiny adjoining cupboard and shut the door. "A good folderfiler needs good gossip," Scribben murmured, "and with this monster, it's life and death." He then opened a small hatch through which they could observe the chancellor's office.

"So, what's on your mind, Bilbury?" Lord Edmund asked.

"You know very well! You've told the king I'll spray the East End with Stinkykill from my air machine." Bilbury waved his arms in the air. "What the *irumbado stercus* were you thinking?"

"Gracious! I thought you'd be pleased," Edmund replied with a smile. "A chance to show off. Isn't that what you love to do, show off?"

"You know damn well my air machine isn't ready yet!" Bilbury shouted.

"My dear friend," Edmund said "I thought a little nudge might help you over the finish line. I only promised because I thought a target date might focus the mind, so to say." The smile on Edmund's face was forced, grotesquely artificial, and clearly intended to aggravate Bilbury.

"You only promised because you want to humiliate me!" Bilbury screamed.

Lord Edmund's face turned dark, vicious. "Yes," he said, his voice several octaves lower now, "perhaps I did, but only after you consorted with Trolleysmash to have me dismissed."

"You *should* be dismissed, you ass!" Bilbury stepped away from Lord Edmund in disgust. "Look at you, your rotting arm, your horrid color, your ridiculous shape, your smell. You're a walking corpse. Why in God's name do you even want this job? Why don't you just go? Buy an estate, retire to the country."

"Retire?" Edmund exclaimed in disbelief. "Are you mad? The Realm needs me! I'm not some cackle-bladder like you! I serve my king!"

"You ridiculous charlatan!" Bilbury shouted and kicked out at Edmund's trike. The trike tipped. As it tumbled to one side, Edmund struck his head on the edge of the table and crumpled to the floor. He ended up sprawled in a heap around a mahogany table leg. There he screamed in agony and rage, soiled himself, and bled profusely from the gash across his forehead.

Hobby Natterer reacted like a rabid dog. The smartypants lunged at Lord Bilbury, a gutting knife in hand, and drove it to the hilt in Bilbury's heart. One might linger from a blow to the stomach or gurgle blood for many minutes from a wound to the lung. A stab to the heart, however, meant almost instant death. Natterer had acted as he'd been trained and inflicted swift and certain death.

Lollipop slapped both hands over her mouth for fear a gasp might have given away their presence. Scribben, his own mouth wide with horror, pulled back from the peephole and looked around desperately as if seeking immediate escape.

The chancellor screamed, "Get me up, get me up!" Natterer stepped over Bilbury's body, raised the trike and then Edmund, and heaved the chancellor onto its saddle.

"I'm so sorry, sir, killing Bilbury like that, I couldn't help my—" Natterer babbled.

"It's great! You saved my life! I'm deeply indebted," Edmund gasped, then grabbed a paperweight from his desk and slammed it into Natterer's face. "Now smash my window!"

"What?" said the staggered smartypants, his nose twisted to one side, blood gushing from his nostrils, down across his mouth and chin and onto the floor.

"I said smash my window. Quickly! It's how the foreign agents got in. They wanted to kill me and managed to kill Bilbury before you fought them off and chased them away. You're a hero. I'll see you're rewarded handsomely."

Natterer tossed a chair through the window behind Edmund's desk and collapsed to the floor.

"Help! Scribben," Edmund screamed, "they've killed Bilbury! You must stop them!"

Scribben looked at Lollipop with terror in his eyes and then bolted from the cupboard. "Coming sir, coming!" he cried.

Chapter Fifty-Four

Talkyhall, Palace of Westminster

Everyone knew what was coming. Since their return from mid-morning tea break, Talkyhall members had become a raucous rabble. The royalist gaggle with their lacy pocket hankies and the Academy's lackies in their boaters and britches screamed like banshees in a concerted effort to prevent Primus Speaker Sellers from recognizing the first orator of the session. In turn, they'd been booed and bellowed into silence by an even more strident majority wearing trilbies and brogues. Eventually, PS Sellers did manage to gavel Talkyhall into silence.

"The Primus Speaker recognizes the honorable member from Biddleford-Fordingreen, Sir Maltvinegar Tartarsauce."

The significance of this moment was not lost on anyone. Even the mezzanine—which had not been occupied since the great mascara debate of '24—was filled to capacity. Spouses and staff and friends and cooks and cleaning biddies crammed the benches, along with an army of scribblers from *The Tittle-Tattler* and *The Daily Trumpery* scratching away on their chalkboards.

Sir Tartarsauce, resplendent in his burgundy waistcoat and knee-high hose, rose, coughed, sipped from a hip flask, and began.

"Honorable members, I first want to share with you intelligence I've just received. I have it on authority that Russian naval forces are approaching the channel, and American airships are rising into the skies over France and heading this way."

Howls of anger filled the chamber.

"Second, I want to acknowledge the passing of a young woman whom you did not know but whose sacrifice you will most assuredly honor in days to come. Her name was Marigold Springpeeper, and she lost her life in an attempt to warn us about the cavalier conduct and criminal conspiracy within our government."

The chamber rang with shouts and insults.

"Furthermore, I'm convinced more young people will soon lose their lives if we do not expose the longstanding pattern of ignorance and indifference to human suffering at the highest levels of the Realm.

"So I ask you, what shall we do, we the portly, the prosperous, the comfortable, the complacent, gathered in this hall today, what shall we do to end the government's reckless arrogance? A recklessness that destroys half our city in an experiment gone wrong. An arrogance that would plunge us into war merely to divert attention from our nation's ills.

"How shall we serve the cause of enlightened governance? *Will* we? Will we have the courage to do something, anything, anything at all? I believe we will.

"In fact, I propose Talkyhall members do precisely what we do best. We talk, but we must talk as we have never talked before. We must speak openly, truthfully, courageously about everything we know from our first-hand knowledge of government. We must talk about the stupidity, the selfishness, the venality we've seen with our own eyes so that no lapse, no gaffe, no graft, no ridiculous prohibition or ill-informed presumption by those in power will ever again go unexposed.

"Never will our talking require more courage or serve a higher purpose than it will in the days to come. Our contribution to the struggle for peace and good order will be to shine a light into dark corners, expose the concealed, and challenge the idiotic.

"And so I rise today, Mr. Speaker, to introduce a resolution, a resolution of historical significance and profound consequence. I propose to this hall that we set aside—now and forever—the ludicrous topics of discussion prescribed by the Lord Chamberlain. Instead, I resolve we set our own agenda for debate, starting with a conversation here and now of the Realm's deteriorating relations with the Republic of America and the Russian Empire.

"Our government would have us stumble into war. If we do not speak out now, the fathers and grandfathers who elected us will see their sons marched off to wage a war without purpose. If we do not speak out now, the wives and mothers of those young men will bear the terrible grief of their pointless loss. We cannot allow this march to bloodshed to continue unchallenged. I find no merit in debating French postcards when the lives of our sons and daughters hang in the balance."

Chapter Fifty-Five

Garter Chamber, Palace of Westminster

As Edmund's steam carriage pulled away from the Academy, hundreds of grey-haired old men peered from the windows. How they'd howled when he'd announced the lockdown. "For your own safety, you will remain in your rooms for the foreseeable future," he'd shouted. "Automata will deliver your meals and empty your chamber pots." He might as well have been singing in a hurricane because the wailing and weeping of a thousand terrified old men had drowned out his words.

***

A raw, damp, bone-splitting chill had every creature in Westminster Palace in its grasp. The Garter chamber was as cold as a butcher's congealator. No one dared set a coal fire for fear an open chimney flue might admit the toxic miasma that enveloped central London. The king was wrapped in a beaver skin coat. All others were garbed in their traditional Garter regalia and chattering from the cold like monkeys in a mango tree.

The hot water bottle tucked in Lord Edmund's trousers was cooling quickly. Also, his growing nervousness at the sight of the king's grievous agitation was doing little to stave off his own shivers.

"How did this happen?" the king screamed, his voice an octave above its normal range. "You lot, you're supposed to be the wisest minds in the Realm and my most trusted councilors, and yet you let this happen! And you, Lord Edmund, this new projectile of yours was supposed to intimidate the Russians, and instead, we have their entire fleet sailing down our east coast—"

"Fishermen from Inverness report fifty warships en route," piped in Admiral Trolleysmash, "and not just little boats—big boats, really big boats."

First Sea Lord of the Admiralty, bah. Ding-a-ling wouldn't know a coracle from a corvette.

"It's your fault, Lord Edmund. I blame you!" the king bellowed. His tone then turned petulant. "Why didn't you hit Russia with that first shot of yours? Why strike the Americans, for *stercus* sake? Never mind, I don't want to know. The damage is done."

"Majesty, you described my choice of target as a masterstroke," Lord Edmund replied.

"That was before I knew how everyone would react. Now I see it was a terrible choice, terrible," the king whined.

Buoyed by the king's crumbling confidence, Edmund shouted in reply, "But now our course is all the more obvious, Majesty. We can still humble the Russians by striking them right away, just as we'd planned. Isn't that so?"

"That's the other thing I blame you for, Lord Edmund, for being late!" The king was shouting again. "I told you to be ready to hit St. Petersburg in a week, so are you? Can you fire today? No! That's why the Russians are coming. Because your projectile is late."

"But Majesty, you said two weeks, your—"

"Don't contradict me. I know what I said. Did I not say one week, Trolleysmash?"

"One week, Majesty," the Sea Lord replied.

Toady!

"Well, Your Majesty, I … I would have been ready today had we not suffered a tragic loss," Edmund said.

"Loss? What loss?"

"Lord Bilbury has been killed."

Gasps from every council member. Eyes flew wide in shock.

"Bilbury? How?" whispered the King.

"Secret agents, Your Majesty," Lord Edmund replied. "You recall I warned the council last week that secret agents were on their way to attack the Academy? Well, they attacked this morning. They broke into my office, tried to stab me, stabbed Bilbury instead, and ran away."

"That's terrible. Our beloved Bilbury. Wallis will be heartbroken. She and Bilbury were very close, you know."

"Yes, Your Majesty," the Lord Chamberlain said, "very close."

"You'll have to tell her, Liverwort," the king ordered. "Wait, Edmund, did you say these secret agents are still at large?"

"I did, Majesty."

"Am I in danger?" the king asked in a voice barely above a whisper, as though he feared being overheard.

"We have every automaton scouring the city, and the training of our new smartypants, which you authorized, Majesty, is proceeding apace."

"Perhaps ... perhaps this would be a good time for Wallis and me to take that little vacation," the king said, mopping his brow with a hanky from his sleeve. "I've mentioned the idea several times, haven't I, Liverwort?"

"Often, yes, Majesty," the Lord Chamberlain replied, "but perhaps now would not be a good time, not just yet anyway. In the days to come, we will almost certainly require your direction on several pressing matters."

"But why do you need *me*?" the king whined like a small child being denied a sweet. "Everyone ignores my wishes anyway. I wanted Edmund to strike St. Petersburg, but no. I wanted Bilbury to spray the East End, but the damned man has up and died. I swear he did it to spite me."

"Your Majesty," Lord Edmund interjected, "it was an unfortunate coincidence that Bilbury and I were meeting on the matter of Stinkykill when the assassins broke into my office. As a testament to the dear man, I propose we proceed with his spray. Since we shan't have Bilbury's flying machine to deliver it, I suggest we employ automata."

"All right, yes, yes, just get it done. I'm sure the rioters will return to their homes when the smell is gone," the king said. "Oh, and fire that damned projectile!"

"In two days, Majesty," Lord Edmund replied.

"And while we're discussing the launch," said the Lord Chamberlain, "I'm going to suggest that you move the launch site from Hyde Park back to the Academy estate. That way, you won't have to haul your cannon and projectile across the city. Ought to save you some time. The sooner we have our war, the better. Don't you agree, Edmund?"

"Certainly," replied Lord Edmund with a grimace as a pain like a razor ripped through his innards.

Chapter Fifty-Six

London East End

The Tittle-Tattler canal barge was tied alongside the Tidworth Locke. There, the innkeeper of the nearby Dog and Gun Public House delivered a message from Sir Vinny to the Earthedgers. A scribbler on *The Tittle-Tattler*'s staff would meet them the following morning in Highgate Cemetery. He'd await them by the monument to the Right Reverend Karl Marx, former Bishop of the Lutheran Church in Britain. "Can't miss it", the message read, "big man, enormous beard, huge head of hair."

My crewmates were busy loading our equipment onto the pony cart we'd rented from a local greengrocer. Paralyzed by grief, however, I was still abed in the barge's lounge, my face buried in a pillow. Captain Codkiss was clearly irritated with me.

"Stalwart, my lad, I've had enough of this. Marigold's loss has broken all our hearts. But you're only making matters worse for everyone with your wallowing."

"I ... I know, Captain, and I'm sorry, but ...."

"But nothing, lad. It's been three days now. We can't have this. You know how dangerous this mission is. It was your idea. For it to succeed, we must all do our part. You have to start pulling your weight. We can't continue feeding you, moving your gear about, hell, wiping your ass. We could leave you here to sit in The Dog and Gun until we return for you, or you could paddle up and down the canal in a coracle and write your poetry, if you wish. But you must do something."

I whimpered like a whingeing child. "It's just . . . first Mother, then Father, and now Marigold. I've lost them all."

"That's a lot of loss to navigate for one so young, I know that. I've lost loved ones too. I'm a good deal older than you and I still feel the ache ... like a yawning emptiness where once there was love. But in the worst of storms, lad, unless the captain takes a firm hand to the tiller, he condemns his ship to the rocks."

"I'm no captain, sir. And I don't know how to get past this."

"You can begin by not thinking of yourself all the time. We need you to step up. Earthedge needs you."

"No one needs me, sir. All I've done is sweep the deck and push away growlers. I'm not a leader. I know that's what Father wanted, but I'm not."

"I'm not asking you to be a leader. I'm asking you to do your share." Until now, the captain's tone had been sharp, impatient. But as he sat down beside me, his tone changed.

"Ever wondered why I talk like Blackbeard much of the time?" he asked.

I rolled over to face him. My eyes burned from all the tears I'd shed, and my throat was raw from sobbing.

"My dear wife and I, we lost a son." The captain swallowed hard. "Eight he was, just a lad, full of beans and treacle. We lost him to a wasting disease. I was lecturing on Robert Louis Stevenson back then. My office was filled with seafaring bric-a-brac: narwhal tusks, harpoons, blocks and tackle, ships in bottles. My boy became convinced I was a pirate." The captain paused to blow his nose. "When we learned he was ill, we had to accept our boy wasn't going to grow up to become a medicator or astronomer or courtjabber or any of the things we might have wished for him. That's when I realized … it's not what parents want their children to become that matters. It's what children believe their parents already are. A hero. A gentle giant. A magician. As my boy lay dying, he believed I was a pirate. Last thing he said to me? "Argh, Captain, we sail for Treasure Island." And so I became his pirate, and a pirate I remain … in remembrance of my son."

Captain Codkiss took my hand, squeezed it, and said, "Don't ever feel you must become what your father might have wanted. Instead, become the man you'll one day want your own son to believe you are. And start being that man today."

**

Earthedge

It was a cool, damp morning. The air was fresh, clean, after a night of thunderstorms. The path through Highgate Cemetery lay deep in dead leaves and downed branches. Up ahead, standing by the granite bust of a truly fearsome fellow was a young man in ink-stained trousers and a colorfully striped jersey with holes in its elbows. He was accompanied by three automata painted blue and orange.

The presence of the automata gave us pause. Till then, I'd been so lost in grief that I'd barely registered our circumstances. But now I was suddenly alert to the possibility of danger ahead. Apprehension raised goosebumps on my arms.

Is this a trap? Has Sir Vinny betrayed us?

"Hello there," the young man called out.

We approached cautiously. "Why the automata?" the captain asked.

"Oh, don't worry about them. Automata normally deliver our broadsheets, hence our company colors. Today, they're for your protection. We might need them where we're going."[46]

We glanced at one another and moved forward cautiously.

The captain extended his hand and said, "I take it you're our greeter."

"Whiskers Forrest-Glen, sir. Yes, Sir Vinny has assigned me to guide you to your quarters."

It must be a nickname. Whiskers has less hair on his chin than me.

"I'm a scribbler at *The Tittle-Tattler*, and once we've got you settled, I'm supposed to ask you a few questions for a column on your intentions here in the capital, if that's okay."

---

[46] Although the Royal Academy had hoped to market its automata as the future of work and to create a lucrative new revenue stream for itself, the automata proved to be so awkward and slow at every task, only one or two sectors of society ever showed much interest. Police services acquired a number for traffic control; nursing homes, a few to carry their elderly residents to the toilet twice a day; and broadsheet publishers for deliverymen, once the velocity of their throw to a cottage doorstep had been moderated and the numerous early cases of damage and injury had been settled.

"As long as you print nothing before we've finished what we've come to do," replied the captain.

We walked our pony cart to the cemetery gate, where a steam carriage was waiting with two more scribblers aboard. Once the gear had been transferred to the carriage, one of Whiskers' colleagues was dispatched to return the pony cart to The Dog and Gun. At the same time, together with the two scribblers, we set off for the center of London.

***

The nearer we drew to the city center, the more appalling the stench became. The air burned my eyes, irritated my skin, and stung my nose and throat. We donned our goggles and carving masks. Everywhere there were ruins, fires, dogs snarling and fighting over bones of indeterminate origin, and worse. Starved, pathetic skeletal creatures wandered about like specters, searching the ruins for any crumb, anything of value, any memory.

As we travelled deeper into the East End, piles of debris grew ever larger. Eventually, the lanes became impassable. We had to disembark the steam carriage, leave the automata to guard it, and make our way on foot through the ruins with as much gear on our backs as we could manage.

"Sir Maltvinegar has made arrangements for you to stay in one of the few buildings still intact in the East End."

The site to which we were led was vast: a dozen buildings, half a dozen chimney stacks, many small shacks. All were either partially or entirely collapsed, and several had been ravaged by fire. Some fires still smoldered. Many of the ruins were also coated in bright yellow powder.

"This was a fireworks factory," Whiskers explained, "owned by a friend of Sir Vinny's. Not much of the factory left but its laboratory is still intact, and that's where you'll be staying. Little chance any Academy automata or robbies will come looking for you there."

Ahead was a one-story, windowless cinder-block building with a single entry. Whiskers produced a key, unlocked an enormous padlock and heaved open the heavy iron door. Inside, he lit a coal gas lantern. A dozen beds had been set up. There was a coal-burning stove, shelves of food, heaps of clothing on a large table, along with scrap metal, rags, even the twisted remains of some sort of winged craft, and most important—tools, lots of tools.

Whiskers must have noted my interest in the winged contraption. "It's the work of Lord Bilbury, an Academy member who'd been trying to fly for years. During one of his failed attempts, the craft crashed in the Thames. The next day, a robbie river patrol spotted the wreckage washed up on the bank of the Thames. Not sure how it got here, though."

"Hmm," I replied. I was curious to know what Bottomly Fireplug might make of this contraption.[47]

"We've also provided this," continued Whiskers as he walked up to a large wall map of London. "I've circled the Academy in red, here, so when you're planning your next steps, you'll know where you're going."

We all gathered around the map to surveil our situation. "So not too far from the Royal Academy then?" Captain Codkiss asked.

"Well, actually, it's uphill most of the way, and every route from here to there will be dangerous. Crowds are camped here, here, and here. When you're ready, I'll send men to escort you, although I understand you have weapons the likes of which we've never seen."

"We don't want to use them on innocent souls," the captain replied.

"No, of course not, but the desperate can no longer tell friend from foe."

We moved around the room in silence, examining our beds, supplies, and tools.

"Oh," Whiskers said, "another thing. As you requested, Sir Vinny made inquiries about recent arrivals in Boggshead. He learned from friends in the west country that another party of strangers is heading for London. He has

---

[47] Bottomly Fireplug, a former florist, had been working for some time on a promising new source of propulsion for our skipscooters, which he called "exploding cans and fans." Out of a block of iron, Bottomly carved two chambers in which tin cans slid up and down as minute amounts of coal gas exploded beneath them. As the cans moved in the two chambers, they rotated a bar to which Bottomly fixed a large propellor. His intention had been to have the propeller move a skipscooter, but I wondered what he'd make of the propeller on this flying machine.

sent word for them to join you here, and he's dispatched another scribbler to meet them out on the Great Roman Road."

"That's wonderful news," exclaimed the captain.

Suddenly, there was a hammering on the iron door.

Whiskers moved cautiously toward the door and called out, "Yes?"

"Whiskers, it's Quill," came the reply. Whiskers pulled back the crossbar and pushed open the door.

The young man calling himself Quill stepped inside. He was followed by several very colorfully dressed figures whom I did not immediately recognize.

Then Burpee shouted, "Annadeena, Pewter, Paddler, Bottomly. What a sight you are! And Covert, you made it too!"

Chapter Fifty-Seven

The Royal and Ancient Academy

"You will not leave this laboratory, hear me?" Hobby Natterer growled. "Leave, and I swear you'll be so messed up you won't disobey anyone ever again."

It galled Natterer having to make threats like that at a knobfiddler. Browbeating a knobfiddler was the job of a junior smartypants, not him. No, he should have been ordering greybeards about, hunting villains, rooting out dilly-dallyers and theoreticookoos, and the many other academikrooks who defied the Academy. For some reason, however, Lord Edmund had attached inordinate importance to the work of this girly guttersnipe and then stuck him with her watchkeeping.

Lollipop smiled. "Leaving, are you? Is there somewhere else you have to be?"

The instant the chancellor is done with you, Missy, I'm going to rip that smirk from your face, along with your nose, ears and teeth.

"You know damn well, little lady. It's spray day!" Natterer sang the words and rubbed his hands together with glee. "Better pray your folks are out of town because by teatime, London will be swimming in Stinkykill." Hobby turned and left the calculating engine laboratory, locking the door behind him.

He was not supposed to let the bitch out of his sight, but what choice did he have? He dared not bring her along. It would be damaging to have his new recruits see this slip of a girl insulting their boss, especially before they departed on their first mission.

What would his pa have thought now, to see him commanding the might of the Royal Academy? "Yer no better 'an yer mum, ye drunk bastard," his pa had shouted at him as Hobby'd left home for his impracticum. And for a time, the truth of his pa's description had been borne out. Weak like his ma, he'd drunk his way through three years of study until the threat of expulsion had at last shaken him, and he'd buckled down and squeaked through his finals. Now here he was, commanding the defense of the most prestigious institution in the land. A hard man just like his pa.

***

The dozen new smartypants were lined up in the grand courtyard facing the Palladian staircase. They were kitted out in ill-fitting tartan trousers, shirts of faded blue with tattered yellow trim, and cracked and discolored ammo belts. They also wore dented tinpot helmets from which dangled ribbons of gauze in place of the customary noxious gas filtraters. Recruited so hurriedly, there hadn't been time to find them new uniforms. Instead, they were decked in returned, damaged, or irreparably stained gear for their Passing-off-the-Square ceremony. It wasn't going to matter though, since their first mission was bound to be a messy one.

Enjoying every second of his new authority, Hobby marched down the Palladian stairs whistling the *Radetzky March* and came to a halt in front of the twelve. He placed a hand on his left hip, cocked his head to the right, and spoke. "Your mission, my courageous warriors, will be to accompany our automata on their march into the city center."

Behind the dozen smartypants were fifty automata lined up five abreast, tanks of Stinkykill slung on their backs and spray hoses across their tin chests. They were in turn ringed by another thirty or so automata, each carrying a gum Arabic shooter.

"You will accompany our automata to Kippertiddling Square, rewinding their clockworks every twenty minutes or so as you march. At Kippertiddling, you will wind them one last time and set them on their way. They are programmed to fan out and spray every lane and alleyway, every market and circus, every terrace, court, and yard, from Shoreditch to Greenwich.

"En route, you will disarm and administer rough justice to any worthless drudge who tries to delay your progress. Use whatever force you deem appropriate to complete your mission. Now, march on and make the Academy proud."

Earthedge

The automata sprang to life, turned around, and trudged off in lockstep down the long avenue toward the Academy gate. The dozen smartypants fell in behind the automata. Hobby watched the small army exit the estate and turn down Snapthrottle Hill until the last figure disappeared into the city's green fog.

Now we wait.

Hobby's first diversion was a pleasant lunch in the empty greybeards' dining hall, a meal of cockles and mussels followed by Spotted Dick and custard. Fat and full, he had a sip of Oban and a short nap in his room and then returned to the calculating engine laboratory to check on his charge.

***

"Not here? What do you mean, she's not here?" Hobby shouted at the pasty-faced knobfiddler with the potbelly. "Before I left, I locked this door myself ... from the outside!"

"Yes, sir, but Miss Lollipop wasn't here when you did. Just us."

"But I talked to her," he said, confused, perplexed by the knobfiddler's assurances. "I warned her not to leave."

"No, sir, you warned us not to leave. Miss Lollipop wasn't here."

"What are you playing at," he bellowed, "eh, what you trying to pull?"

"Nothing, sir. But we'll play whatever you wish, sir."

Hobby pushed Basenote to the ground, kicked him and screamed, "Don't get smart with me, you fat turd."

Just then, a greeting clerk from the great hall reception booth came running into the laboratory. "Mr. Natterer, sir, Mr. Natterer, they're coming back."

"What? Who's coming back?"

"Your smartypants, sir, they're coming through the gates."

A chill ran down Hobby's spine. "Already? They can't be," he muttered as he took off at a gallop.

***

Eleven smartypants, soaked with sweat and Stinkykill, their clothes torn and soiled, staggered into the courtyard and then headed off in the direction of their guardroom. Three had suffered severe burns and were obviously in shock. The rest had lesser injuries of one sort or another.

"Halt," Hobby shouted, "back here now! Form up!"

The smartypants stumbled back to the Palladian stairs and formed a rough line.

"What the *stercus* happened to you? Where are the automata?"

"Sir," one of their number called out in a shaky voice, "we was ambushed, sir."

"Ambushed?" Hobby couldn't believe his ears. "Step forward, man. Explain."

The young fellow in singed clothing moved forward painfully. "Yes, sir. We gots to Kippertiddling Square with no problems, then we winds the automata clockworks for the last time and starts them off. But the lanes there narrow as they twist around the old churchyard. And as the automata squeeze together to get through the pinch point and into Wimpole Street, there is this sudden burst of light, huge it was, and then this great bang, like lightning. And them gum Arabic guns what the automatons is carryin', every one of them goes off at the same time.

"Gum Arabic sprays out everywhere. The automatons carrying them guns tumble into the glue, and the others carrying the Stinkykill fall over them. Eighty of them in a heap. And covered in gum Arabic they is.

"Then there's this second blast and a third and a fourth. We covers our eyes and ears, but we's blinded. And when we can see again, we discovers them tanks of Stinkykill is busted, and the stuff is running everywhere. The automatons is rolling about in gum and Stinkykill. The Stinkykill then starts eating into their tin plating and into the cobblestones. If we get Stinkykill on our boots, they begins to steam.

"That's when the firin' starts. These here bolts of lightning is coming out of alleyways and windows. So we starts running back up Bobbleshuttle Lane. We can hear crowds cheering as we runs past. Not sure who they was cheering for."

At first, Hobby was merely speechless, but then as the reality of the defeat sank in, he became nauseated. He turned away as the cockles rose in his throat only to discover Lord Edmund on the portico stairs above him, his face purple with rage.

Chapter Fifty-Eight

East End

As we made our way back to the fireworks factory through the ruins of East London, we chanted, "Vic-tor-eee, Vic-tor-eee!" like rugby toughs after thrashing the French. Crumbled walls and toppled towers echoed with our battle cry. "Vic-tor-eee, Vic-tor-eee!" It was the first time in days I'd felt anything remotely resembling joy. I went into battle not knowing my own heart. I'd emerged elated. We Earthedgers had tested ourselves against overwhelming numbers and succeeded beyond our wildest imaginings.

"Won't be as easy the next time," cautioned Captain Codkiss. "We've shown our hand. Even so, we've drawn first blood, and they're going to be terrified to meet us again. So savor the moment, me hearties!"

With that, we took up our chant once again. "Vic-tor-eee, Vic-tor-eee!"

***

We certainly hadn't anticipated confronting the Academy quite so soon. After our first unsettled night in London, we'd broken our fast at dawn, gone for a short reconnoiter around the factory site, and started inventorying our equipment and weaponry when the scribbler, Whiskers, had come racing into the shed. He'd been on his way with bottles of hot tea for everyone when he'd encountered the Academy contingent marching in our direction. He'd known immediately what the Academy army was planning and what he had to do about it.

He raced into our shed. "You've got to stop them!" he'd shouted. "They're going to spray Stinkykill."

"Who? Who's spraying what?" asked the captain.

"Academy automata, they're going to spray Stinkykill over the East End. It's an odor killer, but after the East End explosion went so terribly wrong, everyone's afraid Stinkykill will be equally catastrophic if the Academy's involved."

"And you want us to stop them?" asked Burpee.

"Can you?"

The captain looked us all in our faces, turned back to the scribbler, and said, "I guess we could try."

We'd hurriedly gathered weapons and without any planning, raced out to meet the Academy force. The three of us carrying shockshooters had taken up positions on either side of Wimpole Lane. I'd concealed myself in the window of a small fish shop. The smell had been appalling but the spot afforded me a clear line of fire up the lane. Others with methane grenades had climbed to the second floors of buildings not yet toppled and so we'd waited. Covert Millrace, who was still recovering from his injuries at the hands of Hobby Natterer, stood watch at the churchyard.

When the contingent of automata squeezed around the churchyard and entered Wimpole Lane, we'd known instantly we were hopelessly outnumbered. But then Cogsy Eyebeam had a stroke of genius. Cogsy recognized the infamous gum Arabic shooters from his service in the 5th Middlesex Grenadiers during the third American war and he knew too well their vulnerabilities. "We fire together," he'd shouted. "On my count!"

The simultaneous blast from our three shockshooters had so rattled the mechanisms of the unstable gum Arabic rifles that they'd begun discharging of their own accord. Soon the automata were covered in thick, sticky strands of gum. As we waited for our shockshooters to recharge, we watched in amazement as rank after rank of the tin men tumbled one upon another in one great heap of thrashing mechanicals and gum Arabic until their clockwork mechanisms ran down.

Suddenly, a tank of Stinkykill ruptured.

"The tanks," Cogsy bellowed, "shoot the tanks!" And so we'd discharged our shooters into the remaining tanks. Soon the automata were lost in a stew of Stinkykill and gum Arabic. The dozen smartypants, who'd been stunned by the blinding flashes of our shockshooters and the sight of their hapless automata, began firing their rifles wildly. We responded by turning our shockshooters on the smartypants. Too rattled to stay and fight, the dozen smartypants took off at a run back up Bobbleshuttle Lane.

From the first sounds of conflict, crowds of filthy and emaciated East Enders had tumbled out of their makeshift shelters and into the lanes and alleyways. There they bayed at the fleeing smartypants and pelted them with rotting food and rubble.

***

So now we were preparing for more demanding tests to come.

None of us, save for Cogsy, had ever known armed conflict. Captain Codkiss had everyone in stitches as he described the only time he'd ever done battle. Eons earlier, after a late-night pub crawl, he and a band of fellow students had crossed a gang of foundry workers coming off shift. They'd fought in the streets and squares and lanes till well past noon, when robbies arrived to take them all into custody.

With such credentials, everyone readily ceded command of our small force to Captain Codkiss.

"As I see it," he said, "we face four challenges, each difficult and together almost impossible, impossible that is, except for the likes of you."

We grinned and patted one another on the back.

"First, we're going to have to neutralize the remaining Academy automata. Trouble is, we have no idea how many more tin men there might be. Second, we have to defeat the smartypants. Again, we don't know how many there are, but we have to assume they'll use their rifles more effectively the next time. Third, we've got to destroy their projectiles when we don't know how many they've built or how close to launch they are. And fourth, I think we have to destroy the Academy's capacity to threaten Earthedge now and forever."

The captain's assessment of the situation was like a bucket of ice water tossed in everyone's face. We didn't speak for some time.

Annadeena broke the silence. "Stalwart," she said, "it was your suggestion we do this. How do you propose we proceed?"

At first, I was taken aback by her question. Was there an implied responsibility in her remark, an accusation? But then I saw the warmth in her face. She actually wanted to hear what I had to say.

"Well," I said, then paused. Suddenly, our way ahead became obvious. "First, I think we can assume the smartypants who killed Marigold...." For a moment, the words caught in my throat. "I ... I think we can assume that the Natterer fellow made it back to the Academy and has warned the chancellor of our intentions. Second, I expect he's also described our weaponry. So I don't suppose our victory this morning will have revealed anything Natterer didn't already know, only perhaps that we have arrived."

"Meaning surprise will not be a factor in our favor a second time," Burpee responded.

"No, our shockshooters won't surprise them a second time, not if we use them in the same fashion, that is."

"In the same fashion? You mean we need to use them in some new way?" Cogsy asked.

"Right, just as you had us fire our shockshooters simultaneously at the automata. That was so brilliant!"

Everyone applauded Cogsy.

"So clever!"

"You were great!"

"So smart!"

Cogsy grinned.

I continued, my excitement building as I spoke, "I think we'll need to use all our resources like that ... in new and unexpected ways. It's clear to me the only way a handful of us can defeat hundreds of them is if we utterly overwhelm them with our creativity."

There were smiles across the laboratory, then applause. "Then creative we shall be," said Captain Codkiss.

"Right!" said Covert, "Creative is who we are!"

"And so our priority this afternoon will be to ready our new arsenal," Captain Codkiss asserted. "We'll take two days to service, repair, and craft our new weaponry. As Stalwart has said, we must be bonkerly creative, moonraker mad. The more surprises we can inflict on the Academy, the better we'll fare."

Earthedge

The captain then assigned everyone to teams and announced, "A more creative force a commander could not ask for. You shall conceive with zeal and create with abandon. Our only requirement is that your results must terrify and confuse."

And so we set to work.

Whiskers, the scribbler, passed the afternoon wandering about the laboratory, taking notes and sketching images of our curious new weaponry. He had a million questions concerning Earthedge science and our way of life. There came the point when his inquiries hindered our work, and we decided it was time he left.

Captain Codkiss was walking the young scribbler to the door when there came a knock.

We fell silent. "Yes?" the scribbler called out.

The voice was too faint to be heard through the heavy iron door.

"Who are you?" Whiskers shouted a second time.

Again the voice was too weak to be understood. "I think it's a woman," the scribbler whispered to the room. "Can I open it?"

Captain Codkiss looked back at us all. No one moved.

"Okay," Whiskers muttered, "then I will."

He pushed open the heavy door, and in stepped a young woman.

"My name is Lollipop Crossingguard. I'm a knobfiddler at the Royal Academy. Are you from Earthedge? I really hope you are because you're our only hope for preventing a war."

Chapter Fifty-Nine

War Department HQ, Royal Horseguards' Parade

After the humiliations of the last American war, King Edward had proclaimed a program of renewal and reinvention for the Armed Forces of the Realm. He'd invited private industry to purchase brigades, sponsored public competitions to rename battalions, held lotteries for holiday cruises aboard dreadnoughts, and asked school children to propose fearsome new weaponry. The commitment to renewal was summed up in the War Department's new motto: *Quae damus multum cogitation* (We're giving the matter a lot of thought). Harrods purchased the Black Watch, and Sainsbury's the Catering Corps. Weetabix included an officer's commission in every cereal box, and a royal commission investigated the feasibility of a monkey band and a dragon force. Regrettably, the Realm's coordination of its military resources had not benefited quite as it should have from the new spirit of innovation.

"The Sea Lord wishes a moment of your time, Field Marshall," announced the squaddie, standing to attention in the office doorway of the Chief of War Department Staff.

"Send him through," replied Viscount Treadmill Aimsbroke.

It was quite apparent that Admiral Trolleysmash—a hereditary lord, gentleman farmer, and civilian well into his sixties—now loved the uniforms and ceremony associated with his royal appointment as First Sea Lord. What a shame he couldn't abide the roll of a deck beneath his feet and so had to confine himself to duties ashore. Trolleysmash enjoyed the excitement of preparing for war—all the rushing about, the dressing up, and the many hushed conversations. Like his fellow warriors at War Department HQ, he was especially pleased that none of the preparations for war actually required him to travel more than ten feet from his office.

"Nasty afternoon," said Trolleysmash as he entered the office of his colleague, "March winds, spring showers, and all that, eh what, Tready?"

"Ah. Dingaling," Aimsbroke replied, looking up from a stack of papers. "Have you seen these reports from the National Police Service? Seems they've decided to withdraw their robbies from central London. The crowds are simply too large and too rowdy. Worse than finals night at the Threadneedle Dog Show, if you can believe it."

Unlike several other colleagues at War Department HQ who held ceremonial rather than earned rank, the Chief of the War Department, Viscount Aimsbroke, was a career officer. A former boy scout, army cadet, and commandant of the Quartermaster Corps, Aimsbroke had earned his appointment the hard way—by hosting Queen Wallis at his home in Bath for several summer weekends of quoits and cards and shopping.

"About those rowdies," Trolleysmash said, "a rider has arrived from the Royal Academy with a plea. Edmund is begging for troops. It seems he's had some sort of run-in with the London rabble over Stinkykill. He suspects the agents who topped poor old Bilbury are behind the clash. Whether it's true or not, he's asking if we can spare some troops?"

"No, sorry old man, not a one," Aimsbroke replied. "They're deployed at the moment ... escorting the king and queen out to Windsor for safekeeping."

"And they're the only troops you have in Greater London? No barracks-full just sitting about? What about the Quality Street Cavalry? I saw them watering their horses in Green Park this morning."

"Again, sorry, no. They're on their way to Salisbury. Everyone's busy... and here I must ask for your complete confidence." Aimsbroke got up and shut his office door. "They're all busy moving our new cannonvans."

"Your what?"

"Some time back, I authorized a weapons development program for the army, and my boffins came up with the cannonvan."

"Without the Academy's approval?" Trolleysmash exclaimed.

"I simply couldn't wait any longer, what with war looming and all that. So we developed the new cannonvan, a steam-powered, iron-clad, tracked behemoth capable of carrying a dozen squaddies and firing projectiles a hundred miles." Aimsbroke pulled a file from his drawer and emptied several illustrations onto his desk.

"Impressive," muttered Trolleysmash as he examined the drawings.

"Only a few small issues still to be sorted," Aimsbroke said quietly.

"Oh?"

Aimsbroke hesitated before speaking, shook his head, and muttered, "They're a wee bit top-heavy. Tend to tip over on uneven ground. And they're slower than I'd hoped."

"How slow?"

"Two miles an hour top speed."

"And you've acquired how many?"

"Four hundred."

Trolleysmash didn't even try to stifle his gasp.

"Our troops are massing at our weapons range on the Salisbury south downs. Convenient to the coast and all that. But the process is taking far too long. Might require another month for them all to reach Salisbury."

Four hundred enormous engines, belching smoke, moving slower than a man can walk, clogging every lane in Wiltshire, and for a month? The mind boggled.[48] "So, this means, if our war does start soon," said Trolleysmash as he rolled the implications over in his head, "your forces might not be operational in time."

"No, probably not." The two men stared at one another in silence until Aimsbroke asked, "But what about your fleet?"

"Well ...." Trolleysmash sat down across the desk from Aimsbroke and mopped his brow with a crisp white nosewipe. "I regret to say we've had setbacks of our own."

"Oh?"

---

[48] The cannonvans never saw conflict. Purchased as a single lot by Buntlin Holiday Camps, they were relocated to Dorset and converted into cottage accommodations, all four hundred of them, then positioned in four ranks along the cliffs above Lulworth Cove. "If the cliffs give way, you're sure to be safe in one of our ironclad cottages," read the holiday brochure. Their cannon barrels had been removed, laid out from the heights of Lulworth to the beach at Durdledor, and welded together to become Britain's first waterslide.

Earthedge

"Several of our ships off Ireland were testing the Royal Academy's new life preserver—the Queen Wallis floatator. Waste of time. Damned thing kept flipping its wearer upside down in the water. Trouble was, we'd already issued the floatator to every man in the navy. So we had to order all ships in the fleet to scrap them. Well, you remember that ferocious storm in the North Atlantic a few weeks back ... when the semaphore ships were blown from anchor? During that gale, our signal became garbled. Instead of "Fleet to scrap floatator," it became "Fleet to Scapa Flow."

"What, to that remote little bay in the Orkney Islands?"

"Yes."

"So you're saying the entire Royal Navy is up there, in the Orkneys?"

"Bit messy, I can tell you. Three hundred ships at anchor in a port with one pub and two tea shops. Villagers have tried to muddle through. The community hall hosted an afternoon dance. Eleven thousand men showed up. Royal Navy has to pay for a new roof, three fiddles, and a set of bagpipes. On a shooting excursion to the local laird's hunting preserve, seventeen men were wounded, and the laird's prize beagle vanished. Rumor has it his wife's also run off with one of our young officers ... but the laird's most upset about the missing beagle. The Ladies Auxiliary has done its best to entertain our men. They've offered lectures on quilting and tatting, the history of the tartan, and so on. There was some confusion regarding their talk on local birds and wildlife, however. The three ladies presenting had to be hospitalized for the vapors and the local parson suffered a heart attack."

"Surely our ships are on their way home by now."

"You'd think so," replied Trolleysmash. "Turns out there's not enough coal in all the Orkneys to refuel an entire fleet. Have had to send private coal carriers to Scotland before our ships can sail."

"Not in the best of shape, are we?" muttered Aimsbroke.

"No. And the king wants his war immediately," said Trolleysmash. "We have to hope Edmund's projectile frightens our enemies into immediate submission ... or we're in for a rum go."

"Then the sooner Edmund fires the damn thing the better, before someone starts pointing the finger at us."

The two stared at each other until Trolleysmash spoke. "I guess this also means Edmund will have to defend the Academy himself. Of course, he does have his own army, doesn't he."

"And big projectiles. We don't have big projectiles," Aimsbroke added.

"That's right. Lucky sod."

Chapter Sixty

Fireworks Factory, East End

We'd all assumed our hiding place in the East End with its horrid conditions and appalling stench would provide a measure of anonymity, not to mention security—mistakenly, it now appeared. A young woman from the Royal Academy, no less, had simply waltzed up to the door and knocked. How many other Academy agents might have been waiting outside?

"How did you find us?" Captain Codkiss asked.

"I followed you from Wimpole Street."

"But you're from the Academy," Gemeny said.

"I am. I slipped out of the Academy before lunch to contact my parents. When I saw them last, they were leaving London for Iceland. They're hoping to get to Earthedge. I was on my way to the Royal Semaphore shop near Trafalgar Square when I came across you fighting with the Stinkykill army. After that, I followed you here."

I spoke up. "But the fight was hours ago."

"Once I knew where you were, I went on to the semaphore station. I sent a message to the Minisculevik ferry terminal asking if they had any record of my parents' arrival. I waited for a reply but haven't received any so far. I'd urged my parents to leave London, but now they might be in even greater danger. Tomorrow the Academy will launch two projectiles, the first against St. Petersburg to provoke a war with Russia."

"This country isn't ready for a war, that's sure," Captain Codkiss said.

"It's the Garter council," explained the girl, "they think the public will rally round the Crown and the established order once war is declared."

"And the second projectile?" I asked.

"Sorry?"

"You said the Academy will launch a second projectile."

"Oh yes, at Earthedge," she replied.

We all gasped.

"But how?" asked the captain. "Even if the Academy has figured out the math required for a flight over a flat Earth, they can't possibly know how to do it across the barrens."

"I'm afraid they do," the girl admitted. "I worked it out for the Academy chancellor."

Everyone shifted uneasily. I'd been suspicious of the intruder before; now, I was deeply alarmed. This innocent-looking girl might have been a treacherous enemy sent to discover our plans.

She must have sensed my suspicions because she immediately explained. "I was ordered to work with the smartypants you captured to come up with some targeting coordinates."

"With Hobby Natterer? You worked with Hobby Natterer?"

"Yes."

I felt nauseous. This girl had actually admitted to collaborating with Marigold's killer.

"Based on his trip to Earthedge," the girl continued, "he'd done some figuring of his own—it seems he's had some training in mathematography—and I had Grimly Wordsmouth's notes. This morning, we gave the chancellor a rough set of numbers for targeting Earthedge."

"So," said Captain Codkiss, "what yer tellin' us, young lady, is if we're goin' ta stop the Academy, we gotter be doin' it tomorrow morning."

I couldn't believe the captain had been so quick to trust this woman. I couldn't help my own immediate distrust and let it be known. "How can you trust this stranger, Captain?" I almost shouted. "She just admitted she's been working with that monster, Natterer! And now she could be setting a trap for us all."

Ignoring my accusation, the girl addressed the captain directly. "Yes! You have to stop the war as soon as you possibly can." She then turned to me and asked, "Your attack on the automata on Wimpole Street? Did you notice how badly the area was damaged?"

"Ruins, sure."

"One of you hid in a fish shop, my parents' shop. I saw you firing from their parlor."

Earthedge

"Can I ask how you got out of the Academy in the first place?" the captain asked.

"So she saw us fighting. So what?" I grumbled in exasperation. "That proves nothing."

This time the girl ignored me completely. "I got out through the tunnel they're digging for a new women's privy."

"Then you'd know how we might get in?"

"Indeed, yes."

The captain was silent for a moment as he appeared to be considering the implications of the girl's ready access to the Academy. "All right, everyone, get back to your work," he suddenly announced. "Your creations will have to be finished well before dawn. And little lady, let's you and I talk."

I could barely constrain myself at the horrifying sight of Natterer's collaborator consorting with Captain Codkiss.

***

Near midnight, the captain and the girl ended their discussions and announced their conclusions.

"So, this is what Miss Crossingguard and I propose. In three teams, we'll enter the Academy grounds," he said. "Once inside, each team will make its preparations as stealthily as possible. You'll wait for my signal. When the battle begins, each team will carry out its mission: the first to neutralize automata, the second to confront smartypants, and the third to destroy the Academy's explosives laboratory. With the three new messaging units Covert has assembled for us, we'll be able to coordinate our assault."

"And I'm going to take care of the projectiles," said the girl. "I'll re-target them to do no damage. But now I have to get back to the Academy."

What she was proposing sounded too much like a trick to prevent us from destroying the projectiles. "Wait," I blurted out. "Why re-target the projectiles? Why not just blow them up?"

"Because with all the explosives they contain," the girl replied, "blowing both up at the launch site would destroy half of Middlesex."

"So we want them launched but targeted where they'll do no harm," explained the captain. "Questions?"

It had been on my mind for days. I felt at that moment I simply had to ask, "Will we shoot to kill?" What I really wanted to ask was whether I could kill Marigold's murderer.

The room was silent until Captain Codkiss spoke. "We're going into battle in defense of our homes and friends and families. We'll be vastly outnumbered with only our creativity to save us. When the moment comes, I trust you will each do what your heart directs."

Each person was lost in their own imaginings—of chaos, gunfire, explosions, screams—of the cacophony of war and the terrible choices we might have to make.

"Right then," the captain said. "We're ready."

"And I'll make sure the broadsheets are present for the assault," Whiskers exclaimed. "This is going to be great!"

Captain Codkiss shook his head. "No. Have no illusions. This is going to be terrible. Conflict always is." Then he added, "Stalwart, will you accompany Miss Crossingguard back to the Academy?"

***

After a nauseating hike in an icy, fetid fog across the ruined city and up Snapthrottle Hill, we were crouched in a deep, weed-filled ditch alongside the estate's stone wall. The wall was veiled in ivy and topped with broken glass. A smartypants, oblivious to our presence and sipping on a flask, staggered past us by.

"Most smartypants are so bored," the girl whispered. "Endless patrols, pointless drills. Nothing ever happens, not before now anyway."

I couldn't quite make out her face, until for just a brief moment, her eyes sparkled in a shaft of moonlight. Full of fire, determination. But could she be trusted?

We crept along the ditch for almost a league until we came to a gorse thicket. Crossingguard removed her jersey, wrapped it around her hand, and then pulled thorny branches away from the base of the wall until she'd revealed a small tunnel.

"Sure you want to go back in?" I asked.

"If I don't, they'll torture my colleagues."

"But you're the one the chancellor needs. You do his calculating."

"It's not like I have a choice."

Or perhaps you do.

"So you're quite smart then," I said, "doing calculations no one else can manage."

"Lord Edmund gave me Grimly Wordsmouth's papers to work from."

"Ah, after Father died, we wondered what had become of his early notes."

"You're Grimly Wordsmouth's son?"

"Yes."

"You don't look anything like him. I've seen sketches. He was short."

"My mother was tall, a poet," I replied.

"Are you a poet too?"

"Not sure what I am." I shifted uneasily. I wasn't comfortable speaking so ... so casually ... with someone who might turn out to be an enemy.

"Natterer was supposed to kill you," she said.

She's forthright, that's for sure.

"He killed a ... a close friend instead."

"Who?"

"Her name was Marigold Springpeeper."

"She was important to you?"

"Yes."

"I'm sorry."

"Natterer will pay."

She didn't immediately react but then said, "Wait, you're not thinking of trying to get even tomorrow, are you? Because we can't afford any freebooting. You go off on your own and you'll be risking the lives of your friends."

"Are you protecting that monster?"

"No, I'm trying to protect your friends ... from your recklessness," she whispered as she disappeared into the tunnel.

I watched her dash across the rough meadow and down into an excavation. She was either very courageous or very treacherous. Everything we'd hoped to achieve depended on a girl about whom we knew nothing ... except that she had already helped a murderer place our village squarely in the Academy's sights. With that chilling thought, I turned and headed back to the fireworks laboratory. There were less than four hours till dawn.

***

Smudge pots lit Lollipop's way along the trench and into the tunnel. She eased around the excavation for the cesspit, clambered up the ladder at the side of the sluice, and pushed open the grate into the privy's lower cistern. Waste would eventually flow through it, but for now, it was empty and pitch black. She drew a candle from a pocket with one hand while searching for her tinder box with the other.

Suddenly a tiny flame flared up in the darkness, and a voice said, "Allow me, young lady."

Chapter Sixty-One

Garter Council

In the king's absence, the Lord Chamberlain, Harrold Liverwort, chaired the Garter council. Free of the King's scrutiny, he didn't have to constrain his contempt for the whole parasitic lot of them.

Liverwort recognized the Earl of Treetrimmings.

"Have you seen this, Liverwort? *The Tittle-Tattler* is calling for the dissolution of the Order of the Garter and the transfer of its authority to Talkyhall. They claim the transfer will be for the well-being of our Realm." As he finished reading, Treetrimmings thumped the table in anger.

"Seen it, yes. It's nothing," replied Liverwort. "Just Tartarsauce blowing smoke again. We're keeping an eye on things."

"What is the rabble in Talkyhall up to?" asked Flaccid Balderdash, the Marquis of Stonestocking. "I hear stories of every sort. They're getting ready for a coup, or so I was told over lunch."

"You need not trouble your waterworks, Balderdash," Liverwort sneered. "Since Tartarsauce's resolution to debate actual public policy passed Talkyhall, nothing much else has happened. I gather Primus Speaker Sellers is meeting with several cronies to craft a proposition for constitutional change. Tartarsauce is behind that too. But once we declare war, we'll take him into custody."

"So it's more urgent than ever we get this damned war started," said Viscount Aimsbroke. "Is our fleet in a position to engage the Russians yet, Trolleysmash?"

Trolleysmash's glance shot daggers. "A day away," he replied. "Can your troops shoot down the American airships?"

"Alas, no. They're still out of range."

Balderdash interjected, "Liverwort, why the damned wait to declare war? Why can't we do it now and arrest that traitorous Talkyhall mob immediately?"

"Because, Balderdash," replied the Lord Chamberlain with unconcealed irritation, "as you've just heard, our forces aren't ready for a fight." He turned and glowered at Trolleysmash. "And I frankly doubt they ever will be!"

"Now see here, Liverwort." Trolleysmash tried to appear indignant, but there wasn't much conviction in his tone.

"That's rather cruel," protested Aimsbroke in little more than a whisper.

"Oh shut up the both of you!" shouted the Lord Chamberlain. "Does anyone doubt Edmund's projectile is the only hope we have of frightening our enemies into an early surrender and of avoiding another calamitous conflict?"

A few shook their heads and several muttered "nay." Mortified and humiliated, Trolleysmash and Aimsbroke slumped back in their chairs.

"So we're agreed," the Lord Chamberlain growled, "everything rests on Edmund's projectiles. As soon as he blows up St. Petersburg, we'll tell the Americans they're next and demand our enemies' immediate surrender. We'll also declare the War Measures Act, order troops into the streets to clear away demonstrators, and prorogue Talkyhall. That's our plan. That's what I shall tell the king. And that's what we shall bloody well do!"

Again, there were muted sounds of agreement from across the Chamber.

"Uh, while we're on the subject of launchings and the like," said Forecaster Fogbank, 8th Earl of Squishysides. "Uh … I don't think I can afford the time to attend the launch. My son's regiment has been called up and I need to see his tailor."

"Nor I, nor I," said a chorus of other members.

"Fine," replied the Lord Chamberlain. "I'll send word to Edmund he is to launch as soon as possible and that he need not wait for Garter members to attend. Our armed forces have been activated, but defense of the Realm relies entirely on the Academy's projectile." Swept up in his own rhetoric, the Lord Chamberlain continued. "I shall tell Edmund to strike our enemies with unprecedented savagery to ensure their immediate surrender."

Hearty applause from every Council member.

"Oh, and I'll let Edmund know he has the blessings and full confidence of the King … who, incidentally I'm told, has now left Windsor for a brief holiday in Scotland."

Chapter Sixty-Two

Royal and Ancient Academy

Lollipop screamed as her third finger splintered, or at least she thought she screamed because someone was screaming, and other than Natterer, she was the only person in the room. Yet somehow, she didn't actually feel the pain. She was aware his pliers had already crushed two fingers because she could see the damage. Shards of bone protruded through the flesh. The strap binding her arm to the table was smeared with blood. And yet she felt nothing. It was as though she'd drifted away somewhere. She was watching her new friends, the Earthedgers, toil over their curious weapons, watching them chat and laugh, watching the Wordsmouth boy sweep a shock of hair from his face, and watching his icy blue eyes.

Natterer's first effort to beat information out of Lollipop had been predictable. He'd slapped her, punched her, struck her with his belt, knocked her to the floor, and kicked her. A rib might have snapped, but she'd given him nothing.

She couldn't help the tears, but she was determined not to sob, not even to speak. She wasn't going to give Natterer the satisfaction of seeing her grovel no matter how many times he bellowed in her face, "Who did you see? What have you done?"

When he began crushing her fingers, she'd mercifully succumbed to shock and drifted away into delusion.

Scribben gasped as he entered the room. "My gracious, Natterer, what are you doing?"

"The bitch escaped. She was gone the entire afternoon and evening. I need to know what damage she's done."

Lollipop murmured through her battered lips, "I was just checking on my parents. That's all."

"Of course she'd say that," shouted Hobby, "but how do we know she hasn't fiddled with the projectiles? We can't launch until we know."

"The chancellor will know if the projectiles' settings have been changed," replied Scribben. "As for the launch, that's the chancellor's call. But when you meet with him, you can explain that Miss Crossingguard got out … because Lord Edmund wants to see you right now."

There was a look of desperation in Hobby's eyes. "Why?"

"It's almost dawn. He needs you to roust the greybeards and march the lot of them into the theater for his instructions."

"Surely the automata can do that."

"No. Lord Edmund wants you to do it and to make sure everything is ready for the launch. He wants to fire the space cannons as soon as it's light."

"All right, yes," Hobby muttered as he checked Lollipop's lashings. "I'll dispatch you later," he whispered in her ear.

"Oh yes," Lollipop said, "that's right. You like to kill women, don't you?"

He stood, seemingly shocked by the remark. "What … what did you say?"

"You killed that girl from Earthedge."

"Is she dead? No, no, I didn't mean to kill—" Natterer actually appeared to be rattled by the idea.

"But you did anyway, you monster!"

"I swear, I didn't mean to. Wait, how do you know about the girl? And how do you know she's dead? So you *have* seen them, haven't you, the Earthedgers!"

"Lord Edmund's waiting," said Scribben.

Natterer glared at Lollipop, then turned on his heels and left.

Once he was gone, Lollipop begged, "Please, Scribben, you have to untie me. You know this war is wrong. Please."

Scribben gawked at her, confused, uncertain. "No, I can't, I just can't."

"Then at least tell the calculators in the engine room where I am, please," she begged. "Surely you can do that much."

Chapter Sixty-Three

Fireworks Factory, East End

The bells of St Mary-le-Bow Church struck the hour just as Whiskers the scribbler banged on the laboratory door.[49] "It's four," he shouted. "Hurry, we only have two hours to sunrise."

Exhausted, we staggered out of the laboratory under the weight of our gear. With all the fabricating and planning we'd had to do overnight, no one had slept a wink.

My head was heavy, stomach sour, and mood darker still. I'd barely returned from the Academy and hadn't for an instant been able to put the image of my hands around Natterer's throat out of my mind.

"There's a carriage waiting through that alleyway," Whiskers said as he pointed down a narrow passage between two brick sheds, each of which might have toppled at any moment.

A carriage indeed. It was a charabanc with seats for twenty drawn by four Clydesdales. "Weren't sure how much space you'd need for your weaponry," Whiskers explained.

"And those men?" I asked, pointing at the four fellows seated nervously at the back of the wagon.

"Scribblers, like me."

"This'll do fine, my lad," said the captain. "Right, onward into the fray!"

***

---

[49] To say the bells of St Mary-le-Bow struck the hour is a bit of an overstatement. The facts are that only a portion of Christopher Wren's tower had withstood the East End blast and its bells had fallen from the bell chamber into the crypt, where they'd shattered. Beefeaters from the Tower of London, who'd not been on duty the day of the blast, had taken to striking the bells' remains with battle-axes hourly in remembrance of their fallen brethren.

We climbed Trundle Cobble Lane as far as The Boil Bottom Public House, a league from the Academy gatehouse. There we met up with Pewter Doubting. He'd gone on ahead and spent the past hour scouting the estate.

"They're expecting us," Pewter began. "All the trees along the entrance avenue have been cut down to create barricades across the great lawn. Automata and smartypants are lined up in two phalanxes behind the barricades. First, the automata. They're installed about halfway down the grand avenue in three lines of fifty tin men each. They're carrying those gum Arabic rifles again. That's the good news. Next are the smartypants, lined up about eighty fathoms before the Academy courtyard. The bad news is they're carrying proper rifles. I also had a look behind the Academy building. Just as that young woman said, many small wings extend from it. It's hard to tell one from another. Still, I think I've identified the explosives laboratory by its smell … sulfur, and lots of it."

"What about the projectiles? Did you see them?" asked the captain.

"No, couldn't in the dark, but there's a rail line extending from one of the larger wings and running off into the darkness. I didn't have time to follow it, but I suspect the rails are used to move the projectiles to their launch site."

"Good, that's good." The captain clapped Pewter on the back and then turned to the rest of us. "Right, this is how we go. Team One, you'll install your equipment across the great lawn between the gatehouse and the automata. And when you're done, you'll proceed along the side of the estate to the main building and place your explosives as close to the Palladian staircase as you can. Team Two, you'll place your gear between the automata and the smartypants. Then you'll creep up the other side of the Estate and aim your special shooters across the front of the building. And Team Three, you'll stand by at the corner of the building to triage any glitches in our plan. Barring none, on my signal you'll proceed to the privy tunnels, enter the Academy and locate the explosives laboratory and destroy it. Fingers crossed, our new friend will have taken care of the projectiles by the time you get to the lab. So, is everybody clear?"

We'd been through the plan a dozen times in the past hour. Truth to tell, I had only one objective in my mind, however—Hobby Natterer.

"Right then," continued the captain, "I'll be concealed along the south wall with Covert's message machine. Annadeena will remain with me ready to jump in wherever she's needed. She'll also tend to our wounded so come back to our location if you need help."

"And what about us, captain?" Whiskers asked as he nodded in the direction of his associates, the scribblers.

"Don't leave the pub until you hear the first sounds of conflict. Then you can move up the hill to the gatehouse and watch. But you mustn't arrive before conflict starts because if the guards see you, they'll alert their colleagues."

"And what about the Crossingguard woman?" I asked. "Do we look for her?"

Since she might lead me to Natterer.

"No. She said she'll find us," the captain replied. "She'll know we're coming when she hears our first assault."

We transferred our gear from the charabanc to shoulder sacks, spinal slings, and handcarts and set off on our respective assignments.

Now we were in our element. Twilight. We trudged across meadows, wove through stands of trees, climbed over hillocks and down through gullies in the last hours of darkness. With just the first streaks of purple across the horizon, we saw more clearly than in the glare of day. We were confident we could move about and make preparations right under the very nose of the enemy. At least that was our plan.

Chapter Sixty-Four

Royal and Ancient Academy

Basenote raced into the mathematography corridor shouting, "Miss Crossingguard, can you hear me?"

"In here," she tried to reply, "Help me, please," but she managed little more than a whisper before she passed out.

"Miss Crossingguard! Miss Crossingguard, please!"

Basenote ran from one room to another: the workspace cluster, the chalkboards collection, and the bibliotary. When at last he reached the calculating lab and found it locked, he battered the door, first with a chair, then with a bucket full of sand and pipe tobacco, and finally with a fire ax. After several sharp blows, the lock gave way, and he rushed into the room.

"Lollipop!" he cried in horror.

Still tied to a chair with her forearm strapped to a small table alongside, she sat slumped unconscious, blood from her crushed fingers dripping into a pool at her feet. "Lollipop," he said softly as he gently propped her upright and untied her bindings.

Her face was pale as a sheet. Her eyes fluttered open, and she looked around, confused, stunned. But then she screamed.

"Oh Lollipop," Basenote said as he cradled her mangled hand in his.

Her screaming stopped eventually. She moaned, gritted her teeth, and whispered, "Thank you."

Basenote smiled. "Sorry I took so long. Scribben said you were in mathematography somewhere and that you were hurt." As he spoke, Basenote found a towel at the sink, soaked it, and gently wrapped her fingers. "We've got to set your fingers or … or something."

Through gritted teeth, Lollipop asked, "Has the assault started yet?"

"What assault?"

"And the projectiles? Where are they?"

Basenote shook his head. "Miss Crossingguard, you can't worry about them now, your hand—"

"The projectiles! Where are they?" she cried out.

Shocked, Basenote backed away. "They ... I think they're rolling them to the launch site."

Lollipop tightened the towel around her hand, grimacing and groaning as she did. "And the guidance mechanism, you've inserted it?"

Basenote nodded.

"Help me with this, please," she said as she attempted to knot the towel in place. Basenote tore a length of cloth from his shirt and tied it carefully around Lollipop's hand.

"I'm sorry, I didn't mean to yell," Lollipop whispered with a tiny smile. "You're a dear friend."

"That's okay."

"Before you loaded the guidance mechanisms, did anybody touch the programming cards I gave you?" Lollipop attempted to stand.

"No, don't think so." Basenote took her arm as he spoke. "Why? Where are you going? You can't go anywhere. You're hurt."

"We've got to go to rocketry. We have to make sure the targeting cards haven't been changed."

"I don't understand. I thought we wanted to stop the launch."

"No ... not now ... not before ...."

"Before what?" Basenote asked. As Lollipop tried to walk, Basenote flinched at her obvious suffering.

"Before all hell breaks loose," Lollipop replied as she staggered toward the door.

Chapter Sixty-Five

Royal and Ancient Academy

Automata marched through the corridors on each of the Academy's residential floors, banging on doors, sounding fire claxons, and bellowing, "Honorab...hon...rise, go to...announce...Toft Theee...announce...announce...." A thousand greybeards in nightgowns wandered into the halls, rubbing their eyes, confused, perplexed, appalled at the indignity of this early reveille, and of course, demanding their tea.

"There'll be tea soon enough," shouted Scribben, who was galloping from floor to floor in a vain attempt to expedite the assembly. "But for now, please go to the theater. Please, it's urgent."

Automata started shoving the greybeards. Several foolishly pushed back, and in a matter of minutes, dozens were toppling over one another in the corridors and tumbling headlong down the stairs. Shouts became screams. Greybeards stampeded through the Hall of Heroes, knocking paintings from the walls and marble busts to the floor, until Hobby Natterer fired several shots into the ceiling. The shouting and screaming and running about ceased immediately.

"Thank you, Gentlemen," Natterer bellowed, "so now please proceed in an orderly manner to the Mary Toft Theater. Your tea and toast will be served after the chancellor's remarks, not before, so shut the *stercus* up! Thank you."

Automata surrounded the horde of greybeards as they marched like condemned men into the theater.

The chancellor's onyx plafond had been hoisted into place for the occasion along with the suspended gilt staircase. Edmund pedaled to center stage, looked at the stairs, and realized his predicament. Natterer grabbed two other smartypants and they rushed to Edmund's aid. The two lifted Lord Edmund from his trike and carried him up the staircase. Hobby followed with a footstool from the theater wing. The chancellor was placed on the stool mid-plafond, and the three smartypants retreated back down the stairs. Lord Edmund might have hoped the plafond enhanced his dignity and the profundity of the moment. From below, however, he looked like a portly child squatting on a potty. Even so, no one was laughing.

"Gentlemen, distinguished greybeards, as your chancellor, it is my honor to bring news from the palace. The king has entrusted us with a magnificent opportunity. Today our science is going to bring triumph and glory to the Realm and victory over its enemies. We are about to launch two projectiles. They are being rolled to the space cannons as I speak. Their launch will mark both the beginning ... and the end of conflict with our adversaries. Once we have demonstrated our unparalleled might, our enemies will have no choice but to acknowledge our global dominance."

There was much muttering across the theater.

"But I've heard there are crowds in the streets," someone in the audience dared to call out.

"I've heard that too," shouted another.

"And what about the stories of an American airship over the channel?"

"Airships are of no consequence. We can shoot them down whenever we wish," Edmund replied.

"But what about the crowds?" still others shouted.

"The moment we launch projectiles, we shall be at war. The king will declare the War Measures Act, and the army will sweep into the streets to clear away the rabble," Edmund yelled over the greybeards' rising chatter. "But from you, I require one thing," he bellowed, "that you stay out of the way. If your tea is late—"

The muttering became noticeably louder and angrier at the news their morning tea might be delayed.

"—if your tea is late, be patient. You will receive it eventually. More importantly, you are to remain in your rooms until further notice. Understood? This measure is temporary. Everything will return to normal by mid-morning. You have—"

An enormous explosion rocked the theater.

Edmund tumbled from his stool and came dangerously close to rolling off the plafond. Hobby Natterer raced up the stairs to catch the chancellor.

Greybeards screamed, leapt from their seats and scrambled in every direction. Aisles quickly clogged with heaps of tripping and tumbling old men. The theater filled with dust and falling debris.

"What was that?" Edmund shouted over the din from the crowd as Hobby carried him down the stairs.

"The front doors," a smartypants cried out, "someone has blown open the front doors … with a cannonball!"

Chapter Sixty-Six

The Great Lawn, Royal and Ancient Academy

"Bedazzles will be so proud," Burpee muttered to himself as he reloaded the culverin.

Several hundred yards away, Captain Codkiss raised his head above the tall grass and grinned. Even at this distance, it was clear the Palladian staircase and main entrance to the Academy were but a memory, reduced as they had been to a single enormous smoldering black hole. "Well done, Burpee," he said and crouched back down. Pulling the signaling device closer to his knees, he began squeezing the input ball. "Right everyone," he whispered, "rain hell."

The culverin blast had echoed across the Middlesex hills but was no more. Panicked shouting persisted at the front of the Academy complex. In general, however, the meadow had fallen still once again. And then ….

BOOOOOOM!

The silence was shattered by the crash of a drum so loud it shook one's teeth to the roots. It was so loud the sound wave smashed into one's chest like a rib-cracking body blow from Killer Yeats, the Irish Hammer. So loud one's eardrums were pulverized in a single excruciating second. We'd been warned to cover our ears, but the burst of sound didn't end with that first crash. Oh no. The merciless, maddening drumming continued, on and on, on and on.

BOOOOOOOM BOOOOOOOM BOOOOOOOM ….

Pewter was seated in the dewy grass, his ears stuffed with lichen, holding a child's drum between his knees and grinning like a street urchin with a warm bun. With his right hand, Pewter struck the drum's velum top to the beat of "Goosey Goosey Gander," and in his left, he held the phonocollector. All the while, he kept a steady eye on the Gain display of the exagifier. "Even better than we'd hoped," Pewter said to himself.

Windows in the Academy edifice shattered. Automata jerked spasmodically and collapsed under the ongoing sonic assault. Their clockwork mechanisms trembled and tottered, fractured, and spun apart. Soon, the line of automata three-figures deep across the great lawn was one long writhing heap of tin, cogs, levers, and gum Arabic.

Smartypants, lined up across the meadow, screamed in agony and covered their ears against the merciless drumming. They stuffed rags and socks and barrel wadding into their ears. Some did attempt to communicate with one another by shouts and hand signals. Several waved in the direction of the automata since that's where the merciless drumming seemed to originate. A few even shot toward the automata for fear they'd already been overrun by the unseen attackers.

Captain Codkiss again squeezed the signaling ball and muttered, "Right, Gemeny, your turn. Light up the night."

Following the blast from the culverin and the odd flash from a smartypants' gun barrel, the night had remained dark. There was no moon. Few stars were visible through the chill morning haze that overhung the estate. Still dazed and panic-stricken by the maddening drumbeat, the phalanx of smartypants arrayed across the great lawn could make out little of the automata's fate in the darkness except for the unnatural, writhing elongated shape that had replaced their ranks. Then ….

From behind the smartypants, in the direction of the Academy buildings, the night sky suddenly lit up like an eruption. Smartypants spun about and found themselves looking into lights as bright and as scorching as the sun.

Gemeny giggled as the dazzling lamps proceeded to grow ever more intense.

Smartypants were blinded, their eyes burned. They sobbed at the excruciating damage done to their sight. They threw themselves to the ground and buried their faces in the cool grass. And then Gemeny's lights began to strobe, to flash too quickly for one's senses to cope. Many smartypants became nauseated, dazed, dumbfounded by the dizzying display. Vomiting, stumbling about, passing out, the force of smartypants fast resembled a heap of feckless bar brawlers.

Earthedge

The few smartypants not blinded or sickened by the lights clambered from their trenches and began a mad dash back to the Academy. They didn't get far.

From both ends of the Academy complex, great bolts of crackling, jagged lightning suddenly erupted. The bolts darted and danced across the front of the building. There they crashed into the lightning bolts erupting from the opposite end of the complex in violent explosions of white-hot light. Smartypants who crossed the barrier of lightning dazzled like firecrackers, danced like crazed marionettes, smoldered and fizzled, and eventually collapsed on the scorched lawn.

Then the color bombs exploded. Pewter and I had found abandoned piles of chemicals in the ruins of the fireworks factory, which Pew recognized as colorants for fireworks. We'd combined every conceivable colorant and explosive concoction to create a rainbow of destruction.

By this time, the morning sky was deep blue. Crimson streaked the horizon. With a deafening bang, the first bomb exploded and sent a thousand tiny golden droplets of fire raining down on the ruined courtyard. The concussive force of the blast shattered every remaining pane of glass for leagues in all directions. Then up went the silver shot, followed by the green and the blue and another gold and a second silver. All sent cascades of color showering down on the Academy estate and outshining the rising sun.

The front of the Academy was shattered, broken; whole sections of its walls had already collapsed, columns had tumbled, flames were licking out of many windows, and voices from inside could be heard pleading for help. The drumming had ceased but now another cacophony battered the estate.

"GET OUT, GET OUT, GET OUT," ordered a thunderous voice. "IF YOU VALUE YOUR LIFE, YOU WILL RUN."

Greybeards, covered in dust and bleeding from their many cuts and gashes, stumbled out of the Academy. They clambered through its ruined doorway and over heaps of shattered masonry. There they staggered about the courtyard and lawn like drunkards.

At that moment, a lone smartypants raced out the doorway, clambered onto a heap of debris and bellowed, "There! Look there!"

Dawn now, and the great lawn was visible as far as the gatehouse. The lone smartypants on the heap of stones was pointing past his colleagues' broken ranks and over the line of ruined automata, on beyond to a small group of figures standing in the long grass.

Captain Codkiss and Annadeena had been joined by Burpee, Gemeny, and the others. The captain wasn't about to let this smartypants' rallying cry have any effect.

"Fire!" the captain shouted, and the barrel of the culverin flashed once again. Its shot screamed over the meadow like the keening of banshees announcing death. We could not have imagined a sixteenth century weapon was capable of launching such a true volley.

The cast-iron cannon ball crashed into the MacPherson Tower.[50] Its hit opened a large ragged hole immediately below the bell chamber. The bell rang with the blow, then fell silent. First, a few bricks fell away, then more, then a cascade, and finally, the entire tower crumbled into the courtyard. The great bell shattered. And greybeards and smartypants alike scattered like jackrabbits.

The lone smartypants on the heap of debris didn't run for cover. "Look there," he bellowed again as he leapt from one heap of stones to another, "they're right in front of you! After them, for *stercus* sake!" A few of his colleagues paused in their flight, picked up their rifles and moved cautiously toward the captain and his crewmates.

***

---

[50] The tower was named for scholar, James MacPherson. In 1761, MacPherson announced the discovery of an epic on Fingal written by a third-century Celtic bard named Ossian. In December of that year, MacPherson published *Fingal, an Ancient Epic Poem in Six Books,* together with *Several Other Poems composed by Ossian, the Son of Fingal,* and translated from the ancient Gaelic Language. The authenticity of the translations was immediately challenged by Irish historians, but MacPherson prevailed and Ossian was often cited as the preeminent example of a noble savage, a primitive soul uncorrupted by the temptations and vices of the modern age.

From our hidey-hole beside the complex, Pewter, Covert, and I glimpsed the captain and the others take up their gear and disappear down into the long grass.

The bellowing smartypants was frantically urging his men on. Hobby Natterer! It was Hobby Natterer, I suddenly realized, and I was about to leap from our hiding spot to confront him when Pewter Doubting grabbed my arm and whispered, "Message machine, it's glowing."

I took the ball in my hand and felt it vibrate. "Over to you," signaled the captain. Natterer would have to wait.

We ran full tilt around the side of the building and toward the excavations for the new privy. In the distance, I could just make out the projectiles being pushed by several automata and smartypants down the rails toward a cluster of outbuildings. We were tempted to confront the projectile work party directly, but that was not our assignment. Not yet anyway. First, we had to find the explosives laboratory. Then, if the girl hadn't managed to re-target the projectiles, we were going to have to somehow stop the launch.

We dove into the tunnel. Along with our shockshooters, I was carrying the message machine, Covert the watchycallit, and Pewter his newly adapted shockcannon. We raced through the dank passageway, up into the waste chamber, and on into the privy. Outside, there was no sign of movement along the muddy path to the ladies' doorway in the rear of the Academy building. Even so, we ran as fast as we could. And sure enough, the track was being watched. Shots rang out. Someone was firing from an upper window. Covert spied the sniper and aimed his shockshooter. Its blast shattered the window frame, driving the sniper back into the building, giving us time enough to crash through the ladies' door and into the Academy.

Covert studied the watchycallit and said, "Explosives lab is this way," and off we went.

The rear of the Academy showed some of the effects of the massive damage done to its front—broken plaster, shattered windows, twisted doorframes. Destruction back here wasn't quite as extensive, however. In fact, many of the building's inhabitants had retreated to its deepest recesses for safety. We encountered gaggles of quaking greybeards crouched in tiny storerooms and squealing like terrified children. We raced past them without a word.

On beyond the greybeards we came across a half-dozen knobfiddlers, hiding beneath beds and in cupboards in their tiny quarters.

"You're Lollipop's friends," one called out. "We are too. Please don't shoot."

"Explosives laboratory, where is it?" I shouted.

"Main floor, north wing, big extension out the back. Large metal door."

Just as the Lollipop girl had described. "Okay, good. And Lollipop? Know where she is?"

"No. Haven't seen her, not today."

"Maybe in rocketry?" said another.

"Where's that?"

"Another large extension sticking out the back, right above us, wing R, it'll say."

So explosives laboratory first, then rocketry ... then Natterer.

We galloped to the nearest staircase and headed up to the main level. There were many more people here, some wandering about aimlessly, stunned, in shock apparently, but others were brandishing rifles. A group of smartypants had gathered in the entrance hall near the breached doorway. Their attention was focused on the courtyard and the lawn beyond as they tried to create a defensive barrier against an anticipated frontal assault.

"There, look there!" shouted one smartypants pointing right at us. His colleagues spun about and then dove for their rifles.

We threw ourselves behind fractured columns and heaps of stone. "Pewter," I cried. "Now's the time!"

I heard the spatter and crackle of Pewter's adapted shooter—his shockcannon—as it built up a mighty charge. Covert and I fired our own shockshooters, blasting walls and ceilings, sending a shower of debris down upon the smartypants, and giving Pewter the cover he needed to stand and aim. A deafening clatter erupted from his weapon, then bolts of electricity like the heads of a hydra, and finally, from the shockcannon's barrel burst a mass of copper wiring. Like a monstrous snake, the copper flew as a single long rope upward toward the vaulted ceiling of the entrance hall. But then suddenly, high overhead, it unfurled to become an enormous circular net some ten fathoms in diameter. The net dropped to the floor, enshrouding both the defensive barrier and smartypants attempting to build it. For a moment, the smartypants struggled against the tangle of copper netting. But then Pewter pressed a second button on the stock of his cannon and the netting crackled and sizzled and lit up like a thousand tiny stars.

Beneath the netting, smartypants screamed and writhed about like slugs in salt. Eventually, they fell still and silent, exhausted, stunned, unconscious.

"Right, to the explosives laboratory," I said. But I had another target in mind, the only one I really cared about … Hobby Natterer.

Soon, very soon….

Chapter Sixty-Seven

Aboard USAS *Bolsadeviento*

The USAS *Bolsadeviento*, or B-1, was the creation of the naval aircraft factory in New Jersey. Commissioned in 1947, she was non-rigid, steam-powered, helium-filled, and carried a crew of thirteen. Stationed near St Malo in France, the airship's customary mission was to overfly channel shipping to verify UK adherence concerning its coal imports under the Come-by-Chance Armistice. Captain Haggis McCasanfuilt had spent thirty-plus years in "the silent service." In America's last war, as armaments officer aboard the USAS *Fatty Arbuckle*, he'd personally dropped seventeen bombs on British targets. Memories of the London firestorm tormented him still.

It was not yet dawn. The captain was dozing in his cabin directly over the bridge. Haggis was jolted awake by his first officer rapping heavily on the hatchway in the captain's floor.

"Captain, sir," the first officer called up to him, "urgent semaphore message from the Goodwin Sands Lightship."

"Right," the captain replied as he heaved his seventeen-stone frame from the hammock, buttoned the waist of his trousers and opened the cabin hatch. "Message from the lightship?" he asked, staring down at the young lieutenant. "Go ahead, son, read it."

> From Field Marshall the Viscount Treadmill Aimsbroke, Chief of War Department Staff to Captain Haggis McCasanfuilt of the USAS *Bolsadeviento*.
> We bring greetings from His Majesty, Edward VIII, King of Britain, Scotland, Northern Ireland, and His Dominions. We commend you for remaining outside our territorial airspace. Provocation at this time would serve no one's interest. That said, there is always the grim possibility we may inadvertently stumble into conflict. If this is so, then I have a very big favor to ask.

Earthedge

If there is to be conflict, could you give us a day or so's grace before you drop troops onto English soil so that I can sort out a minor logistical issue? No one would wish our battles to be less than sportsmanlike, eh what? I'd be ever so grateful for the slight delay.

 Yours faithfully, Tready Aimsbroke
 Viscount

"What in pigswaller does it mean?" muttered the captain as he climbed down the ladder into the bridge. "Is it some sort of joke? What the hell is a logistical issue, and why in pigswaller should I care?"

"Could it be some sort of code, sir?" the first officer suggested.

"Mmm," mutters Haggis. "Who's the intel officer on this mission?"

"Second Lieutenant Nosehair, sir."

Stercus, how'd that happen?

"Well roust the man," ordered the captain. At the bridge hatchway, a marine on duty disappeared at a run down the passage to the crew's quarters.

The bridge of the USAS *Bolsadeviento* was airy, with enormous portholes on all sides. A helmsman stood at the wheel, a navigator at the map table, and the first officer at the captain's side. Haggis went to the starboard portals and stared out into the night. "That's Brighton down there. Can tell by the lights on the pier."

"Aye, sir," the navigator replied.

"Lay in a course for the Thames estuary. I want eyes on the Brits' War Department HQ."

Nosehair arrived. "Captain?"

"What do you make of this?" the captain asked as he handed the communiqué to the intel officer.

Nosehair read the curious signal, making the occasional hmm, ooh, and tut-tut as he did so.

"Well, you're right to be suspicious," he said at last. "It's clearly in code. When you've gathered intelligence as long as I have, you get a nose . . . a sense for these things."

"So, what does it mean?" the captain asked. There was a note of impatience in his question.

"Give me a minute, sir," said Nosehair. "I . . . uh . . . I need to check recent bulletins and texts and intel thingies back at my hammock."

"Yes, yes, but make it quick."

Nosehair left the bridge at the double.

Minutes slipped by. The only sounds on the bridge were the whistle of the wind through an ill-fitting porthole and the distant thrum of the steam engines at the stern of the ship. Haggis always found it reassuring to see the smoke trail behind his vessel.

"Altitude?" he asked.

"Sir, six thousand feet, sir," replied the helmsman.

Dawn now. In the first faint rays of daylight, the sea below was no longer black but gun-metal grey.

"Is that a Russian ship down there?" muttered the captain. "*Stercus*, right up the Brits' arses. Helm, hold her here. Get men on the scopes. Eyes on the UK War Dept HQ. Any suspicious movement, I want to know immediately."

As the first officer left the bridge, Nosehair came running back in.

"Well, I've gone through all my intel stuff," said a breathless Nosehair, "and it seems obvious the message is part of a clever plan. I read this to mean the Brits have no intention of launching hostilities any time soon. Quite the contrary, I believe the Brits are hoping through some clever ruse to provoke us into firing the first shot."

"Oh?" the captain replied.

"The message, sir, they'll want to use it to curry public support. 'See?' they'll say, 'we asked the Yanks to hold fire, but no, they shot first. Not our fault.'"

"And you get all that from this message?"

"Oh yes, sir," replied Nosehair. "When you've been in the intel business for as long as I—"

"I know, you get a nose for this sort of thing," the captain said. "And you're confident if we don't allow ourselves to be provoked, there'll be no conflict."

Earthedge

"Positive, sir." Nosehair, clearly pleased with his analysis, smiled as he looked about the bridge. "No conflict, not yet, sir."

"Captain!" the First Officer shouted from the passageway, "We're seeing combat, sir!"

"Combat where? The Brits' HQ?"

"No sir, the Royal Academy. Not too much yet, sir, still kinda dark, but we are seeing gunfire and explosions."

"The Academy, they're the bunch that nearly sank the Mae West," murmured the captain. "Is it the Russians? Have they attacked?"

"Don't think so, sir. But hey, sir, jeez, I can't be certain—still a little too dark—but that sure looks like two more of them projectile things … see, there, on them rails at the back of that building, sir. Seems like they're getting ready to lift them into those two giant cannons."

"No conflict, my ass. All right, we'll sweep over the site, have a look-see," the captain ordered. "If they're planning to launch more projectiles, I want to be right on top of them when they do."

"Whoa," shouted the first officer, "huge explosion! Seems like someone just hit the Academy magazine!"

"You know, flying over London will mean entering their airspace, Captain," cautioned the helmsman.

"We're entering on compassionate grounds. We've observed a terrible explosion and want to help if we can," the captain replied.

"Will people believe that?" the first officer asked.

"This could be the Brits' ruse to draw us into conflict, sir," murmured Lieutenant Nosehair.

"Just do it," the captain grumbled.

Chapter Sixty-Eight

Royal and Ancient Academy Rocketry Laboratory

Edmund had no sooner left the entrance hall than another colossal blast rocked the Academy. Behind him, he heard the dozen smartypants who'd been attempting to barricade the devastated entrance now scream in agony and cry for help. Edmund had no help to give. At all costs, he had to get to rocketry. Progress down the corridor was terrifyingly slow. Plaster, broken furniture, three wounded smartypants, and several collapsed old gents rendered the rocketry hall almost impassable. He'd also been expecting a blast from an Earthedger's lightning shooter to strike him from behind at any moment, but at last he reached the rocketry door.

To clear a passage, the automaton accompanying Edmund had to kick an unconscious greybeard to one side. However, just as Edmund entered the laboratory, there was a deafening boom, a blast far greater than any previous. Every bit of broken glass in the complex was shattered into still smaller fragments. Shards flew in all directions, embedding themselves in walls, floors and furniture. The door afforded Edmund a measure of protection, but the greybeard at his feet was not so fortunate. In the aftermath of the explosion, as the building shook violently, doors fell from their hinges, furniture toppled, and Edmund's portrait—a fixture in every laboratory—tumbled to the ground. Badly shaken but uninjured, Edmund took a moment to regain his senses and then pedaled across the broken glass and crumbled plaster to peer out one of the shattered windows. The location of the blast was unmistakable. Where once had stood the explosives wing, there was now only a smoldering pit.

"Uh ... so you're here," Lollipop Crossingguard said as she limped into the room. "I thought you'd be with your projectiles."

"You," Edmund growled, "what's happened to you?"

"Your madman, Natterer."

Basenote, who had a piece of glass embedded in his thigh, staggered into the room, gritting his teeth and attempting to pull the shard from his flesh as he walked. "Arrgh!" he shouted as it came free. He dropped the glass, looked up, and discovered the chancellor staring at Lollipop with a homicidal glare.

"And then he set you free?" Edmund asked. "Why are you still here?"

"We wanted to watch the launch," Lollipop replied, her voice calm and defiant.

"Why?" Edmund's eyes narrowed with suspicion. His voice dropped. "What have you done?"

At that moment, Natterer appeared in the doorway. He leaned against the doorframe to catch his breath. "That last blast caught us by surprise, but I've gathered several smartypants, and we're—" He stopped mid-sentence when he spotted Lollipop. "How the hell did you escape?" he shouted and charged at her.

Hobby was just about to strike Lollipop when Edmund said, "Wait! You said she escaped? From where?"

"I'd tied her up in mathematography. I was doing a little finger-snapping …."

"Why?" Edmund asked. "Why?" he shrieked again.

"Yes, tell him why," Lollipop said.

"Because …because …." Clearly, Hobby was unwilling to admit Lollipop had escaped his surveillance.

"Because he lost sight of me," Lollipop answered with a wry smile. "And after you'd warned him not to, Lord Edmund."

"Is this true?" Edmund asked the smartypants.

"She left the estate," Hobby whined, his voice rising in desperation. "She's been in touch with the Earthedgers."

"He's guessing. I went out to check on my parents, that's all."

Hobby shouted, "She's lying, I swear! She knows … she knows things only the edgers could have told her. She must have met up with them."

"He's the one who's lying," Lollipop said. "I don't know any edgers."

Edward pedaled across the room and up to Lollipop, and said, "Either he's lying … or you are. How will I ever know?" Suddenly, Edward grabbed Lollipop's bandaged hand and squeezed. She screamed and sobbed for breath.

"Of course, I know who's lying," Edmund sneered. "Natterer is an ass for letting you out of his sight, but he would never lie to me. No, you're lying. You escaped the Academy and now you're going to tell me what you did."

"Nothing!" she cried out. Edmund squeezed her hand a second time. She shrieked and gasped. "I told you. I went to … to check on my parents."

"Enough. Enough! I know your parents left London days ago. What did you do?" He released her hand only to slap her hard across the face. "Did you touch the projectiles? Did you change the targeting coordinates?" He struck her again and again until blood flowed in a steady stream from her mouth and nose.

"I never went … near the projectiles," she whispered through her swollen lips.

"Did she go near the projectiles?" Edmund bellowed at Hobby.

"I … I don't know, I don't think so."

"We have to know. We have to find out. You!" Edmund shouted at Basenote.

Basenote slumped to the floor, holding his hand over the gaping wound in his leg. "Sir, I know nothing. I found Miss Crossingguard bound up in mathematography and untied her. That's all."

"He's telling the truth," Lollipop whispered.

Edmund turned to Hobby. "Signal the launch crew. Ask if the flight control clockworks or the programming cards have been tampered with. Go now!"

"But sir, I don't know semaphore—"

"Find someone who does, you fool!"

"Right," Natterer said as he raced out of the room.

The crack of rifle fire and the hiss and crackle of shockshooter blasts beyond the laboratory door drew ever closer.

Eventually, Hobby came running back in. "Sir, the Earthedgers, they've retaken the grand entrance. We're going to have to move. And I'm told an American airship has appeared over the city."

"Over London? Is it dropping bombs?"

"No sir."

"Then war has not yet been declared. All right, so what did the launch team say?" Edmund asked. "Has anyone tampered with the projectiles?"

"They can't tell, sir."

"Damn those blithernits! We can't launch if she's changed the coordinates, and we won't get our declaration of war unless we do." Shaking his head, Edmund glared at Lollipop and muttered something unintelligible.

Outside in the corridor, lightning bolts whizzed past the laboratory door.

"Please, sir, we have to move," Natterer whimpered.

"That's it! That's what we'll do," Edmund cried out. "We'll go to the launch site and I'll reprogram the projectiles to hit that airship. No complicated math in that, and we'll have our war."

He pedaled back to Lollipop, whacked her across the face, and said, "You're about to die, young lady, and for what? The Realm will have its war. We shall deal with your new friends soon enough. The damage they've inflicted is only minor, and I shall rebuild the Academy more grand and powerful than ever before."

The words were no sooner out of Lord Edmund's mouth than the world went mad. A deafening blast followed by a maelstrom of stone, plaster, and glass, and then clouds of dense smoke and dust raced through the Academy. The floor beneath their feet rolled like the deck of a ship in a storm-tossed sea. The ceilings above them buckled and cracked and rained plaster and lathe down upon them like an avalanche in the Alps.

Chapter Sixty-Nine

Royal and Ancient Academy Estate Gatehouse

The moment Bedazzles's culverin blasted away the doors of the Academy, the four scribblers raced up Snapthrottle Hill to the gatehouse, there to witness the Earthedgers' assault.

Deafened by the blaring drums, gatehouse guards had first been stunned and then bewildered by the cacophony. After a moment's hesitation, they'd packed their ears with crumpled paper, grabbed their rifles and started up the avenue toward the courtyard and Palladian staircase. But then, as blinding lights suddenly illuminated the night, they'd panicked and fled back down the avenue, past the writhing heap of mangled automata and out of the estate, leaving the gates wide open as they ran away.

At first, the scribblers moved gingerly through the gates, but then one climbed onto the gatehouse roof for a better view over the great lawn. Others followed. From their vantage, they could see the automata had already been reduced to one long heap of writhing tin limbs. They watched as the smartypants were first sickened by the flashing lights and then reduced to quivering idiots by the wall of shockshooter fire.

The scribblers were overawed by the series of explosions that filled the dawn sky with every color in the rainbow, then terrified as a second cannon blast sent the MacPherson Tower crashing to the ground. They witnessed greybeards abandoning the Academy building, then scampering away on wobbly legs across the lawn and down the avenue toward the gate.

It briefly appeared the smartypants might regroup but then a massive explosion, far larger than any previous, rocked the entire estate.

And now they were witnessing the strangest sights of all. First, from out of the heavy grey clouds enshrouding the old city, an American airship emerged, its unmistakable shape striking fear into the hearts of the many Londoners who'd endured the relentless firebombing during the last American war. The airship was now all but stationary below the cloud layer.

And then a tiny flying machine appeared from out of the early morning mists. It skimmed the tops of the elmwood forests surrounding the Academy estate. The machine was far too small for its enormous fan to be powered by any known type of steam engine. It putt-putted along, weaving and turning, rising and swooping like a goldfinch over a grassy meadow. Silhouetted against the grey morning sky, its passenger was seen to momentarily wave. Then the curious vehicle went into a heart-stopping dive. It swooped down over the Academy edifice, and a small sack or ball of some sort fell from the machine's underbelly. For a brief moment, all was quiet as the flying machine climbed gracefully and then turned slowly toward the silvery horizon.

In the wink of an eye, the calm was shattered. A single enormous ball of fire rose into the heavens, and the entire north end of the Academy vanished. The fiery orb was followed by a thunderous roar that rolled across the Middlesex hills. And only as the cloud of flaming debris and smoke began to clear did it become apparent the Mary Toft Theater had been wiped from the face of the Earth.

The flying machine slowly puttered away into the watery light of dawn. Its pilot gave one last wave to someone apparently concealed in the meadow below before his craft was once again lost in the morning mists.

Chapter Seventy

Behind the Royal and Ancient Academy

"Get me up, get me up!" Lord Edmund screamed as he regained consciousness. He found himself sprawled across broken beams and fractured plaster moldings. Crawling off the beam, Edmund realized he was bleeding from a large head wound. The force of the blast had thrown Edmund across the laboratory, where he now wriggled about the floor like a goldfish flipped from its bowl.

Nearby, Hobby Natterer stood dumbfounded, motionless, staring helplessly at his shattered left arm. He was covered from head to toe in plaster dust, save for the line of drool dangling from his open mouth.

"Natterer! Natterer!" the chancellor shouted.

Natterer's head moved slightly. Like a man sleepwalking, he slowly turned his head in Edmund's direction. His face bore no expression, no hint of recognition, no apparent concern. Natterer blinked several times, and as some semblance of awareness returned, he asked softly, "What ... what happened?"

"How the hell should I know," Edmund shouted, "a bomb of some kind."

"We should ... we should run."

"No, you fool, we can't run," Edmund replied. "We have a job to do."

Like an automaton himself, Hobby walked slowly toward Edmund. As the fog in his brain began to lift, he looked around the scene of devastation that had been the rocketry department. That bitch, the mathematography girl, lay buried beneath rubble, with only her face visible amid all the broken bricks and plaster. The potbellied boy from the calculating engine was pinned against the wall. Two automata were trapped beneath beams and one remained standing, motionless, and covered in dust.

"Get me up, you fool," Edmund ordered. "We've got to get to the projectiles!"

"My arm," said Hobby, staring at the shredded sleeve of his shirt and the exposed bones and tissue beneath. Curiously, he didn't feel a thing, just a bit of a chill.

"Never mind your damned arm. Bring my trike."

Hobby was slowly coming to his senses. "Trike won't work in all this mess, sir."

"All right, that automaton. Wind it up. It can carry me."

Outside the laboratory, rifle fire and shockshooter blasts had resumed.

"Getting closer, sir," said Hobby as he switched on the automaton. It staggered across the rubble and hoisted Edmund into its arms.

"Right, let's go," the chancellor ordered, his broad rump dangling between the automaton's arms.

"Where to, sir?" asked a bewildered Natterer.

"I told you! To the launch site, fool."

"But that's a league away, sir, across open ground. We'll be nesting swans, sir, easy targets."

"Then you'll just have to fire back, won't you, you ass! That's why you have a gun, isn't it?" Edmund shouted. "Find more smartypants to help. We have to get to the projectiles. We've got to shoot down that airship."

Chapter Seventy-One

Royal and Ancient Academy Cellar

The captain's warning gave us only moments to prepare for the coming destruction of the Mary Toft Theater. Covert, Pewter, and I managed to secure ourselves in the gents' locker room. The palatial convenience boasted Grecian tiles, massage tables, spacious cubicles with marble flushbowls, walnut lockers with gold hangers, and perfumed thermal baths. We toppled lockers to create a bunker, and there we waited for Bottomly's flying machine to do its worst.

Its worst was more devastating than we could ever have imagined. After the blast, we climbed out from beneath our walnut bolthole to find walls flattened, baths ruptured, and doors torn away. Up on the ground floor, we discovered the entire north wing of the Academy was a thing of the past. Gone too were any remaining smartypants in the entrance hall.

Its pedestal was all that remained of a pillar that once rose several stories up to the vaulted ceiling of the entrance hall. We hid behind it and set up the messaging machine. To the captain, I signaled, "Would seem the Academy is almost ours. Proceeding with caution. Building not structurally sound. Sending everyone outside. Don't know what surprises await."

By which I meant, I didn't know where Hobby Natterer was hiding.

"Well done," came the captain's reply. "Any sign of Miss Crossingguard?"

"No," I signal back, although I still didn't understand why the captain was concerned about her. We were clearly up to the job of destroying the projectiles. We didn't need an untrustworthy slip of a girl.

The captain's next message came as a shock.

> Received semaphore from American airship overhead. Its crew spotted explosions at Academy. Has come to offer humanitarian aid. Also warns any aggressive moves on our part will be deemed

declaration of war. The girl said she was going to re-target the projectiles. But even if she has, a launch will almost certainly provoke the Americans.

"So, should we blow them up?" I replied.

"No," came the captain's immediate response. "Explosives too dangerous. Only option is to stop launch. Means you must find the girl."

A nervous chill seized my heart.

But what if the girl has betrayed us? What if she hasn't re-targeted the projectiles and we can't stop their launch? What do we do then? Hunt her down? Take revenge?

Chapter Seventy-Two

Royal and Ancient Academy Rocketry Laboratory

We spotted several smartypants disappearing around the corner at the far end of the corridor. Knobfiddlers had advised us this hallway would lead directly to rocketry and there we might find the young woman, Lollipop Crossingguard. The captain might have believed she was what she claimed to be, an ally and friend of our cause, but I feared she was just as likely to be a treacherous enemy. Worse, she might be an ally of the man who'd murdered Marigold. I feared she was up ahead, waiting in ambush with the smartypants we'd just seen.

Most doors in the corridor had been blown off their hinges by the recent explosions. Many were blocked by fallen plaster and splintered woodwork. Even so, we cleared each doorway and entered every room. But then, from a room several doorways ahead, we heard a frantic cry.

It was a man's voice. "Please, you've got to stay awake, please Lollipop, you mustn't die."

We raced to the room and discovered a young potbellied man lifting splintered furniture and large pieces of lathe and plaster from the body of an unconscious Lollipop Crossingguard.

"Is she ... is she alive?" I asked. So, she wasn't waiting in ambush then. But that meant we needed her. We needed her desperately. If she died, how would we ever prevent the launch?

"Please, you've got to help me free her," the knobfiddler pleaded.

"Yes, but is she alive?" I knelt at her side. Her face was a mass of cuts and bruises and her hand was wrapped in a bloody towel. A moment ago, I'd feared this girl might be my enemy, but now ... now I was suddenly overcome by a wave of concern for her. Who had done this to her?

"I think she's alive, just barely. But it's a wonder," the young man said as he pulled debris from the girl's bloodied and twisted body. "She's been beaten by Lord Edmund, had her fingers cracked by that smartypants, Natterer, and now been blown up by you lot."

As we lifted a massive piece of the ceiling plaster from her chest, Lollipop drew a short sharp breath and opened her eyes.

The knobfiddler and I raised Lollipop into a sitting position. Then I took her bandaged hand—and she let out a most blood-curdling scream and flopped backward, insensible once again.

"Her fingers, it's her fingers," cried the young man. "Natterer, he shattered them. Look there. See?" The knobfiddler loosened the cloth wrapped around her fingers.

I almost gagged at the sight. "Why ... why did Natterer do that?"

"Because she left the estate yesterday and because she wouldn't say who she'd met or whether she'd tampered with the projectiles."

"Brave," is all I was able to say.

"Yes," replied her friend, "the bravest."

"Can you help us?" I asked the young man. "We've been ordered to stop the launch at any cost."

Lollipop's eyes opened. "No, please," she said in a frail voice. "Please, you mustn't stop the launch."

"Are you ... are you all right?" I asked.

"Did you hear me? Don't stop the launch. I've already changed their targeting."

"But Lollipop," said her friend, "Lord Edmund's on his way to the launch site right now to make his own changes. He intends to target an American airship. It's right overhead."

Lollipop said, "Then we have to stop *him*," as she tried to stand.

"I can see them!" Pewter Doubting shouted. Pewter was crouched by a window overlooking the back lawn.

I raced to the window. From there, we could see the rocketry rails and, in the distance, the launch complex itself. The railway lines followed a muddy track for a league and then ran alongside several tin sheds. The rails turned to the right, went around the far end of the huts, and disappeared.

"Is that Lord Edmund being carried by that automaton?" asked Pewter.

A bullet smashed into the window frame spraying stone and glass fragments all over the laboratory.

"Where the hell?" I exclaimed.

"There! See?" Pewter said, peeking carefully over the edge of the shattered frame. "Smartypants, several of them, following behind the chancellor fella. They're shooting at us."

I crouched below the window, carefully raised my head to see, and sure enough, I spotted Hobby Natterer among the smartypants. "I have to get him," I shouted. Staying low, I darted back across the room to grab my shockshooter from the floor beside Lollipop.

"No, you can't!" Pew shouted. "You'll be dead the moment you step outside. Their rifles have a far greater range than your shockshooter."

With her uninjured hand, Lollipop grasped my arm. "Stalwart, we can't just stop Natterer. We have to stop Edmund," she whispered.

"Natterer is all I'm interested in."

"Use your brains," she said angrily. "If we stop Edmund, we stop Natterer. You'll still have your revenge."

"What revenge?" Pewter asked, "Who's talking about revenge?"

I was suddenly embarrassed. Lollipop was staring right at me, and I at her. Bloodied, buried beneath the debris, in agony, and yet there it was in her eyes, her incredible strength, her extraordinary courage.

"No one," I said. "Okay, so how do we stop the chancellor?"

"Could you use your shockshooters?" Lollipop asked.

"No, they only have a range of fifty fathoms or so," Pewter replied.

"And there's no way for us to launch the projectiles from here? Before Edmund reaches them, I mean?" I asked.

"No. You have to ignite a trail of black powder that runs from the launch shed to the cannon with a spark," answered the young man at Lollipop's side.

"With a spark," I repeated. And then it came to me. "A spark, yes."

"What are you thinking?" Covert asked.

"Well, our shockshooters emit a bolt of lightning." I began sorting out the issues in my head as I spoke. "But the bolt actually travels much farther than the fifty fathoms we're able to aim it, much farther, more than a league in fact. However—"

Covert interrupted excitedly, "However, if we could predict where the bolt will eventually go, then . . . then we just might be able to ignite the black powder."

"Right," I exclaimed. "It's a fractal! My father had this friend, Benoit Mandel something," I muttered as I grabbed a piece of paper from the debris on the floor. "Uncle Benny, I called him. Anyway, he told Dad that lightning's path is a fractal."

"A what?" Lollipop asks.

"A fractal," I replied. "Covert, quick, set up the message machine. I need Gemeny."

Chapter Seventy-Three

Royal and Ancient Academy Projectile Launch Site

His spine was twisted almost to cracking, he had no feeling in his legs, and he was gripping the metal chest plate of the automaton so tightly its ragged tin edge was slicing into his fingers. But he had to hang on. He had to make it to the launch site. He would not be humiliated by Wordsmouth's thugs. He would not disappoint the king. Lord Edmund, Chancellor of the Royal and Ancient Academy, had pledged to his beloved monarch to launch the Academy projectiles—and launch them he would. The king had said He was relying on Edmund to save the Realm, and nothing—NOTHING—was going to prevent him from justifying the king's confidence.

Tacky showmen like Bilbury, clotheshorses like Trolleysmash, and fraudsters like the lord chamberlain might let the king down, but Lord Edmund of Muckyheath would not. Oh no, he would not. All his life, Edmund had known his true worth to the nation when others—prettier, snootier, smarmier—had doubted it, questioned his competence, and whispered their libelous suspicions behind his back. Well, he was going to have the last laugh. Once and for all, he was going to prove his worth as a Garter councilor even if it was the last thing he did. Perhaps he should have left instructions with Scribben for a national day of mourning in the event of—

Suddenly the automaton stopped, its arms fell to its sides, and Edmund dropped face-first into the mud.

"What the …," he spluttered as he struggled to pull his face from the muck. "Why in hell?" he bellowed, wiping his mouth with his working hand and spitting filth at the legs of the automaton. The lifeless tin man stood over him as stiff as a scarecrow. *"Stercus, stercus, stercus!"* Edmund screamed. "Wind the damn thing," he bellowed at the smartypants. "Wind it, hurry!"

Hobby raced to the automaton, wound the cog between its shoulder blades, and flipped the toggle. The automaton lifted Edmund from the dirt, but because the mud-caked chancellor was so slippery, it had to bundle

Edmund over its shoulder like a sack of dirty laundry. Edmund could hardly breathe, and remnants of the previous evening's dinner dribbled from his mouth as he bounced along on the automaton's shoulder. But he wasn't going to complain. Getting to the launch site was all that mattered.

Down he tumbled a second time. This time the automaton fell with him, tripped up by the condition of the trail. The tin man was sprawled in the mud, its legs still mindlessly marching along and flinging mud in every direction.

"Get us up!" Edmund screamed. "Get us up!" It took two smartypants to get the automaton back on its feet and Edmund up into its arms once again. "Now, you two, support the automaton. Don't let him stumble again. He stumbles, you die! Understood?"

Progress was excruciatingly slow. Fortunately, there was no sign of pursuit. "Watch that door," Edmund shouted at the smartypants. "Any sign of movement, you shoot to kill."

Lightning bolts from an Earthedger's weapon struck the Earth some distance behind them, sending sparks and flashes scattering in all directions. Apparently, Edmund and company were now out of the Earthedgers' range.

What a stroke of luck, the airship showing up. Edmund looked up into the early morning sky. Huge thing, the airship, and so gaudy with its ridiculous stars and stripes up there, slowly circling like an overfed vulture. Well, its luck was about to run out. No way the Academy projectiles could miss the airship at this range.

"As soon as we reach the sheds, take me straight to the cannons," Edmund ordered Natterer.

"Not to the firing shed?"

"No, to the cannons. I'm sure that girl has changed the projectiles' targeting, so I have to re-target them. It shouldn't be hard to hit that ship. We bring down that airship and we have our war."

Chapter Seventy-Four

Royal and Ancient Academy Rocketry Laboratory

"Sorry, but I don't know fractal geometry," Gemeny replied to my signal, "Your father mentioned fractals, but he never explained."

My heart sank as I answered her message. "Okay, thanks." But there was no way I could do the math alone.

"Stalwart," Lollipop asked, "what are these fractal things?"

"A fractal's a kind of pattern. When it's subdivided, each part of the fractal has exactly the same properties as the whole. It's like what we see all the time in nature; like a fern, for example, or the branches of a tree."

As I spoke, I examined my shockshooter and its various settings and, at the same time, wracked my brain for some memory of Father's musings on fractals. When Father'd been excited by something, he couldn't help but drone on about it.

"My father called fractals the new geometry, the geometry for nature. His friend Benny came up with the name. Benny described fractals as a way to see infinity. He and Dad and several other math fanatics met Wednesday nights over pilsner and smoked meat at Benny's deli to tackle math problems together."

"And your dad taught you this new geometry?"

"Covert, could you increase the gain on this shooter to maybe 50?" I asked, "and maybe switch the load to the lower branch of the burst?" I then turned back to Lollipop, "Sorry, what?"

"Your dad knew this fractal stuff?"

"Oh yeah. When we were hiding in the Highlands, Father and I'd go up into the hills and do the fractal math for wildflowers and insects … and lightning."

"And you think a shockshooter blast might obey the rules of this fractal geometry?" asked Lollipop's knobfiddler friend.

"Maybe, but I don't know for sure."

Earthedge

"But we could try. If you can do the calculating," Lollipop said softly.

"Me? No, not me," I replied as I watched Covert open the shockshooter gain control and make the adjustment. "That's good."

"Chancellor's almost at the sheds," shouted Pewter. "Running out of time."

"Stalwart, Stalwart, look at me," said Lollipop.

I looked up from my scribblings and into this girl's lovely face, and for an instant, I saw the same fire in her eyes that had so captivated me in Marigold's.

"Stalwart, no one else can do this. You ... you have to try."

"You will do miracles. I know you will," I hear Marigold say.

"Oh damn," I muttered, and then, "Okay, so while I do the math, Covert, you and Pewter, you've got to mount my shooter in the window and set it to max. How far is the launch pad?"

"Guessing maybe a league?" Pewter said. "That Edmund fella, he's got maybe fifty fathoms to go."

I scribbled furiously. At first, I was breathless with nervous excitement, then stunned how it all somehow started to come back to me, the algorithms, the variables, the distortions, Dad, Mother . . . .

I hear their voices, sense their presence, feel Mother's fingers run through my hair, Dad's arm around my shoulder. I smell his soap, feel the scratch of the heather beneath my legs, the rasp of Dad's jersey on my cheek, the chill breeze dancing down the slopes of Ben Nevis, fluttering the pages of our workbook. I hear him say, "Now let's see you calculate that daisy. And remember, lad, all you can do is . . . ."

"I know, try. But I'm . . . I'm just not sure," I muttered.

But then . . . Marigold whispers to me, *"You will do miracles . . . if you try . . . try as we might have tried . . . together."*

And it's done!

Chapter Seventy-Five

Projectile Launch Site

"There!" roared Lord Edmund as he thumped his one good hand against the automaton's breastplate, "take me there, yes, by the cannon, you brainless tin can." The automaton trudged up to the base of the space cannon and dropped Edmund into the mud for the third time. Coughing and spluttering, Edmund lifted his face from the muck, muttering, "You're doing it on purpose. Who programmed you? Who? Is it someone's idea of a joke? I'll have his dangly-bits on a skewer when this is all over."

Two smartypants assigned to the launch detail scurried to the chancellor's aid.

"Lord Edmund, forgive us, your Lordship, we didn't know what to do, sir, we can't tell, sir. We can't tell if anything's been tampered with."

"Lift me up, damn you, up," Edmund grumbled. The smartypants hoisted him from the ground. "Higher, you fools, I need to see the projectile's targeting cards."

Much grunting and groaning ensued as the smartypants hauled Edmund up the stairs to the cannon barrel and heaved him onto their shoulders.

"There, right, now a touch higher, good, that's good."

At last, Edmund was able to lean over the edge of the cannon and peer down at the projectile nested within the barrel mere inches beneath its rim. From there he could see the targeting receptacle, a small, foot-square hatch closed by four bolts on the side of the projectile's little pointy tip.

"Oh, *stercus*, no!" Edmund shouted. "The bolts! They're loose, didn't you notice? They've been removed and only partially reinserted. You couldn't see that? You idiots! Even one of these damned tin men could tell what that girl has done! Higher, damn you, lift me higher. I have to reach the hatch! And pass me a screw turny-thing, I've got to get the targeting cards ou—"

At that moment, a blazing light engulfed the launch site, a white light so intense it was as though the Earth had suddenly been consumed by a star.

Time slowed. The chancellor's first thought was, 'Ah, the limelight at last.' But then, from his outstretched arm, from amidst its blistering and bubbling flesh, he watched his bones emerge. Crackling white flames danced down his blackening arm and swept across his chest.

He felt nothing, knew no fear, and had only a vague sense of curiosity at this bizarre turn of events. But then he noticed that Hobby Natterer at the base of the cannon was beginning to melt. Natterer's mouth opened wide, but no sound came out. Hobby's cheeks dripped from his skull like hot tar running down the hull of a ship.

Edmund was falling now, down toward the boiling, bubbling mud, as the smartypants who'd been holding him aloft were turned to ash.

From above the rim of the space cannon, there appeared a flicker of intense yellow flame. It began to grow, grow like a dandelion opening at dawn, like a sunflower in the summer heat bursting into bloom. The yellow sunflower grew ever larger, enveloping first the cannon, then Edmund, then all about him, until its petals consumed the whole world. Everything disappeared in a whirlwind of golden light. Edmund's last coherent thought was *in a blaze of glory* before the innumerable tiny pieces of his being were transfigured into points of excruciating pain. Only then did Lord Edmund mercifully vanish in a scarlet mist amid the swirling gold.

Chapter Seventy-Six

Aboard USAS *Bolsadeviento*

"Holy crap! Sorry sir, but there's so much goin' on down there!" cried the seaman on the scope.

"Details, man," Haggis ordered.

"Well, sir, first the big doors on that Academy building gets blown to bits. Then there's all these flashing lights and lightning bolts and colorful explosions. Then this tower gets flattened. Then some big shed sticking out the back blows up like it was packed with bombs or stuff. Then this flying machine comes chugging over the estate, and the whole damn north end of the place gets blown to kingdom come. Cripes, that's some fight them limeys are havin', sir."

"Yeah, but who's fighting who? That's what we need to know," murmured the captain.

"Sir, another semaphore message from the Goodwind Sands Lightship, sir," reported the first officer. "They're asking if we could be so kind as to let them know what's happening at the Academy?"

"What the . . .? They don't know? It's their goddamn city!" barked Haggis. "Great gater's gonads, what a load of tulip-waving, meadow dancing, skiptrippers they are. Look, send them another semaphore message. This time, say they can play their little game of namby-pamby, 'scusey-me, tea-sipping, baby finger in the goddamn air, dollytalk all they want. But the moment any of their guys threaten my ship, they won't know what the bullturd hit them. And send the same signal to the guys down in that field, whoever the hell they are. This little game of theirs is fooling no one. They're getting ready for something big. I can feel it."

"Aye, sir," replied the first officer.

"And send a carrier pigeon back to St. Malo. Say I intend to exercise my executive authority and respond in kind if attacked. And get some guys on our mortars. Tell them to stand by for my signal."

"Holy crap, sir. Huge blast from one of them lightning guns, sir, huge sir, biggest yet. Looks like it fried a whole bunch a' fellas near them cannons. Whoa, here we go, sir! Projectiles in the air! Projectiles in the air!"

"Trajectory?"

"Coming straight at us, sir, five thousand feet, four thousand …."

"Do we drop ordnance, sir?" shouted the first officer.

"No, hold fire," answered Haggis.

"Three thousand, two … no wait, they're turning!" screamed the seaman on the scope, "jeez, they're turning, sir! Leveling out now, sir, they're heading out over the channel."

"South? They're heading south?"

"Aye, sir."

"What the Billie's baubles are they up to?"

Chapter Seventy-Seven

Loire Valley, Château de Pleurnicher

It was going to be a glorious spring day in the Loire. He'd bicycle the six miles into Monts mid-morning to pick up a selection of fresh cheeses and breads and to order another case of gin for Her Majesty. One could never have enough gin in stock for Queen Wallis.

Bosquette had received word only the previous day that the king and queen would arrive by steam charabanc that afternoon. He'd not been given the customary two-weeks' notice to prepare for a royal holiday in the French countryside. But not to worry. The chateau was always immaculate and the kitchens were always abundantly provisioned. And fortunately, he'd re-stocked the Balmoral trunk with its requisite Celtic paraphernalia just the previous week: a new haggis, three new bottles of whisky, thistles, muddy boots, a torn kilt, and several knitted socks with holes in the toes.

It offended Bosquette that a British monarch felt compelled to conceal his visits to France from his own subjects by pretending he'd holidayed in bone-chilling, skin-scratching, stomach-churning Scotland. But if King Edward thought he needed to include Scottish bits and pieces in his luggage on his return to London to pull off the ruse, it was the king's prerogative. Besides, that was the British for you: devious, always creeping about, keeping their secrets.

Bosquette would finish picking flowers for the vestibule and then select produce for the dinner party planned for that evening. Chef Lyon trusted him entirely to do the choosing. Chateau staff would arrive at noon, plenty of time to remove the sheets from the furniture, air the building, and prepare for the evening affair. It was going to be a lovely soiree. King Edward had sent word on ahead to invite a dozen local friends and celebrities for a small dinner party. Their guests would arrive around 6:00 for drinks on the garden terrace and dine in the Orangery at 9:00. No word yet whether the string quartet was going to make it, but that might be just as well since all their fingering and fiddling tended to make Queen Wallis quite nauseous. Better to have Jacques, her upstairs attendant, perform Joplin on the piano than upset her with Schumann. Perhaps he'd best cancel the booking for the quartet altogether on his way into town for the gin.

Bosquette straightened up, gathered the flowers he'd cut into his arms, and looked fondly across the broad lawns at the castle itself. Château de Pleurnicher was a fine-looking property. He'd lived in the area all of his life. The château had always been a thing of pride for the locals, even when it passed into the hands of the British monarch. A 600-year-old estate, Château de Pleurnicher had already been substantially renovated by its previous owner, Charles Baudoin, a Franco-American industrialist, when the king and queen purchased it as the site of their secret nuptials. All its eight bedrooms were fitted with the new Crapper water closets and had American bathtubs, which could be filled and emptied in under a minute. It had orchards, a woodlot, swimming pool, gymnasium, a golf course and a tennis court, and of course, the most extensive liquor cellar in the region, designed expressly for Her Majesty.

Visits by His Majesty the King were always a pleasure. He was such a genial fellow. Truth to tell, however, the longer the royals remained, the more wearing Her Majesty became—but he wasn't going to think about that now. Things were going so well, he wouldn't let any dark thoughts ruin such a fine day. The air was filled with birdsong and the sweet scent of his bouquet. The trees rustled in the gentle breeze. The sky was the most beautiful blue with just a few white, puffy....

What was that? That high-pitched buzz. It was growing in intensity. There, up there, coming out of that cloud, a great black ball with paddles on it. Hurtling across the sky. And it had a smoke trail like it was on fire. Now it was dropping, dropping toward the château.

***

The blast knocked Bosquette face-first into the flower patch. He didn't move for several minutes as the ringing in his ears subsided and the painful pounding in his head lessened somewhat. Gradually he lifted his face from the roses, wiping dirt and blood from his eyes and spitting blossoms from his mouth. As his vision cleared, he got to his knees, brushed dirt and grass cuttings and the remnants of his bouquet from his trousers and shirtfront and stood up. The sight took his breath away.

Where moments earlier had stood the stately château, now there was only a smoking ruin. Fragments of its centuries-old walls were still standing, and several small fires were still smoldering in the ruins of the Orangery and the long gallery. But nothing was left of Château de Pleurnicher above its ground floor.

"Oh dear," Bosquette mutters, "that will take a lot of cleaning up before the king arrives."

Chapter Seventy-Eight

Royal and Ancient Academy Rocketry Laboratory

Pewter, Covert, and I watched in awe as the two projectiles emerged from the cannons, spewing waves of flame and then rising from the Earth, slowly at first, then gaining speed as they climbed into the grey morning sky. Their roar was deafening.

Even at this distance, I witnessed Hobby Natterer and Lord Edmund being consumed by the eruption of fire. The sight left me . . . cold.

"Did it work? Did it work?" Lollipop exclaimed as best she could from the floor and the heap of debris beneath which she was still pinned.

"You're damned right," hooted Pewter. "Stalwart's numbers worked an absolute treat."

"That's nice," sighed Lollipop and then closed her eyes.

The estate had fallen silent. The crack and crackle of shockshooter blasts had ended. The few automata still intact were standing about, motionless. A handful of smartypants had thrown down their rifles and were heading for the front of the building.

Pewter sent a message to the captain advising our teammates they need not be concerned about the projectiles. They'd been dispatched out over the channel en route to inconsequential targets.

"Robbies are coming up Snapthrottle Hill," replied the captain. "We're heading back to the fireworks factory. We'll meet you there and make our arrangements for departure."

I took a last look out the window at the blackened patch of grass by the launch shed where once had stood Lord Edmund and Hobby Natterer. I should have felt some satisfaction, but I didn't. They were gone, it was over, and that was that. Now my concern, I realized, was not for the life that I'd wanted to take, but for the life of the brave young woman to whom we Earthedgers owed ours.

I crossed the room and bent down beside her. Her eyes were still closed. Her potbellied friend had found a damp cloth somewhere and was gently wiping plaster dust from her face.

"I want to thank you," I said to her, "and to apologize."

She opened her eyes and whispered, "Apologize? What for?"

The friend gave his cloth to me and then tried to adjust the bandage on Lollipop's hand to fully cover her injuries.

"I … I thought you were on their side."

"Ah well, and I thought you were a self-absorbed pretty boy. So we're even."

"You thought I was pretty?"

She looked into my eyes and smiled.

"Say," I asked, "where are the projectiles going anyway?"

Her eyes suddenly filled with horror. "Oh biscuits! How long have they been in the air?" she yelled.

"I don't know, ten minutes maybe. Why?" Her alarm was disquieting, frightening.

"We've got to get out of here!" She pushed the cloth away from her face and struggled to escape from beneath the remaining debris. "Help me up, quick, please!"

"No, you can't get up, not yet," I said firmly. "A medicator needs to look at you."

"No," she screamed, "we've got to get out of here!"

That's when I first heard the faint high-pitched buzz.

"What's that?" I asked.

"Really? You can't guess?" Lollipop shouted as she pushed aside a slab of plaster and tried to stand.

"Oh no!" I exclaimed. "Don't tell me you made the Academy the target!"

"Only for one of the projectiles."

"Oh, well, that's all right then," I exclaimed. "Why did you do that? Were you mad?"

"Maybe because I thought your assault would fail. That's why."

"So," I muttered as I lifted her into my arms, "it turns out we didn't trust each other, not one bit."

Grimacing in pain, she whispered, "And now we have to run for our lives … together."

"Must say, Miss Crossingguard," I gasped as I clutched her to my chest and clambered over heaps of plaster and splintered wood, "this is no way to begin a friendship."

Chapter Seventy-Nine

Grounds of the Royal Academy

We escaped through a maintenance corridor beneath Lord Edmund's office and out the south end of the Academy. At the edge of the great lawn, I paused with Miss Crossingguard still in my arms and spun about just in time to see the projectile descend through the cloud cover and disappear into the crater that had been the Mary Toft Theater.

Trees splintered and shrubbery burst into flame. A massive plume of debris rose high above the blast site and darkened the sky. All around us terrified greybeards, knobfiddlers, and smartypants dove for cover.

I dropped Miss Crossingguard as gently as I could into the long grass alongside the fractured wall of a garden shed and arched myself over her as a shield against the deluge of debris which was sure to come. When the blast's deafening shock wave struck, it was all I could do to avoid crushing her beneath me. My head rang with the thunderous crash. Masonry, plaster, splintered wood, and shattered glass rained down upon us. Shards lacerated my back. Rocks and pebbles battered my skull.

Then a terrible shudder like an earthquake rumbled through the ground beneath us and we were bounced and thrown about like kiddies on a bed. Lollipop screamed with the agonizing violence of the movement.

The powerful quake rolled on across the entire estate. The few Academy walls still standing began to sway. Cracks appeared in their masonry. Each time the masonry broke, it sounded like a gunshot. Bricks tumbled to the Earth, a few at first, then an avalanche, followed by a torrent of fractured archways and windowsills, cornices, and gables. Like bowling pins, the teetering walls of the ancient Academy collapsed one after the other until, at last, none remained standing.

Whether the few figures remaining in the landscape were smartypants, greybeards, or knobfiddlers one couldn't tell for all the blood and dust that caked them. As the quake rolled on, they clambered to their feet and hurried away toward the gates. I lifted Miss Crossingguard into my arms once again and did the same.

A disgusting smell suddenly enveloped the estate. "Is that you?" whispered Lollipop with a devilish grin. But then we gagged and choked, and our eyes burned with the stench. The air filled with a putrid green mist, its tiny droplets creating an oily film on everything they touched, us included. The film stung as it settled on our skin.

Pewter Doubting appeared out of the mist. He'd been following us from the rocketry laboratory but had vanished in the chaos. It now seemed he'd gone back to help Lollipop's friend, the injured knobfiddler with the lacerated leg. Pewter was practically carrying the potbellied knobfiddler as they stumbled toward us.

"The projectile," gasped the knobfiddler, "it burst the effluent pipes that feed the Bilbury mill. Thames sewage is flooding unchecked over the entire estate."

"How appropriate," I muttered. Miss Crossingguard responded with a chuckle and a smile.

Chapter Eighty

Palace of Westminster

In a pea-soup fog and a freezing drizzle, Garter council members were summoned to Westminster Palace by the Lord Chamberlain to witness the passing of an era. The mood among members was as bone-chilling as the weather outside. This assembly was likely to be the Order of the Garter's last. In the council's anteroom, a delegation of Talkyhall members awaited the Order of the Garter's Articles of Dissolution. Every Garter member was required to sign the articles. None dared decline. But the Talkyhall delegation was also awaiting another more momentous signature on a far more important document, the Royal Warrant of Abdication.

"We've been over this, Majesty," said Lord Chamberlain Liverwort, his growing impatience apparent to everyone present. "You must sign the Royal Warrant because Talkyhall members demand it. The Russian and the Americans also expect it. And the London mob outside the palace doors will accept nothing less."

"I just don't understand why everyone is so angry with me. I was only trying to defend the Realm."

"Against enemies you sought to provoke," said Lord Trolleysmash, with uncharacteristic forthrightness.

"All right, so that might have been a mistake but . . . but someone destroyed my beloved chateau. Why aren't the people hunting for those criminals?"

"Majesty, there's little public sympathy for your loss of a French castle," replied Trolleysmash.

There was heavy pounding on the chamber doors. "Majesty," Liverwort bellowed, "Talkyhall delegates are losing their patience. Please! Sign the damned document . . . Sire."

Earthedge

Edward looked at Liverwort with childlike hurt. The king's eyes were the size of pie plates. Tears rolled down his cheeks as he picked up the letter and read. "We're rather hard on poor Edmund, aren't we?" he said meekly.

"The damned fool and all his promises," muttered the Lord Chamberlain. "A madman, he deserves Your Majesty's condemnation and more. Besides, let's be frank. The more blame we shift to Edmund, the less we'll bear."

"I . . . I suppose you're right. If he hadn't promised us his projectiles, I probably wouldn't have . . . . Oh, I don't know . . . oh well. To tell the truth, I never really liked the man. And he smelt so badly."

"We're wasting time, Sire," grumbled Liverwort. "If we're to save the monarchy and the rest of our system of privilege and titles, then the warrant must reach Talkyhall in time for their so-called Session of Installation this evening."

"Can I write my own letter to my people, or do you have to review that too?"

"Once you've signed the Royal Warrant of Abdication, you can write whatever the hell you wish."

"So, if I understand, the very moment I sign this document, I'm no longer king, is that right? Oh, Wallis is going to be so angry with me."

"Correct, but it also means you can live wherever you want, in France or New York or Timbuktu. And you're going to receive a handsome annual stipend. But if you delay much longer, Talkyhall may rescind its largesse."

"Do I get to be called King *Emeritus*?"

"No, but you can be a prince if you wish."

"Prince Edward . . . mmm, I guess that's all right. And my medals, do I get to keep them? They look so fetching at parties."

"Yes, yes, you can keep the medals!" shouted Liverwort, "and the capes and the porcelain dinner service. Now sign, please. I've got an airship to catch."

"Where are you off to, Harrold?" asked Trolleysmash. The lord's familiarity was a mark of the new democratic tone which had suddenly seized the Garter Council.

"Venice. I've bought a cafe on the Grand Canal with my friend Harry from the liquor cellar."

"Well, I'm going back home," said the former sea lord. "Should never have become involved with boats. Don't mind standing in water to fish but standing on water is unnatural."

Chapter Eighty-One

Balmoral Castle

To my loyal subjects,

My wife Wallis and I are mindful that the greatest bulwark of any nation against tyranny and betrayal is its free press. Never has this been truer than it is today. As you have no doubt read in our many patriotic broadsheets, the United Kingdom has of late been grievously betrayed. One of our longest-lived and most prestigious institutions, the Royal and Ancient Academy of Knowledge, and its treacherous chancellor, Lord Edmund of Muckyheath, have done our Realm a grievous disservice.

For a millennium, the Academy was entrusted with the care and nurturing of our nation's scientific inquiry. Instead, under the perverted leadership of Lord Edmund, the Academy in recent years became a cauldron of conspiracy. It connived with certain members of the Garter council to bring our Realm into needless conflict with other nations. I am as shocked and horrified by the Academy's actions as you are. I am also deeply disappointed in the failure of my Garter council to adequately govern its members, oversee the Academy, and inform me of its affairs.

Given the sense of utter betrayal that I feel in men I once trusted to serve me selflessly, and with nothing but love and affection for the people of our Realm, I can no longer continue as your monarch. My mandate to the Garter council was to create prosperity and peace for my subjects. Instead, they sought only conflict and chaos. My confidence was obviously misplaced, my judgment clearly flawed, and since I can no longer trust my own instincts, I feel I must renounce my crown. Our Realm needs a new hand on the tiller.

For this reason, I have asked my darling niece, Elizabeth Windsor, to assume the throne. As my last act as your king, I have requested Primus Speaker Peter Sellers and Talkyhall members to draw up the terms of succession and constitutional governance for Elizabeth's reign.

Long Live Queen Elizabeth, God bless you all, and may God bless our beloved Realm.

Edward VIII

Chapter Eighty-Two

London

Earthedgers were invited to attend the new queen's inaugural address to Talkyhall.

Until then, the former Princess Elizabeth had lived a quiet country life at her estate in Northumbria. There she'd ridden horses and overseen her nation-wide network of boarding kennels called Doggies Rule. The proceeds had supported her two charities, the Royal Horse Breeders' Institute and The Corgis Benevolent Fund.

Summoned quite suddenly into national prominence, she had not yet put aside her farmyard ways and arrived for her Talkyhall appearance wearing a tartan headscarf, waxed canvas overcoat, muddied tweed skirt, and galoshes. Her husband, formerly a naval officer and sailing instructor with some Greek royal connection or other, was somewhat the worse for a morning of shooting and cider with his chums. As Elizabeth was escorted to the speaker's dais, she acknowledged us Earthedgers with a few polite words. "Have you had tea? Lovely weather, what? Do try the jam roly-poly." Her swubby-lubby, as the queen called her husband, trailed behind and wandered about. He addressed Gemeny as Sonny Boy, asked Annadeena if she was our maid, and complimented Lollipop on her fine pair of "lady melons."

The queen's address was a gracious and masterful performance. Her expression of gratitude to the people of Earthedge for our "heroic defense of the peaceful and honorable kingdom against a tyrannous conspiracy" was heartfelt. The oration may have been the queen's, but the words were crafted by Sir Maltvinegar Tartarsauce. He remained our dearest friend and closest ally in Dinnerplate.

In the days following the Academy assault, we Earthedgers were feted across London. Our exploits were lauded in every broadsheet, our technologies dissevered and discussed in every pub, and the virtues of our community of unbridled minds debated and dissected in every social club and chattering society from one end of the Realm to the other. While the nation may have been grateful for our victory over the hated Academy, public opinion was divided over the merits of having such a powerful neighbor living just beyond the veil of confusion, out there, lurking in the twilight, planning heaven knows what. People seemed to believe our victory had been too decisive for comfort.

Governmental reform was proceeding apace. Primus Speaker Sellers and his Chancellor of the Exchequer, Sir Maltvinegar, had drafted a set of constitutional reforms they were to propose to the upcoming Talkyhall Conference on Governance. Most proposals enjoyed broad support in and out of government. One proposal, however, did not. Sir Vinny wished to recognize Earthedge as an autonomous community among nations and grant it special advisory status to the United Kingdom. How, went the popular dissent, could a handful of people, rebels all—who lived in perpetual darkness, ate the most appalling food, wore diaphanous clothing, and practiced ungodly rituals by the light of their electrical lanterns—ever be trusted to give wholesome advice to the Realm's ancient legislature?

By the time we were ready to depart for home, invitations had dwindled, public accolades were few, and our contacts with the people of Dinnerplate were becoming increasingly chilly. Things took a decidedly dark turn when the *Foxhunt* broadsheet fomented a rumor that Earthedgers referred to the UK as Dinnerplate because we harbored some unholy culinary intentions toward the innocent souls of the unwitting Realm. After that, we couldn't get out of London fast enough.

Chapter Eighty-Three

Montelordie Estate

"There's not much from our earlier days that I miss," said the captain as he sipped his latte, "but I do miss mornings like this."

The French doors of the breakfast room were open, and the lace curtains were dancing in a light breeze off the duck pond. Birdsong at that early hour was as resonant as a symphony. The horizon still bore the golden afterglow of sunrise.

"Come sit," said the captain, and so I put my cup down on a carved teak chest and pulled an armchair alongside his so as to face the gardens.

"You're up early," he remarked.

"The thought of leaving," I replied. But that wasn't entirely true. More so, it was the thought of Marigold, being back here, the place of her suffering, my many memories of her, and my loss. Damn! I was doing it again, thinking only of myself. The pain of her loss was everyone's. But so, as I have learned, were the opportunities for healing—enduring friendships, new acquaintances, wonders, adventures, mornings like this.

"You've done well, young man. Your father would be proud."

In another time, that remark might have rankled.

"I've been thinking about something you said," the captain continued, "back aboard the canal barge when you were...."

"When I was wallowing, yes." I shifted uncomfortably at the awkward memory.

"You said your father expected you to be a leader. It occurred to me that you might have misunderstood, that you might have thought he wanted you to be giving orders one day. I can assure you that's not what he meant. I don't think your father gave an order in his life."

But if giving orders isn't leadership, then what is?

"No, your father led, not by ordering us about, but by his example, the example of his determination, curiosity, and commitment to the truth."

Lead by example ... hmm.

"Just the way you did, young Stalwart, with your timely suggestions and your courage."

After that, the captain and I sat in silence, sipping our coffees and listening to the breeze in the birches. Marigold would have loved a morning such as this. I wiped a tear from my cheek.

"And so now you're beginning your own voyage."

"We've so much still to see," I replied.

That morning, the others were leaving aboard Sir Vinny's canal boat for Boggshead and then boarding the ferry to Iceland. From there, they were planning to travel across the barrens on Bottomly Fireplug's new Exploding Cans and Fans skipscooter.

There was so much to do back in Earthedge. Letters posted to the Royal Danish Mail shop in Minisculevik requesting permission to visit the edge of the Earth had overwhelmed its staff. Earthedgers couldn't say no, but we were concerned that rapid growth might smother our tiny community. As a temporary measure, we intended to require visitors to trek rather than skipscooter to Earthedge. The prospect of such hardship was sure to weed the worthy from the worthless. We had also received news that the smartypants who'd been set ashore far down the edge after their abortive raid had returned in dire straits and were begging for help. Gemeny was returning Marigold's ashes to her mothers and we had already begun planning a festival of stargazing and storytelling to celebrate her life. There was going to be so much to occupy everyone.

Pewter Doubting was not leaving for home just yet. He was staying behind to assist Sir Vinny with electrificating his presses. *The Tittle-Tattler* had begun publishing four pages filled with coverage and analysis of Talkyhall discussions. In a poll of topics for upcoming Talkyhall debate, however, the most popular subject remained French postcards, and the most popular section of the enlarged *Tittle-Tattler* was the Corseted Model of the Day illustration.

The door to the breakfast room opened and in came Lollipop Crossingguard. Her hand was heavily bandaged. Sir Vinny's medicator had managed to reset most of the bones in her fingers and said her many other injuries were all healing well. How she'd borne the agony of the surgery on her hand had astounded everyone. Her warm smile of greeting betrayed none of the pain she must still have been feeling. The more I observed this young woman, the more extraordinary she became.

Lollipop was dressed in a pale blue tunic decorated with strands of rose-colored fish leather and azure stones.

"This looks all right?" she asked. "Annadeena offered me one of her outfits for the trip." Lollipop walked to the side of my chair. "She tells me your cloth is so much stronger or warmer or something."

"It suits you," I murmured. And it did, beautifully.

She stepped to the window. "I love the birdsong."

And I loved the way the sunlight shimmered through her tunic. How had I not noticed before? Her figure was breathtaking.

A flock of swifts twisted and turned in the cloudless sky before sweeping down into the chimney of an old outbuilding alongside the walled garden.

"Fractals," Lollipop whispered.

"What?" I ask.

"The flight of the birds," she said and then grinned.

Two people exempted from the new travel restrictions were Lollipop's parents. She'd received word from Iceland they were well and awaiting her arrival. Captain Codkiss was to locate them, invite them to travel to Earthedge with him, and explain why they weren't going to see Lollipop for some time.

Burpee, Annadeena, and I weren't planning on returning to Earthedge quite yet. We wanted to go back to Sir Vinny's cave and retrace our journey through the Earth in search of the Beatrice. We wanted to sail our beloved vessel back to Earthedge, where she belonged, gathering relics as we went. And Lollipop Crossingguard was coming with us.

When eventually we got back to Earthedge, I meant to study Father's notes, some of which Lollipop had received from Lord Edmund, and others I'd found in the ruins of the chancellor's office. Through his work, I hoped to kindle in myself something of Father's adventuresome spirit and unwavering commitment to the truth, qualities I'd resented in him during our time together. I also wanted to delve deeper into fractals and explore the extraordinary notion that the universe might be one enormous fractal—and Lollipop was going to help.

No, that's not true. *We* were going to explore a fractal universe *together... as a team.*

When I'd invited Lollipop to come to Earthedge and study fractals with me, she'd replied, "You realize what this could mean . . . . We might one day see infinity together."

And my heart had skipped a beat.

Walk-ons

What vanity it is
To believe we are each
The central figure in our own story.
When we are far likelier
To be bit players,
Mere walk-ons,
In a narrative
More complex,
More heroic,
Than we can imagine.
We are like
Middling Russian dolls,
Nested somewhere
Inside a construct
So much larger than ourselves.

—Stalwart Wordsmouth

Characters

For those readers who like to keep track of all the players in a story, here is a complete list of both the consequential and inconsequential characters in Earthedge.

Major Players (you'll want to remember them)

    Stalwart Wordsmouth
    Earthedger, our hero

    Marigold Springpeeper
    Earthedger, Stalwart's girlfriend

    Lollipop Crossingguard
    Algorythy, Royal Academy

    Lord Edmund of Muckyheath
    Chancellor, Royal and Ancient Academy

    Hobby Natterer
    Academy smartypants

Supporting Players (you're likely to become quite familiar with them)

    Grimly Wordsmouth
    Earthedger, father of Stalwart

    Captain Armature Codkiss
    Earthedger, captain of the Beatrice

    Annadeena Guesswhich
    Earthedger, science officer, owner of the Beatrice

    Burpee Kettle
    Earthedger, Beatrice crew member

Hopeful Wayward
Earthedger, Beatrice crew member

Gemeny Farcryer
Earthedger, Beatrice navigator

Sir Maltvinegar Tartarsauce
Member of Talkyhall, Publisher

Scribben
Aide to Lord Edmund

Lord Bilbury
Garter member

Edward VIII
King of UK

Wallis Simpson
Queen of UK

Sir Harrold Liverwort
Edward's Lord Chamberlain

Lord Trolleysmash of Duckdrooping
First Sea Lord of the Admiralty

Basenote Bugspray
Acting head, Academy computing engine team

Minor Players (a generally entertaining, but largely forgettable, group)

Raindrop Macintosh
Earthedge mayor, Stalwart's guardian

Melody Fullbottle
Earthedger, Rocksplitters' publican

Bedazzles Middlefinger
Earthedger

Pewter Doubting
Earthedger

Deem Worthy
Earthedger

Captain Amendment Hardknock
Earthedger, Captain of the Sunstone

Bloordrag Lorgeld
Minisculevik ship chandler

Recliner Broadbutt
US Undersecretary of Official Stories

Skip Blarneyson
US Secretary of State

Captain Haggis McCasanfuilt
USAS *Bolsadeviento*

Alexei Romanov II
Tsar of Russia

Baron Needlesovich
Russian Minister of Riches

Prince Pockmarkoff
Russian Marshall of the Army

Field Marshall Treadmill Aimsbroke
Chief of UK War Department

Mrs. Crossingguard
Lollipop's mother

Mr. Crossingguard
Lollipop's father

Covert Millrace
Earthedger, inventor of the message machine

Earthedge

Others A (this lot will be here and gone before you know it)

Dr. Tulip Wateringcan
Head of Earthedge school

Pullover Shears
Earthedger, Owner of Sunstone

Cogsy Eyebeam
Earthedger

Amirgo Gistring
Earthedger

Whiskers Forrest-Glen
Scribbler with The Tittle-Tattler

Admiral Rainslicker
Chairman of the American *ScrambledEggs*

Sub. Lt. Articles Nozehair
US Intelligence officer

Baron Balletshutz von Tapdanzer
Russian Imperial Department of Royal Inquiry

Ronald Reagan
US Plenipotentiary to the Russian Court

Frisbinnovich
Russian Winter Palace footman

Polkovnik Sergei Horseizset
Russian Cossack Colonel

Wavey Marshgas
Knobfiddler

Meadowlark Morningsong
Knobfiddler

Mildew Fogbank
Earthedger, Marigold's 1st Mother

Anemone Bellpull
Earthedger, Marigold's 2nd Mother

Cobweb Linenchest
Earthedger, Marigold's 3rd Mother

Others B (they leave barely a trace on our stage)

Ruthy Wordsmouth
Earthedger, poet, Stalwart's mother

Raglan Bookbinder
Earthedger

Middley Porter
Earthedger

Opal Amethyst
Earthedger

Persia Magenta
Earthedger

Morgood
Earthedger

Amos Uply
Earthedger, inventor of the exagifier, deceased

Gilgilly Kneecap
Earthedger, inventor of the shockshooter

Bottomly Fireplug
Earthedger, inventor of the cans and fans
(internal combustion) engine

Lilly Seedling
Earthedger

Earthedge

Potted Edelweiss
Earthedger

Hengert Lorgeld
Wife of Bloordrag

Abated Giddyford
Former head of calculating engine team

Reginald Sir Footplaster-Barnswallow
Garter council member

Coupon Shoppingcart
Undersecretary Broadbutt's assistant

Ambassador Popover
Russian ambassador to the Court of Westminster

Mrs. Pickle and sons, Wobbley and Nobbley
The Crossingguards' neighbors on Wimpole Street

Acknowledgments

In devising this story, I was fortunate to have the generous assistance of several good friends. I'm grateful to my Long Fiction Writing Group: Wendy Patterson, Jason MacDonald, Monica Furness, Thomas Young, Kim Covert and Rhéal Nadeau. Their searching and insightful comments on every section of the book were both invaluable and a testament to their own skillful authorship. I want to thank Ian Logie who was among the first to read the entire manuscript. His observations concerning key characters, the use of humor in the story, and important plot points were indispensable. And finally, I'm grateful to my good friend Bill Poole, who is always willing to read my stuff no matter how taxing it must be on his extraordinary mind.

About the Author

Ivan Blake was born in England and immigrated with his family to Canada when he was five. He did his graduate studies at the University of Chicago and taught in universities for fifteen years before joining the Canadian Public Service. He served the Government of Canada for twenty years and then went on to lecture and advise governments all over the world. He now travels and writes solely for pleasure, and delights in reading, wines and his grandchildren.

Upcoming New Release!

IVAN BLAKE

THE MAN WHO MADE AN ANGEL

**We need not be angels ourselves
to bring forth the angelic in others.**
A Wiltshire aphorism

It's !921. A Canadian doctoral student flees to a war-ravaged Germany in the vain hope of escaping the unbearable grief of a recent family tragedy. He plans to hide from his pain in the archives of a shuttered university, but finds little respite in a country so rapidly descending into madness. Until, that is, he meets an elderly professor living in the bowels of the empty university. The old man, once a biologist, is determined to heal the German spirit by performing a truly inspiring scientific miracle. The student becomes swept up in the professor's scheme – until he discovers the appalling lengths to which the old man will go to achieve his goal. The young man must choose, either to surrender to his own weakness and instability or rise to the moment -- in spite of the terrible and enduring price he'll have to pay.

In the manner of Guillermo del Toro's Pan's Labyrinth, *The Man Who Made an Angel* is a deeply moving historical dark fantasy about loss, obsession, weakness, and the redemptive power of compassion.

For more information
visit: www.SpeakingVolumes.us

Now Available!

IVAN BLAKE

THE MORTSAFEMAN TRILOGY
BOOKS 1 - 3

**For more information
visit:** www.SpeakingVolumes.us

Now Available!

RAY DAN PARKER

The Tom Williams Saga
Books 1-4

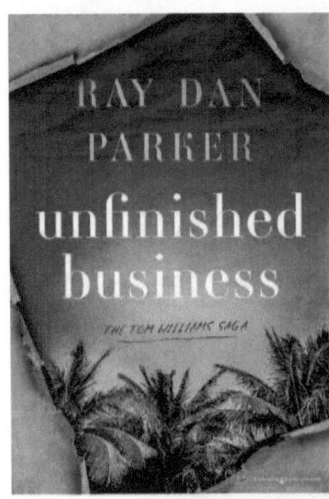 

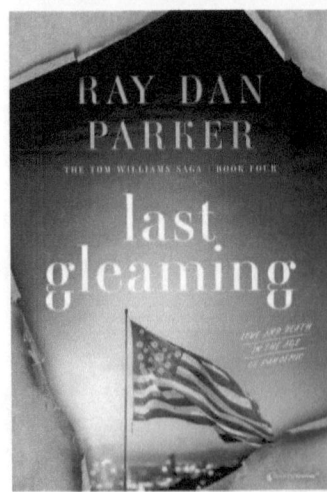 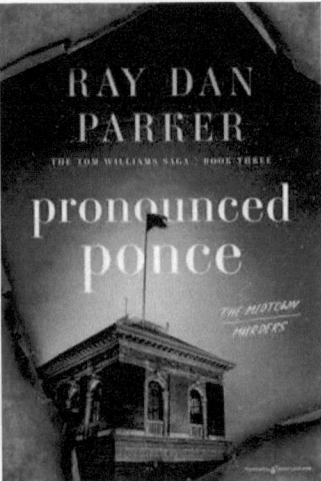

**For more information
visit:** www.SpeakingVolumes.us

Now Available!

LUIS FIGUEREDO

Pierce Evangelista Thrillers
Books 1-3

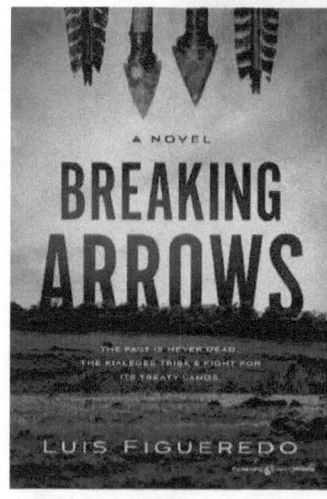

**For more information
visit: www.SpeakingVolumes.us**

Now Available!

B. W. JACKSON

The Rise *of* Lazarus
Book 1

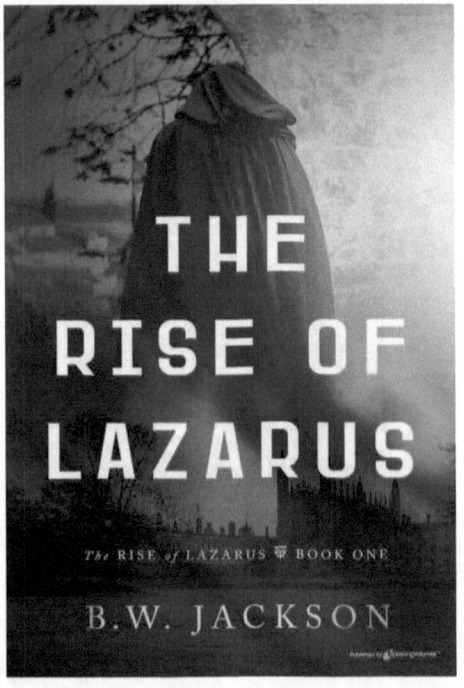

**For more information
visit: www.SpeakingVolumes.us**

www.ingramcontent.com/pod-product-compliance
Lightning Source LLC
LaVergne TN
LVHW091617070526
838199LV00044B/833